J
R

KINGDOM OF THE SERPENT

1

JACK OF RAVENS

MARK CHADBOURN

an imprint of **Prometheus Books**
Amherst, NY

For Gordon John Chadbourn (1930—2005)
Visiting the Summerlands

Published 2012 by Pyr®, an imprint of Prometheus Books

Cover illustration © John Picacio
Jacket design by Nicole Lecht

Inquiries should be addressed to
Pyr
59 John Glenn Drive
Amherst, New York 14228–2119
VOICE: 716–691–0133
FAX: 716–691–0137
WWW.PYRSF.COM

16 15 14 13 12   5 4 3 2 1

Library of Congress Cataloging-in-Publication Data

Chadbourn, Mark.
    Jack of ravens / by Mark Chadbourn.
        p. cm. — (Kingdom of the serpent series ; 1)
    First published: London : Gollancz, an imprint of Orion Publishing Group, 2006.
    ISBN 978–1–61614–607–8 (pbk.)
    ISBN 978–1–61614–608–5 (ebook)
    1. Mythology, Celtic—Fiction. I. Title.

PR6053.H23J33 2012
823'.914—dc23

2011046709

Printed in the United States of America

Thanks to:

David Rowe, Tim Smit and the team at The Eden Project; Lizzy Hill, keeper of the archives; Seraph, Patma, Jayne and other members of the Mark Chadbourn Message Board for Latin translations; Sandy Auden for support.

For more information about the author and his work visit:

www.markchadbourn.net

CONTENTS

PROLOGUE

Three women huddle in a dark place, their features swathed in shadow. They work diligently, one spinning threads, one measuring them. The third waits with a pair of shears. And as they go about their business, they sing in high, unsettling voices, of what was, of what is, and of what will be, and their songs change constantly, like the sea, like the sand on the beach.

The Daughters of the Night know this: nothing is as it seems. There are hidden patterns in the weft and weave of human existence. Only one thing can be trusted: the heart; and some threads that bind shall not be broken, however far they stretch across time or space.

Their song begins anew. The shears are poised . . .

CHAPTER ONE
THE GREAT DOMINIONS

1

Spectral mist drifted across the rolling grassland. The thin light of approaching dawn filtered through in shades of gold and pink, the whole world glowing as if newly formed. The only sound was the breeze; the stillness that followed a terrible storm had cupped the world in its palms.

Out of the gently shifting fog wandered Jack Churchill, as pale as a ghost, which in a way he was, hair as black as crow's wings, a face that combined sensitivity and strength, sadness and hope in equal measure. His torn, bloodstained clothes revealed numerous minor wounds. And in his hand he loosely carried a sword that might not have been a sword at all.

He didn't know where he was going, or from where he had come. Only one thing filled his mind: the image of a young woman with long, dark hair and a face as pale as his own; a name: *Ruth*; a sense of a deep and powerful love that gave meaning to his existence.

Exhaustion enveloped him, but the malaise went deeper than his weary bones; it felt as though the gentle fog had permeated his head, swaddling memories that only recently had been clear and sharp. He knew his name, that all who knew him called him Church. He recalled the basic details of his life—his work as an archaeologist, his family, his friends, his flat in South London—but the circumstances that had led him to that lonely landscape in such a dire condition were muddled and fading fast.

The grassland sloped away before him. He could smell wet vegetation, perhaps a hint of the sea.

Find a road, his subconscious told him. *Hitch a lift. Get away. Get to Ruth, before it's too late . . . for her, for you.*

As he wrestled with his memory, he glimpsed movement in the drifting white—spectral shapes, there then gone, like circling wolves.

"Who's there?"

The echoes of his question were muffled by the fog, but the sound of his voice stirred something in him. He came to a halt and glanced down at the weapon in his hand. His eyes played tricks on him. Though every sensation told him he was holding a sword, for the briefest second he thought he was gripping a strange crystal formation glowing with a powerful blue light. His eyes blurred, static shimmered across his mind and then it really was a sword, the blade imprinted with strange, delicate runes, black against the silvery steel, the pommel an ornately carved dragon's head.

The incongruity was disturbing; even more troubling was the realisation that he had not considered it unusual until now. Why did he have an ancient weapon? Why all the blood? Had he murdered someone?

His dazed incomprehension was interrupted by an inhuman roar thundering across the landscape. As the hairs prickled on the back of his neck, Church gripped the sword tightly, easily.

Whatever had made the sound was lost in the mist. *An animal*, Church told himself, though it sounded like no animal he had ever heard before. Uneasy, he slowly backed away from what he thought was the source of the noise. The mist was disorienting, and when the roar came again, it was unnervingly near at hand. Deep tremors accompanied it, as though an industrial machine was pounding away.

Church chose a direction at random and ran down the gradual slope, dodging gorse bushes and outcroppings of lichen-covered rock. By the time he realised he'd made the wrong choice, there were people running somewhere nearby, their fearful shouts punctuating the now-deafening roar. The ground shook so forcefully that Church could barely keep his feet.

Church had only a split second to throw himself to one side as *something* hurtled towards him. Crashing to the damp grass, he glimpsed a huge, dark mass that felt like a juggernaut whistling by only inches away.

A cry of terrible pain cut brutally short echoed nearby. Church's unease turned to full-blown anxiety. An enormous shadow fell over him.

Looming above him, the top half lost in the reaches of the mist, was a giant figure that Church estimated must have been at least twenty-five feet tall. Yet it was not, by any description, a man. The legs that shook the ground were made of branches, earth, rocks, creepers and clumps of gorse. With a sound like the ground being torn open, the thing bent down rapidly and Church was confronted by a face constructed from a similar jumble of organic and inorganic matter, red eyes glowing from the depths.

He was rooted for a second too long. Fingers as strong as ironwood clamped around his chest. He felt his ribs start to crack as the giant lifted him off the ground.

Six men brandishing swords, spears and shields ran from the mist to attack the giant. Despite his pain, Church was shocked by their appearance. Five of the men had whitened hair, spiked and tied in ponytails, while the sixth wore a bronze horned helmet. They were all naked from the waist up, their torsos tattooed with blue circles and swirls above loose-fitting tartan trousers.

The warriors brutally gouged out chunks of the matter that made up the giant's form. Roars of pain and anger followed each assault.

Church was on the verge of blacking out from the pressure on his ribs when the giant finally loosened its grip to defend itself. A voice deep inside him, calm and blue as a summer sky, told him he could launch his own attack. Extending his sword arm, Church was surprised to see the blade now limned with a thin sapphire light that occasionally became tiny dancing flames. He thought he could hear it singing, a gentle susurration that soothed him.

The giant's red eyes glowed with the intensity of hot coals in reaction to the sword. Church lashed out at its wrist, and wood and rock showered into the air. When its grasp loosened further, Church dropped, landed on his feet and bounded away. With a fierce roar, the giant disappeared into the mist.

The warriors eyed him uneasily as they readied themselves to repel another attack.

"Who are you?" Church said breathlessly. "What's going on here?" His words only served to disturb them further.

The vibrations running up Church's legs were growing stronger. He turned slowly, waiting. Hidden by the shifting grey, the giant was circling them, its attack strategy more cautious. In Church's hand, the sword sang soothingly. Eerily, it felt as though ethereal tendrils were flowing from the hilt, easing through his skin and muscle and bone and working their way up his arm.

The roar made Church's ears ring. An instant later, the giant hurtled out of the mist like a train. As one of the warriors raised his spear, the giant's mighty fist propelled him through the air, turning his chest to jelly. Another fighter, stunned by the speed and ferocity of the attack, was plucked up, his head torn off with a flick of the giant's wrist, both parts tossed carelessly aside.

The other warriors were as quick as rats. They scattered, then turned and attacked the giant savagely with fluid motions as they dodged its huge legs, but their weapons made little impact.

Church was shocked to realise that of all the remaining warriors, the giant had decided to focus on him alone. As he threw himself out of the giant's path, one of its rushing legs clipped his heel and sent him spinning hard into the ground.

The giant was on him instantly, its roar so loud it made his skull ache. Church reacted instinctively, though later he had the odd feeling that the sword had moved on its own. Now ablaze with blue flames, the blade swung in an arc, and when it hit the giant's leg, there was an eruption of fire and a shower of wood, rock and soil. A loud crack signalled the breaking of what remained.

The giant teetered, then pitched forward, its shadow descending like night, talons of oak and ash lunging for Church. His sword came up, a beacon in the approaching dark. Church braced himself, and at the last moment rolled to avoid the bulk of the giant's torso, driving the blade into its neck and up into its head.

The force of the impact threw Church back several yards, and when he finally clambered to his feet, dazed, the giant lay still. Church had a fleeting image of soil accumulating over the years and grass growing over it, until all that was left was a mound on the landscape and a distant legend about giants resting in the earth.

Church came back to reality sharply, the palpable feeling of dislocation making him queasy. The strangely dressed warriors gathered around, their expressions alternating between fear and awe.

"Please . . . tell me what's happening here," Church said. "What was that thing?"

The men looked at each other before the one in the helmet stepped forward. He was in his early twenties with strong, thoughtful features. He glanced several times at Church's sword while he struggled to find the right words, but when he did finally speak, Church was stunned to hear sounds he had only previously heard in the sterile confines of a university lecture theatre: the Gaulish Celtic language.

Church attempted a rough translation, but only a few words were understandable. Most noticeable was the name Nuada Airgetlamh, which the young man said when he gestured hesitantly to the sword in Church's hand; he appeared to be implying that it was the fabled weapon of the Celtic god Nuada.

Unable to comprehend what had happened to him, Church moved away from the young men and wandered down the slope until he reached a point where the dawn sun had started to burn off the mist. The green landscape reached down to a shimmering blue sea, the coast lined with thick trees. It could have been anywhere. He became aware of the sweetly fragrant air without even a hint of pollution. Few places in Britain would have such a pure atmosphere.

"What's happened?" he said, disturbed.

2

The following few hours passed in a blur. Church remembered traipsing across grassland surrounded by the warriors until they came to a copse where several horses were tethered. He was helped onto the back of one and then the group set off south. Through the haze, Church realised a painful truth: there were no roads, no service stations, no towns, no villages, no hamlets, no planes passing overhead. Just an unspoiled landscape of grass, gorse bushes and trees.

3

Church woke on a rough bed of straw in a shadowy place that smelled of mud, smoke and animals. A woman in her early twenties was tending a fire in the central hearth area. Her long brown hair was plaited into pigtails and tied with ribbons, and while certainly attractive, her features had been hardened by the stresses of life. Her long dress was of the deepest green, the fabric thick to protect her from the elements. She nodded impassively to Church when she saw him looking at her and said a word of greeting, which he translated as "Giantkiller."

"Jack," he replied, tapping his chest. Dismissing this immediately with a shake of his head, he amended, "Church."

She repeated his name hesitantly in her thick accent and then proffered, "Etain," resting her hand on her left breast.

Church began to struggle to his feet, but Etain came over quickly and respectfully pressed him back onto the straw. Cautiously, she pulled his shirt away from his shoulder to reveal some of the many small wounds that peppered his frame. She paused, uncertain, before easing the shirt off his upper arm to reveal a black, spider-like object about an inch across embedded in his flesh. It wasn't painful; in fact the whole area was numb. Puzzled, Church moved to touch it, and as his fingers brushed it, the tiny black legs clenched and dug deeper into his skin. He jerked his hand back as if it had been burned: the thing was alive.

"Bad," Etain said. "Poison."

Sickened, Church examined the thing as best he could from his limited perspective. It appeared to be made of shiny metal rather than organic material, but he thought he could see a pair of eyes on the edge of the carapace. His initial reaction was to try to find some sharp implement with which to prise the creature out, but Etain saw his anxiety and placed a calming hand on the back of his own.

"Wait," she said. "The healer will help." There was more, but although Church had studied the language, most of it had been in written form and Etain spoke so quickly it was difficult to draw meaning from her words.

Fighting to understand what was happening, Church struggled to his feet and pushed past the solicitous Etain to get some fresh air. He walked into a small open-air courtyard with several rooms leading off it. One contained a sump to collect rainwater; another was a larder; the rest were living quarters. The building as a whole was almost circular and constructed of stone walls with a high straw roof. Church could see other similar structures beyond.

Etain followed him curiously as he made his way out into a small street that wound around the handful of homesteads. Playing children and adults going about their business stopped to stare. As he looked around in a daze, Church thought he recognised the layout of the settlement and its position in the landscape.

He swung his arm wide in a gesture Etain could understand.

"Cerniu," she said, indicating the land towards the horizon.

Church translated easily: "Cornwall." Then he pointed towards the homesteads, suddenly not wanting to hear what Etain would call them.

"Carn Euny," she said.

With a shiver, Church recalled visiting the settlement while studying for his degree. All that had remained were low walls of grass-topped stone, worn down by the centuries that had passed since Carn Euny had been a thriving community. He refused to accept what the facts were asking him to consider: that somehow he was in the Iron Age, more than 2,300 years before he had been born.

In a wild panic, he ran out of the village and up onto higher ground, hoping to catch sight of a road, or a modern house, or hear the distant rumble of traffic.

Finally Etain caught up with him. His incoherent thoughts briefly coalesced when he searched her face. Was she really long-dead, and everyone she knew and loved? The thought that followed naturally hit Church hard: if she was dead, he too must be dead with her, long before he was born, lost to everyone he knew.

4

For the next three days, Church tried to rest and recuperate. His wounds were all superficial, apart from the sickening black spider that continued to burrow into his flesh whenever he made any attempt to remove it. While it did not cause any immediate pain, Church was convinced it was somehow involved in the disappearance of his memory, which still continued to fade in random patches. Etain told him bluntly that it was killing him.

On the second day, unable to restrain himself, he attempted to gouge it out with a hot knife, but only succeeded in burning his skin. The spider dug its legs so deeply into his flesh that he felt an ache at the bone.

The mysteries of his existence tormented him with unanswerable questions: how had he walked out of his modern life and into a landscape more than 2,000 years earlier? What was the black spider and where had it come from? Where had he gained the sword, which left the villagers in such awe that they refused to enter the room where it was stored? And why had he forgotten all the details of the recent past that might have explained his situation?

His own emotions see-sawed wildly: shock, anger, depression, frustration and a desperate yearning for what he had left behind. One feeling burned brighter than all the others: how much he missed Ruth Gallagher, the woman he loved. He remembered her pale face, her hopeful, dark eyes that hinted at internal scars, her tumbling brown hair. He remembered her cathedral-like importance in his life and that somehow they had finally come together after a period of strife; that he was bereft without her. He recalled her last, grief-stricken words: "I'll love you. Always, Church. Always." But all other detail had faded, and he was afraid that as long as the spider continued to suck out what was important to him, it was only a matter of time until the rest of Ruth would be gone, too. In that strange place, so far from everything he knew, adrift in loneliness and confusion, that memory was the only thing that gave him the strength to continue.

Unable to make sense of anything, he found it easier to cope if he didn't try. And so he spent his time getting to know the people who had taken him in, and sharpening his use of their language. Part of the Dumnonii tribe, they were farmers who occasionally traded the lumps of Cornish tin they found in the local streams at the nearby port of Ictis, which Church knew as the modern-day St Michael's Mount. They were, as historical records said, friendly to strangers but fiercely combative when threatened. But though they told him much about their existence, whenever anything he felt was important came up in conversation they walked away, muttering that it was neither their place nor the time to discuss such things. It infuriated Church, but they could not be persuaded to change their views. "They are waiting," Etain told him, but for whom and for how long was never defined.

Etain was his guide, introducing him to the good-natured families who made up the settlement, with whom he would attempt to converse in the Brythonic Celtic language interspersed with untranslatable modern English words. Her nature was naturally sphinx-like and many times Church found himself using her as little more than a sounding board for his own troubled thoughts. It eased his mind somewhat and she appeared unconcerned about it, so he couldn't see the harm. Yet he was always cautious about revealing too much of his origins for fear of disturbing the villagers; displacement in time was troubling enough for him to understand.

"I remember just about everything from the early part of my life," he mused to himself one morning as he and Etain returned from an exploration of the surrounding countryside. "University, studying archaeology, feeling disillusioned when I graduated. Then hacking out bits of journalism for technical manuals. I had a girlfriend, Marianne. She was killed. It took me a long, long time to deal with that."

Etain listened apparently without understanding a single thing he was saying, but she appeared content to let him speak if it made him happy.

"After that I recall a misty morning, like the one when I arrived here . . . and a river . . . and . . . that's it. After that, there're faces, images, bits and pieces, nothing I can put together to make any sense. And I remember Ruth—"

"Your love." Etain stooped to pluck a wild flower from beside the path.

"I can remember what she looked like, the kind of person she was . . . strong, thoughtful, kind. I remember that she was a solicitor. But I can't remember how we met, or anything we did together, or how I fell in love with her. I just know that I *was* in love with her. The feeling is so strong, but it's cut off from everything around it. It feels as if she's a ghost, haunting my life." Church fought back another wave of disorientation.

"Stay true to your heart. It is wiser than your head."

Church glanced at Etain, but she didn't return his look. "That's very profound."

They were interrupted by three of Etain's friends who were bickering as they wandered out of the village. Ailidh was barely out of her teens, but heavily pregnant. A good-natured young woman, Etain doted on her like an aunt. Owein's muscular, lumbering frame belied his sharp intelligence, while his friend Branwen was flinty with a sharp tongue that could cut anyone down.

"Etain, help me." Ailidh laughed. "They will not let me work."

"You must rest," Owein insisted, clearly troubled by the discussion. "The baby will be here soon. You must save your strength."

"My hands are still strong." Ailidh showed them to Etain and Church. "We must all labour while summer is here."

Branwen shook her head with unconcealed contempt. "Then let her. If she brings her child forth in the fields or at the stream, he can help with the labours."

Etain took Ailidh's shoulders and turned her around. "Owein and Branwen are right. Your days are short. The birth will take you to the edge of death. If you are too weak, you will not return."

Ailidh made a childish expression of disdain, but obviously valued Etain's opinion. She stomped back along the track to the village.

Owein shook his head wearily at Church. "Women never listen."

"That is because they must close their ears so they do not go mad from the witterings of men," Branwen said sharply.

They continued their argument all the way back to the village. Etain shared a wry smile with Church, and it was a moment of awakening for him. He had always unconsciously considered the people of the past as an alien race, but they were hardly different from modern people at all.

The warriors Church had saved from the giant tended to their horses in a makeshift camp on the outskirts of the settlement. They were not from Carn Euny. They kept themselves to themselves, but while they told Church politely that they had travelled for several days to protect the village, they too kept the important details infuriatingly secret. Their leader Tannis, however, was intrigued by Church and showed a deep respect whenever they conversed. He always greeted Church as "Giant killer," however much Church tried to escape the title.

In the moments when Church felt the insanity of his situation threatening to run away with him, he would find solace in the wild, sun-drenched

Cornish landscape, unspoiled and filled with wildlife. On the lonely uplands, he would sit and watch the distant sea, feeling lost and desperate.

The nights were the best. Then the villagers would gather around a fire in one of the homes and drink a strong brew while swapping tales of their gods and heroes. They were raucous events filled with great humour. Church sat on the fringes, but from the stolen glances he knew everyone was deeply aware of his presence, though they tried their best not to make him feel uncomfortable. After several draughts of the powerful drink he no longer cared, about anything.

It intrigued him to learn that their society was just as he had been taught in his university classes. There was an equality amongst the men and women that was surprising for such an ancient culture. The women were unafraid to speak their minds, and the men listened intently and with respect to their views. Indeed, some of the women present put forth their views more forcefully than their male counterparts, and were even more raucous in their enjoyment of the nightly festivities.

They were a lusty group. The storytelling eventually devolved into arguments and fist fights amongst the men, which tumbled out into the muddy street to be resolved. But once it was over, the men returned, bloody and bruised, and immediately appeared to be the best of friends once more. Regularly, men and women would walk outside for a bout of noisy lovemaking, the sounds often interrupting the stories, and the assembled group would cheer loudly. When the couple returned, they wore it as a badge, with no embarrassment.

On the night of the third day, a ferocious storm swept in from the Atlantic. Thunder banged loudly and white lightning flashes burned away the dark, while the wind whipped around the roundhouses that were scant protection against the elements. Yet with the central fire stoked and the sparks surging up to the tiny hole in the roof, and all the villagers huddled together to hear tales of a darker bent, it was undeniably cosy.

As the warm glow of the alcohol suffused him, Church vacated his seat at the back and slipped out. A maudlin feeling had been creeping up on him all day. He hated his inactivity and his inability to find a solution to his predicament. He wasn't someone who could lie back and let life wash over him.

In the doorway, he watched lightning play across the horizon as the rain fell heavily. Spindly trees bowed in the face of the wind, and the swirling clouds were caught starkly in each flash. Something about the wild work of nature comforted him.

"There is beauty in the wildest thing." Etain was at his side, her cloak pulled tightly around her. The voluminous swathes of cloth made her face appear unusually delicate.

"The villagers have got you to spy on me, haven't they?"

She showed no emotion. A long moment passed, filled only with the driving beat of the rain pounding all around, as she stared towards the black horizon. Finally she said, "Our lives have been harsh. In recent times, many have died. But we have survived, and as this new age dawns, we will not allow ourselves to fall back again."

"I don't understand," Church said.

Her eyes reflected the flare of the lightning. "The gods have withdrawn. We will never be herded by them again. This land is ours now, as it was in the beginning. We all stand together, men and women, shoulder to shoulder, brother and sister, carving out our own path."

"You think I've come from the gods—a spy, or an agent of some kind, to watch you and report back." Church knew how dearly the Celts held their religious stories, one of the richest mythologies in any world culture, filled with symbolism and wisdom. The gods were stitched into the very fabric of Celtic life and death.

"You carry the sword of Nuada Airgetlamh."

"But I'm human, like you."

"The gods take many shapes. And only a representative of the gods could wield such a weapon of power."

Church couldn't argue with her logic. The sword troubled him, too: where had it come from? Why was he carrying it? The blue light that limned the blade. The way it felt alive in his hand. His fleeting glimpse of it as something that was not a sword at all.

"You used it to slay one of the great giants of Kernow, and yet you say you are a man, like Finn, who falls in the mud every morn when he tries to catch his mare?" Etain's smile was knowing. "Yes, I am charged to watch you Jack, Giantkiller, because we will not abide the gods ruining us any longer, after so many seasons of ruin. We will not see our children stolen from their cribs, or our women unwillingly impregnated, or our men turned into goats or stags or trees."

"Do I have to worry that you might kill me in my sleep to keep your people safe?"

"I do not think you are a threat to us, Jack, Giantkiller." Another smile, wise and teasing at the same time. "But my mind could be changed on the matter." She stared deeply into his eyes for a moment, but Church couldn't divine the emotions that skimmed fleetingly across her features. She may well have said more, but Tannis appeared at the door, drunk and coughing up a mouthful of phlegm. Etain nodded to the new arrival and pushed past him back indoors.

"That one wants to offer you the friendship of the thighs," Tannis said with a wink.

Church ignored him. "Do you think I'm a threat sent from the gods?"

Tannis mused, staring into the depths of the storm. "I saw you fight. You are a warrior. You saved my men, for the giant Cormoran would not have relented until they were all crushed. The giants do not like humans, like many of the things from Otherworld."

The giant still loomed large in Church's thoughts, another of the many things he couldn't explain.

Tannis nodded thoughtfully. "I would show my back to you, Jack, Giantkiller. And I would fight beside you again."

In the split second during which another flash of lightning turned the world white, Church's attention was caught by a curious sight. It looked as if there was a surge of black fire away on the rolling grassland above the village, about two miles distant. It showed up starkly in contrast with the lightning, but was gone so quickly that Church couldn't be sure whether it was anything more than the after-burn of the glare on his retina. For some inexplicable reason it set his nerves on edge. At the same time, the spider-thing burrowing into his arm clenched as if in response.

Tannis followed Church's glare into the impenetrable storm. "You saw something?"

"I don't know. Maybe." If it had been something tangible, the night was too dark to look for it again until the next lightning flash. "You're not from Carn Euny," Church noted, changing the subject. "These people are farmers and traders. You and your band are warriors."

"When the word went out about the Great Battle, we were dispatched to protect those who were closest to the field."

"What battle?"

Tannis eyed Church curiously. "Between the Tuatha Dé Danann and the Fomorii."

Church was puzzled. He presumed Tannis was talking about the Second Battle of Magh Tuireadh, a major event in Celtic mythology when the god-like Tuatha Dé Danann finally defeated the demonic Fomorii and slew their leader Balor, the one-eyed god of death. "You believe that actually happened?" Church asked hesitantly.

"It took place these four days past. On the night before you came upon us."

More superstition, Church thought. There was no point questioning it. "Then you'll be leaving soon?"

"No. We are waiting."

"Everyone's waiting. What for?"

Tannis grinned. "Does it concern you?" He punctuated the question with a laugh, slapped Church on the back and returned to the raucous noise emanating from inside the house.

Church let the unceasing rhythm of the rain ease his troubled thoughts for a few more minutes. In another lightning flash, he thought he saw the black fire again, though he knew it could easily have been his imagination. He immediately went back inside, shutting the door tightly. But for the rest of the night he found himself listening intently to every sound made by each gust and eddy of the wind against the building, strangely fearing it was a hand trying the door, searching for a way in through the window.

He didn't know why he thought that. He didn't know anything any more. Nor did he know why a scraping fear was clawing its way slowly up from the deepest part of him, whispering words of warning: run away. Run away, Jack, Giantkiller.

5

The storm blew itself out during the night. Church was woken sharply by Etain, at the edge of the communal hut where he had drunk himself into a stupor of forgetfulness.

"What is it?" he groaned.

"You must come." It was all she said before departing quickly.

Church emerged into a bright dawn of fiery reds and shimmering golds. All of the villagers were gathered around a mound on the north side of the settlement, and Church could see they were laughing and cheering. As he neared he saw they were all drinking again, clashing their mugs with gusto. The reason for the party only became clear when he saw Ailidh sitting amongst the loudest group, clutching a swaddled bundle to her. She looked pale and exhausted, her cheeks tearstained.

Church went over to congratulate her, but as he peered into the bundle, he saw that the child's face was blue. Ailidh's eyes confirmed his fears.

"I'm sorry," he said. Through the idyllic days and nights he had spent with these people so far he had forgotten the harsh realities of life during that time.

"No," she replied. "Only joy."

Owein clapped Church on the shoulder and thrust a drink into his hand. "A time for celebration, Giantkiller."

As Owein wandered off, singing, Etain took Church's arm and led him to the edge of the group.

"I don't understand," he said simply.

"We cry at the birth and rejoice at the death," she replied. "That is our way. Ailidh's child lives in peace in the Summerlands now. He will not have to suffer this world."

Church knew the Celts believed in the soul, and in a cycle of reincarnation. At death, the soul would pass to T'ir n'a n'Og, the Otherworld, where the gods lived, where it would wait to be reborn into the world.

"I understand." He sipped his drink, wishing he could find comfort in similar notions.

Etain surveyed the tranquil landscape. "You do not share our beliefs. I know that you come from far away where other things are held dearly. But if you think the gods only live in stories, you are wrong."

Church said nothing.

"The Tuatha Dé Danann have been all around us since the First-Times. They have golden skin and beautiful faces, but inside they are cold and hard and they would treat us in a way that we would not treat our animals. They see this world as their dominion, one of the Great Dominions. They believe they can take what they want, and do what they will. But that must change, for we have suffered long enough."

Church listened carefully, saying nothing that would show his disbelief. He understood that the Celts saw the world as a magical place, filled not just with gods, but with spirits and strange beasts. After encountering the giant, he could not dismiss their worldview so easily, but he still hoped for a rational explanation.

"The . . . gods fought a great battle here recently—the Second Battle of Magh Tuireadh?" he asked.

She nodded. "They defeated their great enemy, the Fomorii, the Night-walkers. But they have suffered greatly, too, and they have returned to T'ir n'a n'Og to lick their wounds. They will be back. But until then we have

24

time to forge our own destiny, free of their influence." She raised her face, proud and defiant, and pressed his cup to his lips. "So drink now, for our poor, frail kind, and know that we will find strength. And we will not be broken down again."

As Etain rejoined the others, Church was left with a great admiration for her, and for the community. They understood and accepted the hardship of their life, even if they did characterise it as the work of the gods, and they remained unbowed, determined to rise above it.

Lost to his thoughts, he was startled when he saw something peculiar peeking at him from behind a nearby tree. At first glimpse it looked like a man, but it appeared to be covered with brown fur, like seal-skin. He hurried over to investigate but found nothing, at the tree or anywhere nearby. *Just a figment*, he thought, but he was left with an impression of mischievous eyes and a dark, toothy grin.

6

Church returned to the roundhouse and removed the sword from where it had been hidden. He had decided to carry the weapon with him at all times. He tried to explain to himself that he was in a dangerous time when death was always close, but there was another, deeper reason, like a stain on his subconscious. His fingers tingled as they reached for the sword, and not just with anticipation. When they closed around the hilt, the faint blue light edging the blade lit up the dark corner of the hut.

Sitting around in the village until the next drinking session would mean being alone with his thoughts. Activity was the only answer to keep the ache at bay. He took the opportunity of Etain's immersion in her daily chores to slip out of the village and made his way over the grassland to higher ground.

Beyond the well-trodden area close to the settlement, the landscape became wild: long grass, rocky outcroppings, vast clusters of spiky yellow-flowered gorse and shadowy, near-impenetrable copses. Church enjoyed the exertion after the long days of recuperation. When he reached the high ground, he looked back towards the village, a small oasis of humanity in the wildness of nature. The land glowed green and gold in the morning sun. A symphony of whooshes and rustles and whispers soothed him as the Atlantic wind blew in, filled with the fragrance of growing things. Songbirds joined the wild melody, adding complex high notes. No discordant sounds, no sour odours of pollution. His senses had been numbed by modern living, but in that moment they came alive and he tasted a remarkable peace that he had never experienced before.

Jewelled butterflies and humming bees rose up from his path as he forced his way through the long grass towards his destination. As he neared, his mood darkened. On a hillock where a lone hawthorn tree had been twisted into the shape of a hideous old man by the blasting wind, he paused and looked around. He was sure this was the spot where he had glimpsed the peculiar burst of black fire. He didn't know what he had expected to find, but his deep, secret mind wouldn't leave him alone until he had gone there. From the hillock he had a clear view of Carn Euny, but it would not have been visible in the dark of the storm.

"You shun your own kind."

Church started at the voice. The seductive, honeyed tones came from a beautiful woman in a dark-green dress, her auburn hair blowing in the wind. Her skin had a rich, golden hue, but her features were hard. Church thought he saw a shadow of contempt in her expression. She sat on a rock, examining a pack of cards that she should not have had there, at that time.

"Where did you come from?" he asked.

The woman haughtily ignored Church's question. "Have you turned your back on your own kind?" she stressed.

Church shook his head, not understanding. "My own kind? You mean the people of Carn Euny?"

"At the Second Battle of Magh Tuireadh, you fought with a courage and skill that surpassed those of the Fragile Creatures with whom you associate. You have moved beyond them now. Why should you stand with them?"

Church was stunned for a moment, as he tried to assimilate the woman's words. "*I* fought at the battle—"

The woman sized him up. "You do not remember? You do not recall our meeting before the battle?"

Church shook his head. "We met?"

The woman's forensic gaze held Church fast until he felt himself squirming beneath it. "I find you strange and troublesome," she said. "What is your name?"

Her attitude was irritating, but Church contained himself. "Jack Churchill. And you are . . . ?"

Her smile was unsettling. "You may call me Niamh."

"You're from another village nearby?" Church turned and scanned the area, knowing how well the roundhouses merged into the landscape. But there were no telltale smoke trails from any fires apart from the ones that hung over Carn Euny. When he turned back, Niamh was gone, and there was no sign of her anywhere nearby.

7

Church planned to ask Etain about Niamh, but she was soon forgotten as events unfolded. Despite the warmth of the summer day, he felt a growing chill. The memory of the burst of black fire blossomed in his thoughts like a sable rose. The spider in his arm felt as if it had settled deeper, and there was now a coldness running from it deep into his bones that made him feel vaguely nauseous. He would have to remove it soon, even if it meant carving it free with a knife. The maddening ache of his missing memories left him on edge, troubled by an itch he couldn't scratch. All in all, he felt so thrown off balance that he couldn't begin to see what he was going to do next.

When he arrived back in Carn Euny, he was surprised to find the residents in a state of mounting excitement. The children ran back and forth, in and out of each other's houses, whooping and calling. The adults stood around, talking in quiet but animated voices.

Tannis was tethering his horse to the post near the communal house.

"What's got everyone so worked up?" Church asked.

Tannis pointed to the east. Beneath the glare of the sun, Church could just make out a figure in the distance, slowly walking towards Carn Euny.

"*Druidae*," Tannis said with a subtly nuanced smile: there was respect, certainly, but also apprehension, perhaps even fear.

As the figure approached, Church gradually made out a man in his mid-fifties, dressed in olive-coloured robes splattered with the mud of his journey. He used a staff to propel his forceful pace. His hair was chestnut brown streaked with silver, wild and untamed, his beard incongruously clipped and tidy.

When he reached the edge of the village, three elders greeted him with deference, a quiet word and a slight bow. He barely acknowledged them. Instead, his eyes swept back and forth across the gathered crowd, his face steely. He muttered something. One of the elders turned and pointed directly at Church.

The children gathered in silence and followed as the elders ushered the druid into the meeting house. Everyone waited outside the door, only whispers passing amongst them.

"He's come for me, hasn't he?" Church said.

Tannis's reaction was unsettling in its simplicity. His smile faded and he placed a reassuring hand on Church's arm. "Stay true to yourself, brother. That is the only advice I can give."

Church wandered over to sit on the grassy knoll just beyond the village boundary. The sun warmed him, the whisper of wind in the grass as soothing as ever, but the idyllic setting no longer worked its magic on his troubled mind.

As he brooded, Etain came up and sat quietly beside him.

"You did a good job of keeping me here until your grand inquisitor could arrive," Church said.

"We have to be sure," Etain said, though there was a hint of regret behind her words. "We can no longer be at the mercy of those who would trap us in hardship and suffering."

Church wondered what the druid's plans were. Torture? He didn't believe that, though the Romans attributed brutal practices to the druidic class. In truth, the druids had much in common with the Hindu Brahmans, an intellectual caste that encompassed both learning and priestly traditions. Druids insisted that all their knowledge was passed down orally so it wouldn't fall into the wrong hands, and that practice had left a void at the heart of their history. Some academics even argued that the druids came from a culture that preceded the Celtic tribes, bringing with them an ancient knowledge that had elevated them to a place of respect amongst the Keltoi. Church placed his hope in the belief that if they were intellectuals they would not resort to violence. But this was a hard, bloodstained world and he couldn't be sure. At least he had his sword, which quietly hummed its pleasant song to him from where it hung against his thigh.

"Do not be afraid," Etain said, as if she could read his thoughts. Her hand crept to rest on the back of his, and when he looked at her, her eyes were dark and numinous. "I have belief in you."

They were interrupted by a tall, elderly man. "Your presence is requested," he said to Church.

The druid sat in the centre of the meeting house, next to the fire, drinking heartily from a jug of the strong alcoholic beverage and gorging on dried meats and fruits from the village store. He motioned to a rush mat opposite. "Sit," he said with his mouth full, then waved his hand furiously until all the villagers had vacated the building.

When they were alone, he studied Church over the rim of his cup and then wiped his beard with the back of his hand. "My name is Conoran," he said, "and you are Jack, Giantkiller, also known as Church."

"I am. And you are here to test me."

Conoran smiled and nodded. "Good. Then the land is clear and the skies blue." Conoran's eyes were still unreadable, but there was a warmth in his gaze that put Church more at ease.

"You want to know if I'm one of the gods' agents sent here to spy on you, or just a man."

"There is no *just*, little boy. A mortal is a good thing to be. The most important thing."

"How are we to go about this? An interrogation?"

Conoran mused while he sipped on his drink. "Let us talk. You walked out of the morning mists into the world of man carrying the sword of Nuada Airgetlamh—the weapon of a god. And it speaks to you . . . and it is yours. You slew one of the great giants of Kernow, made of earth and tree and the great green heart of the wild, constructed of the very stuff of the world. You slew it, yet no man has ever been able to slay one of the giants of Kernow before." The druid ended with a broad smile.

Church considered his comments and replied, "When you put it like that . . ."

Conoran laughed. "My kind have a secret name," he said. "Amongst ourselves, we are called the Culture. We existed long before the tribes and we shall be here long after they are gone. Our knowledge is beyond your imagination . . ." He paused, tugged gently at his beard. "Or perhaps not. You are not of this place, little brother. You use our words, but speak with a strange voice. Your skin is soft, your hands uncalloused. Your garments are beyond the ability of even our most skilled weavers—"

"And you think that makes me a spy from the gods," Church began his argument, but Conoran raised a silencing hand.

"The Culture has a long memory, and our knowledge is great. We can recognise a mortal when we see one. You are mortal, but you are . . . strange. I would say there is something special about you, little brother. Something that is mortal, yet more than mortal. A quality . . . a light shining out of you. And in my eyes, it is blue."

Church felt a shiver of recognition at the druid's words, but frustratingly it originated in the part of his memory that had been locked off.

"You are not like us, yet you are like us," the druid continued. "You are not from the gods, yet you are not from this world. Speak. Tell me the truth. Now." The firelight reflected in his eyes.

"I am from this world." Church paused, considered how best to continue, then leaned forward and scratched a line in the hard-packed-mud floor. "Time," he said, glancing at Conoran to see if he understood the concept. The druid's expression suggested he did. Church etched a point on the far left of the line. "Here we are now, you and me, talking." He scratched another point on the far right. "Here is my home. I have no idea how I got from there to here." He tapped his head. "A lot of my memory has been wiped away."

Conoran nodded thoughtfully. "Space and time are prisons that we all need to escape. You have achieved a great thing."

Church fought back a swell of emotion. "I don't care. I just want to go home." Another flash of Ruth, her face strong and defiant.

"Show me your arm." Conoran gestured to where the black spider nestled in Church's flesh.

Church removed his shirt and Conoran examined the thing without touching it, his expression dark. Finally he sat back and said, "There is much mystery here. The mists must be rolled back. Remember: nothing happens without a reason. You are here for a reason. That thing is in your arm for a reason. A great plan is unfolding, but we can see only one tiny part of it."

"So I'm accepted?" Church replaced his shirt.

Conoran ignored his question. "First we must remove that creature. I will make arrangements."

He marched out of the room without a backward glance.

8

It was a perfect summer night, bright and balmy from the heat of the day, with a million stars glittering overhead and the moon as bright as a lantern. A soft breeze occasionally brought scents of the cooling countryside.

Carn Euny had been transformed. Torches blazed along the main thoroughfare, the flickering shadows making the village hazy and unreal. Church stood with the community silent at his back. The atmosphere was pregnant with anticipation.

Finally Conoran emerged from a nearby house where he had been performing his ritual of preparation. With a flamboyant gesture, he tossed a handful of leaves and twigs onto a small fire that blazed at the head of the street. There was a brief flash accompanied by a murmur of awe from the crowd, and then a heavy aroma filled the air. It reminded Church of incense.

"Are you prepared for the journey into the world beyond?" Conoran asked Church solemnly.

Church nodded. When he had agreed to the ritual he had expected it to be a diverting piece of entertainment, but he was surprised by how affecting it truly was. Every nerve in his body felt electrified.

Conoran held his hand out, palm upwards. On it lay a small pile of dried mushrooms. Church knew that many ancient cultures used some kind of hallucinogen to enhance the religious experience—even the early Christian sects were supposed to have used psychedelic mushrooms in their rituals—but he was apprehensive about their effect.

"Take them," Conoran urged, with a flinty tone that suggested there could be no refusal.

Church reticently popped the mushrooms into his mouth and swallowed. At his back, someone began to bang a drum of animal hide, then another, and another. The sharp notes of a bone flute rose up.

As the rhythmic music built, Conoran led the procession through the settlement, Church close behind him. It ended at the entrance to a mysterious tunnel that Church had inspected earlier. It was a fogou, a feature of several Cornish Iron Age settlements; archaeological debate about their use ranged from a grain store or shelter from marauding enemies to some ritual purpose. Church now knew it was the latter.

Conoran motioned to the dark hole. "Enter now, and be prepared to be born into a new world and a new life."

Church felt a flicker of anxiety as the first flush of the mushrooms hit his system. Lying on his belly, he slithered like a snake into the dark.

The tunnel opened into a larger space, but not high enough to stand upright. The darkness was so intense it had a palpable quality; Church felt as if he was floating in space. He became acutely aware of the beat of his heart and the rush of blood through his arteries and veins.

"Move along the tunnel." Conoran's disembodied voice floated eerily around.

Church edged forward, one hand outstretched in front of him, the other dragging along the cold stone corbels of the wall for guidance. He worried that there might be some secret pit ahead, that the whole ritual was an elaborate trap to rid the community of the dangerous stranger in their midst.

The tunnel turned this way and that, or appeared to in the dark, so that

Church could no longer recall the way out. Eventually he came to a place where the roof and floor came together to form a funnel.

"Crawl into the gap."

Church jumped. Conoran was right behind him.

Church crawled until he was wedged in a foetal position inside a tiny chamber, and there he realised the significance of Conoran's words about being born into a new world. The tunnel acted symbolically like the birth channel. After the ritual he would emerge into the light, to start a new life after the mind-altering experience.

The drums throbbed distantly like the slow beat of an enormous heart. The sound of the bone flute ebbed and flowed like the thrum of a vascular system.

"Jack, Giantkiller, known as Church. Let me tell you about Existence," Conoran began in measured tones. "There is one rule in our secret studies, and it is this: no here or there exists, no in or out. There is only us. Everything you see in the world around, every rock and tree and blade of grass, is fluid. The world is only the way you perceive it because that is how we need it to be, at this moment. We make our own world."

"You're saying this is all just a dream," Church said languorously. He felt strangely like laughing. "We dream the world this way."

"All living things are a part of Existence. The Blue Fire burns in everything, roaring through like life's-blood."

Church had a strange vision: standing on a balmy night, looking over the rolling countryside as streams of Blue Fire raced across the grass in lines, interlinking, forming a huge grid that echoed inside him as much as without.

"The Fiery Network," he muttered.

Was it a dream, or had he truly experienced this, the memory now lost to the abyss in his head?

"You know of this," Conoran said, pleased. "I knew that would be the case. It is secret knowledge, passed down only through the Culture, yet you know. The lines of power run through the earth, from stone circle to cromlech, from sacred spring to hilltop. And the lines run through us, too.

"They are the source of all magic. They are our inspiration, and our defence against the forces that would destroy us."

"Ley lines," Church muttered. He was starting to drift.

Conoran continued with renewed vigour. "Then know this: Existence has another side, as dark as the Blue Fire is bright, as filled with despair and dread as we are filled with hope. From this darkness spring forth the Formorii, the shape-shifting monstrous enemy of the golden-skinned Tuatha Dé Danann. And the black spider, even now crawling from your arm into your very soul, is from that darkness, too."

Church felt a chill run deep into his heart, though he didn't fully understand Conoran's words. The spider in his arm squirmed sickeningly.

"Why is it attacking me?" Church said. He grew nauseous at the insistent wriggling in his flesh. The spider was becoming more active, as though it sensed a threat. Church's thoughts fragmented, his memory grew dim around the edges, and the abiding cold consumed everything.

Suddenly Conoran's voice boomed, then receded as if he had radically shifted to another place, distant yet simultaneously near at hand. "You came to us with the sword of a god. Now you must fight to free yourself from the corrupting touch or be lost for all time."

Church was shocked to realise he could no longer feel the corbels at his back. He was standing in the dark, possibly in the approach tunnel, though he had no sense of having moved. "Conoran?" he called into the echoing gloom. There was no response.

Two other sensations hit Church sharply: he was now holding his sword, the blue glow providing a dim light by which he could see; and he could no longer feel the spider burrowing into his arm.

Cautiously, he reached out to touch the cold wall stones. The drum heartbeat and the whispering echoes of the bone flute were gone, too. A deep silence lay over everything.

Church took a hesitant step forward. If he could find the exit, he could discover where everyone had gone and what odd game Conoran was playing. His thoughts were interrupted by a rapid scuttling motion in the gloom ahead. He had a horrible feeling that he knew what was in the tunnel with him. His breath was taken away by the size of it, bigger even than him. He gripped the sword with both hands, the pounding of his heart filling his head.

More scurrying, the *click-click-click* of legs rattling on stone, oddly metallic. Church sensed the attack before he saw it. The spider launched from the dark, and he dropped to his knees, swinging the sword, cutting air. The spider swept over him, the size of a car, and disappeared into the shadows as quickly as it had come.

Church moved through the fogou trying to get his bearings, but it appeared to be much larger than he had imagined, with side tunnels branching into a labyrinthine network. Soon he couldn't tell where the spider was, or whether he was hunting it, or it him. Long periods of silence were punctuated by the rattling of legs that sounded close at hand one moment, then far away a second later.

He rounded a bend and the light of his sword revealed it, gleaming with a black sheen, eyes turned on him, dark and maleficent. Its maw was open, toxins sizzling at the tips of razor-sharp fangs.

The spider struck with devastating speed, moving from floor to wall to ceiling, knocking Church to his knees with its bulk. The serrated edge on one of its legs tore through his shoulder and he cried out as the pain burned deep into him. When he swung the sword up sharply, the spider was already gone. The blade raised a shower of sparks as it clanged against the corbels.

For minutes that felt like hours, Church dived out of the creature's way, tearing open knees and elbows on the stones, striking as fast as he could, but never fast enough. Occasionally he would nick its steely flesh, raising a venomous cry deep in his own head; and once he struck quickly and strongly enough to hack off a length of leg that twitched with a life of its own on the floor.

He hoped to carry on whittling the thing down, but as he ducked an attack, he turned his ankle and fell to the floor, his sword skidding out of his hand. The spider was on him in an instant, its bulk pinning him down so that he couldn't reach the sword, its legs skewering his flesh. Its eyes hovered over his face. A thousand tiny Churches were reflected back.

It struck rapidly, driving its fangs into Church's arm. The agony was excruciating as his flesh ruptured and the poison rapidly flooded his system. On his pale flesh, the thin blue veins began to turn black as the toxins moved inexorably towards his heart and head. A jarring whispering echoed deep in his skull. The words were alien and came and went like a badly tuned radio, but they carried with them images that threatened to overwhelm him with dread and despair. The spider's consciousness had invaded his system along with the poison, a viral intelligence within the very molecular make-up of the toxin.

After a sickening, hanging moment, a black wave sucked Church along in its wake. The language infiltrating his skull was emotional, speaking of the end of everything, of a vast hole in Existence that pulled in all light, all matter, all hopes and dreams. Church found himself walking across a blasted landscape where ghost-images hovered before winking out. Church saw modern cities fallen into shadow, and Ruth filled with a crushing grief. There were other men and women he felt he should know but didn't.

It would have been easy to give in to the deluge of hopelessness, but instead Church became more aware of qualities that had shaped him. He recalled his despair at the death of his girlfriend Marianne, and how he had overcome that to find some hope for the future. He uncovered a strength forged by hardship. And in that instant he felt the sword in his hand.

He didn't know whether he had found it in the throes of his delirium, or if it had magically appeared there, but he acted instantly, thrusting upward where he remembered the spider being.

An echoing shriek filled his head and the black wave receded. When his mind cleared, Church lay with the spider's body across his legs, ichor leaking all over him. But that impression faded just as quickly, and once more he was in the tiny nook at the end of the fogou with the heartbeat drums echoing through the ground. A dream within a dream within a dream.

And he was still dying.

9

What followed came in flashes as if he were viewing intermittent frames on a reel of film. Being carried out of the fogou, seeing the powder-blue and pink flush of a dawn sky, with a few stars and a ghost-moon still hovering. Lying next to the fire in a roundhouse with Etain leaning over him, tears in her eyes. A foul stench from a pot bubbling over the fire, and an anxious Conoran throwing unseen things into the brew. Tannis bowing before him, making some oath that Church couldn't translate.

A long period of darkness followed, and when Church next came to consciousness, the fragmentary nature of reality had subsided but the pain and exhaustion in his limbs was near-unbearable. Church fumbled for where the spider had been embedded in his arm, felt nothing.

"Death stalks you." Conoran loomed over Church, his pale eyes gleaming in the firelight. "Are you ready for the next step of your journey?"

"Yes." Church's voice sounded as if it came from a different person. "But I'm not ready to die."

"You must fan whatever flames lie within you if you are to pull your spark back from the dark."

"What do I have to do?" Church found his strength creeping back, but he still could not lift his head.

Conoran considered his response. "You are to meet the god above gods and plead for your life."

10

In the dark before dawn, Church found himself carted from the roundhouse and fastened to a stretcher of wood and straw harnessed to Tannis's horse. They set off at a slow pace that still amplified every rut and bump in the main street, and was barely less uncomfortable when they passed onto the sweeping grassland. Church was vaguely aware of other riders accompanying him, but their identities remained unknown.

For a while he was transfixed by the stars and for a moment touched a sweeping sense of wonder rarely felt outside childhood. But after an hour or so, branches closed in overhead, bringing with them a feeling of claustrophobia and a dull background drone of dread.

Tannis clearly felt it, too, for he said quietly but insistently, "Go slow. We are no longer alone."

The rocking motion became a crawl, the thud of hooves barely a whisper. Church could hear the breeze rustling through the upper branches and the tinkle of a nearby stream, but nothing else. It was too dark, and death increasingly tugged at his sleeve.

"The dark powers do not want us to reach Boskawen-Un." It was Conoran's voice.

"They come for Jack, Giantkiller?" Etain this time.

"He is a threat to them. They recognise this. That is why the Poison-Spider was set in his body. They did not wish a direct confrontation," Conoran replied.

"Then he must be a great warrior indeed," Tannis said with awe.

Church faded out for a while, and when he fought his way back to consciousness the atmosphere had grown even more tense.

"Where? Towards the west?" It was Etain's friend Owein, cautious and intelligent.

"No. Look north." Branwen, as flinty and insistent as ever.

"What are they?" A touch of horror in Etain's voice. "Are they men or beasts?"

"No time now to discuss their nature," Conoran said. "With the Giantkiller near death, we do not have the strength to fight them."

"Gods." Owein's voice was scared. "See how they move through the trees? So fast and low. Surely they must have come from beneath the sea. Are they Fomorii?"

"Enough talk!" Conoran snapped. "Tannis, draw your slingshot."

Church heard the creak of animal hide, and then the harsh clack of a flint being struck. A second later there was a whoosh and a crackle. A bright ball of light flared in the gloom before arcing across Church's line of vision and disappearing into the trees. The tinder-dry summer wood flared up and quickly became a deafening roar. Above the crackling flames, Church heard a terrible sound, like furious pigs disturbed during feast.

"Ride with the wind beneath you!" Conoran bellowed.

Church was rushed along, bouncing so wildly he was convinced he would be jolted unconscious any moment. Somehow his delirium preserved him, and after ten minutes he dreamed a river took him to a night-land where a single boatman waited.

Eventually they came to a halt. He could only guess that their pursuers had fallen back. Someone lit a fire, which drove some of the aching chill from his bones, but its red light was uncommonly thin and he felt as though he was looking at it down a long tunnel. The others must have wandered away to forage for food, for their voices retreated to a distant tremor.

For a long time Church hovered in that limbo until the overwhelming odour of engine oil mysteriously appeared. An old woman's face loomed over him, eyes red-rimmed in a face so filthy it looked as though the grime had been accumulating for decades. Her wiry hair was greasy and matted, and her breath was so foul it made Church gag.

"Gods answer to gods, answer to gods," she whispered in a voice like rending metal, "and somehow the Voice of Existence trickles through to men." Church felt as if he was lying next to a massive generator; the atmosphere was distorted, infused with such an overpowering dread that he felt he might go insane with the intensity of emotion. "Hold hard. You must see the dawn," the woman continued.

And then she was gone in the blink of an eye, leaving Church unsure whether she had really been there.

11

"It comes." Conoran's voice made Church start; he had been convinced he was alone.

"What comes?" Church said weakly.

Conoran appeared in Church's frame of vision. "You fight hard, Jack, Giantkiller. I was certain you would be dead before the dawn. But look, its first rays break. All is not lost."

Tannis and Owein freed Church from the stretcher and propped him up. A thin line of silver lay to the east. In the firelight, Church could see they were sitting on a grassy bank, looking down on a thick forest of gorse. Just visible beyond it was a circle of scrubby yellowing grass, worn by many a foot. Several ghosts stood inside the circle, immobile. It took Church a few seconds to realise they were standing stones, glowing spectrally in the first glimmer of light.

"Boskawen-Un," Conoran said reverently. "We must get you into the circle before the sun comes up."

Tannis and Owein helped Church to his feet. His head spun and he couldn't stand without their support.

"What was hunting us?" Church's thready voice was almost lost to the breeze.

"There will be time for that later." Conoran looked over his shoulder to the north. "If you survive what is to come, they will be waiting."

Other outlying stones became visible around the central circle as Tannis and Owein helped Church down the slope to a thin path through the protecting gorse.

Once they were in the circle, Church was surprised to feel a potent atmosphere suck the tension from his limbs. It was the same sensation he felt whenever he held his sword.

Conoran turned to face the golden sun now half-risen above the horizon and bowed his head. "For too long the days have been dark," he said. "Let it be so no longer."

"Look at him—a weak, straggly thing," Branwen said harshly of Church. "He does not have the strength to endure what lies ahead."

"He has more strength than you, or I, or any of us." Etain marched forward defiantly and kissed Church on the lips. When she pulled back, tears rimmed her eyes. "I would give you my life if it were enough," she said so only he could hear. "But only your own heart will suffice."

When she backed away, Conoran began to lead Church towards the circle's westernmost stone, the only one made of white quartz.

"I don't think I can make it," Church said. The darkness was closing in around him again.

"You will," Conoran said sharply. "This is no longer just about you. It is about the people of this land, and their survival into the long days to come."

"You are sure?" Owein said. "This is what the gods spoke of."

"This is what the gods fear."

Conoran directed Tannis and Owein to haul Church to the white quartz stone, where they left him clinging on with the last of his strength. He felt as though the remnants of his life were trickling out of him, the trickle growing faster by the moment.

"Ruth," he whispered into the returning delirium. "I love you."

Church's world shrank to the ring of stones and the white quartz pillar, the whisper of the wind on the grass, the fragrance of the yellow gorse blossom.

"You place too great a burden on him. It is not just." Etain's sad, angry voice came from somewhere behind him, a world away.

"Existence has placed the burden," Conoran replied, an anxious edge to his voice. "Existence has chosen its vessel. All lies within this man's grasp, if he can but rise to the challenge."

The words fanned a spark within Church. He gripped the quartz stone tighter and attempted to haul himself upright. He no longer knew where he was, or why he was, or what was expected of him.

"Look." Branwen's hushed voice was laced with fear. "They have found us. There is no escape now."

Church forced himself to peer beyond the limits of the circle. The surrounding countryside was alive with movement; red glimmered in the wan light eking above the skyline—some kind of uniform.

"Then our survival lies with this one," Conoran stated.

"This cannot be right," Branwen persisted.

"Do not question him." Tannis's voice was steady. In the fields beyond rose up the rhythmic beat of a hundred voices chanting a low war call.

Warm breath tingled Church's ear and he smelled Etain's fragrance. "I hold you in my heart, Jack, Giantkiller," she whispered. "You will save us all."

And then the sun crested the horizon and the world caught fire.

It wasn't the ruddy fire of a homestead hearth, but the brilliant blue of a summer sky. At first Church thought it was another hallucination, yet when he let go of the quartz stone the image faded, returning with a blaze when he grasped the rock again.

When the sun touched the quartz stone, lines of licking sapphire flames ran out from the stone circle in all directions, interconnecting at various points to create a vast network and echoing the dream that had come to Church in the fogou. Other lines soared up into the sky over the stone circle, forming a glowing cathedral of light. The blackness of the poison gradually ebbed away and strength began to return to Church's limbs. He was amazed to see a filigree of blue lines on his own skin, like the meridians used by acupuncturists. The same network, within and without.

Church had an impression of the lines of force running out along the spine of Cornwall, across the Somerset Levels to Glastonbury, to Stonehenge and Avebury, and beyond, across the entire world. And more, Church could see the Blue Fire stretching out across the vast gulf of the years, connecting the future and the past. There and here, then and now, all linked; time and space united.

The force of the vision shook Church to the core. It had the familiarity of a returning memory, and Church couldn't decide whether he and every other human being had always known about the Blue Fire, encoded in the genes, or if it was peculiar to his own lost memory.

Once the euphoria had ebbed and Church discovered he now had the strength to stand upright, he peered beyond the circle's comforting perimeter once more. The azure incandescence revealed the approaching threat in stark relief. Moving rapidly across the countryside was a small army of inhuman creatures, squat and brutish with greenish skin, long black hair and monstrous features. It wasn't their supernatural aspect that shocked Church, but the fact that the uniforms he had thought he glimpsed earlier were human skin and body parts worn as clothes.

"Redcaps," he said, half-remembering the legends of the creatures that had once stalked the border counties.

"What now, Giantkiller?" Conoran said with concern.

Church fought back the poison still licking at the edges of his consciousness and wondered why everyone was suddenly relying on him.

"Knock three times if you want in."

Church started at the unfamiliar voice emerging as if from the air around him. None of the others showed they had heard it; they were fixated on the rampaging Redcaps, fear evident in their faces. Only Etain looked at Church with pleading eyes.

Church's head swam. The voice had been in modern English. Another hallucination?

The Redcaps were already crashing into the circle of spiky gorse, their low war chant turning hungry as they scented blood.

Church reacted instinctively, slapping one hand three times on the white quartz stone.

Instantly there was a rumbling beneath his feet as a section of turf tore open in the centre of the circle. It rose up like a gaping maw in a shower of earth and stones. The Redcaps hesitated in confusion.

"Come on!" Church said to the others, unsure if it was the right thing to do but rapidly running out of options. He leaped into the dark hole. The other five followed his lead without a second thought, and then the ground thundered shut behind them.

12

"Stand your ground. Do not be afraid." Conoran's voice was resolute, but its timbre was muffled by the acoustics of the rocky tunnel in which they found themselves.

"To what monstrous place have you brought us, Giantkiller?" Owein asked. "Is this the underworld home of the Fomorii? Have you led us into the arms of those dark gods?"

"Be silent," Etain said sharply. "The Giantkiller has saved our lives."

"What were those creatures?" Tannis asked.

"As far as I was concerned they were just myths . . . stories . . . not real at all," Church said. "Looks as if the stories had some basis in fact." Like the legends of giants terrorising Cornwall, and the stories of ley lines linking ancient sites. Everything that was happening to him had the slick, ungraspable feeling of a dream.

"Let's see where this tunnel leads," he said, hiding his disorientation.

The air was electric. He could taste iron in his mouth, and there was a feeling of being at the side of the ocean or on a mountaintop. The others followed him in silence, helping him upright whenever the poison overcame the restorative powers of the Blue Fire. He felt permanently queasy as the black and the blue fought for dominance inside him, and he knew that his death had only been delayed, not rescinded.

As they progressed, Church began to feel as if the tunnel was not in the earth at all, but somewhere else entirely. His suspicion was sharply confirmed when they ventured into a large chamber seemingly hewn from the rock. It was permeated by blue light, and for the first time they could see clearly.

Tannis touched Church's arm and pointed upwards. "Proof, my friend, that since you arrived amongst us you have turned our world upside down."

Above their heads hung the floor of the chamber—they were standing on the ceiling of an inverted room with a flagstone floor, walls covered with delicately etched Celtic designs, supporting columns and a stone brazier in which blue flames flickered. On the far side of the room was an upside-down doorway that looked inaccessible from where they were standing.

"Should we sprout wings and fly?" Owein asked in disbelief.

"Let us return," Branwen pressed. "Those beasts will have departed by now. We can make our way back to Carn Euny by the light of the day."

"No," Conoran said. "Only here can the Giantkiller cure himself of the poison that infects him. Only here can he learn the path he must tread."

"Tell me, good Conoran," Tannis said warmly, "if this is a question that will not offend you: how do you know these things?"

"The Culture has many secrets passed down to us from the First Days, when man was an infant and the rules were first carved in the earth."

"If we must venture on, how do we rise above ourselves?" Etain looked around for a solution.

"Walk."

Once again, Church started at the same mysterious voice he had heard at the quartz stone, and as before it was for his ears only. This time he had no qualms about responding. He searched the nearest wall until he found what appeared to be a foothold. Resting his foot in the hollow, he pushed up, searching for another foothold. There was none, but he was surprised to find himself balanced effortlessly with his second foot merely touching the wall, perpendicular to the ceiling on which he had been standing, as if gravity had given up on him. The others watched uneasily as Church took another step. His stomach did a flip as he began walking up the sheer rock face.

"Evil!" Branwen hissed, and made a protective sign in the air.

"The normal rules don't apply here," Church said. "I think you can follow me."

Etain pressed forward without hesitation and walked up the wall until she was at Church's side ten feet above the ceiling. The others followed hesitantly.

Finally they were standing on the floor of the upside-down room. Branwen turned to one side and vomited, before wiping her mouth and uttering a curse-word that Church didn't understand. He realised everyone was waiting for him to lead the way, but as he cautiously headed towards the far door, the blue flames in the brazier roared up into a column of fire that reached far above their heads. Church was shocked to see a face floating in its midst.

"Finally. You really take some prompting." The flames made the features swim so it was difficult for Church to get a clear view, but he had an impression of a young, clean-shaven man with short, dark hair.

"Who are you?" Church asked, once he had got over the unreality of talking to a pillar of fire.

"You can call me Hal." The voice was English, the inflection definitely twenty-first century.

"As in the computer in *2001: A Space Odyssey*?"

"If you like. 'Open the bomb bay doors, HAL.'"

Church knew instinctively that the being in the flames was teasing him, but there was no sense of malice. "It was you who told me how to get into this place, and to walk up the wall."

"That's my job. Part of it, at least."

"And what else is your job? To drive me insane? Because everything else that's happened to me recently seems to be trying to do that."

The features were disrupted by a surge of flame, and the voice fizzed and receded before returning, as if echoing through vast, empty halls. "I'm here to help you, Church."

"How do you know my name?"

"I know everything about you. Everything about everything. Well, at least to the point where the dark and the light converge, but that's another story."

"If you know so much, tell me what's been taken from my memory."

Hal faded again, and when he returned Church thought he detected a note of sadness in his voice. "Not so long ago I would have told you everything you wanted to know, but now . . . I can see the bigger picture."

Church laughed derisively.

"You wouldn't understand, and I don't blame you for that. It's all a matter of perspective. What I've learned is that not-knowing is part of knowing. That sounds like some kind of double-speak, but it's not. The only way we learn and change and grow—because that's what life is all about, and believe me, this is *really* about life—is by experiencing the journey ourselves."

"You sound like some fairground medium," Church said.

"I'm sorry, but somehow the real, basic truths always end up coming across like that. I think it's our built-in cynical streak."

"Our?" Church thought he glimpsed a flicker of a smile in the blue.

"Let me put it another way," Hal continued. "When your mother told you, 'Don't touch, it's hot,' did you listen? Course you didn't, because it's a fact of life that nobody learns anything important by being told. You have to feel the pain yourself."

"That's reassuring."

"All I'm saying, Church, is that you're on a journey of discovery on lots of different levels. And what you'll learn about yourself will be just as important as the facts you uncover." Again the note of sadness. "If I told you what you needed to know, you'd only get half of the equation."

"So basically you're next to useless."

When Hal spoke again, his voice had grown grave. "You're on a long journey. A long, *long* journey, and it won't be easy. I could save you a lot of hardship along the way, but there will be times when you can go down one path or another, and you've got to make those choices yourself or you won't be any use when you get to the end of the road."

"And what am I supposed to do when I arrive?"

Another pause during which the shadows in the room appeared to grow darker. "Storm clouds are gathering, Church. That's another cliché, but it's the best way I can describe it. If you don't believe in Evil, Church, Evil as a force of intelligence, you ought to start now. It's gathering its strength, waiting for the right moment. Everything's at stake, Church—everything you believe in, everything that matters. That power knows you're a threat to it—"

"Me?" Church said incredulously.

"And you are. It'll do anything to stop you. Even now it's searching, scanning Existence, sending its agents out to track you down. In fact, you've met some of them already—"

"The Redcaps."

"They don't act alone. You'll soon find out how widespread that threat is, and exactly what you're facing. Stand firm, Church. Don't turn away. Existence needs you. According to what I know about you, I reckon you'll make the right choices along the way."

"But you can't be sure."

"No. I can't."

Church thought he saw other faces buried deeper in the flickering fire. A feeling of hope emanated from them. "Is there anything you can tell me that will help?"

"Not now. But you'll encounter me again. There'll be moments when you'll really need me, and then I'll try to do what I can."

"That's if I make it that far. I'm dying—"

"It's a spiritual poison. The Enemy landed a lucky blow when you first dropped into this place—one of its agents stuck you with a black spider. The aim was to get you off the board right away. Your resilience has brought you this far. If you walk through that door, you'll find what you need to clear the poison. You won't get back the memories it stole, but you'll be ready for the fight."

Church eyed the door with uncertainty. The real dangers clearly lay in the things Hal could not bring himself to say.

"Go through the door, Church. Take the first step on your quest. You've got a vast gulf to cross and a million hardships to overcome before you can rest. Just one word of advice: when things get darkest, don't turn away from the light. Don't ever give up hope. If you do, you're gone. All is lost."

The column of fire retreated into the brazier, and Hal's voice was replaced by a ringing silence. The others were examining the Celtic motifs on the wall, and Church got the impression that the whole conversation with Hal had happened in a fraction of a second.

13

The door was made of polished granite. Church couldn't imagine who had made it, or constructed the chamber in which they stood. In the centre of the door at head height was a graven image of a serpent eating its own tail: an ouroboros, an ancient symbol for the cyclical and eternal nature of life. Level with his waist were the imprints of five hands of varying sizes. Church's own hand fitted the central imprint perfectly, but none of the others. There was no handle on the door.

"I think we each need to put a hand here," Church mused. "The door could be fitted with some kind of balance. The right pressure might move it."

When there was no response, he looked back. Tannis, Owein, Etain and Branwen stared at the door apprehensively. Conoran watched Church with a cold, expectant eye.

"What's wrong?" Church asked.

"It has the mark of the dragon," Owein said.

"You must enter alone. We will not follow." Branwen rubbed her hands together feverishly.

"I can't do it on my own." A rush of nausea from the poison swept through him. "All right, just help me push the door open. I'll go in alone."

The look of fear in their faces made him feel guilty; he had forgotten that for all their emotional and intellectual sophistication, they were still the product of superstitious times.

Conoran pointed one slender finger at Church. "If they open the door they must enter."

"You know more than you're saying." The poison and disorientation made Church snap with irritation.

Conoran's eyes glowed with a cold light that made Church regret his tone.

"You haven't come this far just for me," he said to the others. The delirium was growing worse again. "You've done it for your people. You think I can help defend them against the gods, and you may be right. But if you walk away now, I won't be able to do anything because I'll be dead. And what will happen then if the gods return?" Church felt a twinge at the shameless emotional manipulation, but he could see in their eyes that it was working.

"Your family and friends need you. Your tribe needs you," he continued. "I know you're scared of what lies ahead, but I'll stand with you. You've seen me fight. You know what I can do with this." He touched the sword, which sang quietly in response. "Together we can survive this. Didn't I help you escape the Redcaps?" He ran out of steam as poison-pain burned his heart, but he could see he had done enough. Conoran was smiling.

Tannis stepped forward and pressed his right hand into a snugly fitting hollow. "I stand with you, Jack, Giantkiller." He smiled warmly, all trace of fear expunged now that he had made his choice.

"And I." Etain's smile was shy, but her eyes blazed when she looked at Church.

Owein followed suit, and then finally—reluctantly—Branwen. All of their hands fitted perfectly into one or other of the hollows.

"Almost as if it was meant to be," Conoran said wryly.

A short period of anticipation gave way to a crackle of blue sparks as the door swung open.

"I await your return," Conoran said.

Church braced himself, then crossed the threshold.

What had appeared to be simply entering another room felt like moving to a different place entirely. The clammy underground air was replaced by a balmy summer warmth. Sand crunched beneath Church's feet and a night sky dappled with unfamiliar constellations hung overhead. Gradually, he became accustomed to his surroundings. A hot breeze brought with it the scent of steaming vegetation. Ahead he could see palm trees silhouetted against the sky: an oasis; a garden.

"Where are we?" Etain whispered in awe.

"The desert, I think," Church said.

A blue light amongst the trees pulled them towards it. The others drew their weapons with trepidation.

Church pushed through spiky-leaved bushes until he arrived at a lake. But instead of water it was filled with Blue Fire moving as though it were a liquid. A dark shape swam sinuously in its depths, but Church's attention was drawn to a woman who stood in the centre of the lake, seemingly on the very surface of the flaming energy. Her skin was pale, her hair black, her eyes as blue as the fire.

"Greetings, Quincunx." Church flinched; though the woman's lips had moved, the voice was deep like a man's, perhaps not quite human. "The first of many," she continued with a smile.

The surface behind her broke and a head rose on a long serpentine neck. It had scales and tines and horns and a form that reminded Church of pictures in books he had read as a child. Fire licked around its open mouth, and beneath the surface leathern wings were just visible amongst the coils of its body. Yet the strangest thing was that the creature appeared to be made of the Blue Fire itself. Now and then, Church glimpsed its vascular system beneath the flickering sapphire skin.

Behind Church, the others cowered. "Strike it now," Branwen hissed, "before it slays us with its breath."

"Do not be afraid," the woman said, and it seemed to Church that the beast was somehow speaking through her. "I am here to give you knowledge and purpose."

"Can you cure me?" Church asked.

The woman and the beast jointly turned their attention to him. "You are filled with the black poison of the Devourer of All Things. Your time is nearly done." A pause, then: "Step forward."

Church obeyed. Etain and Tannis leaped forward to prevent Church from burning himself in the flames, but he was surprised to find the Blue Fire cool. Euphoria rushed through him, and he could feel the poison being scoured from his system.

"Thank you," he said. It didn't seem enough. Whatever the fire was doing to him, he felt he could overcome any obstacle.

"And you can, if the Blue Fire burns in your heart." The woman appeared to be privy to every thought that passed through his head. "Existence needs champions," she continued. "There is a great struggle ahead. Battle and suffering and death. But also wonder. And magic. Will you be the first?"

Everyone was too awed to speak, so the woman asked again: "Will you stand for Existence against the dark? Will you carry the Pendragon Spirit in your heart, and keep it alive so that it can move freely from champion to champion across the ocean of time? Will you be my Brothers and Sisters, the first of many?"

Filled with the rush of the Blue Fire, Church felt himself speaking. "I will."

The woman smiled. "You are already the first amongst all, Jack Churchill. But there must be five. Always five. The Quincunx must be complete if the full power of Existence is to manifest."

Tannis looked to Church. "If my good friend and leader says he will, then I must follow." Tannis grinned broadly and stepped into the fire. The minute it touched him, a moan of ecstasy left his lips. "Ah! I never knew! Brothers, sisters—follow me. Drink of this lake. Taste this power."

Hesitantly, the others followed until they all stood in the lake. Their fear was soon forgotten. Instead, they grinned at each other, and hugged and kissed. Church felt a part of them, as if they had always known each other and always would. Etain fell into his arms and kissed him with a pure love, before moving on to Tannis, and Owein, and finally Branwen.

Church saw a blue star burning brightly in each of their chests, not floating on the surface, but buried inside. He realised with awe that he was looking through the physical to the essence of each one, the ghost in the machine. It was beautiful and immeasurably powerful and honest. Though memories faded and bodies decayed, he knew he would never forget the revelation until his dying day.

"Now and for evermore, champions all," the woman said with a soft, soothing sibilance. "The spark of Blue Fire within you all has become a flame to drive out the darkest shadows. Where there is despair, you will bring hope. Where there is weakness, you will bring strength. Where there is fear, you will bring courage. The Pendragon Spirit has created an unbreakable bond that links this Quincunx, and all future champions of Existence, for all time. You are Brothers and Sisters. Be free."

The incandescence became brighter, and then brighter still, rising up from the lake of fire until Church could see nothing but blue. The blue of summer skies, the blue of a peaceful ocean. Tranquil, eternal, majestic.

14

Church woke on the warm grass at the centre of Boskawen-Un. The setting sun made the sky a blaze of scarlet. Tannis, Etain, Owein and Branwen stirred around him, muttering the last remnants of a fading dream that still filled them with wonder.

"Finally." Conoran sat with his back to one of the stones. He glowered, but a smile lurked just behind his stern expression.

"Sunset?" Church struggled to comprehend how a day had been lost.

"The rules of our world do not apply in that place. Time moves like smoke in the breeze, back and forth and then not there at all."

"What place do you speak of?" Owein looked around, blinking. "We were in a cavern beneath Boskawen-Un."

"If you believe that, you are more stupid than you appear," Conoran said.

Realisation of what they had experienced came to them as one and they all looked at each other in amazement.

"We are Brothers and Sisters of Dragons," Tannis said, scarcely believing.

"But what does that mean?" Etain said.

Church tried to make sense of what they had been told. "We're joined, on some deep level. There's something inside us—the Pendragon Spirit—that marks us out as champions—"

"Of Existence," Branwen finished. "Life."

Owein flexed one hand, examining his skin for some superficial sign of what they had experienced. "It makes us stronger, perhaps. Wiser—"

"It means you have a job to do," Conoran said curtly. "No more drifting through days without purpose. You have received a great gift, but there is a price to pay, and that price is no more peace until the work is finished."

Tannis and the others continued to smile at each other, but only Church understood the truth in Conoran's words. Conoran saw him weighing this and said, "And you, Giantkiller, have received the greatest gift of all: your life. Against that, this price is nothing."

"But what does it *mean*?" Branwen pressed. "What lies ahead for us now?"

"That," Tannis said, "we shall soon discover."

As the shadows lengthened, they collected themselves and sought out their horses in nearby copses, still skittish after the passing of the Redcaps. Conoran's grim mood had returned, and he had taken to glancing at the sliver of red on the horizon.

"You think the Redcaps are going to be waiting for us on the way back?" Church asked.

"When you are weak and ineffectual, the powers that exist in the worlds around us have no need to notice you. But the more you rise up, the more they will pay attention. And those powers do not brook challenges from humankind."

Church reached silent agreement with Etain that he would ride back with her, and when their eyes met he could feel something crackling between them. As he climbed onto the back of her horse and slipped his arms around her slim, muscular waist, her scent enveloped him and every nerve came alive. He brushed his nose against her hair and fought the urge to kiss her.

It was a powerful attraction, but instinctive, driven by the changes inside them and the knowledge that they were now a minority of five, separated from the rest of the human race by their shared experience. Church made himself focus on Ruth, but without his memories to give her weight, she was as insubstantial as a ghost, however strong his feelings. How could that compete with the earthiness of Etain, with her real and fiery passions?

For an hour they rode in silence across the cooling Cornish countryside, fireflies glowing green in the long grass, and the moon bright and thoughtful. With the warm aroma of the gorse and the trees, and the soft licks of breeze, it felt like moving across the surface of a dream.

Church thought, *There will never be another time like this.* No smell of pollution, no constant background drone of traffic, no stress of a mundane, unfulfilling job. There was only the land, where the Blue Fire crackled just beneath the surface, and the people in tune with it.

Church urged Etain to bring their mount alongside Conoran's. "You knew about the Blue Fire," Church said.

"All know of the Blue Fire. All can feel it. Few can see it. Fewer still know what it truly is."

"Which is?"

"The lifeblood of Existence," Conoran replied. "It binds us all together, all the people of this land. And it binds us to the deer in the forest and the wolf on the moor, to the hawk in the sky and the mouse in the grass, and to the grass, and to the sky, and to the trees. All one, Jack, Giantkiller. A body bigger than any giant you could slay. A mind . . ." He made an expansive gesture, but could not find the words. "We are within Existence, and we are Existence, and Existence is our soul." Conoran leaned towards Church conspiratorially. "And the Blue Fire links you to the Otherworld, Jack,

Giantkiller, to T'ir n'a n'Og, and all the worlds beyond. Those who live there can now see the Pendragon Spirit burning brightly within you, like a beacon in the night."

Church ignored his rhetoric. "You did a good job of not answering me."

Conoran laughed. "You are a wise man, Giantkiller. You would make a good member of the Culture. Yes, my people know of the Blue Fire. It is part of our body of knowledge, passed down through each generation in our colleges. And it was known by the ones who preceded us, who set up the markers on the landscape where the Blue Fire is strongest."

Etain had been listening to the conversation carefully. "And we are now champions of this great power," she said with incredulity.

"Existence needs champions now," Conoran said gravely. "The seasons are turning. A time of great devastation is coming, a time of reckoning."

"And we must fight?" Etain's voice trembled. "I can see why you were chosen, Jack—you are a great hero. The fire burned within you even before you met the Beast. But the rest of us—"

"You wouldn't have been chosen if you weren't up to the job." Church tried to sooth the jumping shadows he saw in her eyes. "And I have a feeling that *Existence* doesn't make mistakes."

"No," Conoran interjected. "Only humans."

The sound of Branwen and Owein bickering rose up from the rear of their column. "Be quiet," Tannis hissed. "Do you want to bring the enemy upon us?"

"This one has been given a great gift yet acts like a small child," Branwen said contemptuously.

Owein snorted and tried not to look embarrassed. "I just said we should have asked what was wanted of us before we took the Pendragon Spirit."

"I was wrong. You are not a small child. You are an old woman scared of a storm," Branwen spat.

"Quiet," Tannis hissed again. "You are both old women."

Church felt a prickling in the pit of his stomach and quickly surveyed the sparsely wooded area through which they moved. The bright moonlight illuminated the scrubby grass, raising phantom shades. Nothing moved. The only sound was the gentle tread of their horses' hooves on the sward.

Tannis noticed Church's alertness. "You see the enemy?" he asked quietly.

"No, but I can feel something—can you?"

Tannis raised his head as if sniffing the wind. "Yes, something foul." A look of surprise crossed his face. "I smell blood."

Church understood: all their senses were becoming heightened. "Red-caps," he said. "They're lying in wait somewhere." Yet he couldn't imagine where. The only movement in the landscape was a few drifting strands of mist amongst the trees.

Owein brought his horse up alongside Church and Etain's. "I hear nothing."

"There's nothing there——" Church began.

"No, I hear *nothing*—no screech of owls, no bats in the trees, no move-ment of branches in the wind."

Church realised that Owein was right. The whole area felt deadened. Church's attention moved back to the drifting mist. It was now clinging to the bottoms of the trunks and had taken on a faint, unnatural greenish colour.

Church felt a weight in his chest that reminded him unpleasantly of the spider-poison. "Ride!" he shouted. The word had barely left his lips when it dropped like a stone in the sound-deadened zone. No one else had heard him. Their attention was fixed on the eerie green mist, which was now billowing towards them.

Church saw Branwen mouth, "Goddess be with me," felt Etain stiffen against him. They were all mesmerised.

A sudden shift in time jolted him: the mist was now neck-high and only fifty feet away; and again, now only twenty feet away. Shapes moved inside it.

Church's attention was caught by activity to one side. On a ragged out-cropping of granite stood a tall, thin man in black robes wearing an emotion-less silver mask that caught the moonlight. He carved intricate patterns in the air with sweeps of his robed arms.

Church only had a second to register this before there was a ferocious roar and five Redcaps erupted from the mist. They were as fast as thoroughbred horses, their muscled legs shaking the ground. Close up, the sight of the human body parts stitched together was sickening.

There was no chance to flee. Church jumped from the horse and drew his blade. It released a keening sound, showering blue sparks everywhere. A Redcap hit Church like a wrecking ball before he even had chance to swing the sword. The impact smashed him to the ground, and the Redcap was instantly upon him like a wild animal, head shaking furiously as its jaws snapped for his throat. The only thing that kept Church alive was the blade, which he had managed to get between him and the Redcap as he fell.

The iron smell of blood was heavy in the air and congealed gobbets show-ered down on Church from the flayed human skin flapping madly against the

Recap's head: a Celtic tattoo, a navel, on the Redcap's shoulder a piece of scalp with hair still attached. And beneath that, something black and gleaming: a spider like the one that had been fixed to Church's arm.

Piggy eyes glared down at him as the jaws clamped closer. Its breath smelled like a butcher's shop. Suddenly all motion stopped, and a gout of stinking blood burst from the Redcap's mouth and splattered across Church's face.

Etain's knife was buried in the Redcap's ear. She must have struck the blow a few seconds earlier and it had taken that long for the Redcap to realise it was dead, for she was already a few feet away.

When Church threw the Redcap off him, she darted forward to retrieve the knife, flashing him a look of unadulterated pleasure at having saved his life.

The Redcaps ran back and forth like jungle cats. Conoran had managed to spur his horse fifty yards away, but it was clear the Redcaps were only interested in the Brothers and Sisters of Dragons.

Tannis, Owein and Branwen had abandoned their horses and were performing an intricate ballet as they ducked attacks and lashed out with their weapons. With his axe, Owein took the top off one of the Redcaps' heads. Branwen rammed her spear in another's back, while Tannis took on the remaining two with his sword. But the Redcaps were too fast and too powerful and would not be contained for long.

The deadened atmosphere had faded with the attack. "Don't waste time with them!" Church yelled as he sliced away the lower jaw of the Redcap that was thrashing around with Branwen's spear still protruding from it. "They're being controlled!" He pointed to the man in the silver mask.

Tannis, Branwen and Etain followed Church as he bounded forwards, but they were halted by Owein's terrible cry. He was pinned to the floor by two Redcaps in a feeding frenzy, and blood was showering into the air.

Church took off both of the Redcaps' heads with one furious swing. He wrenched Owein out from under the still-thrashing mass and was sickened to see bare bone through the skin of Owein's upper arm where most of the muscle had been torn free.

"I will protect him," Tannis said breathlessly. "Go after the leader."

Seemingly oblivious to Church's attack, the black-robed figure continued to weave patterns in the air. But as Church neared, sword raised, the leader turned towards him and Church was brought up sharp by the unnerving sight of the black robe crumpling to the ground as if it contained nothing.

Rivers of spiders flooded out of the robe, disappearing into the landscape. Within seconds only cloth remained; even the mask had been carried away.

"He was made out of spiders," Church said incredulously as Etain arrived at his side.

A triumphant cry from Tannis told them the remaining Redcap had retreated into the green mist, and soon that too was gone.

"We beat them," Branwen said in disbelief, but any jubilation drained away when Tannis approached carrying Owein's bloody form.

15

Etain and Conoran emerged from the hut, their expressions grim. Church had waited quietly in the dark of the street while they tended to Owein.

"He cannot last long," Conoran said quietly. "Too much flesh has been lost from his upper arm, even down to the bone . . . too much blood."

Etain brushed away a tear, the strain of the evening evident in her face. "Is this how Existence works?" she asked. "It demands a balance. Your life was saved, Jack, Giantkiller, so Owein must lose his?"

"I don't believe that to be true," Church said.

They stood silently, unable to give voice to their momentous experience. All around them, Carn Euny slept, oblivious. Eventually Etain said, "It makes no sense to me, for Owein to lose his life so soon after being chosen as a champion of Existence—"

"We are not meant to understand the rules of Existence," Conoran said. "We see only one small part of the sweep of the plan, like a fish in a pool who thinks the world is made of water and that the faces that occasionally look down into the depths are the gods of the fish-world."

Tannis arrived from feeding and watering the horses. He could see that the news was not good. "What now for us? The Fabulous Beast said there need to be five for the Pendragon Spirit to achieve its full potential."

"Perhaps another champion will arise," Conoran mused.

Branwen made her way down the street from wherever she had been hiding since their return. Her face was streaked with tears. During their journey home from Boskawen-Un, Church realized she had feelings for Owein that she buried beneath her fractious exterior. Tannis called her gently, but she ignored him and slipped into the hut where Owein was caught between delirium and coma.

"Look at us," Etain said bitterly. "Already broken and torn asunder. What kind of champions are we? Is this the best Existence could do?"

No one answered her question, and after a moment Tannis bid them good night and Conoran followed. Church knew he wouldn't be able to sleep with so many questions still troubling him. Etain led him to a spot just outside the village where they lay on the grass looking up at the stars and the smoke drifting from the hearths of Carn Euny.

"Now you cannot leave us, Jack, Giantkiller," she said after a while.

"What do you mean?"

"From the moment you appeared in our midst, I have waited for the time when you would walk out of my life." Etain's voice was low and dreamy. Church looked at her, but she kept her eyes on the stars. Her face was as pale as the moon, and shadows pooled in her eyes and added lustre to her hair. Her breasts rose and fell slowly. "Now you and I—and all of us—are joined by the Blue Fire. We are one. It will pull us together, however far apart we might be."

Church knew this to be true, in the way that he now knew many things on an unconscious level. Though the feeling of unity raised his spirits, he also felt deeply sad. Did it mean he would never be allowed to return to his own time, to see Ruth again, to reclaim the life he had lost? Was he now fated to live out his days and be forgotten long before anyone he cared for ever existed?

"I'll do what's expected of me while I'm here," he said, "but I'm never going to stop looking for a way back home. And to Ruth." He felt Etain flinch.

"We judge a person by what they hold inside them," Etain said, "and you are a good man to keep such a powerful love pure in your heart. But Conoran says your home is not one day's ride away, nor many, but exists across the unending sea of days. Can you not see that your love is hopeless? You are hurting yourself by holding on to it. And those around you who care for you." She moistened her lips. "Let it go. Accept your loss." A desperate yearning was wrapped in her final sentence. "I could make your heart sing too, Jack, Giantkiller." She gently touched his face with her cool fingers.

"I know you could," Church responded quietly, "but I love Ruth. I'm never going to give up hope. However many miles, however many years I have to cross, I'm going to get back to her. Nothing's going to stand in my way."

"Then hear this," she said passionately. "However many miles I walk and fight at your side, however many years it takes to prove my love to you, I will shoulder that burden. Because I know that in this time and in this place our souls are bound together. Judge me by what I hold inside myself."

In that moment, the deep affection Church felt for her crystallised. She would never replace Ruth, but there was an undeniable connection between them.

"Come quick!"

The mood was shattered by the cry. Church and Etain ran back to the main street where Branwen waited anxiously in the doorway to Owein's hut. Church feared the worst until he saw the hopeful light in Branwen's face. She dragged Church into the smoky, warm confines and thrust him towards Owein, who lay on a mat wrapped in blankets. He appeared to be sleeping more peacefully.

"Look at his wound!" Branwen pleaded.

Church lifted the dressing: the deep gash was healing much faster than was possible. Already the bone was hidden beneath reknitted flesh. At that rate it would only be a matter of days before the gash was gone completely.

"It is the Pendragon Spirit." Conoran stood behind Church. "The Blue Fire can heal the flesh as well as the spirit. But to see such a wound heal so quickly!"

While the others gathered around Owein with renewed hope, Conoran motioned for Church to follow him back out into the night. "The cycles of Existence move slowly, but this is a new beginning. A time of hope, a new dawn," Conoran said passionately. "And I believe in my heart that this is the first step out of infancy for humankind and onto the long road to the heart of Existence. You have a tremendous responsibility. Do not let us down."

Church said nothing.

"I must return to my people," Conoran said, distracted. "There is much preparation to make, lectures at the colleges, new lessons to teach the way forward. There is a responsibility on the Culture, too, for we must supply the support you will need on your quest. Yes, yes!" He roamed around, deep in thought. "The Culture may not be around for all time, or invaders may drive us into hiding. We must prepare! There are other wise men and women in other cultures. They must carry on the knowledge in their own beliefs. They must be . . . Watchmen, preparing the way, warning of danger!"

He came back to Church, his eyes bright. "And if the gods ever dare to return to force humankind to suffer and slave, you Brothers and Sisters of Dragons will be there to repel them!"

"I'm touched by your faith."

Conoran missed Church's wry tone as he launched into another rush of notions. "Defences must be prepared for such an incursion. Weapons hidden.

For what if the gods return in years to come when we have grown indolent and content?" He glanced at Church's side. "Your sword . . . It is one of four great weapons of the gods, as told of in our stories. We must find the others and hide them away for when they are most needed." He paused. "Would you give this weapon to the cause?"

Church hesitated. He'd already grown attached to the unearthly blade and the way it soothed him.

"Existence will present you with another one, Jack, Giantkiller." Conoran's gaze was heavy and Church couldn't refuse him.

"All right. It's only a sword."

"I must return. Prepare." Conoran was several yards along the street when he rushed back and clasped Church's arm forcefully. "I wish you well! Great things lie ahead!"

And then he turned and disappeared into the night.

16

The legend of the warrior-king and his band of Brothers and Sisters of Dragons passed quickly amongst the Celts from the Dumnonii in the West to the Iceni in the East, from the southern Atrebates to the Caledoni in the far north. For Church it was a time that dispelled any lingering doubts that a rational, ordered universe existed. Things that in his own time had been consigned to story books or bad dreams preyed on humanity, and he began to comprehend the secret history that lay behind the myths and legends of many cultures.

On the south coast they tracked a lamia to its lair and killed it in a four-hour battle. An infestation of vampiric Baobhan Sith was driven out of a South Wales village. In the fenlands, something with leathery wings, razor-sharp teeth and the pleading cry of a frightened child was destroyed in a midnight raid. Villages were saved, women and children rescued, magical items found and hidden for future use.

And in time they became greater than people, their exploits trumpeted from mouth to mouth, growing in the telling; stories of wonder and magic, of heroes who could never be defeated, of the king, Jack, the Giantkiller, who would always defend the land in its darkest hour; all people had to do was blow the trumpet, call his name three times into the wind.

And the shadows would fall back and never return. And the things that lurked in the night and the wild places would be driven beneath the sea and under the hill.

And for the first time since its infancy, humankind could sleep peacefully in its beds.

All was right with the world.

17

"They don't make these like they used to." Church tossed the shattered sword out through the open doorway.

Tannis clapped him on the shoulder. "You do not know your own strength, Giantkiller. That was one of the strongest blades ever forged by my people."

"I need a new sword. A good one." Church eased out the tension in his shoulders that came from too long on horseback riding across the grasslands of southern Britain. "I wish I'd never agreed to give up the god-sword."

Owein thrust a goblet of alcoholic brew into Church's hand. "For now, rest, drink, make merry. There has been little of those things in recent days."

"We are champions," Branwen chimed in. "There must be some reward for our great deeds. The people are not grateful enough." She stretched out on a reed bed, nursing a sprained arm from the most recent battle, then reached out lazily and picked one of the first apples of the season from a wooden bowl beside her.

Church disagreed. They were treated with deference wherever they passed; and while hospitality to strangers was a cornerstone of Celtic society, the finest food and drink were presented to them, along with gifts of gold and jewels. By any standard, they could be fabulously wealthy.

But there was another aspect that disturbed him. Outside the door, Carn Euny was bathed in sun as it had been for most of the summer. When he had first arrived, the village had welcomed him warmly, the children calling his name and running around his feet, while the adults had invited him into their houses. But now they looked at him oddly, respectful of his position and abilities, but also treating him with faint unease. He was no longer like them. He was an outsider; an alien breed; a hero.

The others felt it, too, but it troubled Etain the most. Church had discovered her crying quietly one day. She briefly spoke of her loneliness, but then refused to talk any more because she couldn't accept their isolation from the community.

"Where is Etain?" He realised he had not seen her for the last two hours.

"Gone to recount our latest exploits to the *filid*," Owein said with a hint of drunkenness. "Soon there will be new songs to sing about the wonders of the Brothers and Sisters of Dragons."

Church slipped out to find her, enjoying the opportunity to be alone with his thoughts. Despite the sun, the air was sharp with the first chill of the approaching winter. Across the Cornish countryside the leaves were turning golden and orange, and the storms that regularly swept in off the Atlantic were growing wilder.

He met Etain walking back along the main street. Her face at rest looked unaccountably sad, but she smiled warmly when she saw him. "The *filid* has crafted the best song yet," she said. "Everyone will be in fine voice tonight."

"I was thinking we should spend some more time looking for that spider-thing that set the Redcaps on us." It wasn't what he had meant to say, but since her expression of affection he occasionally found himself awkward around her.

Etain made a face. "We have found nothing since that night. I thought it was decided that another search would be pointless?"

"Sooner or later he's going to come looking for us again—"

"I will talk to the others." Etain began walking towards the roundhouse, then paused, troubled. "I feel something bad is coming."

"Anything more?" In recent weeks, Etain had experienced instinctive flashes that bordered on the psychic, as if some dormant ability was slowly surfacing.

Scanning the green landscape with its gnarled, twisted trees rearing away from the wind, she hugged her arms around her. "Perhaps it is just the winter closing in." She flashed him a smile and hurried to the comfort of the hearth.

Mulling over her words, Church wandered to the edge of the village and beyond. Once the houses had disappeared behind the trees and gorse, a song drifted to him on the wind, desperately beautiful and instilling in him an unbearable yearning. He had no choice but to follow it across the rolling grasslands for almost half a mile. Finally he came to the honey-skinned woman with the incongruous pack of cards who he had met on the hilltop earlier in the summer. She stood beneath an old hawthorn, her beauty as radiant as the sun. When she saw him, her singing was replaced by an enigmatic smile.

"You came," she said with faint humour.

"Where are you from?" Church recalled she had said her name was Niamh. "It's a long walk to the next village."

"I have come from a place further away than you could imagine yet only a heartbeat from here." She surveyed Church with familiar haughtiness, then motioned to a bundle of cloth on the ground. "Sit. Join with me in food and drink for a while."

Church was both irritated by her arrogance and entranced by her beauty. He sat next to her as she unwrapped the cloth to reveal a crystal decanter of water that sparkled in the autumn sun, two crystal goblets and some bread. The water was unlike any he had tasted in his life, filled with subtle, complex favours that invigorated him. The bread, too, was especially nourishing.

"I saw you with that girl," Niamh said when Church had eaten and drunk his fill. "Are you in love?"

Church didn't like her smile, which had an odd triumphant tinge. "Are you spying on me?"

"Oh, yes," she said, unabashed. "I have watched you since our first encounter. You intrigue me. The Blue Fire burns strongly inside you."

"Maybe I should be honoured by your interest, but I'm not. You've obviously got a lot of time on your hands."

"Time is all I have. It means nothing and everything to one of the Tuatha Dé Danann."

Church tried to work out if this was some game. "You're saying you're a god?"

"We call ourselves the Golden Ones. It is the people of the tribes who named us Tuatha Dé Danann. We are travellers, lost in the Far Lands, unable to find our way back to our homeland. That fills us with a great sadness that we can never escape."

Church glimpsed the briefest hint of that sadness in her face. "The people here think you were all driven back to T'ir n'a n'Og after you defeated the Fomorii at the Second Battle of Magh Tuireadh—"

"Driven?" she said contemptuously. "Nothing could make the Golden Ones do what they did not wish. We chose to go as part of the pact. It was decided we would leave these Fixed Lands to your people, for a time at least. But many of my kind like this world and its bountiful riches, and we shall choose to visit from time to time, if it pleases us."

"Good to hear it. Thank you for the bread and water. Now I have to be getting back."

"I desire that you should return to T'ir n'a n'Og with me. See the wonders of the Far Lands. Experience sensations beyond your dreams."

"It's tempting, but I think I'll decline." Church's attention was caught by what appeared to be a flash of black lightning in the vicinity of Carn Euny. It reminded him of what he had seen on the night of the storm more than three months ago, and filled him with a deep dread. "I have to go." He could smell something bitter and unpleasant on the wind.

"You are worried about the girl?" Niamh said. "And about those Fragile Creatures who took you in like a stray animal?"

Church strode down the slope. Niamh called after him, "Did you enjoy my food and drink, Brother of Dragons? It was *not* given freely. It was *not* given without obligation."

Suddenly Church could not move his arms or legs. An abiding fear sprang up in him at what he had done.

18

The sun was setting in an angry red blaze when Church came to his senses. Niamh was long gone. He ran wildly down the slope, thoughts careering through his head: about how the gods of Celtic myth were diminished over the centuries until they were classed as fairies, their Otherworldly home became fairy mounds, their rituals dances under moonlight around a toad-stool ring. But their random cruelty never diminished; the name of the Fair Folk was never taken in vain.

And Church recalled how they lured mortals to their fairy homes and forced them to dance for 200 years. And how their food and drink was enchanted—once tasted it could hold a man in thrall to the wishes of the Fair Folk for the rest of his days.

Not given freely. Not given without obligation.

Carn Euny was eerily deserted as Church skidded down the grass slope and dashed past the midden into the main street. He called out, but no one answered or came to investigate. No children played; no dogs barked. Instead, tasks were abandoned half-complete: the preparation of the evening meal, the water buckets being brought back from the spring.

Church made his way to the roundhouse given over to the Brothers and Sisters of Dragons to see if Tannis or one of the others had left a message as to where everyone had gone. The house was as still as the rest of the village, but the moment he stepped across the threshold his entire world fell apart.

It was a charnel house. Blood had been splashed up the walls and pooled on the floor, and dripped in a sickening rhythm from the roof to sizzle on the embers of the fire. Amongst it lay the bodies of his friends, all slaughtered: Tannis, Owein, Branwen and Etain, the one that crushed his spirit the most.

Church grasped her in his arms so that her blood smeared across his face and clothes. He prayed that there was some flicker of life that the Pendragon Spirit could fan into a flame, but she was already cold, her consciousness long gone. He cried for her and for the others. He cried for himself.

For a long time he sat there, lost to the shock and the grief, until eventually he saw the mark of the murderer scrawled on the wall in blood. One word: *SCUM*.

An English word. A word from his own time.

19

Church staggered out into the twilit street where Niamh was waiting for him.

He was filled with fury when he saw her. "I could have saved them if you'd let me go!"

"Or you could have died with them."

"Who did this?"

She smiled coldly, said nothing. His grief and despair threatened to wash his thoughts away and he covered his face to drive out the terrible images.

"Come with me," she said. It was not a request, and even if he had had the will he could not refuse.

In his daze, he sensed movement in the shadows beside one of the round-houses. It was a boy, Oengus, to whom Church had told stories on many a morning. As he approached, Church could see the whites of his eyes. He was scared, but his curiosity overrode his fear as he noticed the smear of Etain's blood across Church's clothes. "You are mortally wounded?"

Niamh answered for Church. "His wound is much deeper than you could ever know. It runs to the very heart of him."

"Are you leaving?" the boy asked.

"He is." Niamh eyed Oengus with a curious contempt. "Say your good-byes."

"And you are going to the Isle of Apples?" The boy's eyes grew wider still.

Niamh gave a mocking smile. "Your warrior-king sails across the ocean to fair Avalon."

"And will we never see him again?"

"I am sure he will return when you need him most. In your darkest hour, call his name." Another sly smile.

"Find the others now, Oengus," Church said flatly. "Tell them to keep safe. Watch out for enemies."

The boy fled into the night. Niamh's smile chilled Church to the bone. "The ravens are ready to feast here. They follow you, Jack Churchill, always hungry." She gave a mocking bow. "Jack of Ravens."

Church hung his head.

"Say goodbye to this dreary place of never-changing. You have a new home now."

Without a backward glance she walked out of the village. Church followed. Beneath the hawthorn tree, he looked back to where Carn Euny lay and realised that, despite being dispossessed, he had been happy there.

"This world is gone," Niamh said.

She snapped her fingers and night fell.

CHAPTER TWO
ASI ES LA VIDA

1

Entering Fairyland was like stepping from a dark dungeon into a world filled with brilliant sunlight and astonishing detail. Church reeled from the sudden rush of sensory information. Before him the landscape spread out in breathtaking glory: grasslands greener than he had ever seen before, soaring, snow-capped mountains higher and more imposing, trees taller and prouder, the leaves rustling in the breeze as if a symphony were playing. Scents of summer days, meadow flowers and pine forests assailed Church with such force it ignited memories of all the warm, untroubled days of childhood.

"Welcome to the Summerlands," Niamh said archly.

A hawk swooped down to land a few feet away. It surveyed Church with a gimlet eye. "Bless my soul, is this a Fragile Creature?" it said. Church started. "Well, I never! This is news fit to be spread through the air. Does it have a name?"

"It is known by its kind as Jack the Giantkiller," Niamh noted, "and sometimes as Church. He will accompany me to the Court of the Soaring Spirit."

"A Fragile Creature!" the hawk repeated in astonishment before flying off to join some of its comrades circling a mile or so distant.

"The bird spoke," Church said redundantly. His thoughts ran through his overwhelmed mind like sand through fingers.

"Forget all the rules you have learned in the Fixed Lands. They do not apply here." Niamh strode ahead along a flagged path cut into the side of the hill. It wound down into the cool shade of overhanging trees and thick shrubs. Rhododendrons bloomed with wild, improbable colours on either side, and bluebells and poppies clustered in groups, steadfastly disregarding their seasonal rules. They passed a foaming waterfall gushing over a granite overhang. The water ran under the path in a culvert to cascade down the hill-side in a series of further waterfalls.

Eventually the path ended on a grassy lane scarred by wheel ruts where a colourful group waited. It was a caravan of five carts with multicoloured covers and a distinctive flag showing a broken chain. Horses chewed lazily at the grass. Several outriders wearing lightweight armour of silver and ivory waited nearby, their helmets shaped like hawks' heads.

The captain of the guard cantered up. He bowed his head to Niamh before eyeing Church coldly. "Your highness. You have brought a toy back for your entertainment, I see. Should we deliver him to the Court of the Final Word?"

"No, Evgen. This Fragile Creature will accompany us as he is."

Evgen appeared puzzled by this direction, but did not question it. He bowed his head again and returned to the front of the caravan where he waited patiently for Niamh to climb into the back of the central wagon, helped by five beautiful handmaidens. Church made to follow, but Niamh waved him away without looking at him.

"The rear wagon is reserved for your kind," she said.

Church trudged to the back of the caravan and hauled himself into a wagon clearly rougher and less comfortable than Niamh's. He had glimpsed cushions and silk hangings in her wagon; here there was only bare wood, an unpleasant smell of stale urine and one other occupant.

This figure wore clothes of the gaudiest colours, reds and greens, golds, blues, oranges and purples, tight-fitting around the legs, but with a padded bodice and numerous scarves streaming from elbows, shoulders, wrists and ankles. His hair was long and curly and aquamarine in colour, which only made his face more ghastly. His skin was as white as chalk, with the texture of parchment, and his lips were drawn back in a permanent rictus so that he appeared to be laughing at everything he saw. Yet his eyes were at times filled with a terrible sadness, and at others with a soul-destroying horror.

He cast Church one abject, fear-filled look, as if expecting Church to beat him, then buried his head beneath his arms.

Church slumped into a corner as the wagon jerked into life. He allowed the rhythmic rocking motion to soothe him while he patched together his scattered thoughts. His primary concern was to find a foothold in this new version of reality that challenged all his preconceptions: a world of beings who believed they were gods, of parallel dimensions that could be accessed in the blink of an eye. Set against that was the more mundane but no less shocking acceptance that death could come just as suddenly. He recalled laughing and talking with Tannis, Owein and Branwen, his deepening understanding of Etain's feelings, the expression on her face as she hurried to see the others. All so potent and affecting, all torn away while his back was turned, never to be experienced again.

His grief coalesced into a physical pain in his chest, heightened by guilt: if they had not accompanied him to Boskawen-Un, and if he had not encouraged them to enter the hidden chamber, they would not have become Brothers and Sisters of Dragons, and he was convinced their role as champions had led to their murders.

But the one thing he could not get out of his head was that single, ugly word scrawled on the wall of the roundhouse: *SCUM*. Wrapped in it was so much hatred, emphasised by the sheer brutality of the slaughter.

SCUM. It resonated far beyond its simple alignment of letters. Church couldn't escape the possibility that he was not alone in being cast back in time. But if the murderer was another refugee from the twenty-first century, why the hatred and brutality towards people who could not have been known to the killer?

"You have not been sent to torment me, then?"

Church stirred from his thoughts to see his fellow traveller sizing him up with a mixture of curiosity and fear. "Who are you?" he demanded. "*What* are you?" His tone was harsh; he didn't care.

The rictus grin gave the impression that the garish being was laughing at the question, but his eyes showed misery. "How hurtful! What am I, indeed. But that is what I have come to expect."

"I'm sorry."

The stranger searched Church's face and appeared surprised that the apology was sincere. "I am called the Mocker, though my given name is Jerzy."

"Church. Also know as Jack the Giantkiller," he added bitterly. "Though I haven't slain any giants of note for a while. You're a prisoner, too?"

"Prisoner. Entertainer of the masses. Figure of ridicule. Slave. Dancer, juggler, fire-eater, poet, bard, minstrel. Why, my titles are endless." His bitterness dwarfed Church's.

"You've tried to escape?"

Jerzy looked horrified. "You do not escape the Golden Ones! Besides, where could I go with this new face they gifted to me?"

"They did that to you?" Now it was Church's turn to be horrified.

"Your face must fit your life. I was in my cups in the Hunter's Moon, singing a ballad that, by my own admission, was so powerful it moved hardened warriors to tears, when I was spied by the queen's advisors. If I had known they were there I would have kept myself to myself, I can tell you."

"They dragged you off?"

"I was offered a position of tremendous responsibility. How could I refuse?" Tears welled in his eyes and he blinked them away. "I was immediately dispatched to the Court of the Final Word for this . . ." he motioned to his white, grinning face ". . . and to receive my little friend." He tapped his head.

Church made a gesture of puzzlement.

"A Caraprix!"

"I don't know what that is."

"You don't know very much at all, do you?" Jerzy surveyed Church as if he might be dangerously stupid. "A Caraprix is . . ." He searched for the right word. "An associate of the Golden Ones. A small thing—"

"A pet?"

"No, no, no, no! Do not say such things! A Caraprix is small, but can change its shape into anything. No one knows how much they think for themselves, but the Golden Ones need their Caraprix. And by turn, I think, the Caraprix need their Golden Ones."

Church struggled to comprehend. "And you have one?"

"Oh, not in the same way. They put one in my head. It wraps itself around my mind and drinks my thoughts and dreams. If I want to go left it can make me go right. If I want to wake it can make me sleep." Jerzy read the disgust in Church's face. "Oh, it is an honour, no doubt." He didn't sound convinced. "Very few get to encounter a Caraprix so personally. It is only gifted to those considered very important in the grand scheme."

"I understand . . . I think. They use it to control you. So why are you so important?"

"Because I am a bard!" Jerzy replied incredulously. "And like any intelligent beings, the Golden Ones know that stories and songs have power. Why, you can change the way things are, and the way they will be, with a few well-chosen words. You can't have a power like that wandering around without control."

Church decided he liked the strange character; there was suffering aplenty, but also resilience and spirit. Over the following half-hour, Church explained his own situation, while the Mocker spoke of the Far Lands, how the Golden Ones were the most powerful, but only one of a multitude of races, kinds and types. As Jerzy described some of them, Church realised these were the things that had populated mankind's dreams and nightmares since the beginning.

And Jerzy told Church of the Golden Ones' homes, the twenty great courts, each with their own kings, queens, minor royalty, aristocracy and arcane rules and regulations. Each court was characterised by a particular mood or way of thinking, and while there was some friction between the individual courts, only the Court of the Final Word evinced an abiding fear.

Jerzy was about to tell Church why this was so when the wagon ground to a halt and the flap at the rear was thrown to one side. Evgen, the captain of the guard, ordered Church and Jerzy out onto stone flags, where Church was greeted by a sight that took his breath away.

2

The Court of the Soaring Spirit was bigger than any Earthly city Church had ever seen. The caravan had come through a fortified entrance gate at the head of a valley, and the city filled the dale ahead for as far as the eye could see. Despite its name there was something oppressive about the court. The streets were tiny, winding amongst buildings that soared up in every architectural style imaginable, with upper storeys overhanging the lower so that from street level any view of the sky would be minimal. It was a town planner's nightmare, a jumble of roofs pitched this way and that, the buildings so twisted and deformed they looked decrepit with age. From one view it appeared medieval, from another Tudor, with black-stained wooden beams and dirty-grey stone, bottle-glass windows and crumbling chimneys on the point of collapse. It smelled of open sewers and stagnant water and the accumulated damp of centuries.

The sounds, sights and smells combined to give an impression of whispered plotting and secret politics, of private struggles and misery heaped upon misery as residents attempted to fight their way up from the dark slums to a place where they could glimpse the sun.

"Isn't it a place of wonders." Jerzy sighed. Intentionally or not, his fixed grin coloured the statement with irony.

Niamh's grace and glamour were emphasised by the surroundings as she walked towards them from the head of the caravan. Church nodded to the broken-chain banner. "I thought your court stood for freedom." He didn't attempt to hide his contempt.

Niamh spoke as if addressing a child. "We are all prisoners, and we forge our own chains. The love that sets us free holds us fast. Our dreams and ambitions drag us from the wide vista to the prison of a single path. Every choice, every step, is a link in the chain. Every thought is a lock." She motioned to Jerzy. "He has been freed from all those things, from love, from the tyranny of choice and independent thought."

"But you control him."

"As I do you. Yet you are free to wander this city, free to receive sustenance without offering anything in return, free from concern about your choice of path and your future. I have taken that burden upon myself. And so you are free."

Jerzy gave a flamboyant bow. "And I thank you, your highness, from the bottom of my heart."

Church looked from Niamh's icy smile to the sprawling, stinking city and finally realised the extent of his predicament.

3

Freed from obligation for the rest of the day, Jerzy led Church to an inn at the end of a shadowy alley. The Hunter's Moon was a low, labyrinthine pub of numerous rooms and annexes, smoky and stinking of sour ale. The hubbub of voices never dipped. Church was mesmerised by the bizarre clientele: unfeasibly tall, unnervingly short, unnaturally thin and grotesquely fat, horns and tails, scales and wings. Church felt as if he was looking at a pop-up diorama in a nursery story book.

He was introduced to a big, bearded hunter named Bearskin, who had the eyes and odour of an animal; to a tall, needle-thin man with a stovepipe hat who called himself Shadow John; and to a cackling mad old crone by the name of Mother Mary. Jerzy led him to the only vacant table in a nook beside the stone fireplace where a pile of logs blazed to dispel the damp.

They each had a flagon of a potent ale that brought back painful memories of the nights Church had spent around the hearth in Carn Euny.

"Drink up, good friend." The Mocker grinned humourlessly. "The first eight flagons are always the hardest."

"Is that the answer? Drown yourself in an alcoholic haze?"

"There are few pleasures in life. Best to embrace them with open arms." Jerzy took a long draught. His surgically enhanced grimace made it a difficult task and ale flooded out of the corners of his mouth. "Excuse my manners." He wiped his face with the back of his hand.

The barman collecting flagons slapped Jerzy on the back and bellowed, "Hey, it's the Mocker! Tell us a joke!"

Without missing a beat, Jerzy said, "There is no point. Life is meaningless. We strive and we suffer. We shed our tears, always expecting something good just around the corner, but it never materialises. And then we die."

The barman stared in confusion for a moment, until his gaze fell on Jerzy's unflinching grin and he gave a burst of raucous laughter. "Good one, Mocker! And then you die! Good one!"

When he had gone, Jerzy said, "You'll find your little pleasures where you can in the Court of the Soaring Spirit. Steal your moments and hold them dear."

"I don't intend to be around for long."

It was the Mocker's turn to stare before breaking into laughter. When he saw Church was not joking, the sadness returned to his eyes. "There is no escape from the Golden Ones. If you try, if you attempt anything that brings you under suspicion, they will place a Caraprix in your head. And then your life is over. Besides, where would you go?"

"There's a woman waiting for me a long way from here—"

"A love? A true love?"

"Yes. And I'm going to get back to her. Nothing's going to stand in the way of that. Not two thousand years . . . not some overambitious species that think they're gods . . . not monsters or brain-worms or secret assassins."

Though Church's face was expressionless, his voice was taut with a passion that brought a surprising tear to Jerzy's eye. "Why," the Mocker said, his voice cracking, "that is the most remarkable and beautiful thing I have heard in all of the Far Lands. I remember . . . I remember someone . . . before all this . . ." His eyes welled up and he wiped them dry with his ale-sticky hand. "I am sorry, my friend. There are many wonders in the Far Lands, but much that has been forgotten, and one of those things is that pure and powerful love of which you speak. We are all bereft here, and I think we all know it, which is why we hide it so well. There is a reason why so many of the races of the Far Lands are attracted to your world." He sniffed loudly, then blew his nose into a red silk scarf. "This calls for a song. A ballad to break hearts—"

"No." Church held up his hand as the Mocker prepared to sing. "Not a sad song. Something to raise the spirits. To say that I'm getting out of this place." He smiled as inspiration came. "There's a singer in my time . . . dead now, but he had a fantastic voice and a lot of style. Some might have said he was unfashionable, but to me he had old-fashioned class, and that's a quality you just can't manufacture."

"Class," Jerzy repeated.

"Here, let me hum you a few bars. Then I'll teach you the words."

It wasn't long before Jerzy's powerful, emotive voice filled the Hunter's Moon. The first verse failed to penetrate the rumble of voices, but then a wave of silence rolled out until it encompassed the entire inn, every drinker rapt. When the song ended, a deafening cheer demanded more, and by the time Jerzy had run through it three times whole sections of the inn were singing along to "Come Fly With Me," ruminating about the wonders of going down "Acapulco way" and to "Llama land," while a being with a horse's head brayed that "weather-wise, it's such a lovely day."

Church laughed heartily at the hilarious incongruity of the scene, and for a while his laughter masked sharper feelings as the song reminded him of a world that may as well have been on the other side of the universe.

When Church and Jerzy finally stumbled out of the Hunter's Moon, night had fallen and a full moon lit up the clouds in a sliver of sky above the ramshackle, overhanging buildings that turned the street into a chasm. At street level, only irregular, guttering torches provided islands of illumination.

They were both worse for alcohol, and Church mused continually about heading for the city walls and making a break for freedom. Eventually, he gave in to Jerzy's common sense and allowed himself to be led towards Niamh's residence, the Palace of Glorious Light, where a chamber was being prepared for him.

In the distance thunder rumbled and soon fat drops of summer rain were finding their way between the eaves to splatter on the cobbles. The shower quickly became a downpour that gushed from the gutters in torrents. Church and Jerzy sheltered in a wooden porch beside bunches of garlic and lavender hung to dry.

"You'd think in Fairyland someone would have been able to magic away the rain," Church muttered. Jerzy found this amusing and snickered for a full minute.

Church silenced him with a hand to his mouth. A deep cold had materialised in the pit of his stomach: a warning sign, though there was no movement and no sound beyond the driving rain.

"What is wrong?" Jerzy hissed.

"Something's coming." Church clutched at the dry, ancient wood of the porch wall.

Jerzy looked out past the water sheeting off the porch roof. As if on cue, the staccato *clip-clop* of hoofs on the cobbles rose up. Church's heart was pounding so hard he thought it would burst. Blue sparks fizzed around his fingers and when he removed his hand from the wall an imprint was burned in the wood. Jerzy's white face glowed in the gloom. Now he could feel it, too. He clearly wanted to ask Church what was approaching, but the words would not come.

The steady hoof-beats drew nearer. It was the sound of a rider taking his time, surveying the area. From around a sharp bend came a shape darker than the surrounding shadows. Church held his breath as it approached the first circle of torchlight.

The horse appeared first, a strong black stallion liveried in black leather, but with armour on its head and around its eyes, though much of it was crusted with brown rust. The rider too was swathed in black. A sodden cloak hung like bat-wings, and beneath it was a long black tunic, though it was so terribly tattered it appeared to have been stitched together from rags. Underneath that, Church could just glimpse dull flashes of armour, all of it rusted. The cowl of the cloak was pulled low over the rider's head to keep off the driving rain.

Though he did not know why, Church buried himself in the depths of the porch next to Jerzy's now-trembling body.

When the rider was just a few feet away, he reined in his mount so that both man and beast were stock still, listening, smelling, sensing.

He wants me, Church thought. *He can feel the Pendragon Spirit in the same way I can feel whatever drives him.*

And then the rider looked in Church's direction and it felt as if the world was falling away.

It was Etain, her dead, mouldering face accusing him of betrayal. Her eyes burned across the gulf between them, and they spoke of a deep, abiding hatred that even the grave could not soothe.

Church stumbled away from that chilling gaze before she saw him, but she was already urging her horse gently towards the porch. From beneath her cloak she slowly drew a rusty sword that made a grinding noise as it rasped from the scabbard.

Church had no weapon with which to defend himself, but how could he oppose her anyway when deep down he believed she was right to hunt him for vengeance?

Thunder boomed and forked lightning threw the street into stark relief. Church's heart jumped along with it. He might get a little way down the street before Etain ran him down and took off his head with that rusty sword. He might even get a little further, but he knew from what he saw in her face that she would never relent, however far or fast he ran. Sooner or later he would feel the cutting edge of her revenge.

Fear was mounting in Jerzy, too. His grin now looked sick and horrified beneath his terrified eyes, and he clutched Church's shirt pleadingly. Looking around, Church's gaze lighted on a possible escape route.

"Follow me. Keep low," he whispered into Jerzy's ear. Church saw the Mocker silently put all his trust in him, just as Etain and the others had done.

Church bounded into the pouring rain. The horse reacted with a feral hiss, raising its head and baring its teeth with a viciousness uncharacteristic in horses. Etain's sword ripped fully from its scabbard and sliced through the air. Church ducked low and kept running as the sword whisked mere inches above his head. Behind him, Jerzy shrieked like a little girl.

Church had to fight to keep his footing on the wet, slippery cobbles. He splashed through a puddle almost as wide as the street and propelled himself upwards to grab a wrought-iron mounting supporting a creaking sign that read "Hardwick Chalmers, Candlemaker." The mounting was ornate enough for Church to find a handhold and he pulled himself up using the wall for traction. In a second or two, he had hauled himself onto a small slate roof over the candlemaker's main window. He could hear Jerzy whimpering and scratching below; he had failed to gain purchase. Church leaned down, grabbed his hand and dragged him up just as Etain spurred her steed towards them. Jerzy's feet kicked the air just above her head. The roof groaned and threatened to collapse as he crashed onto it.

"We can't stay here!" the Mocker cried.

"No. We climb." Church indicated a path up using window ledge, shutter and a network of rooves on various overhanging annexes that at the second storey were barely a man's width apart.

Jerzy whimpered again. Church's gaze was drawn to Etain, who had thrown off her hood. Her sleek black hair was plastered against her head, and there was a hint of lividity around her jaw and lips. Her eyes were utterly black, radiating malice.

Church tore his gaze away and jumped to a window sill across the way. His feet skidded off the wet wood, forcing him to grab onto a banging shutter for dear life.

Jerzy grabbed the other shutter. "Oh no! I will fall! I will die!" he cried into the storm.

"Just keep climbing!" Church shouted. "We'll get away over the rooftops."

"If we are not struck by lightning or blown off by the gales!" On cue, more lightning flashed and earthed overhead and Jerzy released a terrified howl.

With the rain lashing down like stones, scaling the buildings was slow and perilous. Fingers gripped guttering that threatened to tear out of its fixings, and boots slipped on tiles made glass. The wind channelled between the buildings in savage gusts that plucked at Church and Jerzy when they were at their most precarious. They scrambled and slithered, knocked elbows and knees, became soaked to the skin, every second fearing they were about to fall.

And then, miraculously, they were at the summit. Rooftops stretched out all around, baked-orange tiles, dark-blue slate, sodden wooden planks, punctuated here and there by spires and domes, towers and cupolas on the gothic upper storeys of the larger buildings. The lightning illuminated the scene, a welcome relief after the gloom of ground level. But the wind was stronger up there and the rain was like bullets of ice.

Jerzy pointed to a hulking structure of stone, gold and glass with monolithic walls, ramparts and turrets. "The Palace of Glorious Light," he shouted.

Movement in the gulf between two rooftops caught Church's eye. He expected to see water streaming from a gutter, or lightning shimmering off a window pane. Instead he saw a sight that rooted him in its nightmarish intensity.

The horse was coming up the sheer side of the building, negotiating eaves and overhangs as if it were on the level. Sometimes it would flatten itself, almost crawling like some giant insect. Etain remained mounted on its back, her eyes fixed unblinkingly on her prey. Church could read the bitter betrayal in them with each flash of lightning.

Jerzy's fingers bit into Church's shoulder. "She wants our death. Who is she? Do you know her?"

Church didn't answer. He realized that their only possible escape route was across the rooftops to the palace, a journey of lethal inclines and vertiginous chasms.

He grabbed Jerzy by the shoulders to squeeze the paralysing fear from him. "She'll kill us if she catches us. And that's why you've got to stay with me. Move as fast you can. We can help each other."

The words proved true within minutes. Jerzy grabbed the back of Church's shirt to prevent him from sliding backwards down a steeply pitched roof. Church spread himself out like a starfish to gain some traction, but the rain was running so hard it felt as if he was lying on the bed of a stream. Somehow he made his way back up the pitch of the roof and clutched a leaning chimney stack for support. Propelling himself down the other incline, he let the momentum carry him across the next street.

Jerzy kept pace, running and leaping with all the supple strength of a professional tumbler. Church's muscles burned with every jump, and as his exhaustion increased the chance of making a fatal misstep grew.

At one point the lightning struck so close it demolished a chimney stack mere yards away. Burning brick and blackened shards of pot flew like missiles. Church and Jerzy dived for cover, their momentum almost taking them into a hidden gulf between buildings.

Church made the mistake of looking back. Etain guided her horse eerily over the rooftops, never faltering, never deviating from its relentless path. Yet whatever its supernatural abilities, it was clear the horse could not ride at speed in such precarious circumstances.

Lights glimmered in the numerous windows that dotted the sheer sides of the palace. Just when Church thought they might reach it, Jerzy lost his footing as a tile shattered under his weight. He rolled and bounced down the roof, tearing off other tiles that cascaded into the dark, and came to a halt at the very edge, where he clung to a creaking guttering by his fingertips.

Church could still reach the palace if he abandoned Jerzy. Head down into the rain, Etain was now only two roofs away. Church skidded down the roof and grabbed the Mocker's thin wrist. Pressing his foot into the gutter, he levered Jerzy onto the roof.

"Thank you, thank you, thank you!" the Mocker cried pathetically.

By then it was too late. The sound of cracking tiles signalled Etain's arrival on the next roof, her face fierce and bloodless.

"Preserve me . . ." Jerzy whispered, but the rest of his sentence was lost in a boom of thunder. Etain had drawn her rusted sword and was urging her steed to make the last leap.

As the thunder rolled away, it revealed another sound, like skis on snow. Etain recoiled, an arrow protruding from the centre of her forehead. She pulled it out with a sickening sucking sound and casually tossed the shaft to one side.

But then the air was filled with arrows raining down. Many slammed into Etain and her horse without any effect, but the intensity of the volley was enough to hold her back.

Church and Jerzy scrambled up the roof to see the Palace of Glorious Light alive with archers. Immense nets had been thrown from the ramparts to the surrounding rooftops, and down them descended more archers loosing arrows.

The Mocker bounded joyfully across the remaining distance. Church allowed himself one last backward glance before he reached the safety of the nets.

Arrows protruded from every part of Etain. Her unflinching gaze never left Church until she finally turned her mount around and retreated into the night.

4

Evgen led Church and Jerzy to two neighbouring chambers where they could recover from their ordeal. The rooms were comfortable with fires blazing in the hearths, rugs, tapestries, chests, chairs and a large bed in one corner.

Church dried himself off, but he was too troubled to rest. He repeatedly went to the window to look out across the storm-washed court. Etain was nowhere to be seen, but Church knew she would be back.

Despite the fire, he couldn't rid himself of the chill in his bones and was pleased when a knock at the door signalled Jerzy's arrival. The Mocker's grin was tempered by troubled eyes.

"Tell me, good friend," he said as he huddled in front of the fire, "was that truly a dead thing that hunted us this evening?"

"Definitely dead, but not at peace."

"You knew her. I could see that in her face—and yours. What did you do to bring her back from the Grim Lands?"

The Mocker had given voice to the one question that had haunted Church since he had first seen Etain's dead face. "I don't know," he said. "Unless she wanted revenge." Church unburdened himself of everything—from his arrival in a past time to the discovery of the Pendragon Spirit and the murders of Etain, Tannis, Branwen and Owein.

"I cannot say if she holds you responsible for her death," Jerzy said when Church had finished, "but know this: I hold you responsible for my life. I would be dead now if you had not risked your own existence to save me." His eyes sparkled with amazement that this should have happened.

Church was touched by Jerzy's reaction. "I just saw you in trouble and reacted—"

"Yes. You did not even have to think. That is the wonder of it. I believe we shall be good friends, Jack Churchill." For the first time his grin looked happy.

Their conversation was interrupted by Evgen, who was strangely uneasy.

"Her highness requests your presence in the library." He nodded to Jerzy. "You may come, too."

Evgen's tone made it clear there was no choice in the matter. Church and Jerzy followed him along torch-lit corridors until they came to a large hall lined with shelves of books. Niamh sat at the head of a table surrounded by several other members of the Tuatha Dé Danann, all talking at once. Before her were spread piles of ancient leather-bound books with yellowing pages, scrolls and numerous maps printed in gaudy colours. Niamh waved her coterie away with frustration and summoned Church to her.

At the scooped breast of her gown, Niamh wore a piece of silver jewellery. Church was shocked to see it move of its own accord. At first it shivered, before the edges blurred and it reshaped itself into a silver egg that sprouted legs and scurried over Niamh's breast and onto the table.

Church realised this must be one of the Caraprix of which Jerzy had spoken. He was mesmerised as the creature shifted its form again, growing into an upright, flat oval shape. In its movements, Church recognised a warped echo of the black spider that had burrowed into his arm.

The oval took on a glassy appearance; all Church could think about was Snow White's wicked stepmother asking who was the fairest. The glass grew smoky, and when it cleared a moving image played across the surface.

"I have been informed of your recent troubles." Niamh maintained her haughtiness, but now Church could hear an unfamiliar tone of unease beneath it.

"Our apologies for being such a trouble, Your Highness," Jerzy said with a fawning bow. "We will ensure such a thing does not happen again."

"How can we ensure it?" Church said. "Not that I'm not thankful for the last-minute rescue, but I'm betting you didn't do it out of the goodness of your heart. You just didn't want your possessions harmed."

Niamh waved his comments away. "I would know the nature of the thing that hunted you."

"I don't know what it was or why it was after me," Church half-lied. "Perhaps it's like you, preying on humans just because it can."

Niamh eyed Church forensically before indicating the Caraprix-mirror. "Reports have arrived from the very edges of the Far Lands, where they disappear into the mysterious heart of Existence. The foulest things in all of this realm are being drawn there."

In the mirror, dark shapes tramped across a bleak landscape of volcanic rock and scrubby trees and brush, like ants trailing back to their nest from different directions. Fires sent up thick clouds of greasy smoke that added a hellish tone to the view. Church glimpsed a Redcap, its hair covered by ragged human skin, the remnants of intestines draped around its neck like jewellery. There were other things that Church half-recognised, though whether from his own memory or some bad dream he wasn't sure, and others so horrific he had to look away.

"What is their purpose?" Jerzy saw Niamh's expression harden and added hastily, "If you do not mind me asking, Your Highness."

"That is not yet known, though there have been reports of a structure being formed—a nest, perhaps, for these scurrying creatures."

"Something you can't control?" Church taunted.

Niamh's eyes flashed. "At this time there is no need for the Golden Ones to pay it any attention."

"But you're still worried that what hunted us is connected to it in some way."

"Begone! I find you tiresome. I will summon you again the next time I require entertainment." Her words were designed to sting, but Church found them reassuring; she was not as all-powerful and controlling as she pretended.

5

Church's prison was as big as a city. He was free to roam it, like a convict sent out to the yard to exercise, and like the hero of some jailbreak movie he spent his time searching for an escape route. But the Court of the Soaring Spirit was surrounded by seemingly impenetrable defences, made even more stringent since Etain's incursion. A forty-foot-thick stone wall that soared up the length of a football pitch was broken at regular intervals by watchtowers, and guards patrolled the top relentlessly.

Church had already identified a hierarchy amongst the Tuatha Dé Danann that he couldn't quite comprehend. The Golden Ones of Niamh's rank resembled humans, but were breathtakingly attractive with skin that appeared to radiate a faint golden light. Yet the gods who made up the guards and the more menial ranks had a touch of bland plasticity to their features, as if they were mannequins given life.

Though the Tuatha Dé Danann ruled the court, they were far from the only residents. The court was a seething cauldron of cultures, shapes, sizes and abilities. Church wandered the winding streets in a state of rapt wonder.

He saw short, grizzled men with axes and hammers, complexions pale from being too long underground; women with serpents for hair; others with blazing red eyes that pierced his soul; humanoid creatures with leathery wings and scaly skin; monkeys that smoked and chatted. A new burst of astonishment around every corner, a new chill in every dark alley.

Occasionally he would stop and talk with shopkeepers who appeared more amazed by him than he was by them. Every nugget of information about the strange, twisted rules of that world was a piece of the key that would unlock his shackles. Yet every time he learned something new it only led to further conundrums, and the means of his escape remained elusively just out of reach. The one stark fact that struck him hardest was that only Niamh could release him from the obligation he had placed himself under when he had consumed her food and drink.

That realisation darkened his mood and his thoughts turned to Etain and Ruth, both of them lost to him by an unbridgeable gulf. Though he attempted bravado with Jerzy, he feared he was fated to die without ever seeing Ruth again, and that notion was almost more than he could bear.

Two weeks after his arrival in the Far Lands, Church made his way down Winding Gate Street in the direction of the Hunter's Moon, which he had decided to make his base during his search for an escape. The route was filled with traders from the Market of Wishful Spirit, a travelling band of traders offering just about any object that could be desired, though Jerzy had warned him that the price was often more than anyone would be prepared to pay.

Occasionally, insistent figures in odd costumes that hinted at Elizabethan or Victorian styles tried to grab him from the cover of their stalls. Their voices were mesmerising, the artefacts they pushed towards him more so—dreams in a jar, new eyes that could see across Existence.

During his numerous jaunts around the city, Church had become adept at dodging them while keeping his eyes fixed firmly ahead. But this time he felt a heavy hand fall upon his shoulder. Before he could shake it off, a deep cold radiated from the fingers into the heart of him, and he realised with mounting distress that he could no longer move. Whoever was behind him leaned in to whisper barely audibly as he passed. The tone was urbane and laced with a hint of mockery. Church grew colder still when he realised what had been said: "Ruth will die."

Unable to turn his head, Church had only a fleeting glimpse of a man in a dark overcoat, long, black hair trailing behind him as he weaved his way into the depths of the market crowd ahead.

"You must try to see things from beyond your limited perspective!" Jerzy implored.

Finally recovered from the paralysis and back at the palace, Church looked out of the window across rooftops painted silver by a summer moon. Anxiety tied his stomach in knots. "All I know is that here, a long way from my home, some bastard told me that my girlfriend in the future is going to die. And it wasn't, 'She's going to die like we're all going to die one day.' It was, 'She's going to die because I'll slit her throat and dump her at the side of the road.'"

"Church—"

"And I can't do anything about it!"

"Good friend!" Church turned at Jerzy's sharp tone and was surprised to see concern in the Mocker's face. "Please, do not hurt your heart!"

"What's going on, Jerzy? How did I end up here? Why does everyone want to kill me and the people I care about?"

"You were born in the Fixed Lands and you expect everything to be fixed. But as I told you at our first meeting, the closer one gets to the heart of Existence, the more fluid things become. Even time." Seeing the incomprehension in Church's eyes, Jerzy sighed and tried again. "Time is not the same here in the Far Lands as in your world. It flows back and forth, or remains a constant always now."

Church recalled the folkloric tales of people transported to Fairyland for a night of dancing, only to find on their return that a hundred years had passed. Possibilities dawned on him. "I could while away a few months here and then drop back into my world in my own time."

"If the Queen of the Wasteland frees you from your obligation." His tone suggested Niamh would never agree to this.

"Except that I have no idea how fast time is passing in my world, so if I sit around here for too long I could end up missing it completely. Walk out into some world of flying cars and personal jet packs, and everyone I know dead."

"You must not set your hopes too high," Jerzy cautioned.

"I've got no choice. I have to talk to Niamh."

It was near midnight, and the palace slept. As Church and a reluctant Jerzy trailed along the echoing corridors, guards stood silently, their numbers increasing the closer they came to the royal apartments. Their eyes fell on

Church, but he was not a threat to be challenged. He had the run of the place like a favoured poodle. Sit up. Beg. Play dead. Defiantly, Church increased his pace.

As he neared Niamh's door, the air grew colder and soon he could see sparkles of frost on the stone. Jerzy indicated with an uncertain finger the guard who stood outside. His skin gleamed white, his eyebrows and hair rigid with frost.

"Frozen," Jerzy whispered. "Do not enter, friend Church," Jerzy pressed. "Leave what lies beyond these doors to the Golden Ones."

Despite his apprehension, Church was eager for answers. He marched in. Ice shimmered on the floor, walls and ceilings. The bodies of Niamh's inner guard were scattered in an arc near the door, ribs protruding like dinosaur teeth, slippery organs trailing. A slaughter, quick and brutal. Church wondered briefly what could have the power to dispatch these beings before his attention was caught by a rapid fluttering of golden lights over one of the bodies, then another, and finally over all of them.

They were shimmering moths, composed entirely of light, spiralling up from the bodies to the ceiling and then passing through it like ghosts. As the moths departed, the gods' bodies began to break up, as though they were as insubstantial as light. When the final moth had fluttered away, all the bodies had vanished.

Church snatched up one of the guards' short swords and progressed towards the heavy drapes that sealed off Niamh's bed-chamber. Pulling back the thick fabric, he found Niamh being menaced by the stranger from the market. Church recognised the long, black hair and overcoat, but the face . . . it was a thing of abject horror. Noting Church's arrival, the stranger's lips twisted into a cruel grin revealing needle-sharp animal teeth, stained with blood. Church registered a goatee beard and an aquiline nose, but it was the eyes he would never forget—lidless and fiery red with a small black pupil. When the full force of them was turned on him, Church felt their gaze pierce his very soul.

"Well, this is something I hadn't bargained for." The attacker crooked his arm tighter around Niamh's neck, her beautiful features fragile next to his brutal frame. His right hand was raised ready to strike, the fingers pointed to reveal bloody talons.

"Leave her alone," Church said.

"What's this? Misplaced loyalty? Or have you already grown into your role of lapdog? Jump through hoops for the mistress. Woof, woof!"

Church bristled at the echo of his own thoughts. "She doesn't deserve to die like those others out there."

"That would be a matter of opinion. I think she does deserve to die. I presented her with a perfectly good opportunity and she chose to turn me down. I find that very disrespectful."

Jerzy had been watching the scene, wrapped in the drapes. Tentatively, he stepped forward and tugged gently at Church's arm. His eyes pleaded but he said nothing.

"Speak up, you grinning buffoon!" the intruder said. "Ah, I see. You don't want to be seen to be disloyal in case, by some extremely slight probability, your mistress escapes with her life." The intruder said to Church in a tired voice, "What he's trying to tell you is that you should let her die because then you will both be free of her control. And that sounds eminently sensible to me."

"But even then I'd still be a prisoner," Church replied, "of my guilt." His eyes briefly locked with Niamh's.

"You really have been seduced by her propaganda, haven't you?" the intruder said wearily. He flexed his fingers and prepared to strike.

"Who are you and what do you know about Ruth?"

The intruder's cruel smile grew more enigmatic. "Finally, a discussion that really matters. Of course, the first question is the most important. Let's talk about me. What should you call me? I have many names, and you'll never discover the one that really counts. But for the sake of argument you may call me the Libertarian, because I believe in personal freedom . . . from the rigours of choice, from life itself. See? I too can play the favourite game around these parts."

The Libertarian increased the pressure on Niamh's neck with a twist of cruelty. She clawed at his arm, her breathing shallow.

"I said, let her go." Church raised his sword.

"Ooh, a weapon," the Libertarian said with mock-dismay. He was unthreatened, but he released the pressure of his arm a little so Niamh could gulp air. Church took a step forward. The Libertarian's red gaze became so menacing that Church stopped dead in his tracks.

Summoning his strength, Church asked, "What about Ruth? Tell me."

"Ah, the love of your life, waiting so mournfully at the end of time—"

"What do you mean?"

"A word to the wise: her survival is wholly dependent on you. Interfere in any way and she will die."

"I don't understand. Interfere in what?"

The Libertarian made a faux-puzzled expression. "Now there's the question. Perhaps it would be better not to interfere in anything, just to be on the safe side."

His words triggered a moment of revelation. "You . . . and whoever murdered my friends in Carn Euny . . . and the spider-thing that controlled the Redcaps—you're all together in this." Church added a disturbing codicil: "And Etain, too."

The Libertarian continued to play his part with studied theatricality. "Look at Existence, all nice and shiny and neat and new. Then pull back the surface and, lo, there we are. An army . . . no, that doesn't do us justice—a civilisation. We're all around you, all the time, yet you never see us, not really, not directly. Just an occasional glimpse on the periphery of vision. We live in the cracks between reality. We watch from the shadows, peer from the depths of caves, from drains and sewers, from the dusty windows of empty houses and rooftops at night."

"What do you want?"

"The same as anyone else—food, drink, a roof over our heads." His sarcasm hung in the air for a moment. "We are everywhere. We are legion. There, a quotation that has not yet been written. Or perhaps it is being written as we speak. Ah, the mysteries of Existence." He smiled coldly. "We are the flipside of your world, but the flipside does not always have to stay at the bottom."

Something in the Libertarian's eyes or tone made Church unaccountably fearful. "If you are what you say you are, why are you so concerned about me?"

The Libertarian's eyes narrowed.

"It's the Pendragon Spirit, isn't it?"

Niamh seized the opportunity to break free from the Libertarian's grip. She scrabbled across the floor to Church's side, all her haughtiness gone. "The light burns too brightly in you," she gasped. "They are only brave enough to crush you by subtle means, from a distance."

"Some of us can strike directly," the Libertarian said, "and we will, when the time is right."

"He asked me to destroy you, in the night, while you slept," Niamh said. "I refused. No Golden One would obey such an order."

"If you do it, it has to be of your own free will," Church noted sardonically.

"Our power may be limited now, but it grows with each step closer to the Source," the Libertarian said, before skipping lithely to the open window. He bowed and dived through it.

Church rushed to the window, hoping the killer had leaped to his death, but he could just make out a dark shape disappearing down the side of the sheer wall. The handholds were few and far between, but somehow the Libertarian found them, moving with remarkable speed.

Church turned to Niamh, clearly still dazed by her experience. "Are you okay?" he asked.

The goddess eyed him as if he were speaking a foreign language. "You could have allowed me to be eradicated from Existence. You would have been freed from your obligation."

"I could. But I wouldn't have been able to live with myself."

A flicker of emotion crossed Niamh's normally impassive features, before she snorted, haughty once more.

"I saved your life," Church said. "You can deny it, but it's true. And if you think your life has some value I'd ask for one small thing in reward."

7

The journey took ten days, across a mythic landscape of forests that stretched as far as the eye could see, their secret depths dark and cool and mysterious, and sweeping grasslands skirting the edge of mountains that scraped the sky; through verdant, peaceful glens and past mirror-glass lakes where clouds scudded silently.

The landscape almost served to soothe Church's unease. But at night, as he lay beside the campfire, the deep waters inside him moved with a slow, tidal pull. The Libertarian's words hinted at a hidden pattern behind the mundane reality of his life, but he could not find the connections that would give him understanding.

Jerzy had been his guide, poring over maps given to him by Niamh's advisors and studying the sun and the stars. He had been silent for much of the last leg of their journey, but as they rounded the base of a crag above which eagles soared, he said in a troubled voice, "The tension makes me queasy. When will the queen make her move?"

"What do you mean?"

"Surely you do not expect to reach your destination?"

"Why not?"

"It is not the way of the Golden Ones to give a person what they desire. They love their sport. We will wake one morning in the Court of the Soaring Spirit and find the entire journey a dream. Or as you reach out to knock on the door, the Court of Peaceful Days will turn into a stone at the roadside, or an egg in the nest of one of those eagles. Or—"

"If it's going to happen, it's going to happen. But I think Niamh might just allow me this one thing."

"Why would she do that? It is not her way."

"There was something different about her after the Libertarian left . . . I don't know."

Jerzy shrugged. His fixed grin took the edge off his downcast manner.

Soon after, the Court of Peaceful Days hove into view, a network of inter-connecting, long, low stone buildings with a wood growing all around it, and amongst the residences, and in some places within the buildings themselves, sprouting out of the red-tiled roofs. Flags and banners fluttered from many buildings, while emblems were embedded in the walls. A winding path led to the main door, passing through a solitary wrought-iron gate that soared up nearly fifteen feet, topped with spearheads. The gate swung open soundlessly to allow Church and Jerzy through.

Standing outside the main door, they could hear the measured, heavy beat of drums reverberating from somewhere deep within the complex, never slowing or missing a step, like the beat of a giant heart.

Church was afraid the drumming would obscure his knock on the door, but it opened soon after to reveal two rows of guards in shining silver armour, bristling with swords, spears, halberds, axes and maces. Up near the roof beams, two red and purple globes floated around. They appeared solid, but occasionally passed through each other.

At the end of the ranks stood a woman, also in armour. Her silver breast-plate caught the sun, momentarily blinding Church. When his vision cleared, he saw she was wearing a helmet that covered both cheeks to her jaw-line, curving round the orbits of her eyes to protect her nose, so that her eye-sockets were thrown into shadow. Silver hawk-wings rose up on either side, and from the spike on top hung a red ribbon.

"Welcome," she said in a sonorous voice that rang with the same tone as the pounding drum, "to the Court of Peaceful Days."

Jerzy gave a deep bow. Church nodded slightly. "My name is Jack Churchill. I am here—"

"I know why you are here, Fragile Creature. My sister sent word of your arrival. My name is Rhiannon. I am queen of this great court, and of the army it contains. Come with me."

She turned and strode down a long corridor, the clank of her armour echoing off the walls. They came to a large hall that had the reverential atmosphere of a cathedral. Stained-glass windows depicting brutal moments in battle lined two opposing walls, and incense filled the air.

"I have been charged with providing you with a weapon fitting for my sister's honour guard," Rhiannon said.

Church realised with a sinking heart that rather than reward him, Niamh had simply promoted him.

The hall was filled with rack upon rack of every weapon imaginable, but Rhiannon strode past them all to a large table at the far end. On it lay a sword. A blue glow limned its edge, just like the sword Church had reluctantly given up.

"This is Llyrwyn," Rhiannon stated, "one of the three great swords of Existence. I have yet to comprehend why my sister wishes such an honour on you—a test, perhaps. But here it is."

"Why is it so special?"

"The three great swords are forged from the essence of Existence. They can cut through the foundations of all there is. One is the sword of Nuada Airgetlamh. The second is corrupted, the Blue Fire that burns within it now black. Its whereabouts is unknown. And this is the third."

Church picked up Llyrwyn. Just like the sword of Nuada, for the briefest second it felt as if he was holding another object entirely. Then it hummed a low song of greeting and settled into his hand. The blue light flickered like static discharges in a summer storm.

Rhiannon handed him a scabbard and Church sheathed the sword. "When you no longer need Llyrwyn, you must return it," she said. "That is the only rule."

Church felt strangely comforted by the sword. It warmed his leg where it hung from his belt, whispered quietly into his flesh and bones. Without another word, Rhiannon led Church and Jerzy out of the hall and along a mazy route through corridors filled with marching men, and chambers where soldiers sparred or practised with their weapons. Every room and passageway echoed with the clash of steel and the distant thump of the drum, a martial madhouse where it was barely possible to think.

Finally they came to a room breathtaking in scale. Light flooded through a crystal glass roof eighty feet or more above their heads, and everywhere there fluttered flags and banners denoting victorious past campaigns. In the centre of the hall was a pillar of white marble glowing in the sunlight.

"This is the Wish-Post," Rhiannon announced. "From this point all Existence can be viewed, the solid past and the fluid future, or vice versa, the Fixed Lands, the Far Lands, and all other places, real or imagined. But beware: when you look into the Wish-Post, it looks into you. It will see all lands within as well as without."

Church felt a frisson. This was the moment when he would see Ruth again. His heart beat faster. "How does it work?"

"Stare into it. You will step into the place you wish to visit as a ghost, observing but unable to influence."

"I will be here with you, good friend," Jerzy said quietly.

Barely able to contain his anticipation, Church stared directly at the gleaming surface of the Wish-Post. After a brief moment of disconnection, he felt himself fall through white space.

Then he was standing in the warm light of sunset, smelling exhaust fumes and dust, and the grimy, sweaty odours of a city, the thrum of traffic a constant backdrop. Church recognised the London skyline, and nearby the languorous movement of the grey Thames, tinted red and gold by the setting sun. He was standing on the South Bank in the shade of some trees, not far from Albert Bridge. Nearby a woman was leaning on some railings, watching the river.

Church's heart broke into a thunderous rhythm and he felt drunk— relief, love, yearning, desperation, all churning together. It was Ruth, her long, dark hair a mass of curls and ringlets framing a pale face. She wore the shiny, unflattering overalls of a care home helper, the name of the home stitched in white above her left breast. Church was shocked by how inconsolably sad she appeared. That was not how he remembered her—in his head she was always smiling, filled with hope and passion.

He wanted to ease whatever pain she felt, but when he absently reached out, his hand passed through her. Rhiannon was right—he was a ghost. He wondered if he had done the right thing: to be so close to her yet still unable to connect was almost more painful than being separated by a gulf of more than two millennia.

"Ruth," he whispered. The word caught in his throat. "I love you."

8

For a fleeting moment, Ruth Gallagher had the strangest feeling that someone was watching her, but when she looked around, she was alone. The river was tranquil, yet it didn't provide her with any peace. She felt the same deep sadness that had consumed her for what felt like her entire life. At times she felt as if she was observing what purported to be her life from somewhere unimaginably distant. She'd been to the GP so many times she was sure she was on some malingering list. The doctor always diagnosed depression and offered her an interesting variety of chemical bullets to shoot the black dog. She never took any of them. In her heart she knew he was wrong, as were her few acquaintances who claimed to have some insight into why she suffered. No one had any idea. They never would have any idea, and she would never know herself. It was one of the great, depressing mysteries of life.

Nor did she know why she was drawn so repeatedly to that spot near Albert Bridge. The pull was inexorable, and whenever she stood there she always felt as though some revelation was about to break through the cotton wool of her perception, but it never did. Occasionally she toyed with the idea that she might have a brain tumour, though she felt like a New Age Holden Caulfield. Or perhaps it was some other hideous disease that was sending out psychological tremors before the full quake hit. But she was haunted by the possibility that the answer was depressingly mundane: this was simply the way life was. Feeling dissatisfied, sad, out-of-sorts, unfulfilled was the norm, and the only way to deal with it was to find something to numb the pain.

She wrenched herself away from the sunset and set off across the bridge, still feeling as though someone was walking just a few feet behind. She called in at the first takeaway she found and ate a dismal burger without any enthusiasm before making her way to a bland pub in the maze of backstreets that ran away from the river.

She passed five birds sitting on a wall watching her with beady eyes, unafraid. Only one took flight, hovering over her for several yards before disappearing into the twilight. Five red cars crawled past, one after the other. The fifth pulled in and parked, but no one got out. On the next corner, five children hopped in and out of the gutter in play. One of them smiled at her, covering his left eye until she passed.

Ruth walked on, oblivious.

She sat in the pub for half an hour waiting for her friend to arrive, nursing a vodka and Coke. Though the men in the bar attempted to chat up any single woman who entered, they all left her alone. Ruth knew they could sense something off-putting about her beyond her beaten-down appearance.

Vicky finally put in an appearance at ten-past nine, forty-five minutes later than she had promised. She made no apology. Vicky was a co-worker at the care home, a hard-faced single mother. She had little in common with Ruth, but the two of them had no other friends of note, and sometimes their shifts aligned so they could spend a night together getting miserably drunk.

After an hour and a half and several vodkas, Ruth said, "Do you ever get a feeling you're living a life that isn't really yours?"

Vicky laughed bitterly. "All the time, darlin'. My *real* life is at the side of a pool in Florida. I'm just doing this for a joke."

"No, I mean it. I just don't feel right." Ruth looked around at the other drinkers. "I wonder how many other people feel the same way. Putting up with what they've got instead of doing what they should be doing. Except they don't know what they should be doing."

Vicky snorted derisively. "You're always going on like this. Can't you just shut up and be happy with what you've got? Lots of people would kill for your job."

Ruth drained her glass and stood up. "I'm going to the toilet."

"No need to tell the world."

In the cubicle, Ruth put the toilet lid down and sat on it before letting her head drop into her hands. Vicky was right—she should just accept the way things were. At least that way she might find some kind of peace. When she looked up, her attention was caught by a piece of graffiti on the back of the door, partially obscured by messages of cheap sex and anatomically incorrect drawings: a pentacle.

Ruth was transfixed by it for a long moment as her heart beat faster and faster until she thought it would burst. Leaning forward, she reached out. When her fingers were barely an inch from the scrawled design a blue spark leaped from the tips in a flash and a smell of ozone filled the cubicle. A scorch mark obscured one of the arms of the pentacle.

She returned to the bar in a daze. On the bar stood five glasses, four empty, the fifth being filled with Coke by the barman. Ruth saw it and froze. Blue sparks fizzed across her mind.

One of five, she thought.

Feeling excited and not knowing why, she hurried back to the table to find a man sitting in her place talking animatedly to Vicky. He looked about Ruth's age, his hair black, his looks dark and handsome. He wore an expensive suit and had an air of success about him, but not ostentatiously so.

"Oi, look who it is!" Vicky waved, clearly taken with the new arrival.

"She won't know me," the man said with a self-deprecating grin. "I just moved into the flat next to yours. Saw you leaving this morning. It's a real coincidence I bumped into you here." He shrugged, looked around. "I wouldn't normally come into a dive like this, but . . . I'm glad I did."

Vicky winked at Ruth over his shoulder. Despite herself, Ruth's cheeks flushed.

"I know you're Ruth. My name's Rourke," he said, holding out his hand. "Nobody bothers with my first name. Too embarrassing, to be honest."

Ruth took his hand. "Pleased to meet you." After so long feeling lonely, the charming Mr Rourke gave her a tingle of excitement.

"Is it all right if I have a drink with you?" Rourke asked.

His dark eyes were deep and soothing and made Ruth feel as if she wasn't alone any more.

"Don't mind me," Vicky said sniffily.

"Yeah, have a drink," Ruth said. "Make us both laugh. We bloody well need it."

Rourke smiled, and suddenly the pentacle, the blue spark and the five glasses on the bar were forgotten.

9

In complete confusion, Church found himself retreating through the white nothing-world, despite his consuming desire to keep watching. He didn't want to lose Ruth so soon. The disorientation left him reeling, for the world he had been viewing had felt as real to him as the one in which his body stood. As he tried to make sense of the whirl of emotions and sensations, a wave of joy crashed against him. Seeing Ruth again reignited everything he felt for her so powerfully it was almost painful. If he allowed himself, he could entertain the fantasy that it would have taken no effort to touch her skin, or smell her hair, or even to talk to her.

Yet if he were truthful, he also felt a twinge of jealousy. He saw the way she had looked at Rourke. Had she already forgotten him?

He snapped back into the sunlit chamber, staggering so that Jerzy had to support him.

"You saw her?" Jerzy asked.

Church nodded as he reacclimatised himself. He had felt as if he was in a dream, but now he was back other details began to surface. "She was a Sister of Dragons," he said with a certainty that came from somewhere deeper than the information he had observed, "but she didn't seem to know it. I don't get it."

"But she was safe?"

"She looked as if she was, but there was something not quite right about the whole scenario . . . I don't know." He silently cursed his broken memory. "At least I can keep coming here to check on her. Even if I can't do anything about it."

Church made to walk away from the Wish-Post, but it pulled at the back of his head. He had looked into it, and it into him, and it was not yet prepared to let him go. He decided he would stay there for as long as it took, drinking in every detail, every scene it was offering him.

As he swam in the white, another scene coalesced: a run-down fast-food joint, and leaning over the grill a young woman with rough-cut white-blonde hair, eyes heavy with mascara. Her skin had a vaguely unhealthy tinge, which may have been a result of the strip lights that turned the place into an oasis of artificiality. The woman had a hard face made even harder by the contempt she exuded as she pushed a thin, grey burger around the hotplate.

Who are you? Church thought.

10

"Why do people eat this shit?" Laura DuSantiago could barely stop herself from gagging. She'd decided she was very definitely a vegetarian, but the work was regular and, really, what else could she do?

"I told you, you daft cow—not where the customers can hear." The owner was overweight, short and balding, his arms covered with tattoos.

"Don't worry. They're all too thick to understand plain English." Laura scooped up the burger and flicked it into the warming cabinet. "They shuffle up here every day, following the same routine that's been programmed into them, and stare at me with their fat, stupid faces. And they knowingly risk growing extra breasts thanks to all the hormones stuffed into the shit you serve. You think they have the sense to listen to me?"

"You're well on the way to the sack."

"No, I'm not, because you couldn't get anyone else to do this crappy job on the wage you pay, and you know it."

The owner looked ready to punch Laura, but she pushed past him and stripped off her plastic apron. "Ten o'clock and all's hell. That's my shift over."

"This is your first warning!" the owner bellowed after her as she marched out of the café and into the dingy side street not far from Northampton's main shopping area.

"Yeah, yeah, yeah," she mumbled bitterly, battling down the self-loathing that threatened to break through every minute of every day.

The sodium glare of the street lamps made her feel worse. She wanted to be in a cool, dark wood looking up through the branches to glimpse a clear night sky. She wanted the scents of cooling vegetation, but all she could smell was the rancid odour of fat coming off her clothes.

She wondered where it had all gone wrong. She was sure she must have had dreams some time. Surely she hadn't always planned on a career flipping burgers and a wage that was just enough to cover her rented bedsit in the shittiest part of town, but not enough to buy her time to look for better employment. Not that she had the qualifications to support it. She tried to recall the moment when everything had soured, but her past life was a blur of days in front of the hot griddle and it made her queasy just to consider it.

She didn't have enough cash to get drunk or buy some drugs to expunge her thoughts. She was almost desperate enough to consider giving her dealer a blow job for some E.

In the window of the house where the old hippie woman lived, five candles burned. It wasn't a particularly intriguing image, but it triggered odd stirrings inside her that she recognised with surprise as incipient excitement. As she watched, Hippie Helen appeared to extinguish one of the candles. Laura literally jumped with a surge of electricity that made her feel like sex. She got a strange itch in the tattoo on the back of her right hand—interlocking leaves in a circle—the one she didn't remember getting.

"Hi. How are you doing?"

She turned to see a smiling, handsome face.

"Sorry, didn't mean to frighten you," the man said. "The name's Rourke."

11

Shavi should have gone home a long time ago, but these days it felt as if the offices of Gibson and Layton never closed. In the window he saw the reflection of a handsome Asian face framed by long black hair, a sad expression, a cheap suit; it was him, but not him, somehow. There were too many invoices to go through, too many columns to balance, the whole of the world broken down into numbers, profit and loss. Whenever he got to the end of one client file, another would appear as if by magic. It felt a little bit like purgatory.

Yet he had now managed to reach a state where he could immerse himself in the figures so fully that his *tap-tap-tap* on the calculator became a mechanical act, almost meditative. It allowed his mind to free itself and fly, considering what it might be like to live another life, one with meaning, where worthy deeds were done despite the danger.

And in that state he knew he was not a man who considered cash important. He had an extensive knowledge of diverse spiritual paths, though he had no idea how he had amassed it; his parents were strict in their observance and would not have condoned any study of other religions. It was one of many mysteries clustering around his life.

Everybody in the company recognised he was different. They never involved him in the office gossip or invited him for after-work drinks. The bullies amongst the staff saw his benign, thoughtful nature and mistook it for weakness, attacking him with a thousand barbs of pettiness every day. His resilience drove him through it easily, but it didn't prevent the creeping depression. This was not the way life was supposed to be.

Just after ten and he was the last one in the office. He'd had enough. He pushed back his chair, stripped off his shoes and socks and put on his iPod, winding down before the journey home. The music drifted into his head, some Celtic house, some Balinese temple music, followed by Indian and African beats.

For a while he drifted with his eyes shut. When he opened them, the shock of what he saw brought a convulsion that tore the headphones from his ears. On the desk was a silver picture frame containing a snap of the Avebury stone circle, which he had recently visited. It was an unconventional choice for a desk at that company and had attracted many snide comments from his workmates, but in his more harried moments it calmed him to look at it.

Now, though, the Avebury circle was obscured by a head that appeared to be forcing its way out of the frame, writhing with the pangs of birth. Its features were barely formed, like a clay model with the barest indentations marking eyes, nose and mouth. A white, foaming, gaseous substance leaked out from where the head protruded, and quickly evaporated.

"You called me," it said in a whining, faintly metallic voice. "Brother of Dragons, you called!"

Shavi was struck dumb for a moment. The head mewled as if in pain. Eventually Shavi managed, "What are you?"

"I am from the Invisible World. You called."

"I . . . I did not," Shavi said, but then realised he had been daydreaming, a cry for guidance to rescue him from the misery of his job.

"This world is sour." The head spat and pursed its incipient lips. "I have no taste for it. I cannot understand why you tolerate it, Brother of Dragons, when it is in your power to change it."

Shavi's heart pounded, yet he was surprised to find the encounter was not as terrifying as he would have anticipated before it began. "Brother of Dragons—why do you keep calling me that?"

"Is that your question?" The voice was a little too eager.

"No," Shavi said hurriedly. "I have no question."

"Then I go. But heed my advice, given freely, though you have not heeded such advice in the past: beware the one with cold hands."

The head wriggled back into the picture frame and disappeared with an obscene sucking noise. In the ringing silence of his starkly lit office, Shavi had the unnerving feeling of being cut adrift from mundane reality; yet it was a good feeling, too.

Eagerly he replaced his shoes and socks, picked up his coat and headed down the stairs. Questions raced through his mind and he was keen to start piecing together the answers.

In the quiet street, he came across a blandly handsome man frustratedly pacing back and forth. He turned when he saw Shavi and smiled warmly. "Any idea where I can get a cab?"

"There is a minicab office down towards the crossroads. I was just going there myself."

"Mind if I walk with you? If we're going in the same direction, we can share one. Keep costs down. The name's Rourke."

He held out a friendly hand.

12

This time Church found himself in a flat. The furniture and decoration were threadbare, but it was clean and the occupant had made the best of it. Inexplicably, his attention was drawn to a wardrobe standing against the far wall. One of the doors was ajar, the interior as black as pitch.

He heard a woman humming to herself. Through the open door leading into another room he saw Ruth cross the lounge, tidying up as she went. She appeared happier than the last time he had seen her. Yet she was alone and he felt relieved that Rourke had not come back with her. She hummed a few more bars: it was "Fly Me to the Moon."

Church's attention returned to the wardrobe. What was it about it that bothered him so? It was filled with shadows. His instinct was calling to him. Had Ruth hidden something in there?

He approached the wardrobe slowly. With each step his nerves jangled a little more until they were ringing wildly. He peered into the thin, dark crack, trying to pierce the gloom.

So dark.

Another step, almost close enough to reach the handle. He stretched out an arm unconsciously, knowing in his ghost-like state that he couldn't open the door. One final step . . .

The door slammed shut with a tremendous crash and Church was thrown across the bedroom. From inside the wardrobe, he could hear a sound like low breathing, warning him off.

In the other room, Ruth hummed on, oblivious.

13

Church reeled. Three Rourkes. Or one Rourke in three different places simultaneously.

He grabbed Jerzy's shouders. "I saw three Brothers and Sisters of Dragons. I think they're part of my five. There always have to be five—" He caught his breath. "I think they're in danger . . . Ruth . . . all of them—"

"From what?"

"I don't know. The Wish-Post shows you things, but it doesn't tell you what they mean. I need to try to make some sense of all this."

Church and Jerzy left the Court of Peaceful Days within the hour. A storm rumbled on the horizon, and birds swooped and dived overhead, their cries agitated. Everything he had witnessed through the Wish-Post left Church with a feeling of dread, though he was unsure what he *had* seen.

One thing was true, though: there was nothing he could do about it.

Church arrived back at the Palace of Glorious Light wet and cold and unable to shake the dark mood that had gripped him since he had looked into the Wish-Post. All he wanted was a hot bath and to be left alone with his thoughts. Instead, he had not even dismounted in the rain-lashed cobbled courtyard when Niamh breezed out of the entrance hall wrapped in a thick cloak. Her face was lost inside the heavy shadows of her hood until the flare of a torch revealed an expression that was more troubled than any Church had seen before.

Yet when she spoke her voice betrayed no flicker of emotion. "My brother Lugh is missing."

"What's that got to do with me?" Church replied wearily. He jumped from the horse into a large puddle.

"He has disappeared in your world. I can find no trace of him anywhere. That concerns me."

"Maybe he just wants to be alone."

"You will accompany me to the Fixed Lands and there we will search for my brother." She turned on her heel and marched back into the hall. Overhead the thunder boomed and the lightning crackled, and Church had the unmistakable impression of dark forces moving away in the distance.

CHAPTER THREE
FRATRES DRACONUM

1

Eboracum, AD 306

Lamps guttered in windows across the city and water gushed from orange roof tiles into streets turned into a thick, brown swamp by the storm. The wind and rain drowned out all the sounds of the city, but the stink of human filth tossed out into the road could not be obscured even by the aromas of hundreds of evening meals.

Cursing the vile weather for June, Church kept close to the graffiti-scarred walls as he struggled to make his way in the gloom. The bath-house, the forum and the basilica lay behind him. Now he was in the oppressive jumble of houses, inns and small shops that sprawled towards the fort where the Sixth Legion was billeted.

Eventually he located the tavern on one of the side streets and slipped into its cramped, musty interior. The beams were too low and it was filled with too many men crammed onto benches, talking animatedly about the day's rumours. A few played dice, their eyes feverish, while others voraciously consumed plates of cheese and meat after the day's hard labour.

Church loosened his dripping cloak and threw his hood from his head as he pushed his way to the bar. Nobody gave him a second glance. There at the fringes of the Empire they were used to strangers from far-flung parts.

"New to Eboracum?" the barman said gruffly.

"I have travelled a long way. Wine."

The barman poured a goblet of warmed red wine from a large jug. "This is the finest in the Empire," he said.

Church knew it would be a cheap stew from Crete, but it would take the edge off the night. He tossed a copper coin across the bar and felt a twinge of guilt that tomorrow the barman would find himself in possession of a shiny pebble once the glamour had worn off. "You have a room reserved for me," Church said. "A woman and her slave should be waiting."

The barman nodded. "That slave scared my wife. What happened to him?"

"He was badly burned in a fire at his mistress's home." Church knew this would strike a chord: with torches, oil lamps and candles the only source of light, fire was a constant fear. "That is why he covers his face."

"And a good job, too. It is too monstrous for people to see." The barman led Church through a door and up a narrow, twisting stairway. The rooms were as cramped as the bar below and furnished sparsely with a bed, a chair and a table.

Church was ushered into one that reeked of the olive oil burning in the lamp on the window sill. Niamh waited there, wrapped in a voluminous cloak, the hood pulled low to obscure her identity. Jerzy sat on the floor in one corner. His head was swathed in cloth with two eye-holes cut out so that he resembled a latter-day Elephant Man.

"Have you located him?" Niamh asked once the barman had gone.

Church had seen cracks emerge in Niamh's frosty demeanour since the night the Libertarian had penetrated what she'd believed to be unshakeable defences to give her a taste of a previously alien dish: mortality. The deaths of members of her guard had particularly affected her. Over the last few days, hitherto-unseen emotions had been emerging rapidly: unease, doubt, suspicion and perhaps the first nascent hints of fear.

"I spoke to some of the hookers hanging around outside the curia. They hadn't seen or heard anything, and in a place like this news travels as fast as syphilis." Church collapsed on the bed. He was wet, cold and exhausted, and surprised to find himself thinking warmly of the luxuries of the Court of the Soaring Spirit and the balmy climate of T'ir n'a n'Og.

"That is not good enough," Niamh snapped. "You must search harder."

"Tomorrow."

Jerzy flinched like a whipped dog. He looked fearfully at Niamh, expecting retaliation.

"Now," Niamh said.

"You can send me out there, but you can't make me look." Jerzy had told Church how Niamh had once covered him in boils for an imagined slight, but Church had too much self-respect to fawn.

Niamh went to the window and looked out into the driving rain. In a few short centuries she would have a good view of York Minster, and a few centuries after that the Yorkshire countryside that was now shrouded in impenetrable gloom would be ablaze with electric lights, crushed beneath tarmac, industrial estates, shopping centres. But the heart of it would always be Eboracum.

Jerzy lifted his mask, his face glowing like a spectre in the corner of the room. "My Lady, a question?" he ventured cautiously. "Why are you here alone? Surely for a matter of such gravity you should be accompanied by other Golden Ones?"

"The Golden Ones are a proud race, used to being tied to the heart of Existence. We have no beginning, we have no ending. Thus we cannot ever be defeated, or harmed. We cannot be threatened. Nothing troubles us. Nothing demands our attention," Niamh replied, distracted.

"How can you say that?" Church said. "The Libertarian killed several of your people."

After a moment of silence, Niamh replied, "That did not happen."

"Come on—"

Niamh spoke over him. "I discussed the matter with many of my kind and it was agreed that since such a thing could not happen, it did not happen."

Church laughed in amazement. "Humanity's been scared of you for thousands of years, but you're just as pathetic as any group that won't face up to reality."

Niamh turned to Church, her eyes blazing. "And have you faced up to reality? You are my puppet until I decide it is time to cut your strings. You cannot view your distant love unless I say so. Brother of Dragons, indeed! Are you really the best that Existence can find to champion its cause? The ravens still follow you. You have already presided over the deaths of those you lured into helping you. Now your contemporaries are at risk, and still there is nothing you can do about it. *That* is pathetic."

Church flinched. Niamh saw, and smiled.

"Lesser beings should know their place." She returned her attention to the view out of the window. "To attempt to rise above your station will only result in misery."

"There's nothing you can do to stop me helping my friends—" Church began.

Jerzy jumped to his feet, urging Church to remain silent. "Mistress, my good friend meant no disrespect. We are, of course, as concerned for your brother's safety as yourself, and we will do everything within our power to help."

"Then go out again," she said.

"It's pointless," Church snapped. "If a golden-skinned god proclaiming to be Lugh had appeared in Eboracum, the whole town would have been talking about it. I don't even understand why you're so sure he's missing."

"There is a hierarchy amongst the Golden Ones. Those who come first are linked. We feel each other—and I can no longer feel my brother."

"So he could be dead?"

Niamh ignored the question. "My brother visited this place recently. It was the last time I was aware of his presence." Niamh bowed her head slightly so that the hood cast her face into shadow. "You can mingle amongst your own kind, hear their secret words in a way that I could not."

"So now you need me—"

"My relationship with them is one of supplicant and god. I do not need to hear prayers. I want the words they would never dare speak to me."

Church recognised an opportunity in her words. "I'll do what I can to find your brother. And if I do manage to bring him back here I want a reward. I want to be freed from your control. Agreed?"

Niamh thought for a moment and then said, "Agreed."

And that was when Church realised how truly scared she was.

2

Church and Jerzy bought breakfast from the *popinae* that lined the main street where stall holders loudly proclaimed that they had the best food in the Empire, be it sausage or pease pudding. By 9 a.m. the noise was deafening as rival traders fought to be heard amongst the hubbub caused by jugglers, tumblers and other performers. The Romanised British upper class bought their food from the stalls and chatted about the day's tasks, while the prostitutes hurried back and forth, the only business that never closed.

The rain had ended some time around dawn. With Jerzy at his side, Church had been the scouring the streets, talking to everyone he met. No one had heard any rumour suggesting that one of the gods had been seen in the city, though there were other incredible tales—of a man who became a wolf by night and stalked the mausoleums in the cemetery beyond the city walls, and a slave from one of the Iberian tribes who fell into a trance to make dire premonitions.

In his cloth mask, Jerzy attracted a few stares, but there were many other people with serious disabilities—missing limbs, burns, lost eyes and noses, the rigours of disease hacked into their skin. Church noted how the harshness of life in past centuries was often forgotten in his own time, lost behind illustrations of unblemished people in textbooks. Yet there was an energy to life that he had never witnessed on any twenty-first-century street.

"The food is so plain," Jerzy said as he gnawed on a cheese cake.

"That's because you're used to Otherworld meals. You know, you could have stayed there in the lap of luxury. Niamh wasn't forcing you to come to my miserable, grey world."

"But you are my very good friend," the Mocker said, puzzled. "I could not abandon you to strife. We all need someone to watch for the knife in the back when we are concentrating on the smiling face."

Church was touched by Jerzy's loyalty. "You're well versed in the ways of the Tuatha Dé Danann."

"We must look out for each other now, for we have no one else in all the lands. Your friends are adrift beyond the gulf of years. My family and friends . . . well, even if the queen allowed me to see them I would not inflict this freakish visage upon them. Better that time swells between us and they forget I ever existed." His eyes smiled through the holes in the mask. "And there: I have found the humour in this situation. A sour irony. I need time to bring me peace. You wish time to drain away for the same reason. Oh, what a pair we are!"

"There's a saying in my time. People ask how you get through a difficult situation. The trick is to keep breathing. That's all. We keep hopeful, and we keep breathing."

"You are a strange visitor to the Far Lands, friend Church. We know little of hope there. Things are simply the way they are. Yet you believe it can all change."

"I do. And there's another irony for you. In Otherworld, where everyone keeps telling me reality is fluid, nothing ever really changes. And here in the so-called Fixed Lands, we embrace change. We have to. There's nothing else." Church finished his spicy sausage and finally quelled his hunger.

"And you still have hope," Jerzy mused.

"It would be easier to give up, I know that. But then what would be the point in living? Love, affection for our friends—that's what drives us on. That's our Blue Fire. I'll do whatever I can to save the people I care for."

"Even give up your own life?"

Church considered the question, but he already knew the answer. "If I have to."

This time it was impossible to read the emotion in Jerzy's unwavering gaze. Uncomfortable with the attention, Church caught a passing slave going urgently about his master's business. "Tell me," Church said, "who rules the Empire this day?"

The slave looked at Church as if he were mad. "Constantius is Emperor of the West. Any fool knows that. Though for how much longer is unknown. He lies sick now, on his bed, over yonder. And some say it is his death bed." He pointed to the grand buildings near the fort, before roughly pulling himself free and hurrying down the street.

"Constantius . . . in Eboracum, on his death bed. That gives me a time-frame," Church said to Jerzy. "A few years back, Diocletian set up a system of four rulers to share the burden of government in the Empire. Constantius became Western Emperor last year, a year before he died of natural causes here in Eboracum." He gave a sardonic smile. "So only around one thousand seven hundred years to go."

"Good friend, you are broadening my abilities as an entertainer. I am learning a new form of humour. Fixed Lands humour!"

"I wouldn't go trying it out on an audience just yet."

"Will you teach me about your humour? It seems to me, in our conversations, that laughter has a value I do not understand."

"I'm not the best person to ask. I'm a surly, miserable git, to be honest."

"Please."

Church sighed. "I'll tell you about the different kinds of humour if you want, and I'll throw in a few jokes that I remember. That's about all I can promise. But let's face it, there's not a lot to laugh about—"

Jerzy raised a finger. "Ah! But there is, there always is. Perhaps I can teach you something in return?"

Church laughed. "Knock yourself out."

The sun emerged from behind the clouds and illuminated the bustling life of the forum: men and women in togas, traders in rougher clothes, the kilts and leggings of those who had stayed true to their Celtic roots, and the poor bare-chested despite the weather as they struggled to eke out a living.

A rush of power made Church's hands and legs tingle—a message from his unconscious. He scanned the faces of those nearby until he saw a man hurrying through the crowd. His features suggested he came from foreign parts, and he had the tanned, muscular body of a fighter who spent his time in the open air. Church knew instantly that the fellow was the cause of his instinctive response.

He tugged at Jerzy's arm surreptitiously, and then set off in pursuit. Like all Roman towns, Eboracum was built on a grid system so it was easy to follow from a distance. Their target strode purposefully out of the forum along a broad thoroughfare that cut through the two- and three-storey white-washed buildings. At the temple he took a turn along the side of a row of imposing arches that formed the boundary of the religious compound and made his way towards the theatre. It was one of the grandest buildings in town, with a long, three-storey frontage covered with ornate carvings and an enormous doorway the height of three men leading into the dark interior.

The man ducked inside despite it being early in the day when there were no performances taking place. Church and Jerzy followed, though Jerzy was baffled and Church had no real idea what it was about the man that had alerted him. Inside it was cool and dark and smelled of oil lamps and candle wax. A maze of corridors and stairs ran past rooms like huge burrows where theatre staff went about their business, oblivious.

Church lost sight of the man in the warren. After a while they emerged into bright sunlight and ahead of them was the expansive semicircle of the open-air theatre with mountainous tiers of seats reaching up to the summit of grand arches. It was completely deserted, but had the echoing charm of a pre-match football stadium.

"He must still be inside—" Jerzy began before he was cut short by rough hands clamping across his mouth. Church was assaulted from behind just as quickly, and the two of them were subdued by several arms and fists before a sharp blow to the back of the head plunged Church into unconsciousness.

He came round in a small room crowded with several figures. The windows were shuttered and thick, acrid candle smoke filled the air. The large-boned stranger they had been pursuing sat in one corner, gnawing on the remnants of a hambone. His cold gaze never left Church's face.

Church's sword lay on a table, its faint blue glow illuminating the face of a serious young man who was examining it. Nervously, he kept pushing back the black hair that fell in ringlets around his face.

Church quickly sized up the situation. There were four others: a woman with blonde hair pulled severely back into a clasp, her expression frosty; a second woman with olive skin and a mass of curly black hair, beautiful, with a hint of aristocracy, and wearing a toga of the upper classes; a pensive North African man in long, black robes; and a centurion standing near the door. His presence was charismatic, but his expression appeared permanently troubled.

"The sword is filled with the Blue Fire," said the young man. "See the way the light plays along the edge of the blade? It is an object of power."

"Then why does this scrawny one carry it?" the one with the hambone said gruffly. "His arms are barely strong enough to lift it."

"Try me," Church said. "You'll see."

The man threw the hambone to one side and wiped the grease from his mouth. "I never thought I would see the day when I heard an insect speak."

"Why were you following Decebalus?" the centurion asked. He had the authority of a leader and the others all looked to him as they awaited an answer.

When Church didn't respond, Decebalus leaned forward and snatched away Jerzy's mask. Everyone recoiled from the grinning, white visage. The one leaning over the sword crossed himself and mouthed, "Jesu!"

"Please do not hurt me!" Jerzy shrieked. "I am only a simple entertainer."

"He's no threat to you," Church stressed. He saw hands go for daggers and swords, the steel in eyes used to searching for threats in every corner. Only the dark-haired woman remained calm.

"What is he?" the blonde said with disgust.

"He comes from the Otherworld." The dark-haired woman leaned forward to examine Jerzy carefully. "Do you not?"

"Yes . . ." Jerzy said hesitantly.

"And you?" Decebalus said harshly to Church. "Are you one of the beasts who have tormented us since the dark days when the world was formed?"

"I'm a man, like you." Church moderated his tone to try to calm the situation.

"What kind of man wields an object of such power?" the North African asked.

The young man looked from the sword to Church and said uncertainly, "A Brother of Dragons."

"Five is the number," the centurion said, "and there are five of us already."

"You're Brothers of Dragons?" It was Church's turn to be shocked.

"And sisters," the blonde woman said icily.

"This is too much of a coincidence—"

"There are no coincidences," the young man said fiercely. "That is the first rule we are taught. Existence moves us like pieces on a board to where we should be at the right time." His eyes blazed with a fierce intelligence. He motioned to Church's arm. "You have a scar?"

Not understanding how the young man could know, Church cautiously revealed the scar where the spider had been in his arm.

The young man blanched. "Jack, Giantkiller," he said with awe.

"What are you saying, you little runt?" Decebalus demanded.

"Long, long ago, when the Brothers and Sisters of Dragons first emerged from the Blue Fire, my ancestor met the great hero to whom we all owe allegiance: Jack the Giantkiller."

Church looked into the young man's face and saw something he recognised in the line of his jaw or the shape of his eyes. "Conoran," he said. "He was your ancestor."

"The King of the Land," the young man continued, "who disappeared across the water to the Isle of Apples, accompanied by the Golden Lady, to return when we needed him most."

"And this is he?" The North African stared at Church in awe before bowing his head.

"You are Jack, Giantkiller?" the centurion asked.

"He is!" Jerzy chimed in with a note of hysterical relief. "A great hero!"

"I prefer to be called Church."

Dazed, the young man ran his hands through his ringlets. "This is . . . beyond belief! I never thought I would see the day!"

"Your ancestor was a good man," Church said. "He saved my life."

The young man smiled shyly. "My name is Joseph. I am a shepherd in the Church of Christ, and a Watchman. Legends say our society was established by my ancestor before its knowledge spread into all religions."

"It was." Church recalled his final conversation with Conoran, which was only a few months ago by his reckoning. "You have all the secret knowledge of the Culture?"

Joseph nodded. "Knowledge of the stars and the animals and all growing things. Knowledge of the Blue Fire that is in everything. Knowledge of all the lands, both here and beyond the veil, and of the beings who reside there, and the threats that humanity faces in coming times. I am here to ensure we are always prepared."

The centurion shook Church's hand. "I have heard many tales of the Great King Beyond the Water. I am proud to serve you. My name is Marcus Aelius Aquila of the Sixth Legion, stationed here in Eboracum."

Church was stunned that events he had set in motion had taken on a life of their own, rolling out across the centuries right up to his own time. The others introduced themselves with varying degrees of openness. Decebalus had once been one of Rome's enemies in Dacia, the region that would become Romania. The Dacians were renowned as fierce, brutal warriors and Decebalus was clearly of that tradition. Even after the introduction, he continued to regard Church with suspicion.

The dark-haired woman was Lucia Aeternia Constans, originally from

Rome. Her husband had died in undisclosed circumstances. Decebalus called her *strega*, which Church knew meant "witch" though he couldn't tell if it was a description or an insult. She had a seductive though kindly nature and reminded Church a little of Ruth.

The North African was Secullian, another Christian with an introspective nature and a wry sense of humour. He spoke repeatedly of prophecy and magics and how information came to him in what he called "day-sleeps." And finally the blonde-haired woman who was the most closed-off of all of them: her name was Aula Fabricia Candida, born in Britain and married to a scholar now travelling across the Empire. Church couldn't define her role within the group, but she regularly touched an unusual brooch that featured a circle of interlocking leaves.

"You have come because of the dreams?" Marcus asked. "Are these the End-Times of which Joseph speaks?"

"I'm searching for a missing . . . god." Church was unsure how much he should tell them. "Do you know anything about that?"

Lucia leaned in. She smelled of exotic perfume. "There is talk of gods all over the Empire. They come and go, tormenting people as they always have, making their secret plans over our lives. But not here! Not in Eboracum. And this is a land of many gods, for it is a land of travellers who have stayed awhile and brought their gods with them."

"We were all afflicted by terrible dreams in our own mundane worlds," Secullian said, "dreams that brought us here, where we learned of our destiny as Brothers and Sisters of Dragons, Champions of the Blue Fire, of Existence itself."

"What kind of dreams?"

The North African winced. "Dreams of spiders."

"Swarms of them, streaming out from behind the world around us as if it were a theatre set." Decebalus put on a show of bravado, but Church could see the unease behind it.

"Black spiders," Church said. Unconsciously he fingered his scar, recalling what he had confronted in the fogou at Carn Euny, and the thing that had controlled the Redcaps.

Aula touched her brooch again for comfort. "The spiders are eating their way through the world," she said. "Soon there will be nothing left."

There was a long moment of uneasy silence until Joseph said, "We gather here to understand what these portents mean. Will you aid us?"

On the way back to the tavern to report to Niamh, Jerzy capered beside Church like a monkey. "Good friend, I do not understand," he said with frustration. "If you help these people in their task, you will not be free to search for the queen's brother and earn your freedom."

"There'll be time for that later."

"The mistress is not a patient woman, and you need your freedom to help your loved one."

"Of course that's what I want," Church said, a little more sharply than he had intended, "but I can't shake the feeling that there's a bigger threat here. How can I turn my back on that?"

When they reached the forum, they were instantly aware of a radical change in the atmosphere. All the cities of the Empire thrived on gossip and rumour treated as news, swapped in taverns, on the street and in the bathhouses. The forum was abuzz with people talking wildly, running from one group to the next to pass on whatever was exciting them. Church could see from the frowns and the muttered prayers that it was not good news.

An overweight tradesman hauling a full amphora stopped as they approached, unable to contain himself any longer. "It is indeed the end of the world," he gasped.

"What's happening?" Church asked.

"Then you have not heard? A scout returned this morning from the north. He passed through the city walls and went straight to the fort, speaking to no one. But all who saw him said his face was frozen in fear. And now word has emerged from the legato, or so people say. The Ninth Legion! The Ninth Legion is marching back to Eboracum from the very shores of Underworld." The tradesman shuddered, shouldered his amphora and hurried off.

"Why is he so scared?" Jerzy asked.

The time of the Roman occupation had been Church's chief area of study. "The Ninth Legion is the most written about of all Rome's legions. It disappeared nearly two hundred years ago, and in my time scholars are still arguing about what happened to it. There aren't enough records left to uncover the truth. Some say the legion was disbanded, others that it was reassigned to the Netherlands."

"That did not happen?"

"The last positive sighting we have is that the Ninth marched north from

Eboracum to disperse a large group of Celts in Caledonia who had been launching marauding raids on Roman territory. The most famous explanation is that the entire legion of fifteen thousand men was slaughtered while they camped, the bodies burned and the armour melted down to destroy all evidence of their existence."

"Then how could the legion be returning today?" Jerzy asked.

"It can't." But Church could see that the tension in the forum was not abating. Real terror lay in many faces.

Back at the inn, Niamh sat at the sunlit table next to the window, poring over the cards Church had seen her with outside Carn Euny. Her expression was troubled. They were tarot cards, he noted, but some of them were unfamiliar to him. There were the familiar suits—cups, wands, swords and coins—and he instantly linked them to the four great treasures the Tuatha Dé Danann had brought with them from their distant homes, according to myth: the cauldron of Dagda, which became the template for the Holy Grail; the spear of Lugh; the sword Caledfwlch, which Church had been mysteriously carrying when he was found by Tannis and his men; and the Stone of Fal, which let out a scream when the true king of the land put his foot upon it. Yet as he approached the table he could make out another suit: a bird in flight.

"What's that?" he asked. "There are only four suits in the tarot."

"In the cards allowed for the use of Fragile Creatures." Niamh did not lift her eyes from the complex spread. "These cards provide an insight into the workings of Existence. Do you think we would allow their full power to fall into such hands?" She looked up as if seeing Church for the first time. "Five suits. Five. The number of power. Do you not understand anything?"

"I understand that the arrogance of your kind is going to result in a little hubris one day." Near the door, Jerzy whimpered.

"The suit that is denied Fragile Creatures is Ravens. The eaters of the dead, the messengers of the gods. The fifth suit provides true contact with the great beyond. And how fitting it is for you—do the ravens still hover at your back, little Jack?" She stared into Church's face for a long moment, but her arrogance slowly faded like a light being dimmed. She returned to her cards, her fingers toying with lips grown sad. "Any word of my brother?"

"No. Nothing in the cards?"

"I see too much. For you, for me, for all Existence." She swept the cards aside in a burst of emotion, then turned away from him to look over the rooftops. Church retired to the bed, but as he drifted off to sleep he was sure Niamh was crying.

4

Church met Marcus the centurion in the shadow of the basilica just as night came. The rain was falling again and had driven all the tradesmen and hustlers off the excrement-stinking streets.

"They allow you to come and go from the fort?" Church asked as he huddled inside a sodden cloak.

"I have free passage for the moment. Constantius is ill and minds are exercised elsewhere." He glanced up and down the empty street. "You have heard about the Ninth?"

"I've heard the rumours."

"All true. Fifteen members of an advanced scouting party were slaughtered. Only one escaped, but now he too has died. The Ninth Legion has marched back out of hell and is returning to Eboracum."

"And you think this has something to do with your dreams and the reason you've been brought together here?"

"It *is* the reason. And it may well be linked to your missing god. Secullian conducted a ritual at the theatre after you left. He took hashish, some other spices and herbs unknown to me, and slipped into one of his day-sleeps. And then . . ." Marcus tugged at his hood to free the rainwater gathering on top. "Something spoke through him. Something evil. It told us the Ninth Legion now belongs to the Kingdom of the Spider, and it is coming to wipe us all from the face of the Earth." He swallowed painfully, his mouth dry. "Secullian clawed out an eye to escape what was being shown to him inside his head. He is being cared for by the others."

"I'm sorry."

"He will live. Sometimes that is the best we can say."

Though Marcus still carried the deeply troubled air that Church had sensed immediately when they had met earlier, there was a strength of character to him that Church found reassuring. Clearly, Existence knew what it was doing when it chose its champions. "Is your legion planning to ride out to meet them?"

"Indecision is rife. With the Emperor sick, his advisors are obsessed with omens and portents. The men await orders, but fear runs rampant amongst them. Who in their right mind would want to face a legion of the dead? But orders have been sent to secure the gates. The defences are strong."

"You think that'll be enough?"

"I think five Brothers and Sisters of Dragons will not be enough to defeat an entire legion, even with a hero of legend at our side."

"I'd be the first to agree with that. Any suggestions?"

"Aula waits in the cemetery beyond the walls to seek aid or advice."

"From whom?"

"Her patron. He will meet her there shortly. But first—"

From three different directions, guards rushed up to grab them. The sound of their approach had been masked by the driving rain.

"Wait!" Marcus said. "I am Centurion—"

The shaft of a spear glanced his skull and laid him out cold. Church struggled as several arms grasped him, protesting loudly before he too was beaten unconscious.

5

Cold white marble chilled Church's cheek. The room smelled sweet from perfumes thrown on hot coals. He forced his aching body into a sitting position and squinted around. Thick drapes hung on the walls and exquisitely constructed furniture made by the best local artisans stood all around. Church could see at a glance it was quarters for the wealthy.

An elderly man in a white toga held in place by a gold clasp talked with a quiet intensity to two guards near the door. He exuded power and prestige, but there was a weariness to his features, which had a greyish pallor. When he saw that Church was conscious, he motioned for the guards to leave and poured himself a goblet of wine, before sitting to look down on Church with a degree of suspicion.

"I have nothing to do with the Ninth Legion—" Church began.

The dignitary silenced him with a raised hand. "I know."

"Then why have you brought me here? I am a free man. And where is my comrade?"

"He is a traitor who will face swift military justice." The dignitary took a sip of his wine. "I am Numerius Didius Agelastus, advisor to Emperor Constantius. At this moment, the Emperor lies on his sick bed, unable to govern. And so the task falls to me."

"Why have you brought me here?"

"Why?" Numerius's eyes flickered with unease, as if the memory of his motivation was lost to him. He moistened his lips with a flick of a nervous tongue. "Because . . ." Panic flared in his face. "Because—"

"Because I told him to."

Church started at the familiar voice. A man swathed in a thick cloak and hood had entered. The temperature dropped a couple of degrees as the Libertarian threw off his hood to reveal his glaring red eyes. "Brother of Dragons." The greeting was laced with sarcasm. "I never expected to see you again so soon."

Church turned to Numerius. "You can't work with him—he's some kind of devil. Look at his eyes."

Numerius shivered, but did not turn. The Libertarian came over and clapped one hand on Numerius's shoulder before patting it in a patronising manner. Then he gently lifted the fold of Numerius's toga that fell across his shoulder to reveal a black spider embedded into the skin.

"My good friend Numerius Didius Agelastus may see the reason in your words, but I shall win the argument every time."

"You control him with that thing. How many others?"

The Libertarian pretended to count on his fingers, then gave up with a smile.

Church made the connection. "You tried to control me."

"You were doing so well at the Second Battle of Magh Tuireadh, lopping off heads and limbs like a fully trained butcher with that silly little sword-that-is-not-a-sword. One of those lumbering Fomorii cretins managed to impress a Gravix upon you. It removed you from the field of play, but sadly did not turn the course of battle. Nor did it weaken you enough to be slain."

Church recalled Niamh telling him at their first meeting that he had fought in the battle between the Tuatha Dé Danann and their ancient enemies, but he had discounted it as one of her deceptions.

"The Gravix tried its hardest to turn you, but that damnable fire burns too brightly inside you. Oh, if only we could have eliminated you at that point. Alas, it was not to be."

"So you control the Fomorii?"

The Libertarian laughed silently. "We work towards the same aims. You would not find us drinking in the same bar. Or even in the same town."

Church saw his sheathed sword on a table across the room and weighed up whether he could reach it before the Libertarian intercepted him. The Libertarian saw his eye movement and divined his intentions.

"Please," he said with world-weariness, "can we not have a simple conversation? It is very difficult to find in my line of business." He pushed Numerius out of the way and poured himself a goblet of wine. "Not the best I have tasted, but the best for this era."

"This era?" Church repeated. He watched a spidery smile crawl across the Libertarian's face, just as quickly removed. "Your language . . . it's not archaic. You're from the future, like me."

"The future?" the Libertarian sneered. "Oh yes. The 'future.' The 'past.' The 'present.' What a quaint way of seeing things."

Church edged towards the sword. The Libertarian noticed, did nothing. Numerius moved his mouth in a sticky, troubled way as if he were paralysed.

"Keep playing your games—I don't care," Church said. "But if we are both from a different time, how can we operate here and now without changing what's to come?"

The Libertarian mused. "Well, consider this, perhaps: time is a river. One may swim upstream, or downstream, if you like. Or: one throws a rock into that self-same river. The water hits it, flows around it, recovers its original course. There are eddies here and there, but it still continues to the sea."

"You're saying we can make little changes around us, but nothing long-term."

"Or perhaps what your kind call reality changes all the time, but you are unaware of it because you change with it. You alter, and are reborn with new memories of your new reality so you presume it has always been that way. Yet ghosts invade your memories. Impressions of a different place, with a different you, fading even as they come. Dreams of other realities, so strange yet somehow real." His red, lidless stare grew more intense. "Everything is fluid. Nothing is fixed. Poor you! Poor Fragile Creatures! The curse of your existence."

Church made his move for the sword. But instead of trying to intercept him, the Libertarian put one hand around Numerius's throat. Church saw this from the corner of his eye and paused as he reached for the sword. Numerius's eyes were wide and glistening beads of sweat stood out on his brow, but he did not move. The Libertarian's jagged nails cut through soft skin, went deep and deeper still. And then, with one rapid twist of his wrist, he tore. The arterial spray of blood arced across the room. Church would always recall the sound of it hitting the marble, like a pot of paint being thrown at a canvas. One hot gush splashed against the side of his face, blinding one eye, rushing down his neck, soaking his clothes like a summer storm. In shock, he turned and saw the Libertarian gut Numerius with his other hand, letting the discorporated body slide to the floor, a discarded toy. The Libertarian was red from head to toe.

"Fetch your silly little sword," he said. "Enjoy the comfort it gives you, for now."

Church was rooted in shock at the brutality he had witnessed.

"You know I cannot touch you, not yet, not so far from the Source, when I am weaker and your ugly little fire burns so brightly. There is no point attempting to deny that. But we are many, and we are fanning out through all-time, all-reality, to dream things the way they should be. You will be hunted to the moment when you can no longer stem the flow."

"What are you?" Church asked, sickened.

"You ask for names, still?" the Libertarian replied with complete contempt. "You expect me to tell you words of power? And Fragile Creatures are to be the next to climb the ladder to wonder? Truly the ways of Existence are baffling." He laughed. "Know this, then: we are the Army of the Ten Billion Spiders. We nest, we scurry from the shadows, we spin webs to catch little flies! No escape, little Fragile Creature! No escape for you."

"So you're the reason why the Brothers and Sisters of Dragons exist. It's not just about keeping the gods at bay."

"There is some truth in that, and also a great and devastating irony that you have yet to appreciate in its entirety. But you will, and soon."

Church sloughed off the shock and grabbed his sword, but by the time he had drawn it, the Libertarian had gone, the door stood open and the guards without lay butchered in a widening pool of blood.

6

Niamh stood at the window as she had for so long, watching the rain cascade off the rooftops into the muddy streets. Here and there lamps flickered like fireflies sheltering from the storm.

"I can understand why so many of my kind love this world. Even amidst all the horror and the despair and the degradation, tiny beacons of beauty shine through. The way the light falls on a cold day near the ocean, or the smell of a forest at summer's twilight. The sound here, of the rain, the clatter and splash, so many subtleties . . . a symphony." She paused uncertainly. "And I have been thinking of late that perhaps that quiet beauty exists within Fragile Creatures, too, for they are a part of this world. What do you say?"

Jerzy sat on the bed, cross-legged. "I agree with whatever you say, mistress."

Niamh made an irritable noise in her throat. "I suppose I wanted a performing monkey and that is what I have. Do you have any opinions of your own left, Mocker?"

"If that is what my mistress requires."

"How do you find your companion?"

Jerzy considered the question. "He is a man filled with so many shadows, and doubts, and such a great sadness that he barely recognises himself."

"Go on."

"He surprises me, because he does not think only of himself. Indeed, on many occasions that is the last thing of which he thinks. He does not know himself at all, and he cannot see that he is capable of great things."

"But you think he is?"

"Oh yes. Undoubtedly."

"A good man, then?"

"Good-hearted. Fair. True. Unaware of his strengths. Overly conscious of his weaknesses."

"Yet I cannot understand why he pines for that other Fragile Creature when there is little hope they will ever meet again."

"You would not understand, mistress."

"Why not?"

"You are a Golden One. Such things are not known to you."

"What things?"

"Love . . ." Jerzy's voice trailed off. He thought he had begun to sense a hardness in Niamh's voice that signalled one of her unpredictable responses.

Yet once again he was surprised. "Do you think that is true?" she asked, with a note of puzzlement. "We Golden Ones see ourselves as never-ending, never-changing, a fixed axis of Existence. Yet now I wonder . . . If all that is joined to Existence is fluid, then surely we are fluid, too? We change—"

"Without change, there is only stagnation."

Niamh did not appear to notice that he had spoken out of turn. "I fear for my brother's safety. It is a strange, troubling emotion and I do not care to experience it again. Before the Libertarian came to my quarters it was unknown to me. If only I could return to that state again."

"The Libertarian showed you mortality, mistress. He revealed what it means to be a Fragile Creature."

This time Niamh whirled, her eyes blazing. "Be silent, you grinning jackanape! Be still, or I'll return you to the Court of the Final Word to have your tongue removed!"

Jerzy scampered off the bed and cowered in the corner of the room, tears stinging his eyes.

"Where is that pathetic Fragile Creature?" Niamh snapped. She returned to the window to search the empty streets again. "If he does not find my brother, if my brother has already been wiped from the face of Existence, then I will show him mortality. And I will show him such pain on the road to it!"

7

Church wiped off Numerius's blood on the drapes and set off to find Marcus. Outside, he watched legionnaires run past in step towards the main gate. Three of them clutched sizzling torches to light their way, the flames illuminating faces fixed with concern.

It took him forty-five minutes to locate the stockade where enemies of the Empire were imprisoned. It smelled of urine and damp. Church drew his sword to meet any resistance, but in the main guardroom, three men were slumped unconscious.

Further on, a hissing woman's voice floated to him: "Hush! You lumber like a bull with gout!"

"And you screech like a damnable owl!"

Church padded round a bend in the corridor to see the burly Dacian Decebalus holding an axe as big as a ten year old, ready to attack a heavy oak door. The olive-skinned Roman Lucia was attempting to restrain him with angry frustration. "Barbarian!" she snapped.

"Witch!"

"Be still, for the sake of our Lord. Someone will hear." The North African seer Secullian steadied himself against the wall. Dried blood crusted around the edge of an eye patch covering the empty socket where he had plucked out an eyeball during the throes of his vision.

"You're looking for Marcus?"

They all started at Church's question and Lucia rounded on Decebalus. "See! The entire Sixth Legion could have crept upon us under the cover of your thunderous noise!"

Decebalus raised a meaty hand to swipe her, but Lucia ducked out of the way and skipped towards Church. "A fine band of heroes we are. Fighting like children. Failing on every front."

Church could see them all looking to him as if he had the power to turn the tide of events with one sweep of his sword. "This is the right place?" he said.

"I saw it in a vision," Secullian replied weakly. "But sometimes they lie outright, and often they seek to deceive."

"Just break the door down," Church said impatiently. "There's nobody around—they've all gone to meet the Ninth Legion."

"Then the rumours are true." Lucia looked to Secullian uneasily.

Decebalus grinned and spat on his hands. Within moments the door hung from its hinges in splinters.

The room behind it was sparsely appointed, with straw on the floor and a latrine pit in one corner. A pile of sodden rags was heaped to one side. The room was empty.

Decebalus cursed loudly. "I have better visions after six flagons of wine," he snapped at Secullian.

"Wait." Church hoped against hope, knew it was futile. Lucia followed his gaze to the bundle of rags. Her face revealed two things: that she knew exactly what Church had guessed, and that her heart was breaking in two. Church knew instantly that she loved Marcus.

Decebalus plucked up a small sack resting on top of the pile of rags. Blood dripped from the bottom. Decebalus peered inside for a moment. Then he replaced the sack in silence and bowed his head, muttering a prayer to the gods.

"I'm sorry," Church said, but all he could think of was Niamh's words at Carn Euny about the ravens following him.

"We are no longer five," Secullian said. "Our power has been broken."

"I'll make up your number," Church said.

"Then we fight alongside a legend," Decebalus said confidently. "The King Beyond the Water has returned. Our victory is assured."

8

The cemetery markers and mausoleums loomed up like ghosts in the driving rain. Amongst the busts and statues, carvings of griffins and sphinxes glowered down from the tops of tombs.

Church and the others had slipped outside the city walls as the Sixth Legion marched out of the main gates to meet the Ninth head-on.

Secullian crossed himself. Decebalus's eyes flitted nervously back and forth. "We should not be here after dark," he hissed. "The dead will take us into their homes."

Only Lucia moved with confidence. "Hurry," she urged, splashing through the puddles. "Time is short."

In the centre of the cemetery was a paved square where a single tree grew. Sheltering under it was Aula, her hard features almost hidden in an oversized cowl. "I was beginning to think I would have to wait until winter set in."

Lucia went to her, and the tears she had managed to hold back for so long finally streamed down her cheeks. "Marcus is dead," she said simply.

Church had felt that Aula was the coldest of the group, but she hugged Lucia fiercely without a second thought. Her face revealed that the loss cut her just as deeply.

Aula broke free after a moment and said gently, "There will be time for grieving later. We have much to do."

"You have summoned him?" Secullian asked.

"Not yet. I await Joseph . . ." Aula spied Church and said, less than deferentially, "We are truly honoured."

They were distracted by a loud splashing as the shrouded figure of Joseph weaved through the tombs and graves. When he saw Church, Joseph grabbed his hand with an almost pathetic gratitude. "Thank Jesu. Then we have a chance."

"You have the information?" Decebalus asked gruffly.

"The Ninth Legion approach along the Great North Road. They are dead . . . all of them dead, yet alive. I have this from the mouth of a centurion who took a blessing from me before he set off for battle."

"Christians in the Roman army," Aula said, shaking her head. "Truly it is the end of the world."

"Now you must ask your gods for aid, or all is lost," Jospeh insisted.

Aula nodded with a hint of apprehension. "All of you stand back, then. There is no way to tell how he will react to your presence. He can be as wild as the storm that is brewing, or as calm as a summer's day."

Church and the others sheltered in the lea of the surrounding tombs while Aula conducted some ritual around the tree. For a long while there was nothing except the chill of wet cloth against skin and the drumming of rain on stone, and the comforting smell of the wet grasslands and woods that surrounded Eboracum. But then came a sound that Church first thought was the wind over the hills, long, low and chilling. The hairs on the back of his neck stood erect, and gooseflesh ran up and down his arms. When the sound came again, he was convinced it was the cry of a wolf or one of the birds from the moors, or a bear's roar, distorted by the storm.

A shape loomed up amongst the tombs on the edge of the cemetery and loped towards the central tree. Even when it arrived, Church was none the wiser. Antlers sprouted from its head, and bestial eyes glowed with a ruddy light. Church saw animal fur and ivy, hoofs and intertwining branches and leaves all jumbled together, making it impossible to tell if it was an animal disguised by vegetation, or a tree-like being with a hide draped over it.

"You called me, Daughter of the Green." The voice was part-human, partly a low, rumbling roar filled with notes that made Church unsure whether or not it was on the brink of attacking.

Aula bowed before it. "Thank you for answering, great Cernunnos."

That single name told Church what he was seeing: the Celtic nature god whose reach spread throughout the known world, and who became the template for the archetypal, vegetative figure of the Green Man. The air was electric, as if Cernunnos was discharging energy into the atmosphere, and there was a majesty to him that Church had not felt from any of the other gods.

"I beg for your help," Aula said. "My lord, as in times past we face a great danger that threatens us all. We cannot meet it alone."

"You do not trust in yourself, little sister," Cernunnos growled. "Help will be given. But first . . ." He put his head back and sniffed the air. "There is a scent of more of your kind, and of one who is greater still. Come forth."

Cernunnos's baleful glare fell on Church as he edged from the shelter of a tomb. "Yes, you are the one," Cernunnos rumbled. "I heard tell of you in the Far Lands—a Fragile Creature with the power to shake the very pillars of Existence."

In the god's buzzing energy field, Church found it difficult to comprehend what he was being told.

"One of my little sisters presumes to consider you her pet. Surely she must smell the Blue Fire in you? I will watch your progress, little one, for I sense you will grow to shake all the lands—for good or ill, I cannot yet tell."

Cernunnos brought his face down level with Church's. The vegetation moved across his body as if it was alive, and soon Church could only see a pair of gleaming eyes looking out of a field of green. As Church stared into their depths, they stared into him, and as the static fizzed across his mind he lost all touch with reality.

9

Church woke on horseback, his arms secured around a warm body in front of him and a woman's musk in his nose. At first Church thought it was Ruth, then Etain, and finally the chill brought him round fully and he saw he had his arms around Lucia's waist. They were riding slowly through woodland with the rain dripping down through the canopy, the wind blowing all around, awash with the noises of nature. He could just make out the others on horseback ahead, dark shapes bobbing in the darker wood.

"What happened?"

"Ah, so you are awake at last." Lucia's voice was laced with sadness, and Church thought she had been crying. "You flew too close to Aula's god. We are Fragile Creatures, after all—our minds and bodies can only take so much."

"Did the Green Man say he was going to help us?"

"Aula says that of all the gods he loves us as though we are his own children. He has requested aid, from whom I do not know. But he will not abandon us."

"Gods," Church said, still dazed. "They manipulate us, and torment us, and twist us out of shape. Roll on the day when we're our own masters."

"A revolutionary," Lucia said humorously. She sounded better for it.

"Where are we going?"

"To greet the Ninth," she replied with irony, "and celebrate their joyous return home."

At that they both fell silent. The horses continued at a measured tread. They carried no torch to keep themselves hidden, and the going was slow and dangerous in the pitch dark. They were on one of the old, straight tracks the Celts and the people who preceded them had carved into the landscape. It cut straight through the wood, roots twisting up and branches hanging down to make their passage even more precarious.

Briefly, Church had the impression of a figure in the trees watching their passing, but he sensed no threat, only curiosity. There was something familiar in its sleek, lithe appearance, and he remembered seeing something similar outside Carn Euny, just after the gathering that had mourned the stillbirth of the young girl Ailidh's baby. But whatever it was vanished within seconds, and in the tense atmosphere was just as quickly forgotten.

After half an hour they broke out onto moorland where there was nothing to protect them from the full force of the elements.

"This god-forsaken country," Lucia cursed quietly. "In fair Rome the rain is like velvet."

"Why did you come here?" Church asked.

"I was called by the Pendragon Spirit—it takes us to where we are needed. You know we cannot resist it. I hope to return home, one day."

Church understood the plangent tone in her voice.

They came to a halt on a ridge. In the valley below, the full complement of a Roman legion marched in strict time. The thunder of their regimented step and the clank of their shields and armour gave the impression of a single giant machine of destruction moving relentlessly. Church could see why the Roman army was so feared across the known world, but even beyond that there was an unquantifiable menace about the Ninth Legion that chilled him all the more.

Joseph jumped from his horse and ran over to Church. He looked utterly out of his depth. "Are you to lead us in Marcus's place?" he shouted above the gusting wind.

Lucia untied Church's hands so he could climb down. "You're not suggesting five of us should oppose thousands, even if Cernunnos is providing some support?" he said. "We'll be slaughtered in minutes."

"But it is your role," Joseph said, puzzled.

"It's not my role to lead people to their deaths." All of them were looking at him, expectant, demanding; he couldn't turn away. He sighed resignedly. "We need to get a closer look at what we're up against," he said reluctantly.

Decebalus agreed with his tactics, and soon he and Church were skidding down the rain-slick bank to more tree cover further down the hillside.

"The witch troubles me," Decebalus said of Lucia as they moved under the branches. "I do not trust her kind, and I do not like her at my back."

"You've got to get over it," Church said. "The only way the Brothers and Sisters of Dragons can work together is through trust. You have to be a tight unit, ready to risk your lives for each other. Or else you're nothing . . . just five individuals. And what can anyone do alone?"

Decebalus took the lead through the dense wood until they came so close to the advancing legion that they could feel the ground shake. The big barbarian selected an old tree and motioned for Church to follow as he scaled the slippery bark with a speed that belied his size. He used his powerful arms to swing himself up into the large lower branches.

Finally they reached a branch as broad as a table along which they could crawl to a point fifteen feet or so above the place where the outer ranks of the Ninth Legion would pass. Decebalus hung upside down like a monkey to get a better look.

Church gripped the branch tightly as the tree began to sway with the approaching thunderous footfalls. When the first of the legionnaires marched into view, Church was transfixed by the jarring chiaroscuro intensity of the scene. The contrast of black shadows and white was too strong to be realistic.

As the legionnaires drew nearer, Church saw that to a man their faces were shockingly white, not with the bloodless look of fear, but the pure white of snow. And where their veins could be glimpsed, they were as black as ink with the poison that had spread from the metallic spiders embedded in each and every forehead. The legionnaires moved like robots, without the slightest hint of the discomfort that Numerius had shown, and Church realised this must be the final stage of the process that had been intended for him.

Church glanced at Decebalus and quickly realised that his superstition had rushed to the fore, threatening to overwhelm him. When he had thought he was only facing men, Decebalus had been as brave as ever, but now he was pallid and shaking so much he was almost slipping from the branch.

Tugging at Decebalus's sleeve, Church managed to urge him back to the trunk, and soon they were on the ground and scrambling back up the hillside to the others. Decebalus was mute with fear, and Church dispatched him to the horses so the others would not see. After Church explained what they had witnessed, Joseph and Secullian crossed themselves, but Lucia and Aula took it in their stride.

"What now? They are closing fast on Eboracum?" Lucia asked.

All eyes were on Church. "I don't think any Brothers or Sisters of Dragons can be killed by the Army of the Ten Billion Spiders. The Libertarian hinted that they can capture us, torment us, but they can't deal with the Pendragon Spirit. Everyone else can chop us into bloody chunks, but not the thing we're supposed to be opposing, which must really stick in their spider-throats."

They eyed Church, still uncertain.

Decebalus appeared on the fringes of the group. "The only way we are ever going to amount to anything is by trusting each other. That is what sets us apart as champions."

"We'll ride to where the Sixth Legion is preparing to meet the Ninth," Church said. "We'll do what we can there."

As the others returned to their horses, Decebalus said to Church, "I don't believe a word of it, but if it gets them moving that is all that matters."

As Church climbed onto the back of Lucia's horse, she asked quietly, "Do we face our end?" She showed no sign of fear.

Church couldn't lie. "I don't know.",

The Brothers and Sisters of Dragons bore down on the rolling, rain-blasted moorland as the two legions came together like two torrents of floodwater. At the point of impact, armour, weapons, bodies and limbs gushed into the air amidst a tumultuous sound of clashing.

The Sixth Legion held their ground, though Church knew the terrors that must have been running through their minds.

Church, Lucia, Aula, Secullian and Joseph were shocked by the ferocity of the battle along the front line, but Decebalus was unmoved. He urged the others to join the fray. As they closed, they could see that the Sixth Legion was outclassed. The Roman army would be unsurpassed for centuries to come, yet it had met its match in an enemy that was oblivious to fear and pain. The living legionnaires were being slaughtered by the black and white tide. The Sixth's archers loosed their shafts by the hundred, but wherever they struck no one fell. Church saw some of the undead legionnaires turn into marching pin-cushions, arrows protruding from heads and torsos.

"Come! Let us harry their flanks!" Decebalus bellowed. He was away before anyone could respond.

Church lowered Lucia to the ground. "If you've got the abilities I think you've got, use them," Church said. "Protect Aula, Secullian and Joseph. They'll be no good in this kind of fight."

Feeling out of his depth, Church urged his horse towards the battle. He'd learned fighting techniques during his time at Carn Euny, but the part of him that was still the dreamy archaeologist was apprehensive. Yet the Jack Churchill that was being forged in those ancient times was filled with a greater fear: that more would die because of him if he did not act.

On the edge of the battle, Decebalus drove his horse in close and swung his axe. Heads leaped from bodies like sparks flying up a chimney. Decebalus retreated just as quickly before a blow could be laid on him.

Lightning crashed into the midst of the Ninth, blasting bodies asunder. The wind gusted in unnatural eddies, slamming against shields with the force of a battering ram, Lucia was using her Craft to direct nature in their favour.

Church drew his sword and its illumination cut a swathe through the darkness more effectively than any lantern. In the blue glow, Church saw scores of black eyes snap towards him as one. It might have been wishful thinking, but he was sure he saw a glimmer of unease in those still, dead faces.

Shields went up to deflect Church's first three attacks, but eventually he found a way through the defences. His blade sliced through the skull of one of the white-faced legionnaires as if it had no substance. The Blue Fire filled his system, driving out his rational thoughts until he and the sword were one, and in that moment he felt what he was supposed to be—a champion empowered by the energy of Existence.

He fought until his body shook with exhaustion, retreating every time the Ninth's cavalry moved towards him, only to return to the fray moments later. Decebalus fought in a berserker rage, his axe never resting.

Yet despite their attempts to sway the battle, the soldiers of the Ninth Legion were too numerous and too inhuman. They crushed all who lay before them with machine-like efficiency.

"Retreat. Regroup," Decebalus gasped to Church. Blood streamed from many wounds and a broken arrow shaft protruded from one arm. "They will not be held back. We need something more."

Church was so exhausted he could barely lift his sword. "Where's the help Aula promised?"

They retreated to where Lucia and the others waited, and Joseph did what he could to tend their wounds. Lucia was flagging from her exertions with her Craft and had little left to offer.

Under the shelter of an oak, Secullian sat cross-legged in the grip of a trance. He rocked back and forth, speckles of spittle flying from his mouth.

"How long has he been like that?" Church asked.

"Too long, but we are afraid to wake him," Aula said grimly. "He felt some contact from the Otherworld—"

Aula's words caught in her throat as Secullian's remaining eye snapped open, the white glowing in the dark. He raised one trembling arm to point to the battlefield. "Across the worlds they dance . . ."

At that moment, the undead legionnaires overran the Sixth Legion. The moor was covered with the mangled bodies of Roman soldiers. The spider-legionnaires marched over the remnants towards Eboracum.

As Church watched an event history had never recorded, his vision was briefly obscured. When it cleared, at first it looked as if the moon had come down to the rain-lashed earth. A silvery glow suffused the bleak moor. Church blinked once, twice, and then realised what he was seeing. Cernunnos had been true to his word. A new army now stood where the Roman legion had fallen, their armour gleaming silver. Church recognised the banner of the Court of Peaceful Days. At the front, a goddess Church presumed was Rhiannon led a ferocious assault.

"The gods were true to their word. For once." Decebalus flopped wearily onto the sodden turf, oblivious to the lashing rain.

"But will it be enough?" Lucia asked.

"And are we simply exchanging one invading force for another?" Joseph said.

"Bring on the days when we can defend ourselves." Decebalus tore the arrow from his arm with barely a flinch. "Gods. Devils. May a pestilence fall on all of them."

11

The battle raged for nearly two hours until the first light came up on a grey, sodden day. Church's initial hope for an easy victory had quickly waned as he watched the two forces fighting themselves to a standstill. For every white-skinned spider-soldier crushed beneath the onslaught of the silver army of the Court of Peaceful Days, one of the Tuatha Dé Danann was brutally dispatched.

Clouds of golden moths burst upwards towards the lowering heavens at regular intervals. It was a mesmerising sight that had a strange hallucinogenic beauty in the washed-out landscape, yet what it represented chilled Church to the bone. Niamh had been devastated when a handful of her guards had been "wiped from Existence," as she had described it. How, then, would Rhiannon react to hundreds if not thousands of her own court dying?

Secullian stood beside Church, calm now the delirium of his visions had left him. "Who are the enemy, and why do they choose this moment to march on Eboracum?" he asked.

Church couldn't answer either question.

"Where have the Ninth been these past two hundred years?" Lucia joined them, shivering from the rain.

"It wasn't anywhere in this world," Church replied.

Another burst of gold against the gloomy landscape, and another, and another, yet the fierce warriors of the Court of Peaceful Days fought on undaunted as they drove a wedge into the very heart of the Ninth Legion.

"The light is beating the dark," Lucia noted. An owl flew out of the rain and Lucia held out an arm with a leather patch strapped to it. The owl landed and stared at her with eerily intelligent eyes. Lucia stared back, her expression growing more troubled. "Something is coming," she said.

"What's that you say? Another threat?" Decebalus asked.

The words had barely left his lips when Secullian pitched forward, an arrow protruding from his good eye. Decebalus grabbed him before what had happened registered with any of the others.

Stark against the grey skyline over the ridge behind them were four riders, their outlines both familiar and chilling. Etain was there, as dead and hateful as the last time Church had seen her, and Tannis, Branwen and Owein. All of them dead, all of them seeking retribution.

The Libertarian had said that the Army of the Ten Billion Spiders was not yet powerful enough to oppose the Pendragon Spirit, but something else could. And here it was: the original Brothers and Sisters of Dragons, now corrupted into the opposite of everything for which they had once stood.

Joseph rushed to help Secullian, but it was obvious the North African was already dead. Aula fixed a cold eye on the bow that Etain held. "Who are they?" she asked.

"They're us," Church replied.

Etain reined in her horse and began to lead the others down the slippery slope. Decebalus gripped his axe. "Vengeance, then. For Secullian, and Marcus."

Church caught Decebalus's wrist before he could raise the axe. He had a vision of more ravens following him. "There's only four of us left," Church said. "We can't face them in a weakened state—they're too strong."

"You are saying we should run, like conies," Decebalus said with disbelief.

"Back to Eboracum. If we have to make a stand, the defences are better there." He gripped Decebalus's shoulders for emphasis. "Those four are the secret weapons of the Army of the Ten Billion Spiders and they mean to wipe us out. They *need* to do that because the spiders can't touch us, and they can't win while we're around. It's more important we survive today than go out in a blaze of glory."

"Tactics," Decebalus sneered before running to fetch the horses.

Joseph sobbed silently over Secullian. "We must give him a Christian burial so he can join our Lord at the resurrection."

Church rested a hand on the young man's shoulder. "You can come back to do that when the threat has gone," Church said gently. "In the meantime, you've got an important role to play."

Joseph blinked away his tears, puzzled.

Church spoke quietly, insistently. "The Watchmen are in the church to ensure knowledge is passed down through the generations to help us keep the gods at bay if they attack us in the future. Now you need to watch out for the

Army of the Ten Billion Spiders, because the threat is going to get worse in the years ahead."

"What would you have me do?"

"Pass on this order to your brethren: your group must watch out for anyone who bears the mark of the black spider. They're dangerous, and they have to be stopped, in any way possible." Joseph blanched at what Church was implying. Church watched the slow, deliberate advance of Etain and the others. "And you must make sure that all future generations know that things are not unfolding as they should."

"What do you mean?"

"The Army of the Ten Billion Spiders is changing the way things are meant to happen—"

"God's plan?"

Church hesitated. "If you will . . . They're loose in time, altering events . . . I don't know why. The Brothers and Sisters of Dragons in the future need to be aware of this so they can stop it happening. And you and your group need to tell them."

Joseph bowed his head. "I will carry out this task to the best of my abilities. I am honoured—"

"I know, I know. Now go. Ride south. Those four will follow the rest of us and you'll be free to get away."

Joseph smiled shyly, bowed once more, then ran to his horse. Decebalus returned with the other steeds, and soon Church and the remaining Brothers and Sisters of Dragons were racing through the rain towards Eboracum.

"You have a plan when we get within the walls?" Aula said. "Or is it just running, and hiding?"

"There's an inn not far from the gate. I have friends there—"

"That white-faced freak?" Aula said incredulously.

"My friend, Jerzy, and another woman, Niamh. We'll collect them and decide what route to take." He glanced back through the never-ending rain and could just make out four grey shapes, heads down, riding hard. They appeared to be closing.

Decebalus saw them, too, and pulled his horse alongside Church's. "They are fresher than us, their mounts stronger," he yelled. "I will fall back to hold them off."

"No," Church said. "You know this world better than I do. You'll be needed to protect the others. I'll try to find some way to delay our pursuers and meet you at the inn."

Decebalus nodded, paused in thought, and then clapped Church on the shoulder in a gesture that meant more than words. He urged his horse on to join Lucia and Aula while Church dropped back.

Church finally found his place where the track passed between two steep banks and a rocky outcropping overhung the route. Leaving his horse, Church scrambled up the slippery bank as the noise of the four pursuers grew louder. Jamming his sword under the edge of a boulder, he drove down upon it. At first it didn't move, but then the stone began to heave out of the turf. As the hoof-beats began to echo off the opposing banks, he made one final effort and the boulder crashed down onto the track, taking with it a landslip of soil and smaller stones.

Church threw himself down the bank and sprinted to his waiting horse. He was almost upon it when he was hit by a force from behind. Seeing stars, he sprawled across the mud and puddles.

When his vision cleared, a man stood over him, but it was neither Tannis, nor Owein. His hair was long and dark brown, plastered to his head by the rain, his chin bearded. The blackest eyes Church had ever seen stared out of a face like granite. The man was naked to the waist, his muscled torso covered with an array of strikingly vivid tattoos. Also striking was his left hand, which was an ornate mechanical claw that appeared to be made of silver. In his right hand he held a sword much like Church's, but the fire that crackled along the length of the blade was a desolate black.

"Hello, mate," he said in an emotionless South London accent. "It's taken a few years to track you down, but I always knew we'd hook up sooner or later."

Blankly staring, Church tried to draw on the distant echoes that rang in the gulf where his memory should be.

"Don't remember me? I'm hurt. The name's Veitch. Ryan Veitch."

Veitch stepped forward and swung his sword. The last thing Church saw was Veitch's face, filled with venom.

12

Church woke to the creak of wood, the rhythmic splash of water and the tang of salt in the air. His head still rang from where it had taken the flat of Veitch's blade. He was in the dark, damp confines of a ship's hold, surrounded by amphorae, and the swelling motion of the boat told him he was at sea.

Manacles had chafed his wrists raw. He didn't know how long he had been out, but his throat was arid and his muscles ached from where his arms had been fastened behind him.

The first coherent thought that sprang to Church's mind was Veitch. Was he the one who had killed Etain and the others, and had scrawled "SCUM" on the wall? He clearly knew Church. But the weight of his hatred was shocking. What could possibly have happened between them?

After half an hour, an olive-skinned man with wild black hair brought a bowl of oats and honey which he fed to Church roughly. Church tried to engage his jailer in conversation, but the man ignored him, and wouldn't meet Church's eyes.

Sometime later, when the gloom had deepened, Veitch came to visit. He entered like a ghost; Church didn't hear a thing and only noticed accidentally that Veitch was watching him, his hallucinogenic tattoos glowing in the shadows.

"Come to taunt or torture?" Church said.

"Either would work for me." He crossed the space between them with the restrained grace and power of a jungle beast. His sword was sheathed, but Church could still sense it; his stomach churned and his teeth went on edge the closer it came to him.

Veitch leaned on the bulkhead a few feet away, tugging gently on his beard as he eyed Church coldly. Something crackled between them—a weight of history, a connection, rich and deep and complex, but Church had no context in which to place it.

"You're a tough bastard to catch, I'll give you that," Veitch said.

"You killed Etain and the others in Carn Euny."

"Yeah, I did. How's that working out for you? It was, what do you call it?" He sifted his words carefully. "A gesture. A message, from me to you. A million and one things wrapped up in one little picture. Did you get what I was trying to say?"

"How could you do that? They hadn't done anything to you." Church tried to keep his rage under control.

"I wanted it lying on your conscience for all time. Because they wouldn't have died if it hadn't been for you. A lot of people are going to die because of you. And you . . . now I've got you, you're going to die, too."

"What's this all about?"

"Yeah, they told me they'd managed to get part of your memory. Shame. It'd screw you up even more if you really knew why I was doing this. You want the short answer? Revenge."

"What for?"

"Killing me."

Church scanned Veitch's face to see if the tattooed man was joking, but his eyes gave nothing away. "Doesn't look as if it's done you much harm."

"Life's a bitch and then you die. Except death's a bitch too and you keep coming back. An endless cycle of bleedin' misery." He paused thoughtfully, then shrugged. "Let's just say I got myself an upgrade from the Army of the Ten Billion Spiders."

"You've proved you've got a smart mouth and you're good at sneering. Now how about giving me something I can work with?"

"I've got nothing to hide." Veitch pulled up the jailer's stool and sat eye to eye with Church. "You and me used to be mates, back in the days yet to come, when they've invented TV and fucking deodorant. You were the brains and I was the brawn, and one couldn't get along without the other."

"You were a Brother of Dragons."

"See, there you go. Like mustard." Veitch's gaze was drawn to a tattoo of a spider on his forearm. Church could see other illustrations that had an eerie resonance—a dragon; a pentacle, the five points tipped in red; a flaming sword.

"The five of us . . . the best group there'd been in all history," Veitch continued. "The last best hope of the human race. The gods came back to take our world and we fought them off, and all the stinking beasts that came with them. We lost a lot—" he held up his mechanical silver hand and examined it in the half-light "but we won the battle, and that's what counts, right? Only it turns out there was a bigger threat hiding behind the one we saw off. It was supposed to be down to us again—"

"Except you went over to the other side."

Veitch laughed coldly. "Blimey, they did scoop out your brains, didn't they? I went bad? Mate, you turned on me when we were doing our victory dance and you gutted me like a carp . . . and sent the world to hell in a hand-cart at the same time."

"Now I know you're screwing with me. Why would I do that?"

Veitch's smile faded. "Over a woman. She loved me. You wanted her. So you got me out of the way once all the heavy lifting was done."

"Ruth," Church said.

"Ruth Gallagher. The Uber-witch, that's what that bitch Laura always called her. She was beautiful. Smart. Sexy. And she wanted me. Ryan bleedin' Veitch, no-hoper and part-time villain from South London. The best thing that ever happened to me, she was. And you couldn't deal with the fact that she chose me over you. So you stuck me with that fancy magic sword of yours. And you wonder why I've got a bit of a grudge?"

Church was stunned. Veitch could have been lying, but he didn't look as if he was.

"But, here's the . . . irony. That's a good word, isn't it? Irony. You'd done your treacherous business, got the woman of your dreams, and then Existence went and booted you back to the dawn of bleedin' time. You got your punishment, served your 'time.'" He laughed bitterly once more. "Now it's up to me to make sure there's no pot of gold waiting for you at the end."

"So let me get this straight—you've gone over to the other side because of a grudge against me? The Brothers and Sisters of Dragons are supposed to be the champions of life. The spiders are opposed to us, so what does that make them? The end result is that you're standing shoulder to shoulder with something that's fighting against life itself."

"Yeah, well, I'm dead so it's not such a big bleedin' leap, is it? Wanker." Veitch stood up and kicked the stool across the hold. "Got my own Brothers and Sisters now. They aren't too keen on life, or Existence. They aren't going to stab me in the back, or cut me loose when I need them." The hurt in his voice was barely restrained.

"So you've made your own Brothers and Sisters of . . . Spiders. And you've got me now. What's the point of all this?" Church rattled his chains.

Veitch opened his mouth to speak, then caught himself. He gave an enigmatic, humourless smile before walking off into the enveloping dark.

13

Veitch made his way across the creaking deck, cursing quietly every time he had to fight against the swell for his balance. The silver moon marked a path across the dark ocean. England's dismal weather was falling behind; warm days beckoned.

Veitch had thought himself inured to the extremes of human emotion. For a long time he'd been a machine, focusing on the job at hand while keeping his feelings battened down. But seeing Church had brought everything back in one queasy surge, all the pain and the misery, the rage and the relentless urge to kill him. He hated Church even more for making him feel that way.

He made his way to the captain's quarters, which were cramped and filled with the fruity aroma of the oil lamp sizzling on the side. The Libertarian sat with his boots on the table, pouring himself a goblet of red wine. His eyes took on an unnervingly bloody hue in the lamplight.

"And how is our prisoner?" he asked laconically.

Veitch hated his supercilious attitude and the way he often tried to pretend that Veitch was some menial. It wouldn't take much to prompt Veitch to plunge his black blade into the Libertarian's heart.

"He wants to know what's planned for him," Veitch replied sullenly.

"But he's not afraid, is he?" A smile played on the edges of the Libertarian's lips.

"He will be." Veitch knew it was a lie the moment he uttered it. He'd never known Church to be scared of anything; that's why Existence had made him the leader of the Five.

"And how about you? Have you indulged yourself with him? A few taunts . . . a kick here and there to keep the bitterness at bay?" The Libertarian laughed quietly, sipped his wine.

Veitch allowed his hand to slip to his sword; as always it whispered soothing words that calmed him. *Not now, later.* There was always time.

"'Course," Veitch said, "things would be a lot simpler if you could just reach in and snap his neck, or whatever it is you do. Can't, though, can you?"

A flicker of a shadow crossed the Libertarian's face. "The years move fast, and soon I will be able to do what I want. I am a patient man. I can afford to bide my time."

At the back of the cabin was an even smaller room. Veitch entered and closed the door behind him. Two benches faced each other, with a single chair beyond. A candle flickered greasily in one corner. On one bench sat Etain and Tannis, on the other Branwen and Owein. Their eyes snapped towards him as one with an eerie mechanical motion. Their faces were filled with pale horror.

Veitch sat in the chair and stretched, feeling the calm return. "All right, team. How we doin'?" he said.

No one answered.

14

Church didn't see Veitch again for the rest of the long journey. His silent jailer was the only person he encountered, and then at just one meal-time each day. There were times when he was sure the ship was sinking, so rough were the waves that almost turned the vessel on its end, flooding freezing sea water through the hold. At other times, a swell of nine feet or more left Church retching until his stomach was empty.

Eventually the ship reached calmer waters where the temperature grew balmy, and not long after Church heard the hungry cries of gulls. Finally the ship came to rest with a bump, followed by the thunderous grind of the anchor chain running over the deck into the water.

An hour later his jailer tied a stinking sack over Church's head, unlocked his manacles, tied his hands behind his back and hauled him on deck. Church guessed the sack was more for humiliation than to hide his identity; he would be seen as a broken prisoner, not a champion of life.

He was led down a shaking gangplank onto solid ground. The June sun was hot on his shoulders, the atmosphere dry. All around he could hear the sounds of a busy port, the shouts of workmen, the snorts of beasts of burden, the creak of ropes and the crash of wooden crates on stone.

"Where are we?" he asked, not expecting an answer.

Someone leaned in close. "Ostia. Know where that is, smart boy?" It was Veitch.

"The port of Rome," he replied.

15

The journey from Ostia to the centre of Rome took what felt like hours to Church, as he was jolted black and blue in the back of a cart. As they neared, the noise grew louder until it became an unbearable hubbub that must have driven the residents mad. The Romans spent most of their lives on the street, trading, arguing, eating food cooked on portable stoves, and their activities created an atmosphere that was both exciting and oppressive.

Finally the cart came to a halt. "We walk from here," Veitch said. "No wagons in the city during the day."

Church stumbled after a few steps, falling flat on a rutted street ankle-deep in rubbish and excrement. Veitch laughed hard, then dragged Church to his feet and ripped off the sack. "Don't want you breaking your neck before we're done with you," he said.

Despite his predicament, Church felt a rush of excitement at seeing history alive around him. Open-fronted shops lined the crowded street, with apartment blocks—*insulae*—rising up five or six storeys all around. Despite the gulf of centuries, it was not unlike modern cities—noisy, dirty, exciting, fast-living, cosmopolitan.

Veitch led him past dogs scavenging in the rubbish and children playing some kind of dice game with animal knucklebones. "So much for culture," he said. "This place stinks."

Church nodded to a series of large vats simmering in the hot sun. "That would be the *liquamen*—fish sauce made from fermented fish guts. They boil it up everywhere. Or it's those jars of piss." Nearby, an elderly man had pulled his toga aside to urinate in a pot. "They sell it to laundries and fullers for dissolving the animal fats and grease in fresh wool." Church watched Veitch's expression grow thoughtful. "What's on your mind?" Church asked. "Thinking of the best place to murder me?"

"I'm always thinking about that." He surveyed the street scene. "You used to tell me all that kind of bollocks when we were on the same side."

"Learn a lot?"

A pause. "Yeah, I did."

A procession of actors passed by in gaudy costumes and masks. The most striking mask resembled a rising sun with rays spiking out a full foot around the actor's head. Church knew they were preparing for one of the spectacles that marked the week-long *Ludi Apollinares*, the celebration of the god Apollo that would take place in a few short weeks, in July. A connection sparked in his mind: did the timing have something to do with the disappearance of Lugh, another sun god?

"I don't remember doing the things you claim," Church said.

"Trust me. You did."

"I've been thinking it over since you told me. I can't imagine any situation where I would murder an ally . . . a friend."

There was none of the angry denial that Church had anticipated. Veitch said simply, "She's a great woman. Worth killing for."

"Nobody's worth killing for."

"You really have forgotten a lot."

"I know what I feel for her, but—"

"You love her. I love her. The winner is the one left standing at the end."

Church felt uncomfortable talking to Veitch about Ruth and changed the subject. "Are you going to tell me how come you're here, all hale and hearty, if I killed you?"

"Death isn't the end of it, mate. It's not just turning out the light.

It's . . ." He stared dreamily into the middle distance, squinting against the bright Roman light. "It's like leaving a room. You go through a door and you're somewhere else. And then there's another door. And another. There's always more doors."

"So you found your way back, is that what you're saying?"

Veitch nodded to a young man talking animatedly to a bored, white-haired senator. "Let's just say I found myself a patron."

As a group of men passed by noisily, Church turned sharply and head-butted Veitch full in the face. He knew it was probably his only chance to break free. It was difficult to run with his hands tied behind his back, and he hadn't got far when a centurion brought him down.

"Know your place, slave," he snarled. Church tried to throw him off, but the centurion had the leverage to pin Church flat until Veitch caught up. Veitch thanked the centurion and then launched a series of furious kicks at Church. He thought he felt a rib crack, but managed to return a couple of kicks before Veitch booted him in the face and knocked him out.

He came round as Veitch dragged him up to the grand bath-house of Diocletian. "Try that again and I'll break your fucking neck," Veitch hissed.

"If I get the chance, you know I'll do it."

"Just try it. Make me happy."

The scale of the newly built complex took Church's breath away; it covered thirty-two acres and could accommodate up to 3,000 bathers. They passed the crowds swarming at the entrance and went through an open-roofed lounge where men and women sunbathed or took part in traditional Roman pastimes: gossiping, playing board games, wrestling naked, their skin oiled and glistening, or playing the catch game trigon with sand-filled balls.

Several long corridors eventually led them to a private changing room where a man was undressing with the help of two slaves. He had curly black hair, a beard and moustache and skin darker than the average Roman's. There was a subtle air of desperation about him.

He remained aloof, but his eyes betrayed a flicker of fear when he saw Veitch. "Is this the one?"

"Jack Churchill, Brother of Dragons. The first and last."

The man nodded thoughtfully as the slaves removed his toga. A black metallic spider gleamed on his left breast.

"My name is Marcus Aurelius Valerius Maxentius," he said to Church without looking at him. "This city is mine. Soon this Empire will be mine. And you are mine now, as all things shall fall to me."

"Don't bother talking down to him," Veitch said dispassionately. "He's a smartarse. He probably knows more about you than you know about yourself."

Church did know Maxentius. Despite the bravado the Roman exhibited, he was a man defined by failure. He was the son of the emperor Maximian, but had suffered the indignity of being passed over for high office when both Maximian and Diocletian had resigned the previous year.

His future held even worse. In a few weeks, after the death of Constantius in Eboracum, his son Constantine would gain the rank of Caesar, leaving Maxentius out in the cold once again. It would drive Maxentius to months of political intrigue to gain the title of Augustus he so desperately wanted, only to lose it, and his life, in a war with Constantine six years hence.

Church recalled all the textbooks he had read about that turning point in world history. When Constantine's army met Maxentius's forces on the Plain of Mihian outside the gates of Rome, Constantine was said to have sought the aid of the gods and was rewarded by the appearance of a flaming cross in the sky.

The next day, Constantine's men bore crosses on their shields and carried a Christian standard. Maxentius and his men were driven back to a pontoon bridge over the Tiber, which collapsed under their weight. Thousands were drowned, including Maxentius. Constantine went on to become Rome's first Christian emperor and his support led to Christianity becoming the dominant religion of Western Europe. Was this crucial moment in history the reason behind the Army of the Ten Billion Spider's interest?

Maxentius snorted, but Church could see that Veitch's comment troubled him. The Roman walked into the *tepidarium*, beckoning for Veitch to follow.

"The spider is controlling him," Church said, "but he's got more free will than the others I've seen under their influence."

"That's how they need him. Now get your arse in there." Veitch shoved Church roughly.

In the cool air of the large vaulted hall, Maxentius flexed his muscles to acclimatise himself. He gave Church a cursory glance. "He does not look like a fearsome enemy."

"He's the one. Now, you better keep close tabs on him because he's a tricky bastard and if he gets to his sword your guts will be experiencing life on the outside."

"It is one of the three great swords?" Maxentius said hungrily.

"One of them, but not the greatest. Not Caledfwlch. This stupid bastard has hidden that one so he can find it again in the future to defend the land. Before he even knows what it is."

"But it has the power?" Maxentius urged.

"Don't worry, we'll wring it out like a sponge. You'll get everything you want. Things are going to turn out in a whole new way."

There it was: the confirmation Church needed.

"I've had the sword sent to the temple," Veitch continued. "I've got other business here. Can I count on you to get him to the temple without any screw-ups?"

"Of course." Maxentius clapped his hands and several guards emerged from an annexe.

"Sorry, mate," Veitch said to Church superciliously, "but as my old nan used to say, your goose is cooked."

16

The guards propelled Church to the Forum Romanum, which swarmed with life, though only a few paid any attention to his passing. Church bided his time in the hope that an opportunity for escape would present itself.

After a few minutes he was herded down the Argileto, the ancient road between the Basilica Aemilla and the Curia Julia where the senate had met for more than 250 years. There, in a walled compound, stood a temple built of wood, which signified its great age even in a city as ancient as Rome. Two gates at the entrance to the compound stood open, and between them was a bust with four heads.

"Kneel before the god of gods!" One of the guards roughly shoved Church to his knees before the bust.

"The gates are open," another said in a tone reminiscent of a ritualistic chant. "War has been loosed across the land."

Church was hauled to his feet and thrust through one of the gates. The guards waited uneasily at the threshold. "Into the temple!" one of them barked.

Church surveyed the small wooden building. It was almost insignificant against the grander stone constructions all around. Church hesitated, but he had no other place to go. The cracked, age-old door swung open with a juddering creak and Church stepped inside.

It took a while for his eyes to adjust to the darkness. He was in a chamber with a floor of beaten clay, large and airy with several doors on each wall. A spot in the centre of the floor was illuminated by a thin beam of light from a small window in the roof. It was only then that Church realised that the inner dimensions of the room did not fit the building outside which he had stood. The chamber was much larger than it should have been and the doors suggested a complex that would have dwarfed the tiny wooden temple. Behind him, the entrance door was now shut, though he had not heard it close.

An oppressive atmosphere filled the gloomy space. Church sensed some sort of presence close at hand yet always out of view. The tension mounted as though a generator was being cranked, filling the chamber with a sense of impending arrival. A distant scratching rose up behind one of the doors, drawing closer, and behind another, and another, until it sounded as if a multitude was approaching every door.

Doors. Church recalled what the guard had said about kneeling before the *god's god* and he knew where he was: in the Temple of Janus, the dual-faced god of doors and new beginnings. The cult of Janus pre-dated all others in Rome, and in the Empire's list of gods he always came first and carried the surname *Divom Deus*, the god's god. Church had always found it strange that Janus was unique: no god like him appeared in any other mythology.

The scratching had become the pounding of tiny feet rushing towards the doors. Church's breath caught in his throat. One other thought came to him: Janus was also the god of departures, and all that entailed.

One by one the doors began to open. Church fumbled for a handle on the door behind him, but there was none.

The doors swung open with a single, echoing crash. From every opening flooded tiny creatures the size and shape of monkeys but with shiny skin as black as oil and eyes that glowed with a fierce green light. Tumbling and leaping, they swarmed around Church, tearing at his clothes and skin. The sheer weight of their numbers pulled him from his feet and carried him through one of the doors into an even larger hall made of stone.

Tossed and turned on tiny hands, Church occasionally caught sight of a sapphire light and realised it was his sword, hanging in the air, blade down, with no visible means of support. The monkey-creatures dragged him before it and held him tight.

There was movement in the gloom at the back of the chamber, which appeared to stretch on for ever. The apprehension that had been building since he entered the chamber now felt like a rock on his chest.

He's coming, he thought.

Clouds appeared in the air, folding in on themselves before billowing out as though they were being pumped by an invisible machine. They were backlit by an emerald glow, and as they rushed towards him, Church made out a figure in their midst, either taking shape or moving through them.

The turbulent clouds came to a halt nine feet from Church. The emerging figure was dressed in long, flowing robes of what appeared to be black satin, shimmering as if a thousand stars were sewn into the fabric. One thin, long-fingered hand clutched an oversized gold key with a large loop for a handle, and in the other hand was an ironwood stick: one to open the doors and the other to drive away those who had no right to cross the threshold.

At first Church couldn't make out the god's features—they swam like oil and water as his brain sought to perceive something that was beyond perception. His grasping mind superimposed several images: a politician whose name he couldn't recall; someone who resembled Aleister Crowley; Alexander the Great. Finally one set of features coalesced into relief: bone-white skin framed by lank, black hair, gaunt cheeks with an aquiline nose, slanted piercing eyes. The face remained that way for a moment before shifting to a negative image—sable skin, white hair—and then back again. It continued to shift disconcertingly.

"I am the opener and closer of ways," he said in a voice like a knife on glass. "I oversee all beginnings. I am the daybreak and the twilight. I am the chaos that was prevalent when you all began, and the chaos when it all falls to nothing."

Church felt sickened by the waves of power coming off the figure. It was not like the faint electricity he felt near Niamh, but something altogether darker and more terrible.

Janus fixed his dual gaze on Church, who felt it pass through his skull and into his brain. "You are the Brother of Dragons, the first and the last. The Daughters of the Night told me of your existence. Once I had chosen the path upon which I now walk, it was inevitable that you would arrive at my temple." He gave a satisfied smile. "So powerful for a Fragile Creature, yet here, in my temple. If proof were needed that the path of Existence is wrong, it is here."

Church read the meaning in Janus's words. "You're on the spiders' side."

"And here you are, caught in the web."

17

Church felt the pain that swathed him as much on a spiritual and psychological level as he did the wracking agony that filled his limbs. He hung in the air in a dark chamber identical to a hundred other dark chambers through which he had been brought. The walls and ceilings were lost to the gloom; all sense of time had disappeared along with his sense of space.

He recalled Janus dragging those long, thin fingers across his forehead, and then a period of fragmentary unconsciousness when he had been carried by the monkey-creatures to wherever he was now suspended by invisible strings. The sword hung nearby, its faint blue light a comfort. But that light was fading, like Church's own light.

Black bands like the strands of a giant web crisscrossed the chamber. They wrapped around the hilt of his sword, and they were attached to Church's fingers and arms, feet, groin, torso and head, where it felt as if they passed through his skin and bone and into the very depths of his consciousness.

The strands were linked to what looked like a hunk of black meat, sweaty and glistening, high above his head. Every now and then it pulsed, and he felt a corresponding pain deep within him, as though his insides were being sucked out through the strands. He knew what it meant: the Pendragon Spirit was being leached out of him, and from Llyrwyn. Soon he would be a Fragile Creature in every sense, and then the Army of the Ten Billion Spiders could do whatever it wanted to him.

If he strained his head back he could see one strand, thicker than the others, running from the black meat to something that had at first made his head swim in the same way that Janus's features had. Eventually it had come to resemble an Arabian lamp. The genie was being put back in the bottle.

Though he was weakening by the hour, Church still strained to break free, but every time he moved a coil of the black meat cinched a notch tighter around his neck. If he put enough pressure on one of the meaty strands, he hoped he would be able to break it; and if one went, then the others would follow. Gritting his teeth, he tried again. The strand around his throat jerked tighter. His vision swam and he could barely get any air into his lungs.

Rationally, he knew it was hopeless, but he was determined not to give in; too much was relying on him. Making his neck muscles rigid to hold off the ligature, he tried again. The strand stretched but did not break and agony flooded his system. He tried one more time and his air supply was cut off completely. He thrashed impotently for a moment as he choked dryly, and then he blacked out again.

When he came round the ligature had loosened a little.

"I know what you're thinking, mate."

Church jumped at Veitch's voice, coming from somewhere in the shadows.

"'*Boohoo, why is this happening to me? All I wanted to do was help people.*' It's a bastard, isn't it? No good deed shall go unpunished."

Church found it an effort to speak. "You're enjoying being . . . a traitor . . ."

After a period of heavy silence, Veitch replied, "You're the traitor." He tried to modulate his voice, but hurt and anger laced his words. "There's no need to fight about that any more. I've won. You've lost. Game over. You know what I'm going to do now? I'm going back to my little home in the Other-world for some r 'n' r, then I'm going to hook up with my own little band of Brothers and Sisters and spend the next few centuries dropping in and out of this world, killing every single Brother and Sister of Dragons I come across. You can lie here and think about that. Hundreds of them. Maybe thousands. And all their blood is going to be on your hands, just like the first four."

By the time Church had accepted the full implications of Veitch's words, the ringing silence told him he was alone. Overhead the hunk of black meat pulsed and another drop of Pendragon Spirit drained away. A black wash of despair flowed in to replace it.

"Don't give in to it."

Another voice, this time warm, hopeful, familiar. "Who?" Church croaked.

"That hurts. Forgotten so quickly."

Church strained to look around, but he was alone.

"The Romans loved a good deus ex machina, so this is rather fitting. I'm the god from the machine of Existence. I'm always with you, Church—I'm in everything. I'm your very own Jiminy Cricket, here to whisper in your ear when times get darkest. No? Okay, let's open the bomb-bay doors."

"Hal?" Church recalled the voice in the Blue Fire in the strange place beneath Boskawen-Un. "Where are you?"

"I told you—here, there and everywhere." Church heard a hissing sound and noticed a blue glow emanating from the Arabian lamp. "My conscious-ness exists in the Blue Fire, Church, and the Blue Fire is in everything—you, the world, every single human being. It links our world to T'ir n'a n'Og and all the other worlds beyond. It's the lifeblood of Existence, the stuff that holds it all together, so I guess that's what I am, too."

"Come to tell me how I've failed the master plan?"

"Don't talk. Conserve your strength. I told you before that I'm not going to tell you everything—the process of learning is one of the things that's going to make you or break you—but I can give you one or two carrots just to tide you over until dinner time. Okay, as you've probably guessed, I used to be like you: a Fragile Creature—and a Brother of Dragons—but I was one of the next generation after yours, the last in the line. Our team didn't do so well, Church. We failed. Not completely, though. Our one little victory was that I would give up my life to allow my consciousness to enter the Blue Fire. But that's what being a Brother and Sister of Dragons is all about, right? Sacrifice for the greater good. Once I'd entered the Blue, I was outside all the stupid physical laws we're used to. I got to exist in all-times and all-places at once, 'cause that's what the Blue Fire does. And I got to see reality from the outside. Boy, Church, it makes a lot more sense from here, I can tell you."

"Why did you—?"

"Why did I give up the ghost? To bring you back, of course. Your group of Brothers and Sisters of Dragons—you, Ruth, Shavi, Laura, even Veitch— you were the team supreme. Everyone knew that. And if Ruth was the Uber-witch, you were the Uber-king, the first amongst equals. I know you can't see it from your perspective, but you're a good man determined to do good things whatever the personal cost. And you'd be surprised to know how few and far between people like that are."

Church wanted to ask Hal all the other questions rampaging through his mind, but he knew he wouldn't get any answers. "I need to get out of here—"

"Of course you do, and that's where I come in. But don't think I'm going to make a habit of it. If you get yourself into a mess like this again, you fail on your own terms and everything else goes with it. Right?"

"Right."

"The Pendragon Spirit will give you the strength to get free from the web, but the strength won't last. You need to get out of here with the sword *and* the lamp. There's a part of you in there, part of your Pendragon Spirit. You need to get it back inside you if you're going to be any use."

"Okay. I'll do what I can."

"Good. From here on out it's all going to be down to you."

18

Chamber after chamber passed in waves of darkness and pain. On the dull edge of his senses, Church occasionally heard the scurrying of the monkey-creatures, but he never encountered them, and of Janus there was no sign, though the god's presence hung over the entire temple.

Finally he stumbled out into brilliant morning sunlight and the thick, queasy smells and cacophony of Rome at the height of its power. He allowed his eyes to adjust to the radiance only to realise it had all been for nothing. Maxentius's guards were waiting patiently just beyond the open gates.

Within moments, Church was being dragged through the seething streets. He had no strength to fight back, could barely lift the sword that hung limply at his side.

"He should not have exited the temple," one of the guards said. "Maxentius will not be pleased."

"Maxentius does not have to know," another guard said ominously. They fell silent as they weighed their options.

Church glimpsed the actor in the sun mask who he had seen on the way to the temple. He was practising intricate hand and body motions in silence at the side of the street, incongruous in his brilliant yellow toga and wildly ornate headdress.

The crowds pressed heavily on either side. A large man in a hood and cloak lurched against one of the guards supporting Church, prompting a brief, furious foul-mouthed exchange.

The guards moved on. Through his daze, Church caught a surreptitious glance and nod passing between the two guards holding his arms, and then he was being moved towards one of the quieter side streets.

Faces came and went in the throng, some that even looked familiar. Church briefly thought he was back in London, meeting Ruth for the first time.

"Halt! Where are you taking him?"

The guards stopped sheepishly as Maxentius strode up.

"The prisoner escaped from the temple," the guard at Church's right said unconvincingly. "We were bringing him back for further instructions."

Maxentius and the guard engaged in a hushed, strained conversation, but Church's attention was drawn to a strange sight: an owl sitting on top of one of the busts that lined the route. It stared at him with large green eyes.

"Take him back to the temple!" Maxentius barked.

He has a spider in his chest, Church thought obliquely. *Do you know?*

A commotion erupted nearby. The actor in the sun mask was now engaged in a series of breathtaking tumbles that drew an impressed crowd. Smatterings of applause turned into loud cheering.

After the most spectacular tumble, the actor stood with arms outstretched, revelling in the attention of the onlookers, before whipping off his mask with a flourish. The laughter and cheers turned instantly to gasps of horror. The crowd pressed back at the sight of parchment skin and a rictus grin.

"Thank you, thank you, thank you," the Mocker called out. "I live for the adoration of the audience!" He leaped towards the nearest onlookers with a monstrous roar. In an instant everyone was running wildly, their anxiety transmitting rapidly to those who could not even see Jerzy.

Church almost pitched forward as the guards let go of him. Someone caught his arm and urged him gently away. He looked into the frosty face of Aula, who hissed, "Find your feet or I shall leave you here." Her insistent tone cut through his weakness and he moved in her direction.

In the confusion, Church glimpsed the large man in the hood and cloak who had bumped into the guard earlier. It was Decebalus. He pulled his axe from beneath his cloak as he drove through the throng, swinging it fluidly in a flash before returning it to the folds. Maxentius's head flew from his shoulders and bounced across the street. The confusion of the crowd became wild panic.

Aula pulled Church into the unruly mass. "Decebalus was never a man for subtlety," she said sourly. "Why a barbarian was allowed into our group, I will never know. Hurry now. Let us hope the others can employ more subtle diversions."

Lightning crashed from the clear blue sky and within moments storm clouds had swept up to release a torrential downpour. Aula moved Church down a side street, away from the crowd, and Lucia hurried up, her owl familiar flying overhead.

"How did you find me?" Church gasped.

"We are Brothers and Sisters of Dragons," Lucia replied with a smile. "We are not without means."

"Besides, you are the king, are you not?" Aula added with a note of sarcasm. "There are some who seem to think you valuable."

At the city walls a hooded woman waited with a horse and cart. It was Niamh. Her beautiful face betrayed no emotion. Decebalus and Jerzy ran up and helped Church into the back of the cart where he was covered with piles of stinking sackcloth. The last thing he recalled was the gentle rocking motion of the cart as it pulled away, and the sound of slowly fading thunder.

19

A summer moon cast long shadows over an unspoiled landscape filled with the scent of olive trees. It was July, and Church sat on the hillside with a bowl of the warm herbal infusion Aula had prepared for him every night on their journey from Rome. It had helped his recovery immeasurably, and although he was still far from his old self, he could walk unaided once again.

Spread out before him were the standing stones of Fossa, not far from where the modern town of L'Aquila would grow in Abruzzo. The stones looked the same as in the photos he had seen in his own time, and had probably changed little since the Vestini tribe had established them 1,000 years earlier. After all the many changes in his life, he found the continuity of the stones comforting, particularly when he had so much on his mind that was troubling. How would the premature death of Maxentius affect history? Would Constantine find a new enemy to defeat before he turned the Empire to Christianity? Or was this the start of greater instability ahead?

"Your ancestors were an astonishing people." Niamh had come up quietly behind him. Church was surprised to hear respect in her voice.

"Because in the Iron Age they had the ability to align stones for astronomical significance? Or because they survived your people's interference?"

"Both." She sat next to him with her tarot cards and began to lay them out in her favourite divinatory spread. "Because they were capable of great things even *with* my people's interference."

Church took in the scope of the stones. Some were up to twelve feet high, pitched in circles and straight lines, patterns that looked incomprehensible to the untutored eye.

"They knew the places in the earth where the Blue Fire was strongest and they recognised its true nature." Niamh concentrated on the cards. "They built their monuments to mark nodes of power, and they worshipped there, too, for life and Existence was their purpose."

Church noted the cemetery of the Vestini amongst the stones: death and life and spiritual strength joined together in one image.

"They knew these places were a gateway to your home?" he asked.

"They did, and to all the lands beyond."

"I'm sorry I didn't find your brother."

"There is still time. For my kind, there is always time."

"And I want to thank you for coming to rescue me. I suppose it was just a matter of keeping your possessions safe, but thanks anyway."

Niamh turned the cards, said nothing.

"I was working under the assumption that only you Golden Ones gave gods to the Celts, but then I met Janus. Is he one of you? Are you responsible for all Earth's gods?"

Niamh wrestled with her response. "My people believe what they want to believe. That is their way, a natural response to being so close to the heart of Existence."

"Arrogance—"

"They believe they cannot die. They believe nothing in all of Existence can threaten them, because that is how things have always been. And if they receive information that contradicts that stance, they ignore it."

Church was puzzled. There was an edge to Niamh's voice as she fought with the changes taking place within her.

"They believe they are unique," she continued.

"But they're not?"

"We know other races existed in the Far Lands before we arrived from our long-lost home. We have seen their ruined cities on the mountaintops and beneath the waves, and we have heard tell of their names: the Drakusa, the Hyanthis . . ." She shrugged. "Many races exist in the Far Lands, and the Far Lands stretch for ever. Who knows what lives there? Though . . ." She hesitated. "There are rumours of other races related to us living in further corners of the land, but it is not something my people wish to consider."

A shooting star blazed across the sky. Church and Niamh watched it together. She picked a handful of dry grass and released it into the wind. "There is much I wish to learn. Things I must see for myself." A shadow crossed her face as she wrestled with the fading of lifelong certainties. She looked over at the campfire where Decebalus and the others were finishing their evening meal.

"Fragile Creatures . . . your lives always hang by a thread," she mused, "yet they risked everything to rescue you. They see beyond themselves in a way my people never do. They recognise in you a deep seam of goodness that will be mined for the benefit of all Fragile Creatures." Niamh gave Church a quick sideways glance, but would not meet his gaze. "I would know what drives you." A pause. "All of you."

Church finished his drink and levered himself shakily to his feet. "Come on. Let's join them."

"You look well," Decebalus noted as Church approached. "Aula has some uses, then."

"Be still, ox-brain." The blonde woman sighed. She lay next to the fire, staring at the stars.

"Tomorrow morning when Niamh, Jerzy and I cross over to the Otherworld at the standing stones I want you all to come with us," Church said.

"To T'ir n'a n'Og?" Decebalus said in astonishment.

"It's not safe for you here. Veitch and his little spider-gang won't rest until they've hunted you down and killed you. Especially now that you've freed me."

"There is nothing for me here," Lucia said. "I welcome new horizons."

"We can return?" Aula asked. "Occasionally, to see our homeland?"

"The Pendragon Spirit will allow you to transcend the barrier with impunity, as can anyone you bring in your wake," Niamh said.

A broad grin crossed Decebalus's face. "Goddesses. The wine of the gods. New adventures. I say yes!"

Church noticed a pale will-o'-the-wisp floating in the dark further down the hillside and realised it was Jerzy making his way back from exploring the stones.

"That was quite a performance you put on in Rome," Church said as he met him halfway.

"You have yet to see my best, good friend! One day." Jerzy glanced warily past Church to the campfire.

"What is it?"

From inside his jerkin, the Mocker pulled a piece of parchment. The writing covering it was in a language Church had never seen before, but one word stood out: Lugh.

"Where did you get this?"

"In Rome. I spied on a ritual for the sun god—"

"Apollo."

"Yes—when I was trying to steal the sun mask. There were ten men, chanting, drumming, and then one of them was overcome by . . ." He shrugged. "I know not what. He began to speak words I could not understand. The others had clearly experienced it before, though, for one of them was prepared to write it down." He tapped the edge of the parchment and smiled shyly. "I thought you could use it to trade with the mistress for your freedom."

Church was touched. "Thanks, but I'd rather find out what this means before I show it to her." He slipped the parchment into his pocket.

Back at the camp, Church was overcome with exhaustion and made his way to the blankets laid out for him beneath an olive tree. He saw the deep bonds of camaraderie growing between Decebalus, Aula and Lucia and desperately wanted that for himself.

But as he slipped his hand under the blanket he used as a pillow, he discovered that the Arabian lamp was no longer there. No one owned up to taking it—in fact, they all looked honestly surprised—and even though they scoured the area there was no sign of anyone who could have slipped into the camp unseen.

Without the missing Pendragon Spirit he could not be whole, and he would never achieve the power he needed for the coming struggle.

Hopelessness began to tug at his thoughts until he was disturbed by Lucia's exclamation of surprise. She was pointing towards the stones where Church could see blue lights flickering like candles at Evensong.

Decebalus thundered down the hillside like a bull, with Aula and Jerzy in pursuit. Lucia helped Church to his feet and supported him, bringing up the rear. Niamh remained behind.

"Nothing," Decebalus bellowed once they stood amongst the stones. "What trickery is this?"

"No, there!" Aula pointed to a spot above a stone where a blue light had flickered and disappeared.

"And there!" Jerzy indicated another one. He gambolled after it.

The atmosphere had changed. It now felt like a dream, alive with possibilities. Exhilaration rose inside Church unbidden; his fingers tingled and goosebumps prickled over his skin. When he looked round at Lucia, she appeared to have stars glimmering in her dark hair and on her brow. She gave him a warm, peaceful smile, revealing emotions that had been lost to her since she had learned of Marcus's death; it was as if the grief had been lifted right out of her.

"Can you feel it?" she said in a quiet, honeyed voice.

The blue lights were flickering across the breadth of the complex, growing stronger, and as they flared then receded, Church thought he could glimpse faces in them, like the ones that had appeared briefly in the column of fire under Boskawen-Un. Their features were all different: men, women, children.

"The spirits of the dead," Decebalus said in awe, but there was no fear in his voice, nor in any of their faces.

Church felt Lucia stiffen beside him, and when he followed her gaze he saw Marcus shimmering in one of the sapphire lights away in the stones. It could have been an illusion, but it felt real and deeply affecting. Lucia swallowed hard, then moved towards the figure.

Feeling invigorated, Church slumped down at the foot of one of the stones. Decebalus, Aula and Jerzy moved amongst the lights, interacting with the people they encountered, their faces innocent and open like children's as they gave themselves up to the wonder invoked by the potent atmosphere.

The missing lamp was forgotten, and his suffering at the hands of Janus, and all the many hardships he had faced, large or small. In that dreamy, endless moment, all the darkness receded. It was as if the universe was talking directly to him, and what it told him was not to worry about anything: all would be made right, and peace awaited him at the end of it.

He didn't know how long he spent in that warm night with the shades shimmering around him, their soothing whispers mingling with the breeze through the olive trees. Eventually the blue lights winked out one by one, like stars fading as the dawn approached. Lucia appeared out of the night, her expression beatific. She sat beside him, and for a while neither of them could find any words to express the vast mysteries of what they had experienced.

Finally Lucia said, "We are blessed."

"In what way?"

"Across the land, people suffer brief lives. They strive for little reward, and see those they hold in their hearts die, and they watch their own bodies wither. And though they cherish their beliefs, they are haunted by one simple notion: that there might be nothing more. That all the suffering might be for naught. That we appear, we feel pain, we wink out, the blink of an eye that amounts to nothing. But we *know*. This Blue Fire links our group and what is here, in this life, to what lies beyond. We recognise that we exist in a small pool, and beyond its edge there are infinite horizons we barely glimpse. We know that death is not the end. And we know that, however difficult it is to see, there is a reason for it all."

Lazily, she rested her head on his shoulder, and he slipped an arm around her; friends. The magic of that balmy Italian night still hung in the air, and Church knew that whatever happened to him, he would never forget it.

Decebalus lurched up. "I thought I saw Secullian," he said, puzzled. "And he was smiling."

Church glanced at Lucia, who was smiling, too.

"We find comfort in the heart of mystery, for in mystery there is always hope for something better," Lucia said.

"We're going to need to remember that for what lies ahead," Church said. "There's a war coming, and it's going to be brutal and hard. I don't know what the Army of the Ten Billion Spiders really wants, but it looks like they're out to change the ways things were . . . are. They want to alter reality. And they've got the advantage—Janus, one of the oldest and most powerful gods, is on their side." His thoughts turned to his own personal war with Veitch, one that threatened all the Brothers and Sisters of Dragons to come. "How are we supposed to win a battle like that?"

"How are we not?" Lucia replied. "We stand for the Blue Fire, and we carry the colours of the Kingdom of the Serpent. Look around you, remember what we saw and felt this night, and tell me we cannot win. We are champions of a force that is pure and strong, a force that runs to the heart of everything we see and know. And it is always at our shoulder."

Listening to Lucia's words, Church felt a shift deep within him that was like the slow but powerful movement of the ocean. His own desperate predicament, and the deaths of Etain and the others, and all the other suffering he had experienced, had left him wallowing in darkness. But it was all a matter of perspective. He needed to look outwards, where hope burned everywhere, and where the Blue Fire waited to be tapped.

Lucia sat forward, her eyes glimmering with tears in the moonlight. "The deaths of Marcus and Secullian, their sacrifice, are the strength that empowers us. We fight for them. And every death will give us more strength, for every death is a sacrifice." She took Church's hand. "If I die in the days ahead, do not mourn for me, for I will travel into the heart of the mystery. And in my leaving there will be no loss, only victory."

Church leaned back against the stone and thought about her words until the sun came up. In the quiet peace of that night he had learned something profound that would help him in the struggle to come.

CHAPTER FOUR
THE DEAD PLACES

1

While Church recovered at the Palace of Glorious Light, Niamh sequestered herself in her rooms and continued her investigation into the disappearance of her brother with mounting desperation.

One of her first visitors was the god the Celts called Math, a sorcerer from the Court of Soul's Ease who wore a mask with different animal faces on each of four sides. It magically rotated around his head and each time a new face appeared, his voice changed accordingly. His disturbing appearance reminded Church of Janus, and that night he had his first nightmare about his time in Rome.

But even Math could not locate Lugh, and that left Niamh desolate, for Math could see across all the Fixed and Far Lands.

Decebalus, Lucia and Aula adapted quickly to the many wonders of T'ir n'a n'Og and formed a tight-knit group that began to build a reputation across the court for adventuring. But even though they were fellow Brothers and Sisters of Dragons, Church did not place them above suspicion in the disappearance of the Arabian lamp, though he could not comprehend any possible motivation. The missing lamp preyed on him continually. He had to presume it had been stolen for a purpose, but he didn't know where to begin looking for it. In the meantime he felt bereft, as though the missing part of his Pendragon Spirit rendered him some kind of shadowy half-person, unable to affect the world around him.

Niamh visited Church and Jerzy one morning and it was clear she was troubled.

"Bad news about Lugh?" Church asked.

She shook her head. "My fears for my brother's safety tear me apart, but there are so many other responsibilities . . ." She chewed on a nail.

"It's never easy being a leader."

"It was easy," she said. "I had a pampered existence. Difficult decisions were few and far between. Now I feel I must take a lead in establishing my people's opposition to the Enemy—"

"Because no one else is." When she nodded, for the first time Church felt there might just be some common ground between them.

"I have decided we must mount an expedition to the edge of the Far Lands to establish the extent of the Enemy's force, and, if possible, discover who they are, and what they truly want."

"Who are you sending?"

"It has to be people I can . . . rely upon. I hoped you would lead the expedition, and that you would join us, too, Mocker."

"Travel to the Enemy fortress?" Jerzy whimpered.

"All right," Church said, "but I want to take Lucia as well—she has some abilities I could use."

"Agreed. And I will accompany you."

"I don't think that's wise. It could be dangerous—"

Niamh's eyes flashed. "I will not shirk my responsibilities."

Church held up his hands. "Okay, you're the boss. When I'm back on my feet there's a lot I need to find out, starting with Janus's role in all this. Why was he trying to suck the Pendragon Spirit out of me? The Army of the Ten Billion Spiders clearly needed me if they were prepared to transport me halfway across Europe to Janus's temple, and if they managed to keep Veitch at bay, because I tell you, he was ready to slit my throat at a moment's notice."

"You must have offended him a great deal, good friend," Jerzy said.

Inwardly, Church winced as he recalled what Veitch had told him on the ship. It set doubts crawling through his mind: would he really be prepared to kill a friend for the sake of Ruth's love? He couldn't believe it, but the nagging doubt still wouldn't leave him.

As she left, Niamh appeared relieved that Church had agreed to lead the expedition and that also surprised him. Why hadn't she just ordered him, as she had when she made him visit Eboracum to search for her brother? There were mysteries everywhere he turned.

As he recovered from his ordeal, Church felt a growing desire to see Ruth again, and to check on her safety and that of Shavi and Laura. And so, a week and a day after his return, he set off for the Court of Peaceful Days with Jerzy in tow, to view his own time through the Wish-Post. But the moment the court appeared in view, Church realised something was wrong. The martial banners that had fluttered over the red-tiled roofs were gone. Everywhere was still.

The gate was barred with twenty spears forced through the rails to prevent it from opening. A horse skull hung from the lock with the missing banners hanging between its jaws. The constant beat of the war-drum was gone, too, and an uneasy silence lay across the entire court. It appeared deserted.

Church recalled the court's soldiers dying by the thousands on the moors near Eboracum, and regretted his own selfish motivation for visiting without a second thought for the tremendous sacrifice they had made.

Silently, he turned his horse away. He would leave Queen Rhiannon to her mourning. But his unresolved desire to discover what was happening to Shavi, Laura and Ruth cast a long shadow.

2

A thin grey haze over London trapped the exhaust fumes and heat in a sweltering stew that had still not dissipated by the time night fell. Ruth's clothes clung to her as she made her way from the care home to the city centre. The physical discomfort only contributed to her unease. For several nights she had been troubled by a series of dreams that had a strange psychological intensity. They all featured snakes of various kinds, some coiled around a tree whispering words she could never remember when she woke, others as big as trains, rushing across the landscape, becoming rivers before they sank beneath the surface of the earth, where they glowed like blue veins.

Afterwards she was always left with a tremendous yearning, as if someone close to her had been lost at sea, and every day she waited for a return that never came.

The Embankment was strangely peaceful. No cabs or buses were on the road, and only the occasional pedestrian hurried by, keen to get home out of the heat. It would have been quicker to take the Tube, but increasingly she found that the presence of too many people set her on edge. Only on her own did she find peace and the space to probe her jumbled thoughts, but finding isolation in London was a task in itself. Everywhere she turned there was someone. *Watching me*, was always her first instinct, but recently she had decided to take a stand against the creeping paranoia for fear it would inevitably lead to the mental illness that always felt just one step away.

The haze muffled all sounds from the city, so when an owl hooted from a tree nearby, Ruth jumped as if a gun had been fired. It stared at her with large, intense eyes. She felt something odd tickling at the back of her mind, part memory, part an unnerving sense that it had intelligence. She would have laughed if it had not felt so eerie.

"You going to spend all night looking up into the trees?" Rourke was waiting for her beneath one of the lights not far from Blackfriars Bridge.

"There's an owl," she said, but when she went to point it out it was gone.

"Enough with the bird-spotting. Are we going to hit the town or not?" Rourke took her arm before she could answer and guided her towards the Tube.

The fact that she called him Rourke instead of his first name was just one of the anomalies of their nascent relationship. She had been seeing him socially for five weeks since their random meeting in the pub. A drink here, a meal there, a cinema trip. They had held hands and kissed once, on their last date as he dropped Ruth off at her flat.

The real anomaly was that she wasn't wholly sure she liked him. Not that she disliked him, either—her feelings were a little like that foggy night: he passed through her life and left no impression. But he was charming and he always managed to say the right thing. It was a near-miraculous skill. He'd point out her favourite dish on the menu, or suggest they go to see one of her most-loved movies in the late-night screening at the independent cinema. Their conversation almost always seemed to be about things that were close to her heart, which was flattering, but it meant that if she had to admit it, she knew barely anything about him. He was just . . . there.

"I noticed the strangest thing," she said as they reached the top of the stairs leading down into the Tube. "Four cars in a row had only one headlight working, and the fifth had none at all."

"Coincidence," Rourke replied easily.

"It didn't feel like it. It was as if it meant something." She laughed, embarrassed. "That's silly, isn't it?"

"Yes, it is." He gave her hand a squeeze. "The human brain is conditioned to see meaning where there isn't any. We fill in the gaps in reality because we can't stand chaos or the fact that there is no underlying meaning."

"No pattern, then?"

"No pattern."

On the Tube, Ruth spent the first five minutes of their journey unburdening herself about her job, and wishing she had the time or the energy to consider a career change. But her work sucked everything out of her and left her able to do little more than head home to sleep.

"Good job you've got me to brighten things up," Rourke said, and she had to admit that was true; in the bleakness that was her life, he at least provided some vibrancy and interest.

They passed through Leicester Square Station heading towards Tottenham Court Road where they planned to change to the Central Line. Ruth had been briefly wondering why she was incapable of recalling any of her favourite songs when the train ground to a sudden halt and all the lights went out. There was a brief scream and then nervous laughter.

Ruth fumbled in the dark and found Rourke's hand. He gave it another reassuring squeeze. Yet she felt even more on edge; her fingertips and toes buzzed, and an odd sensation of apprehension jangled in her belly.

She freed her fingers to brush a strand of hair from her eyes and as she did so an enormous blue spark leaped from her fingertips to the metal upright at the end of the row of seats. She exclaimed loudly as the flash briefly lit up the entire carriage.

"Ruth? Are you all right?" Rourke hissed as mutterings ran amongst the passengers.

As her eyes cleared after the glare she noticed a similar blue light, this time outside the carriage and further along the tunnel. But this light was constant, like a torch. *Underground staff working on the train*, she guessed. Slowly the light began to move towards her carriage.

Her apprehension began to grow. As the light neared she saw it was coming from an old-fashioned lantern with a blue flame flickering inside it. From her perspective, Ruth couldn't see who was holding the lantern.

Just a lantern, she thought. *An unusual lantern, to be sure, but nothing to concern you.*

"Come on—we should move down the carriage." Rourke had been watching the light, too, and his face was dark and concerned in the azure glow leaking through the windows.

"It's all right," she said, but he had found her hand again and was tugging her to her feet.

They were brought to a halt by the noise of something grating on the outside of the carriage. Ruth's heart was hammering. Now she could make out the shadowy shape holding the lantern: it was a giant.

Rourke attempted to pull her away, but Ruth fought to free her hand—she had to see. The figure loomed closer and now she could see a man at least eight feet tall, with a bushy black beard, long, wild hair and burning eyes. He wore what looked like a sackcloth shift fastened at the waist by a broad leather belt. A thong around his left forearm was covered with small hooks, which he occasionally dragged along the carriage. Ruth's breath caught in her throat.

"Come away!" Rourke shouted.

The giant stopped next to Ruth and brought his face down to the glass so he could make eye contact. Ruth was jolted by what she saw there. The blue lantern light flooded the carriage, making shadows dance with every flicker. Now even Rourke was transfixed.

"There you are, little sister. It is so difficult to see you in this dark world."

Ruth could hear the giant as clearly as if he was standing next to her.

He held the lantern forward. "This is the last light in the world, and once this is gone only darkness will remain."

Ruth felt a surge of panic. Why was he talking to her? What did he want?

"Wake up, little sister. Wake up!" he continued insistently. "This is not the way things were meant to be. You must find yourself quickly . . . keep the light alive . . . before it is too late." He pressed the fingers of his left hand against the window and the glass changed quality and began to run like oil. Slowly his fingers began to move through it.

Ruth stepped back into Rourke's encircling arms.

"We need to get you out of here," he whispered in her ear as he began to tug her gently down the aisle. This time she did not resist.

As she moved away, she saw the giant snap his head to the left. A second later, he withdrew his fingers and he and the blue light began to move back in the direction from which they had come.

Ruth's attention was caught instantly by more movement in the tunnel. It appeared as if a thick black liquid was running horizontally along the wall in the direction of the receding light. But it was not a liquid; there was detail in it and too much rapid motion, and that was when Ruth realised she was seeing an army of black spiders rushing from floor to ceiling towards the giant.

"That's disgusting," she said. "It's not natural."

"There's nothing there," Rourke whispered. "Just shadows. We need to get you home to rest. You must be a bit strung out if you're seeing things."

Ruth was disoriented and shaken, and nodded queasily, but the image of the giant and the spiders wouldn't leave her mind.

3

"I tell you, there's no point being nice to me—I'm not going to sleep with you." Laura DuSantiago was enjoying the hypnotic lights and the way the bass made her stomach tumble. She'd had four vodka and Red Bulls and was letting the music take control.

"I'm not asking you to sleep with me. Just take these." Rourke opened his hand to reveal two tabs of E.

Laura took them and went to pop them in her mouth. Then, for the first time ever, she decided to save them for later. Rourke looked disappointed. "It won't work," she said to him with a frosty smile.

Before he could reply, Laura took the opportunity to dive into a swirl of dancers and dodged through them into one of the numerous tiny rooms that formed a complex around the vast central space of the abandoned warehouse where the rave was taking place.

The ironic thing was that she'd slept with many people like Rourke before, often for much less than a couple of tabs. There was something about Rourke that always put her off, however desperate she was. But she still took his drugs, and he always had plenty of them on him to keep her happy in her never-ending quest to get caned and forget the life she had inflicted on herself. All day frying burgers; barely enough cash to keep a roof over her head. Free drugs were a godsend.

They also helped her forget the many irritating dreams she'd been having recently and the odd feeling of being out of sorts, as if she was just a visitor in her own life.

She ducked through one room after another, knowing Rourke would not be far behind. He was annoying like that, always around, and if not for the drugs she would definitely have told him to stay away.

One room was filled with a group of people tripping. Laura swore at them and picked her way across the bodies to the next room where a couple were having sex. The room after that was a bare concrete shell with smashed beer bottles in one corner and an area where somebody had once lit a small fire. On the far wall was a piece of jarring graffiti: *Look out for the spiders*. She'd seen something like it a couple of times across town recently. *The Army of the Ten Billion Spiders*, one of them had read. She guessed it was a guerrilla publicity campaign for some new band, but she'd never seen any flyers for them performing.

The familiar tread of boots came from the room behind—Rourke en route to entreat her to take her Es like a good girl. It wasn't in Laura's nature to do what she was told, even if it was something she wanted to do. She slipped out of a side door into the night.

A small yard area was scattered with lumps of broken concrete. Beyond it was a sagging chain-link fence and then the comforting darkness of a wooded area where she could lose herself.

Before she could take another step, she heard a strange sound, like wires whipping in the wind. The door through which she had just passed was now covered with a dense wall of ivy and bramble. Someone was pressing against it—Rourke, probably—but the greenery held it fast.

In her confusion she realised her fingers were tingling peculiarly; the skin around the tips was puckered as though they had been too long in water. They gradually grew smooth before her eyes.

You did this, a voice told her, and though it made no sense, some part of her believed it was true.

She jogged towards the tree line, turning to look back when she reached the fence. The vegetation was still covering the door, but from her new perspective she could see the bramble curling upwards in the shape of the number 5, too well defined to be random.

Laura was mesmerised by the figure. In the depths of her, something shifted and answered the call.

4

The lights across Avebury were slowly going out as the villagers turned to sleep. Shavi stood outside the pub, inhaling the scents of the Wiltshire countryside and feeling more alive than he ever remembered being. The ancient landscape of the Downs rolled away to the south beneath the vault of a sky sprinkled with a dazzling stream of stars.

So much had changed in such a short time that he felt as if he was awakening from a deep sleep. When the strange spirit form emerged from the picture on his office desk, he had been bewildered for only a short time. That evening he had mulled over the existence of things beyond the mundane and had come to the conclusion that it made a lot more sense than his life at the offices of Gibson and Layton, Chartered Accountants. When he handed in his resignation the next day to begin his notice period and started to grow his hair longer in preparation for a new lifestyle, he wondered why he had been denying himself for so long.

Throughout it all, he struggled with the advice of Rourke, the man who had entered his life on the same night as the revelation. Rourke was unassuming and pleasant, a sympathetic listener. Everywhere Shavi went, pub or supermarket or just for a walk in the park, Rourke cropped up with a cheery wave and a line of reassuring chat. He questioned Shavi's decision to quit his job and became quite intense during subsequent discussions about Shavi changing the direction of his life. The more Shavi grew in tune with his inner self, the more he found Rourke's presence oppressive, and then negative. It had become a trying task to avoid Rourke and to leave London without the man being aware.

And so Shavi stood there on the brink of—he hoped—something profound. Long black hair now framed his exquisitely handsome Asian features. His workaday suit had been consigned to a charity shop, replaced by loose-fitting cotton clothes, with sandals instead of the black leather shoes that had always made his soles ache.

He had listened to music, lit incense and candles, and most of all thought and dreamed. He had reflected intensely on his inner rhythms and the cycles of his subconscious, becoming more complete with each passing day. After that came the dreams of serpents filled with a coruscating but redeeming power. And finally these were overlaid by one single image falling into stark relief: Avebury's ancient stone circle. It came to him as he drifted off to sleep and was still there when he woke, night after night. It was calling to him. He answered.

Leaving the main street, Shavi made his way through the cool shadows to where the majority of the remaining standing stones stood in a large grassy expanse, bounded on one side by a steep bank. It was peaceful and still. Shavi let his fingers drift over the surface of the megaliths as he passed, his skin tingling with the contact.

As he walked he had the vague impression of movement away in the night near a copse of trees. It was gone the moment he registered it. *A fox?* he thought. Soon after, a shape flitted through a beam of moonlight to hide behind one of the stones, though whether it was man or beast Shavi couldn't tell. He decided the safest thing to do would be to return to the van to get his torch, but before he could turn around he was hit forcefully and dragged into the lee of one of the megaliths.

"What are you doing here?" Foul breath blasted into Shavi's face as a hand closed around his throat.

He allowed himself to go limp to prevent further violence. The attacker eased his grip and Shavi saw it was a man with straggly, grey hair and the sunburned, wind-blasted complexion of someone who spent his life outdoors. He was wiry and exceptionally strong for his age, which Shavi placed post-sixty, though it was difficult to pin it down. He was unwashed and mud splattered his old cheesecloth shirt. His eyes were feral and frightened and reminded Shavi of a wild beast's.

The man brought up a wooden staff with his free hand and placed it quickly across Shavi's throat, pinning him down. If the man increased his weight on the staff he would crush Shavi's neck in an instant.

"Who are you?" he repeated threateningly.

"My name is Shavi."

"What are you doing here at night? Nobody comes here at night. Nobody comes to any of the old sites any more. They're all dead and dried up." His eyes flashed from side to side anxiously; he appeared on the edge of sanity.

Shavi's first thought was that the man was a drunk or a drifter, but there was an indefinable quality to him that made Shavi think again. "I came because of a dream," Shavi said after a second.

The man's erratic movements ceased and he stared deeply into Shavi's eyes. "You dreamed of the stones?"

"Every night."

"And you came because of dreams? You're not lying to me, are you, you bloody young idiot?"

"I am not lying."

"Are you one of them?" His stressed, anxious tics returned in force. "You can't be one of them. They're gone. Lost. Dead. Don't exist any more." He sat back against the stone, nursing his staff in his lap. "What's your name?"

"Shavi."

"Bloody idiot name. Are you one of them?"

"I do not know." The man began to grow agitated again, so Shavi added hastily, "I do know that I am supposed to be here. Something strange has come into my life . . . a feeling that this is not the way things are meant to be."

"The world is the way anyone with the strongest will makes it. That's just the way it is." The hungry gleam in the man's eyes told Shavi his instincts were right: somehow the man was connected to the growing mystery.

"Who are you?" Shavi asked gently.

A flash of paranoia came and went and then the man said roughly, "I've got lots of names, but you can call me the Bone Inspector until you know me better." When he saw Shavi looking at him quizzically, he snapped, "It's a name *and* a job description. I guard the ancient sites all across the country . . . here, Stonehenge, Boskawen-Un, Callanish, all of 'em. Have done for years."

"Guard them from what?"

"None of your business!" He caught himself, punched the turf. "I'm the last in the line of a group that called themselves the Culture. You'd know 'em by another name. They were the keepers of wisdom, passed down from one generation to the next by word of mouth only." The Bone Inspector suddenly jumped to his feet. "We can't stay here talking! They'll be coming for us soon!"

"Who will?"

"The ones who rule the world. I've been running from them, and hiding . . . travelling by night, sleeping in ditches. They want me dead because I'm the only one who knows about the stuff that's been forgotten. Even though they're dead the old sites still have something . . . they help me hide from the ones who're after me."

"You are not making a great deal of sense," Shavi said quietly.

"You think I'm crazy, do you? Well, that shows what you know." He rapped Shavi's head with his knuckles. "Thick."

The Bone Inspector grabbed Shavi and tried to haul him away, but Shavi resisted. "I cannot go. I was brought here for a reason."

"If you stay here, they'll have you. They don't allow anyone to get close to the old ways."

"If you know what is happening, please tell me."

Whatever the Bone Inspector saw in Shavi's eyes calmed him. "All right. I reckon you might be one of them after all. And if you are . . . well, there's hope." He looked around like a cornered animal. "I'll show you, that's what I'll do."

The Bone Inspector bounded away so quickly that Shavi had to scramble to keep up with him. Scraps of the Bone Inspector's crazed mutterings floated back. "Ancient knowledge . . . secrets encoded in the landscape, so it'll never be lost. But you need eyes to see . . . think smart, different from the way you were taught . . ."

Shavi caught up with the fragmentary commentary at one of the stones. The Bone Inspector patted the megalith a little too enthusiastically. "Everything they taught you in school is wrong. There's a secret history that went on behind the scenes of what most people saw. And it's all about this."

"The standing stones?"

"No, you idiot. The stones are just markers."

"For what?"

"The power that's in the land . . . telluric energy, the Blue Fire—the Pendragon Spirit. Call it what you will."

"Ley Lines?"

The Bone Inspector cackled. "The New Age idiots were right all along. Isn't that a punch in the eye? Every sacred site, whether it's a stone circle, a spring or a cathedral, they're places where the spirit fire is strongest, where you can tap into it if you know how. And this place was the most powerful of all."

Shavi glanced at the row of stones disappearing into the gloom. Avebury was such a big megalithic complex that it encompassed the whole of the modern village: rings of stones, two processional avenues snaking out on either side. The books he'd read in recent days told him that archaeologists considered it just part of a vast site that had once stretched for miles, taking in nearby Silbury Hill and scores of other smaller prehistoric remnants.

"They call it a *dracontium*," the Bone Inspector said, "a dragon temple, because the two avenues make a snake in the landscape with the temple at the heart. Dragons . . . serpents—that's just another way of describing the power that runs through the land, and through us, too. There was a time when this whole world was the Kingdom of the Serpent. Now . . ." He shook his head. "You want to see how bad it's got?"

He loped across the clipped grass like a wolf until he reached another stone. "This one's called the Devil's Chair," he said. "Everything is a secret. You have to look past the surface, find the key that unlocks hidden doors. They're everywhere if you know how to look."

"Doors to where?"

"Here, there and everywhere. We run round this three times widdershins. That'll raise whatever sparks of energy are left in the ground. That's the key, you see. The key to everything." His eyes were wild and white in the dark. Too long hiding and running from whomever he thought was pursuing him had taken its toll. He grabbed Shavi. "Once we've done that, you follow me. And don't fall back, all right?"

The Bone Inspector ran anticlockwise around the stone. Shavi followed, unsure whether he was making a fool of himself. After the third circuit, the Bone Inspector spun off towards a steep embankment. He led Shavi down the other side, across a road, through a gate and two rows of concrete pillars that marked the site of stones long since uprooted.

"West Kennet Avenue. Not long now," the Bone Inspector said breathlessly.

A change had come over the atmosphere: it was electric, and Shavi could feel his fingers and toes tingling. The ground rumbled, and to his astonishment he saw the turf rising ahead of him to reveal a gaping hole.

"Underground we go," the Bone Inspector chanted.

They scrambled along a loam-stinking tunnel for fifteen minutes until it widened into a space whose boundaries were lost to the dark. A thin, flickering blue light emanated from faint deposits on the floor.

The Bone Inspector suddenly thrust an arm across Shavi's chest, halting his headlong rush. As Shavi's eyes adjusted to the half-light, he saw he was standing on the edge of a sharp drop.

"Not so long ago that would have been filled with a lake of Blue Fire." A hint of awe laced the Bone Inspector's voice; he sounded saner and more measured now he was underground. "It was magnificent. You felt as if you were a god just standing at the edge."

"Where has it gone?"

"Where's it gone? Where's it gone?" The Bone Inspector rubbed feverish fingers through his lank hair. "If I knew that, I'd know everything. It was dormant before, when men thought science could solve all their problems. It looked as if it was coming back for good, but then . . ." He gripped his skull as if he was trying to crush it. "Why can't I remember? What's wrong with my head?"

"We must stay calm," Shavi said comfortingly.

"Calm? The Blue Fire is the lifeblood of everything! If it's gone, what do you think that means? We're all dead men walking around, only we don't know it. There's only a residue at the old sites—the scum left behind after it went down the drain." The Bone Inspector grabbed Shavi's shirt and hauled him so close that Shavi could smell the old man's foul breath again. "If you really are one of the Five, then you've got to find it. That's your job. Bring back the power in the land. Set us all free!"

Once Shavi had calmed the Bone Inspector, he encouraged him to explain what he meant by "the Five." Soon Shavi had heard about the champions of Existence who came together to protect the land, bound as one by the Pendragon Spirit.

"Five. Always five. That's the magic number," the Bone Inspector said. "When one lot does what's required of them, they sail off into the sunset until the next crisis, when Existence calls another Five."

Shavi didn't know whether to believe the Bone Inspector's story. From anyone else it would have sounded ludicrous, but coming from him, in that place, it rang true somehow. "If I am one of them," Shavi began, "who are the others?"

"How should I know? You always find each other. The Pendragon Spirit calls to its own—that's why you came here. But now, with everything changed, who knows? There might not be enough Blue Fire in the world to bring you all back together."

"If what you are saying is true, how did it get like this?" Shavi mused.

The Bone Inspector wiped snot away with the back of his hand. "It's not just the Blue Fire that's gone. Where are the Fabulous Beasts?"

Shavi gave him a questioning look.

"That's right—scales, wings, breathe fire. They live in the earth, just as the old stories say. They keep the Blue Fire burning, and they feed on it. Some say they *are* it."

"They exist? Like the Chinese said—the spirits of the earth? I would very much like to see one."

"There used to be a big old bugger here . . ." The Bone Inspector shook his head sadly. "You find the Fabulous Beasts, you'll find the Blue Fire. Unless they're all dead. We'd better get out of here. Now you know all this, they'll be looking for you."

"'The ones who run the world?" Shavi said hesitantly.

"Dead-eyed people, watching. Always watching. They want to keep things the way they are. They don't want hope and wonder and magic loose— too dangerous. They want it this way so they can control it. Power for the powerful, and the rest of us be damned."

They returned along the dark tunnel and at the Bone Inspector's command the turf rose up to release them into the warm night. The minute Shavi stepped back onto the ancient West Kennet Avenue he knew something was wrong: the electricity had departed along with the heady rush of magic. Instead there was a faint buzzing like high-voltage power lines.

"Shavi? What are you doing?"

Rourke stood to one side of the concrete markers, hands behind his back. Casually dressed, he looked at ease, as if bumping into Shavi there was the most natural thing in the world.

"Why are you following me?" Shavi asked.

"I'm a friend. I want to look out for you."

"With all due respect, you are, at best, an acquaintance. And I really don't need anyone to look out for me."

The Bone Inspector tugged at Shavi's sleeve. "'E's one of 'em," he hissed. "Keep your distance."

"I'm worried that you're getting into dangerous waters. Out here in the countryside, at night." Rourke tried to peer around Shavi at the Bone

Inspector. "No doubt getting your head filled with all sorts of nonsense by unseemly types."

Rourke appeared benign, but Shavi was picking up unmistakable signs of danger.

"The car's back at the road." Rourke jerked a lazy thumb over his shoulder. "I can give you a lift."

"I have transport."

"I'd like you to come with me, Shavi." Rourke's voice had developed a hard core.

"No." Shavi's single word shattered all pretence.

Rourke approached quickly, but Shavi noted he did not step onto West Kennet Avenue. He kept just beyond the perimeter of the ancient sacred site. "I told you not to make changes to your life," Rourke continued. "You had a good job, a regular income, stability. Now look at you. Frankly, I think all this crazy change has pushed you over the edge."

Though he wasn't sure why, Shavi turned to the Bone Inspector and whispered, "Stay within the site's boundaries until we approach the village. We may then have an opportunity to get to my van."

The Bone Inspector pushed past him. "You don't know the place as well as I do. Keep up—and don't wander off the path."

He bounded off and Shavi followed. As he passed Rourke, Shavi caught sight of something that chilled him: Rourke's face was altering. In the moonlight it looked as if lumps were rising all over it.

After a few more paces, Shavi glanced back: it hadn't been a trick of the light. Rourke's face had started to come apart, the skin splitting to reveal a black, wriggling mass beneath. His eyes burst and unfolded. His mouth gaped wider and wider as the jaw began to disintegrate. To Shavi, it was as if he had been looking at a life-sized photograph of Rourke that was slowly being stripped away to reveal what was hiding behind it.

As a large chunk of cheek disappeared, the face became black and Shavi saw what was really there. Spiders as big as his fist poured forth, with thousands of smaller ones tumbling behind. They drained from Rourke's sleeves and trousers and flowed towards Shavi, until finally Rourke fell apart completely. As the spiders moved across the grass it charred and faded under them. A flat, dead path was left in their wake.

Shavi didn't wait any longer. He ran as fast as he could through the gate and back over the road to the embankment. At the top he looked back and saw the spiders moving almost as fast as he could run.

When he reached the far side of the stone circle, the Bone Inspector was waiting for him. "Where the bloody hell were you? I was just about to go off on my own."

"This way." With a twinge of unease, Shavi broke out of the circle and ran towards the pub. The Bone Inspector followed him into the van, cursing. Through the side window, Shavi could see the spiders streaming towards him. A stone wall fell apart before them as if they had eaten their way through it, but Shavi felt it was more than that: it had been erased.

"Come on, you bloody idiot!" The Bone Inspector bounced up and down in the passenger seat.

The van lurched forward with a screech of tyres. Soon they were speeding through the maze of night-dark country lanes that surrounded Avebury.

Shavi glanced into the rear-view mirror. "We have left them behind."

"Don't you believe it. They'll find you again. That's what they do."

"What do we do now?" Shavi gripped the wheel tightly.

"Aye, well," the Bone Inspector replied, "that's the question."

5

Ruth allowed Rourke to guide her back to her flat with a brief detour to the local for a steadying drink. Her vision of the giant with the lantern obsessed her, but Rourke adamantly denied seeing anything.

Feeling a bit woozy after the three vodkas she'd downed in rapid succession, Ruth stumbled on the way up the stairs. Rourke caught her and wrapped his arms around her.

"Don't worry," he whispered in her ear. "I'll look after you."

The sentiment was absurdly appealing. Ruth felt so disoriented, depressed and detached from the world that it would be a relief for somebody else to carry the heavy weight of her life for a while.

At her door, Rourke hugged her. "Are you going to be okay?" he asked, concerned.

"I'm fine, really." She wasn't, and she thought Rourke knew that, too.

He kissed her gently on the lips. She hesitated and then kissed him back with passion. After a moment of hesitation, he returned the embrace with force.

Heat rose inside her. "Do you want to come in?"

Within moments they were writhing on the sofa, their hands all over each other's bodies. After so long feeling numb, when Rourke brought his hand to her breast and gently squeezed her hard nipple the rush was almost delirious in its intensity. She felt the hardness in his trousers grind into her groin and she spasmed in response. She wanted him inside her. She wanted to feel again. She wanted to love and be loved. She wanted colour in her life, and music, and surges of wild emotion that would make her accept that she was really, truly alive. She didn't want to be trapped in a monochromatic existence any longer, where every experience was cotton-wool padded and it didn't matter to anyone, let alone her, whether she lived or died.

But as soon as the notion entered her head she realised it wasn't Rourke she wanted; it was anyone. Just a warm human body from which she could leach some life and return from the dead.

"I'm sorry." She gently eased him off her. "I can't do this now. I didn't mean to lead you on. I'm just a mess. It's probably not good for you to be with me. Or for anyone to be with me, for that matter."

Rourke straightened his clothes and Ruth was relieved to see he wasn't offended or angry. "Don't worry." He smiled. "I want it to be the right time for both of us."

The sentiment was correct, but there was something calculated about it that was not reflected in his expression. She realised obliquely that while they had been in the throes of passion, it had almost been as if he was running through the motions. The word that came to mind was *hollow*.

After he had gone, she sat on her bed, hugging her knees and feeling so desperately lonely that her stomach ached. She had the strangest feeling that her life was just a role being conducted for hidden cameras; that the real Ruth Gallagher was someone quite different, living an existence that was filled with love, passion and most of all meaning. And more, she felt that in that life there *was* someone else who was more important to her than life itself, someone whose face she could almost see if she just concentrated hard enough . . .

Ruth jerked out of her reverie. She had the oddest sense that the wardrobe door had opened a little, barely perceptibly, but she was sure she had registered movement. The crack was wider than a finger and she could see the darkness within. Gooseflesh ran up her arms for no reason that she could understand.

She tried to recall what she had been considering, but the thought was gone. She went to the kitchen to make herself a herbal tea, and when she returned to the bedroom later she didn't notice that the wardrobe door was shut once more.

6

During the month-long expedition, Church had seen many wonders of the Far Lands: a brass robot 100 feet high who guarded the treasures of ancient races; a city of mirrors that only appeared at sunrise and sunset; a pool where you could see your own dreams made flesh; a garden of sentient exotic blooms that lured unwary travellers to their doom; and a vast array of strange people and stranger creatures: the vampiric Baobhan Sith, cannibalistic boar-men, lizard-women whose song could send you to sleep for 100 years, wolf-men, sorcerers, inch-high men and women with homes in the trunks of trees, basilisks and manticores, flesh-eating unicorns and cats that were wiser than any human he had ever met.

He had sat beneath the billion, billion stars on a warm night looking out over a great plain to mountains that appeared to reach to the heavens. He had slipped into the silent, green depths of the preternatural Forest of the Night and skirted the edge of a burning desert.

During that time he had been forced to confront many threats both to himself and those who travelled with him, for the Far Lands were as dangerous as they were wonderful, and gradually tales of the great exploits of Jack the Giantkiller began to spread amongst the denizens of T'ir n'a n'Og. Though he didn't realise it himself, he was passing into legend, in a place where legend was the currency of the great.

And so they came to what felt like the edge of the world, beyond the great desert where the sky was occasionally filled with swirling psychedelic colours. An inhospitable landscape of volcanic rock and glass and dusty plains stretched out as far as the eye could see.

The constant tolling of a bell told them when they were nearing their destination. Overhead flew clouds of the region's strange carrion birds, their beaks and breasts white, the rest of them as black as oil.

Church crested the final ridge on his belly and wriggled to a good vantage point amongst the razor-sharp rocks. What he saw made his blood run cold. A massive city was being erected in the wasteland, but it was not like any city he had seen before: from a certain angle it appeared to be a giant insect squatting on the landscape, as big as London, yet while parts of it gleamed the shiny black of a carapace, other sections appeared to be constructed from spoiled meat. None of the architecture had any human dimension or design; there were promontories and spikes, domes and sheer faces that appeared to serve no purpose. A wall of the black meat at least 100 feet high ranged across the front of the city and continued around the back, where the incessant construction work was taking place.

"Abomination." Jerzy had wriggled up beside Church. A scarf was wrapped across his frozen mouth to keep out the dust.

The outer surfaces of the city swarmed with figures involved in some unidentifiable activity. They reminded Church of the regimented movements of worker ants. On the plain before the wall marched a vast army, members of the Ninth Legion amongst its ranks.

Niamh appeared next to him, and Church quickly pulled her down before she could be seen. "Don't you have any sense of self-preservation?" he said.

Niamh's fragile features looked out of place in the cruel landscape. "No," she said simply, "for Existence has always protected my people."

They crawled back down the slope to where Lucia was waiting with the horses. "It's big," Church reported to her. "I don't know how many of them there are inside, but if it grows much larger they could overrun this land in an instant."

Lucia wiped a smear of black dust from Church's sweaty brow. "Then all the reports were correct," she said. "Now we know where their forces are camped, we can strike swiftly—"

"Must you continually molest him?" Niamh said to her coldly.

"You may have tricked him into being your slave, but you will never own his soul." Lucia's eyes flashed defiantly.

Church stepped in to quell the tension that had been mounting between the two women throughout the journey. "We can tell your people to raise an army and return here," he said to Niamh.

"There is no point," Niamh said. "It would take a great deal of negotiation simply to bring together the twenty great courts, and even then my people would never agree to a pre-emptive attack. The Golden Ones believe themselves to be so powerful that no one would dare strike against them. But if any ever do, they will respond with force."

"So we have to wait until those things get the first punch in?" Church said.

"Only then will the Golden Ones respond."

"By then it might be too late."

She looked towards the distant horizon that hid her home. "Only then."

7

Church led the way back into the Court of the Soaring Spirit as dusk was falling. Lanterns burning in a million windows transformed the oppressive architecture into a place of magic, and the streets were filled with the aroma of exotic spices from evening meals.

Niamh returned to her quarters immediately. Throughout the entire return journey, she had been brooding over the repercussions of their discovery of the enemy fortress. With each passing day she was less like the goddess who had enticed Church into the Otherworld. Her arrogance and confidence had been shattered and she stalked the corridors of her palace as if death were only one step behind.

The first thing Church did was to seek out Decebalus and Aula, who were drinking in the Hunter's Moon. They had recently returned from their own expedition to explore the Far Lands to the east.

After Church explained about the enemy fortress, he said, "I have a job for you, if you're up for it."

Decebalus raised his flagon. "Anything, brother."

Church told them of Veitch's plan to murder any Brothers and Sisters of Dragons he could find. "If I'm allowed, I'm going to return to our world at regular intervals and bring back any of us I can find—and who are prepared to come."

"After they have carried out whatever mission Existence has planned for them in our world," Aula noted.

Church nodded. "I'm not saying it's going to be easy or successful, but at least I'll be able to save some of them from Veitch. We'll also be able to build up a force, here in the city, for whatever fight we've got ahead of us."

Decebalus nodded approvingly. "An army of Brothers and Sisters of Dragons."

"Well, maybe a squad . . ." Church bent forward so he would not be overheard. "I want the two of you to look after them. Give them all the information they need. Find them somewhere safe to stay, either here or outside the city. And get them ready for whenever they're needed. Will you do that?"

Decebalus grinned and drained his flagon.

"There are worse jobs," Aula said before downing her own drink.

Church quickly returned to the Palace of Glorious Light where the Brothers and Sisters of Dragons had been given quarters in a tower that faced the setting sun. By accident or design, it was far removed from the main living quarters of Niamh's staff.

Lucia had already turned her rooms into a reflection of her character, filled with obscure artefacts, talismans and strange objects she had located in the court's markets and shops. One chamber had been set apart for practising her Craft, and it was there that the owl resided. Church had started to think it was less a bird than something else that had adopted the image as a disguise; it always looked at him with an unnerving intelligence.

Church had also come to realise Lucia's potential. Somehow she was tapping directly into the energy that manifested as the Blue Fire. If she could truly manipulate it, she would be capable of anything.

"Perhaps," she mused as they sat sipping wine while Jerzy practised his juggling, "we are all capable of drawing from that reservoir of power. We only need to find the right key to unlock the part of our mind that has the ability to direct it. For me it is the words of power, the correct hand movements, the rituals. For you—"

"I need to find the lamp containing the missing part of my Pendragon Spirit," Church said. "Without that, I'm not going to be unlocking anything."

"She has it. I am sure of it." Lucia didn't have to specify who *she* was. "She cannot be trusted. The gods have manipulated mortals since the world was formed. She has already manipulated you." A pause while she savoured her wine, and then a statement designed to appear throwaway: "Why do you indulge her?"

"I don't."

"You have not attempted to break her control over you."

"She's agreed to release me if I find her brother."

Another pause, another carefully considered statement: "She is developing a fascination for you."

"As a specimen, maybe. Not in the way you mean."

Lucia smiled at Church's naivety. "I have seen the way she looks at you when you are not aware. Whenever you speak, her attention is drawn to you. She does not treat you like chattel, though by any definition that is what you are."

"She's a goddess." Church finished his wine. "And I'm a man. At the very best it would be social suicide."

Lucia laughed and offered him more wine. Church declined and was surprised by the flicker of sadness in her eyes when he said he was heading back to his chamber.

As Church and Jerzy approached their quarters, Evgen was waiting for them. Church did not trust Niamh's guard captain. He was sure it was only Niamh's patronage that prevented Evgen from eradicating him in an instant.

"You have a visitor," Evgen said in a monotone. "He arrived at the gates of the court shortly after your return."

"I have no idea who that could possibly be."

"He says he knows you. He was a mortal . . . once." Evgen smiled nastily. "He is known in the Far Lands as the pet of the queen of the Court of the Yearning Heart. He has announced himself here as Thomas Learmont of Earlston. Also known as Thomas the Rhymer."

8

"Who is this Fragile Creature?" Jerzy asked as they followed the echoes of Evgen's boots down the winding stone steps.

"It depends if he is who he says he is," Church replied. "Thomas the Rhymer is a figure from the myths of my people, like King Arthur—very much like Arthur, in fact. Both of them were supposed to sleep under a hill until the darkest hour when their people would need them again."

"So he was a great warrior?"

"Not in the same way. According to the old stories, Thomas was kidnapped by the Faerie Queen while he slept under a hawthorn tree. He stayed with the Fair Folk for a while and was given two great gifts: the power of prophecy and the Tongue that Cannot Lie. If you can actually call that a gift. True Thomas, they called him. When he returned home to Scotland he made his mark, achieved legendary status and then disappeared back to Faerie. But that might not have happened yet. Or maybe this is it happening now. I can't get my head around the whole time-not-being-linear thing."

"Perhaps he simply ran out of friends in the Fixed Lands because of all that truth-telling," Jerzy said.

Evgen led them into a large chamber in the castle's guard-tower where a man sat alone, swathed in a cloak with a hood pulled over his head. Evgen nodded to Church and left.

The man stood and removed his hood to reveal a dour face and lank brown hair. Intelligent but troubled grey eyes surveyed them forensically. "This is it, then." His Scottish accent softened his irritable tone. "A naïf and a fool."

"What winning ways," Jerzy said drolly. "We must introduce you to the queen."

"I've been teaching him the humour of our world," Church said. "He particularly likes irony and sarcasm."

"I am glad you are using your time wisely," the stranger said. "After all, you could simply be fighting for humanity and the whole of Existence."

Church tried to read how much the stranger knew, but his eyes gave nothing away.

"I have been *gifted*—" Thomas enunciated the word venomously "—with the ability to see into the future. We are fated to walk the same road, at least for a while."

"Friends, then," Church said.

"Oh, I would not go that far." Thomas the Rhymer smiled tightly.

9

Jerzy raised his flagon. The Hunter's Moon was as packed as ever. "Well, then, Tom—"

"Thomas."

Jerzy's grin was challenging. "No, I think it has to be Tom." He winked at Church. Tom shook his head wearily. "I raise my glass to a hero in the making. A *legend*."

"I think," Tom said pointedly to Church, "your monkey has had more than enough lessons in irony."

Church raised his own flagon ironically. "You are, then, Thomas Learmont."

"Yes."

"And it happened as the story said: you were taken by the Faerie court—?"

"The queen of the Court of the Yearning Heart entertained me until she grew bored with my ways."

"And she gave you the two gifts?"

"Curses, not gifts. It was an act of punishment."

"Punishment for what?"

"For not being . . . entertaining enough. The gods grow bored easily."

Jerzy's mood dampened. "Though it irks me, I fear we have much in common. The Golden Ones like to act as patrons, sometimes friends, even lovers, but they are cruel masters and they have only their own best interests at heart."

"But being able to see the future—" Church began.

Tom shook his head. "To see the misery of growing old, the indignities, the countless occasions of pain and suffering that lie ahead for yourself, your loved ones, your friends? To see your own death? To know when and how and have it haunt your dreams? There is a reason why man was made to drift through his days in ignorance."

Church could now understand the bitterness he sensed in Tom. "What incentive is there to do anything if you know exactly what's going to happen?" he asked.

"Ah, it is not as simple as that, as if anything is. I see static images laid out before me, not live in all their multifaceted glory. It is like walking through an endless gallery where each painting shows a different scene of something that lies ahead. I have no idea how they relate, how any of them come to be. I know not if they are true representations or a warped perspective of what is yet to come. Yet they haunt me still."

"But what you saw led you to seek us out?"

"To seek *you* out."

Church weighed up whether he really wanted to ask the question. "What did you see?"

Tom weighed his reply just as carefully. "A stark choice: between humanity being freed of its shackles, or being confined to the mud for evermore. A war that could destroy men and gods. And you as the deciding factor."

"That's the big picture. What did you see for me?"

For the first time there was a glimpse of sympathy in Tom's eyes. "I think you know the answer to that," he said.

The lull that followed was heavy, and it felt as if the whole of the bar had grown still. Jerzy clapped an arm around Church's shoulders. "Hope, good friend, is the key that unlocks many a door, and we carry it around with us always."

"All right," Church said to Tom. "You're the man with the answers. What do we do now?"

"Now," Tom said, "we prepare to take the upper hand in the coming war."

CHAPTER FIVE
THE SWORDS OF ALBION

1

Venice, 26 December 1586

Fog blanketed the city by the lagoon, but even its chilly, damp embrace could not douse the hot emotions. The carnival was in full swing. Music swept out across Venice from the Piazza San Marco where hundreds of costumed and masked revellers danced in wild abandon or engaged in the subtle art of seduction. Before the Basilica of St Mark the Evangelist, with its towers and dome reaching up to the sky to denote God's glory, men drank wine by the bottle and laughed loudly enough to drown out the fiddle players. Further into the shadows of the ornate building, couples kissed and slipped their hands beneath the folds of each other's clothes, their masks hiding their identities even from themselves.

The Venetian Republic was at the height of its power. The wealthy enjoyed unparalleled access to all the best that life had to offer, free from the threat of war and suffering. And the carnival was the time when they could indulge themselves to the limit, unrestricted by the rules of society.

It was also the time when the boundary between the human world and all other worlds blurred, when mystery and magic ruled and anything could happen.

2

Through the crowds of carousing people moved a man in a dragon mask and a black and gold doublet and breeches with a garter of fine silk from Granada. With him was a woman, her arm looped through his, wearing a cat mask and a dress of deepest scarlet stiff with jewels and embroidery that set off the dusky gold tint of her skin. She paused to watch a skull-masked man in a black costume painted with white bones.

"How do you Fragile Creatures cope with the constant presence of death?" Niamh asked. "Living in its shadow can only bring fear, and that is so debilitating as to leach all pleasure from daily existence, thus removing the very reason for being."

"If you know you're going to die there's no point worrying about it." Church scanned the crowd, but the masks and costumes were so elaborate it was impossible to tell what he was seeing. "You have to make the most of what you've got. Make things good for yourself. More importantly, make things good for the people who come after you so they can lives their lives with a little less pain and suffering."

"How curious," Niamh mused.

"Death focuses the mind. If you don't have to die, you don't have to drive yourself to achieve things quickly because there's always plenty of time. The result is that nothing ever gets done. You drift along, saying, 'Tomorrow, tomorrow, tomorrow.' Life becomes an endless stream of nothing. Frittered away. Worthless. Meaningless. Death gives life meaning."

Niamh observed a trio with lute, viol and recorder accompanying a madrigal. "So you are saying death is good?"

"I'm saying it's the piece in the tapestry that makes the picture complete."

Niamh tapped her toe to the music, deep in thought. "If what you say is true," she began, "then rather than being at the centre of Existence, my people are . . . unnecessary. Pointless. Whatever meaning exists in the great sphere of things can only be divined, and defined, by Fragile Creatures. Death, then, is your curse and your gift." She gave a hollow laugh. "And from that comes the sole conclusion that Fragile Creatures lie above the Golden Ones and not below."

"Crazy, isn't it?" Church said with an irony that Niamh did not register.

Church's attention was drawn by a colourful puppet show before which a group of children sat rapt. The puppetmaster rose up eight feet or more, his long black robes hiding whatever stilts he wore. His white mask featured an enormous nose that arched out like a bird's beak. The puppets were the most amazingly lifelike that Church had ever seen, and it was only when he looked closely that he saw there were no strings. As he tried to see how the illusion was created, the puppetmaster made a flamboyant gesture towards him, and Church realised with shock that his height was entirely natural.

Church turned to Niamh. "Not all of these people are human."

"The denizens of the Far Lands take the opportunity to mingle amongst Fragile Creatures when they can do so undiscovered. Many have a deep affection for the Fixed Lands, and even for your kind. Some come for entertainment. And some for sport."

Church could see she was right. Beautiful men and women with the golden skin of the Tuatha Dé Danann were dancing so gloriously that their feet barely touched the ground. A painfully thin man in a tall hat performed magic tricks. A woman with scales watched from the shadows. And there were others unusual in many ways, their true identities hidden behind the fantastic masks and costumes.

"The fabulous and the strange have been a part of your world since your kind first appeared," Niamh said, "guiding your destiny with a gentle push here, a shove there. Influencing your writers and artists and musicians. Whispering in the ears of kings and religious leaders."

Church considered how many great works and events might have been influenced from beyond. Was that guidance, or interference?

"You people do have your advantages. It's weird to be able to understand the Venetian dialect so easily," Church mused. "And when I speak, my brain tells me I'm talking English, but everyone understands me. Don't get me wrong—I'm grateful for the upgrade. But it's still weird."

Niamh ignored him. "If your new friend had not decided this was a time of crucial events we could enjoy the music," she said blithely. "Would one dance hurt?"

Church relented while still keeping one eye on the shifting crowd. "'Friend' is too strong a word for Tom," he said. "I can't help but think he has his own agenda."

Soon they were whirling around the square in one of the formal dances that the locals loved. Niamh's hand was cool in Church's; her smooth cheek brushed his and her lips breathed warmth onto his ear. He realised she was staring at him in a curious manner, her eyes huge and dark. When she saw he had caught her looking, she broke her gaze and then the dance.

"Enough," she said. "These are dark times for both of us, and it is not right to indulge in frivolity."

Nearby the Mocker juggled burning torches for the pleasure of a small crowd. He wore no mask, though none noticed. He caught Church's eye and nodded towards a man in a harlequin costume slipping determinedly through the crowd. Tom followed at a distance, his dour features hidden behind a wolf's-head.

"Looks like Tom's found our man," Church said. "I'll meet you later."

Niamh caught at his sleeve as he moved away. "Take care," she said, and before the words could register she was gone.

3

Lucia loitered alongside the canal where Tom had told her to keep watch. The sounds of revelry were muted there. Nearby, but hidden by the fog, her owl hooted mournfully. Adjusting her mask, which resembled a beautiful doll with pale skin and bright-red cheeks, she considered using an incantation to bring some light to the gloomy, lonely street. She was still amazed at how powerfully her Craft worked now that she was a Sister of Dragons. When she was a child in Sicilia, learning the words and rituals from her mother, who had learned them from her mother before her, she'd had many small successes: controlling small animals, shifting the moods of friends and enemies, altering the balance of fortune slightly. But it had been nothing like what she could do now. Most of the time she felt almost bursting with power, ready to bend even the weather to her will. It was increasingly addictive.

A man in a skull mask and skeleton costume appeared out of the fog and walked by. He nodded to her and continued on his way before halting under an arch, where he gave a short whistle that ended on an interrogatory note.

Within seconds, a man in a dog mask appeared behind Lucia. She sensed his presence and looked around as another man with a clown mask joined him. Lucia's heart beat a little faster. Before she would have been scared, but her confidence in the Craft filled her with bravado.

The three men surrounded her. "A doll," the Skeleton said, "a toy for our play."

"Lay one finger on me and you will live to regret it," Lucia said defiantly.

The three men looked at each other and laughed, their masks making their actions eerie. The Skeleton drew a small knife and moved towards Lucia, who backed to the edge of the canal. Her heels went over the edge and she teetered, only just catching herself. Brief panic scrambled the words of power she had been about to utter, and that made her panic more acute.

"Canal vermin!" she said, not showing it.

The Skeleton brandished his knife.

From the shadows came a bright English voice laced with wit: "Sheath your blade, good brother, for its size only embarrasses you."

A man in a gaudy harlequin costume stepped into the small circle of light cast by the lone torch. He drew a rapier and flexed the tip against the flags. Lucia could see his balletic poise and strength, but the costume made him look like an unthreatening dandy.

"You see, my weapon is *most* impressive," he said.

The Skeleton continued to advance on Lucia while the others drew their swords and turned to face the Harlequin. Before they could attack, he flamboyantly drew a scarlet silk scarf and presented it to them on the palm of his hand. The men stared at it, dumbfounded. Snapping his head to one side, the Harlequin whisked the scarf into the air. A blinding flash burst as phosphorus dust ignited.

Dazzled, the Dog gamely thrust his sword forward, but the Harlequin parried quickly, returned the thrust and disarmed his attacker. As the sword clattered to the flags, the Harlequin cuffed the Dog unconscious with his hilt. The Clown blinked, but had no time to recover. The Harlequin propelled him into the canal with a kick to the chest.

At the same moment Lucia grabbed the Skeleton's arm and twisted it behind his back. A second later he was in the water, too. She flinched as the Harlequin grabbed her hand.

"This doll has a lively attitude," he said. The two attackers distracted him as they attempted to climb out of the canal. "Enough sport with rats. Best not to dally, lest they travel in packs."

The Harlequin flung Lucia over his shoulder and despite her protests ran along the edge of the canal until he found a secluded alley not far from the revelry at the Piazza San Marco. He lowered Lucia gently to her feet and waited for thanks. Instead he received a sharp slap to the face.

"A kiss would have been preferable," he said, rubbing his cheek.

Lucia bristled. "If I wanted your help I would have shouted for a fool."

The Harlequin was baffled. "I saw a lady in distress. Your life or honour—"

"My life and honour are my own. I need no man to protect them."

"So you think," the Harlequin said dismissively.

"So I *know*." Lucia pulled a knife from her dress and shook it at the Harlequin. He didn't flinch.

"Next time I will leave you to your own devices," he said.

"Good."

As he began to walk away, Lucia asked, "What is an Englishman doing here, in enemy territory?"

"You would rather I had been elsewhere," he said sarcastically, "and left you to the hands of your admirers?"

"A question answers a question," she teased. "I fear you have something to hide."

"Enjoy the carnival, my lady."

As the Harlequin made to leave, Lucia leaped forward and attempted to pluck his mask free. The Harlequin grasped it in time.

"This is not the time for unmasking." He waved a cautionary finger.

A whistle like the one the Skeleton had made echoed nearby, but this one was clearly intended for the Harlequin. He gave Lucia a laddish grin. "Anon, fair doll."

Then he was gone, and Lucia realised that behind her annoyance there was intrigue.

4

In the Piazza San Marco two men met on the edge of the revels away from the torchlight. One wore a hawk mask, the other a fish. They looked around uneasily until the Harlequin hurried up.

"We thought Philip's men had got to you," the Hawk said.

"More like the king's women," the Fish added irritably. "Did some doxy take your fancy?"

"A spot of bother," the Harlequin replied. "Nothing to worry you, Mr Fish. Let us make haste. The king's agents are everywhere."

The three men made their way to the Palazzo Ducale, whose grand faµade stood next to the Basilica, the sacred and the profane cheek by jowl. The Palazzo was the residence of the doge, the city's leader, but also contained many other institutions of the Republic's government.

"This way," the Hawk whispered. "The door is unguarded."

"While you were making love, we were doing the job the queen has charged us with," the Fish said tartly.

The Harlequin led the way to the door. "Good Queen Bess has charged us with succeeding, not talking. And if there was gold for chat, Mr Fish, you would be the richest of us all."

The Harlequin and the Fish formed a barrier while the Hawk dropped to his knees to work the lock.

"Remember," the Harlequin whispered, "the *avogaria*, the law offices, are on the first floor, along with the chancellery, the censors and the *Proweditori della Milizia del Mar*. They will be unoccupied. The ballot chamber where the committee meets to elect the doge and the doge's apartments are on the second floor. That is where we must go."

"Hurry now," the Fish said.

The Hawk tutted. "Genius cannot be rushed. What do you say, Will? An unguarded door at a grand palace? Are the Venetians or the Spaniards the true buffoons?"

"Never underestimate the enemy, Mr Hawk. And no real names. My reputation precedes me. Spain has a bounty on my head."

The Hawk chuckled. "England's greatest spy."

"I fail to see how a spy can operate when everyone knows his name," the Fish noted.

The lock clicked, the door swung open. The Hawk held up a triumphant hand. "Applause, now."

The Fish pushed past him. Will the Harlequin helped the Hawk up and they both slipped inside, pushing the door closed behind them. Across the echoing, marble-floored entrance hall they flitted like ghosts from shadow to shadow. Silently, they climbed two flights of stairs to a grand corridor along which a guard walked nonchalantly. The Fish removed his mask to reveal a shock of red hair and a freckled face. He pulled out a blowpipe and waited for the guard to near before blowing a dart into his neck.

Will and the Hawk dashed out to catch the guard before he hit the floor. "Well done, Francis," Will said, removing his mask to reveal an intelligent face topped by curly black hair.

The Hawk followed suit, wiping sweat from his brow. He was barely out of his teens with the red cheeks and heavy jaw of farming stock.

"Keep your lock-picks to hand, Richard," Will hissed. He sprinted quietly along the corridor, counting off the doors. He indicated the fifth, but when Richard dropped to his knees to work the lock, the door swung open at his touch. He looked at Will in puzzlement, who considered this turn of events for a moment before motioning for them all to enter.

Will closed the door behind them. The room was still and dark apart from one shaft of light from the sole unshuttered window. It illuminated a pedestal with a glass case atop it. In it was a black wooden box.

"There it is," Will said softly.

Richard was filled with awe. "The Box of Anubis," he said in hushed tones, "containing—"

"A plague that can devastate an empire." Francis could not tear his eyes from the box. "Recovered from the sands of Egypt by Spanish marauders."

"So Dee says," Will noted sarcastically. "And Dee claims to talk with angels."

"It would make a fine weapon for England," Francis said. "The Spanish could not threaten us with this in our possession."

"And we cannot threaten the Spanish with it in theirs." Will tried to survey the room, but the conflict of dark and light made it impossible to discern any detail.

"Let us take it and be off. The shadows in this place disturb me," Richard said. He set off for the pedestal.

"Wait!" Will said, reaching out to his comrade.

The quiet of the room was cut by a shrill whistling. Richard's head toppled from his shoulders and bounced noisily across the floor. His body slumped down a moment later.

Will and Francis stared in horror before Francis whispered, "Witchcraft!"

"Spanish deception. Traps." Sickened, Will edged along the wall to a candelabra and lit two candles with his flint. The shadows rushed away from him.

Dropping to a crouch, Will crept forward holding the candelabra above his head. When he neared Richard's decapitated body he noticed a brief glimmer in the air. Slowly, he moved the candles back again. The glimmer reappeared.

"Wires," he said, "strung across the room at different heights, so delicate they are almost invisible." Will followed the line of one wire to where it disappeared into the wall. Holding the candelabra as high as he could, he pressed the wire with one finger until it broke.

High overhead an intricate clockwork mechanism came to life. One of many scythe blades swung down in an arc through the place where Will's neck would have been if he had been standing. It returned to the ceiling. The top of one candle fell off; the lower one remained intact.

"The Spanish have the minds of devils," Francis said. "Would that we were so inventive."

"To the window, Francis," Will said. "We may have need of a rapid exit."

Carefully ducking under any wires, Francis edged around the wall until he could open a window. The sounds of the carnival floated in.

"The rest of the world makes merry while I risk a haircut too far." Using the candle to illuminate the wires, Will manoeuvred through them. A few steps from the pedestal his boot slid on the wooden floor. He caught himself before he fell, balancing on the ball of one foot. His hand brushed against a wire, which trembled but did not break. Will and Francis let out their breath in a sigh of relief.

Reaching the pedestal, Will cautiously opened the glass case. The wooden box had a handle carved in the shape of the head of Anubis, and hieroglyphics were etched on the black wood in gold filigree. Will scanned for other traps, but seeing nothing steeled himself and plucked the box out. He held it up triumphantly.

"How can a plague be trapped inside such a thing?" Francis asked.

"Damnably clever, those pyramid builders."

"I do not believe it."

Will held the box towards Francis. "Would you take a peek inside?"

The door swung open with a clatter and Spanish guards carrying crossbows rushed in and deployed themselves around the room, carefully staying clear of the network of wires.

Will sighed. "'Twas too good to be true. Where is he, then?"

A flamboyant man with a waxed goatee and a red and green diamond costume stepped in. He was charismatic, but with a dark, brooding streak.

"Don Alanzo De Las Posadas," Will said. "'Twas not my wish to draw you from the party."

Don Alanzo smiled. "William Swyfte. How fitting to see you dressed as a clown."

"My friends call me Will, Don Alanzo. Though last time we met you called me 'master.' The wound has healed, I see."

Don Alanzo unconsciously traced a small scar on his cheek. "If I recall, our last fight was curtailed by your cowardly comrades blasting the deck from beneath my feet. You have never bested me in fair swordplay, Swyfte. And you never will."

"Only a matter of time. I will prevail . . . and so will England."

Amused, Don Alanzo pulled back a drape to reveal a lever. He pressed it down and the intricate network of wires rose above head-height. As one, the Spanish guards pointed their crossbows at Will.

Don Alanzo held out a hand. "The box."

"Who told you we were here?"

Don Alanzo waited patiently with hand outstretched.

Will flung the box to Francis. "Quickly, away! I'll hold them off."

Francis caught the box as Will threw himself into the line of crossbows. When the guards didn't fire, Will looked around to see Francis smiling. He was holding out the box for Don Alanzo to take.

"A traitor, then," Will said sadly. "I always gave you the benefit of the doubt, Francis. Remember that." His hand a blur, Will stabbed it towards Francis, propelling the knife that had popped from his sleeve. It embedded in Francis's throat. His look of puzzlement gave way to a frantic gurgling as arterial blood arced across the room. "And remember I saved you a trip to the Tower."

Don Alanzo looked down on Francis's twitching final moments and said simply, "No loss." He turned back to Will with a cruel smile. "Your own death will not be so quick—"

His words were cut short by a distant high-pitched squeaking, drawing closer, and a rattle that was rapidly transforming into a loud drumming.

Will drew his sword while Don Alanzo's attention was turned to the door. It burst open a moment later and an undulating wave of rats rushed across the floor. The guards were attacked by the snapping, shrieking army that swarmed up their legs and into their clothes, tearing at flesh, aiming at eyes, fingers and groins.

Don Alanzo lurched away from the flood, thrusting the back of his hand to his mouth in horror.

Will flexed his rapier and prepared to duel. "You must feel quite at home, Don Alanzo."

Don Alanzo launched a surprise thrust that almost caught Will unawares. "The Devil is with you," he said.

Will pinched his nose. "Your hypocrisy is rank."

As Will advanced, Don Alanzo flicked his rapier above his head. A scythe swept down silently. Will saw it from the corner of his eye and ducked at the last moment, but felt his hair stir in the blade's passing.

"Let us dance, then," he said, all humour now gone.

Don Alanzo and Will launched into a furious duel, thrusting and parrying as they whirled gracefully around the room. With every strike, one or other of them would whisk their rapier up to slice a wire. The scythes swung back and forth in a lethal rhythm, forcing wilder and more athletic steps from Will and Don Alanzo so there was barely time to breathe.

Amidst the cacophonous chaos of attacking rats, clashing swords and swinging scythes, Will registered three people entering the room: the doll-masked woman he had rescued by the canal, a man in a wolf's-head and another in a dragon mask who wielded a sword limned with a faint blue light. Another figure hovered behind them, unrecognisable in the shadows.

Don Alanzo's blade nicked Will's ear: first blood. He could not afford to let his attention wander again, but then he glimpsed something that puzzled him: as Don Alanzo dodged Will's attack, the sway of his hair revealed what appeared to be a large black spider nestling at the nape of his neck.

They continued their equally matched duel for another minute before there was a flash of activity and Will glimpsed the white, grinning face of the figure behind the strangers, which Will was forced to believe was a mask even though its nightmarish qualities were startlingly lifelike. The figure tumbled with breathtaking agility, dodging guards, rats, blades and scythes with ease. With a flourish, he snatched the Anubis Box that Don Alanzo had been clutching to his chest, and with a bound he was at the door and out, his three comrades following rapidly.

Don Alanzo forced Will onto his back foot and then sprinted away in pursuit. Will in turn ran for the window. Wrapped around his waist was a rope with a hook attached to one end. He hoped it would be strong—and long—enough.

5

Church led the others out of the Palazzo Ducale into the swarming Piazza San Marco where Niamh waited. Tom took the Anubis Box from Jerzy and gave it a perfunctory examination as they lost themselves in the crowd.

"Is that what you saw?" Church asked.

Tom nodded. "It's vital to the enemy."

"But you don't know why?"

"Am I expected to do everything around here?" Tom snapped. "Let someone else shoulder the weight for a change."

Since joining the group, Tom's fractious nature had managed to put both Lucia and Jerzy on edge, but the Rhymer's gift of prophecy more than made up for his personality flaws. For the first time Church felt they had gained a little parity with the Army of the Ten Billion Spiders.

"Come," said Lucia. "I grow weary and would rest. Controlling the vermin in such large numbers is exhausting."

They headed away from the crowded piazza into the deserted adjoining streets.

"The boat is waiting," Niamh said, "and then perhaps you will discover whether it was worth risking your lives for this box."

"We'll investigate its merit when we've got time," Church said.

"Perhaps a look inside would help," Niamh noted tartly.

"I would not advise that, my lady." Will stepped from the shadows, the tip of his rapier moving fluidly to Church's throat. "Mine, I think." He took the Anubis Box.

The sound of running feet drew nearer. Don Alanzo and three guards were pushing their way through the crowd. Will backed away slowly, preparing to run.

"You saved my life," Lucia interjected. "Let me now save yours." Will eyed her suspiciously. "We have a boat—"

"Why should I trust you? Anyone who desires this box cannot be wholly pure of heart."

"We have to get it out of the hands of our enemies," Church said.

"An Englishman?" Will was surprised by Church's accent. "Then you stand against Philip of Spain." He thought rapidly before nodding. "Lay on. But the box remains with me, and my sword will make sharp argument with any who disagree."

6

Rowing hard, they reached their vessel moored out in the lagoon ahead of Don Alanzo and his men, and set sail immediately. Will exuded an air of extreme confidence and bonhomie, but Church could tell it masked the steely nature of someone who never let down their guard.

After introductions had been made, Jerzy and Tom set about the steering and navigation with an inordinate amount of bickering that drove Church and Will below deck to find peace.

Lounging in a hammock with one leg trailing, Will observed Church with a wry eye. "It was you who removed the guards from the entrance to the Palazzo Ducale," he said.

"Lucia. She has skill with certain potions and brews."

"And she can deliver them with unerring aim, for who could refuse that one." Will grinned. "So you thought you would let my men do all the hard work and then step in at the last to take the box."

"That's about the size of it."

"Bravo. A man after my own heart. Then I will ask, who are you and why do you want my box? You spoke of thwarting the enemy, but you are not in the queen's employ, unless I am very mistaken."

"You are opposed to King Philip of Spain, who wants Elizabeth removed from the throne and England returned to the fold of Catholicism." Church knew it was a period of great intrigue that had started when Henry VIII had turned his back on Rome and formed of the Church of England. "My enemy is greater than that."

Will was puzzled. "France?"

"Greater than any country. My enemy controls kings and queens. They attempted to control Rome many years ago. They may well now be controlling Philip of Spain."

"To what end?"

Church chose his words carefully. "Power that crosses all borders."

Will nodded. He could understand this. "I am a good judge and you seem like a man of character. I would ask, then, why I have not heard of this enemy, for it is my business to be the queen's eyes across the world."

"A spy," Church noted. Will said nothing. "The enemy operates in the shadows . . . the best way to control. They are the Army of the Ten Billion Spiders—"

Church expected Will to mock, but the spy grew intrigued. "Spiders? That is their totem? I saw what appeared to be a spider on Don Alanzo's neck, here." He tapped his nape.

"That's how they control people. I don't know how it works, but once the spider has been attached, the person does exactly what the Enemy wants but still appears perfectly normal on the surface."

Will considered this, but didn't dismiss it out of hand. "And how did you know my men and I were here this eve to steal the box? Do you spy upon the spies, or was it happenstance—one of God's games?"

Church told Will of Tom's glimpse of the future. He laughed. "The dour one is the hero of the Scots? Why, he would cut his own foot off if you gave him a sword! You spin a strange tale, Master Churchill. I may not wholly believe you, but then I consort with a man who speaks with angels and uses the *elixir vitae* to change base metal into gold."

"And how did you find out about the box?"

"Why, from that self-same friend of angels—Doctor John Dee. You have heard of him, of course."

Church knew Dee had been a controversial figure with a reputation as a black magician and astrologer to Queen Elizabeth I. But Church guessed Will's association with the man was due to Dee's work as one of England's senior spies, who always signed his communiqués "007." In between spy missions and magic, he had invented ciphers, introduced the English-speaking world to Euclidean geometry and developed state-of-the-art navigational techniques. But Church was sure that by this year he had fallen on hard times.

"Isn't he out of favour with the court?" Church asked.

"He is out of favour with the God-fearing men and women of England who have increasingly taken it upon themselves to hang many a black magician or witch, or those they perceive as such, without recourse to the magistrate. Nor is he in favour with the Archbishop of Canterbury, who keeps an eye out for God in this world," Will added sarcastically. "Dee now spends his time abroad, in the employ of rich men, desperately seeking his fortune."

"But he still carries out the queen's work?"

Will smiled. "Dee received word of the box from I know not where. And I was dispatched to retrieve it for England. I am to return it to Dee."

"And Dee says it contains a plague?"

"Dee *says*. Only Dee would know."

"Then we'd better ask him, hadn't we?" Church said. "Where is he?"

7

In the distance, the Carpathian Mountains soared up, black and threatening. In contrast, Krakow stood beautiful and cultured beneath a cloudless night sky lit by a crescent moon. It was a good time to be in the thriving metropolis, which was experiencing a golden age at the centre of a prosperous kingdom that stretched from the Black Sea to the Baltic.

Grand gothic buildings loomed over Church and Tom as they waited for Will in the twisting streets at the heart of the medieval town centre.

"This is an amazing place." Church examined the architecture, which appeared more alive than in the carefully preserved modern context in which he had previously encountered the city. "You've got people travelling here from all over Europe to experience the culture, education and religion and then taking what they've learned back with them. Can't you feel something special in the air?"

Tom grunted non-committally. He still ached from the long journey in the coach that Will had commissioned.

On reflection, Church realised he was sensing more than just the rarefied atmosphere of the city. "The Blue Fire is here," he noted. "I can feel it the same way I did at Boskawen-Un and in Italy."

"Of course," Tom said superciliously. "You may know a great deal with your hindsight on the history of the world, but clearly you do not know everything. Legend has it that a dragon with fiery breath was roused from his slumbers in the caverns beneath where the castle stands. King Krak, who tamed the dragon, founded the city here."

"A metaphor."

Tom snorted. "You think the Blue Fire is a big secret known only to such wise and adept personages as yourself. The truth about it, and the places where it is strongest, is written large in the old stories. If you are clever enough to know where to look."

"Do you think that's why Dee came here?"

"I think he is a powerful and knowledgeable man who has, perhaps, been using the energy unconsciously."

Every now and then Church glimpsed a hidden store of knowledge in Tom, secrets and mysteries that made his agenda difficult to read.

"You must have learned a great deal while you were in the Court of the Yearning Heart," Church said.

"She encouraged me to learn." Tom's tone suggested dark depths that Church could not fathom.

"Not a wholly enjoyable experience, then?"

"Under the queen's orders I was dissected down to the smallest part of me and then put back together, complete with my new abilities." The horror of his experiences shadowed his face. "My torment is beyond imagination."

"The Tuatha Dé Danann are arrogant and cruel, but I've never known them—"

Tom rounded on Church with blazing eyes. "Then you have never been to the Court of the Final Word! The gods have a secret agenda."

"Even Niamh?"

"All of them. Behind their contempt, they fear us. They will lead us on with smiles and promises of heart's desire, or from simple mischief, but their sole aim is to destroy us."

Church couldn't tell whether Tom was speaking the truth or if it was just the bitterness of his experience.

"Most humans are secure in their blind ignorance," Tom spat, "happy to believe they have reached the summit of God's mountain, when in truth they are mice in a vicious universe filled with predators waiting to pounce at every turn."

There were tears in his eyes, of anger or despair, Church couldn't tell. Will chose that moment to hurry up to them, and Tom looked away.

"Dee has agreed to see you," Will said. "You have ignited his curiosity, Master Churchill."

"Are you coming?" Church asked Tom.

"I will await your return."

As Will led Church into the winding maze of streets, Church glanced back to see Tom standing lonely and forlorn, a hero of legend disguised as a broken man.

8

Even at that late hour, Rynek Glowny, the city's sprawling Grand Square, was alive with men and women taking the air. The ten-acre plaza, the largest in Europe, was beautiful, with tall trees framing the gothic Basilica of the Virgin Mary and the leaning tower of the town hall gleaming like silver in the moonlight. The mood was intensely peaceful. They passed the town hall and headed to the corner of Jagiellonska and Sw. Anny, where the Jagiellonian University stood.

"Dee is a master deceiver," Will noted, his tone respectful. "He spends his days performing magic tricks in the street for money while secretly performing his own work in a room provided for him in one of Europe's most prestigious centres of learning."

Dee's room lay on the second floor of the Collegium Maius, the oldest of the university's colleges. It overlooked a large courtyard surrounded by arcades, with a well at the centre. The room itself was a treasure trove of magical artefacts, crumbling leather-bound books, phials and flasks. A brass telescope stood at the open window, while skulls and bones, powders and liquids, parchments and maps cluttered every available space on walls, tables, desks and chairs.

Dee stood poring over a volume, his thin frame and grey skin turning him into one of the relics that filled his quarters. He wore threadbare purple robes and a matching pill hat. His wild, white beard added to the image of eccentricity, but behind his small spectacles his eyes were sharply incisive.

"Is this the one of whom you spoke?" Dee came over, never once taking his eyes from Church's face. He took Church's hand in his bony fingers. "Show me the sword."

It took a moment for Church to register what Dee was asking, and then he pulled Llyrwyn partway from its scabbard. The Blue Fire flickered brightly along the exposed blade, responding to the city's potent atmosphere.

"In the secret knowledge of the adepts there is talk of a great hero who carries a sword like this. He has many names—Jack the Giantkiller, the King Beyond the Water . . . He always appears at the darkest hour of England's history to fight for right, before once again disappearing into the mists." Dee searched Church's face. "Are you this hero?"

"Never believe legends. You'll only be disappointed."

Dee smiled and gently patted the back of Church's hand. Lounging in a large wooden chair, Will looked bemused. "A great hero? You hide your light under a bushel, Master Churchill."

"Enough of your banter, young Swyfte," Dee said. "You are like a bird, always chittering and chattering." Dee swept a pile of papers off a table to reveal the Anubis Box, and set a candle nearby. "So small and insignificant, yet it has the power to destroy us all."

"Does it really contain a plague?" Church asked.

Dee harrumphed and glanced at Will, who was now peeling an apple with his knife. "That was for the benefit of Master Swyfte and his men so they would not be tempted to look inside."

"I am cut to the heart," Will said flatly. "Such a lack of trust from one of my own comrades."

"What *is* inside it, then?" Church moved closer. In the still air of the room, he thought he could feel a deep cold radiating from the box.

"I do not know," Dee said.

"Then how—"

"The angels told him," Will said wryly.

Dee flapped an irritated hand at Will. "There is no point in discussing esoteric matters with a knave immersed so fully in the pleasures of the flesh. But you . . ." He motioned to Church. "You understand the power of the Azure Flame and the force it represents that joins all things, living and inanimate, known and unknown." He did not wait for an answer. "And you know that there are higher powers that live in that force. You know them. You have seen them."

He rifled through some papers and plucked out a black crystal. "On the twenty-first day of November, in the year of our Lord fifteen eighty-two, an angel came to my study window in the form of a boy and gave me this. The stone provides visions for my good friend and partner Edward Kelley—"

Will raised his eyebrows. Dee picked up a paperweight and hurled it. Will ducked, smiling mischievously.

"There are some who consider Edward a charlatan and a drain on my resources," Dee said pointedly, "but I have seen the evidence of his abilities as a medium with my own eyes. With this stone he brings the angels down to earth. On one occasion, Uriel himself came." His voice rose with passion and he dived into another pile of papers, pulling out a thick sheaf. "The manuscript for my *Liber Logaeth*, detailing all the spells I have used to control them—"

"Perhaps you should also have snapped a leash on them to walk them in the streets like dogs," Will noted.

Dee turned his back on Will to talk directly to Church. "The angels revealed to me such secrets! Of the workings of the Blue Fire, and what can be achieved by any man who can bend it to his will! The Blue Fire is the very essence of Gnostic thought. Gnosticism is the ultimate truth—it shows us the inner workings of everything!"

Church was intrigued by the eccentric old man, but Will clearly had little time for Dee's ramblings. "Ah, Gnosticism," he said with irony. "How many times have I heard this little speech? Five? A hundred?" He did a plausible impression of Dee's cracking voice. "Gnosticism is a quest for redeeming knowledge and a quest for oneself."

Dee ignored him. His excitement was palpable. "In the Zohar of the Qaballah we are told of a king with a casket of fabulous treasures who ensured they were guarded by a poisonous serpent. The king entrusted a friend with the secret of how to seize the casket without coming to any harm. The Blessed Holy One, the Qaballah tells us, acted in the same way when he placed a serpent near his sanctuary, telling only his friends the angels the secret of how to remove the serpent and approach the Shekinah. The parable is clear to all eyes: the serpent is not autonomous but acts as God's agent."

"Not quite how the Good Book would have it," Will said.

"Then the Good Book is wrong!"

Church had been allowing Dee to indulge himself, but the story brought echoes of the Fabulous Beast he had encountered beneath Boskawen-Un. "God's agent?" he asked.

"Ah!" Dee raised a finger. "But who is God? The God of the Jews, the God of the Bible, the God of Islam, the God of the ancient Britons? All of them? Or none?"

"He will go on like this all night if you let him," Will said wearily. "To the point, old man, before my hair turns as white as yours."

"The point! The point! The point is that the angels told me of this box and the terrible thing it contained. A thing that would result in the destruction of all there is."

Church eyed the Anubis Box. It was too small to contain anything physically threatening, but he had learned that danger came in surprising shapes. "What should we do with it?"

Dee's elation evaporated. "I intended to ask the angels one more time, but they have not answered my call. I fear there is something amiss in the spheres . . . The angels are lost. If we are to decipher this mystery, we must find the angels."

Will covered his face. "You are dispatching me on another fool's errand. Good Lord, spare me."

Dee smiled slyly. "You do not wish to return to London?"

Will peered at Dee from between his fingers. "You know how to torment me, old man."

Dee pulled out another sheaf of papers. "I must write you a word of power. It is the only way to bend the angels to your will. But you must guard it with your life and repeat it to no man."

"Yes, yes, with my life. With Master Churchill's life. Of course. Why not?" Will said with exasperation.

As Church watched Dee search the sheaf of papers, he noticed something curious. "What is that?" he demanded.

"The angels taught me the language of Enoch that Adam spoke before the Fall. This is the Book of Enoch, dictated to Edward while he was in a trance. It reveals the ultimate mysteries of creation."

Church slowly pulled from his pocket the parchment Jerzy had given him after they had escaped from Rome. He had said it had been dictated by one of the members of the Cult of Apollo who had been in a trance. It was the same strange language as that in the Book of Enoch. Lugh's name stood out amongst the odd words.

Dee grabbed it excitedly. "Where did you get this?"

"Do your angels by any chance have golden skin?" Church asked.

9

January was cold and there was snow in the air, yet the sea was surprisingly calm. Church stood on deck, leaning against the rail, his breath clouding, still surprised at the resources on which Will could draw. Lucia stood next to him, shivering in the depths of her woollen cloak.

"This climate is not for me," she said. "If only we could stay in Roma. It is beautiful this time of year." She glanced at Church. "But we go where the Pendragon Spirit calls. I am starting to think this is a curse. We can never have a life of our own. We shoulder the responsibility of all humanity. We fight and suffer and die so that others can live free. Our own desires, our hopes, our need for love . . . they are all secondary."

"Put that way, it's miserable, but from another perspective it's great. Think about it: you get the chance to save the human race. How many people can say that?"

"But the price! Marcus . . . I had only just begun to know him, as our Five came together, and not nearly well enough. There was so much else we had yet to discover about one another." She wiped away a stray tear.

"Death follows us around. We fight for life, and I think, in a way, that draws death to us. But that's just the way it is, Lucia. That's the road we've got to walk. We've been given this wondrous gift, but there's a price. There's always a price."

She peered into his eyes and forced a sad smile. "You remind me so much of Marcus. So strong, so wise——"

"Maybe you're just seeing the Pendragon Spirit in there. I'm not so great. I'm introspective, a brooder . . . I make stupid mistakes." He looked to the horizon. "I'm just lucky I've got someone who loves me and who I love. That's where I get the strength to keep going."

"And you still believe you will see her again?"

"Every morning when I wake I think of Ruth. And yes, I know all the obstacles that lie ahead, but I can't believe I'll never see her again. Without her it would be so easy to walk away from all this struggling——"

"I wish I could have your hope. Sometimes all I see ahead is darkness."

"You don't have to face it alone." Church nodded to Will, who had just emerged from below deck. "He's a good man. And you know, I think he might be a Brother of Dragons, though he doesn't know it yet. I could be mistaken——"

"He is a pig. Arrogant, lascivious . . ." She gave Church a kiss on the cheek, and then laughed. "Perhaps I will teach him some manners!"

She went over to Will, leaving Church to make his way to Niamh, who stood at the prow with Jerzy, staring across the waves. "You appear to be teaching my jester some strange humour," she said.

"He's a good learner. You're lucky to have him."

Niamh ignored Church's pointed comment. "Why will you not tell me what you learned in Krakow?"

"It's too soon."

"I could make you." Jerzy took an unconscious step away from Niamh's side.

"Of course you could."

For a long moment there was only the sound of the wind and the waves.

"I find you infuriating, Jack Churchill."

A flicker of puzzlement crossed Jerzy's face.

"I try my best."

Niamh put a finger to her lips in thought. "Like all my kind, I have found peace in the stability of Existence. We do not perceive time as you do. We *understand* the way things will play out. Consider: standing on a hilltop and looking to the horizon. You can see the lie of the land, but you cannot make out the detail of the landscape. That is how we see what lies ahead. But now . . ." Her voice trailed off uneasily.

"What do you mean?"

"It is as though a great mist lies across my vision."

"You can't see the future any more?"

"It feels as if nothing will turn out the way it is supposed to. All the landmarks are gone. Everything is fluid."

"Is this our enemy's doing?"

"I do not know," she said. "But it scares me."

10

A heavy blanket of snow lay across London's rooftops, and more was falling from the night sky. Inside their homes the residents remained cosy, with candles flickering behind the diamond-pane windows and smoke drifting from the capital's chimneys. But for Church, Will and Tom, even the stamping of their boots could not bring any warmth.

"Why could we not do this in the summertime?" Tom said.

"There is enough warmth in Lucia to keep me roasting like a chestnut through this winter and the next," Will said.

"Make sure you look after her," Church cautioned. He knew Will and Lucia had grown close during the remainder of the sea journey and they had spent the last hour sequestered in Will's room.

"You are like an elder brother, Master Churchill." His laugh gave way to seriousness. "I will take care of her, have no doubt of that."

The snow lent the city a magical air, hiding the refuse-slimed cobbles of Bankside, though occasionally it was splattered with the contents of jordans emptied from upper-storey windows overhanging the narrow street. But the night was far from quiet. It echoed with the cries of criminals chained to the banks of the Thames so they could endure the obligatory washing of three tides; and the brothels, stewhouses and bull and bear pits that lined the street in the Tudor pleasure-quarter of Southwark were awash with raucous clients. Bawdy women hung half-naked from upper windows, urging passers-by to enter, while drinkers stumbled out into the snow in groups as they passed from one inn to another. Here and there, apprentices fought furiously, spraying blood from cracked noses and split lips. Every conversation was carried on at a bellow.

Church saw Tom watching with horror; the city was a far cry from his rural Scottish borderlands. "The whole city is drunk, all the time," Church explained. "Nobody drinks water. It's strong ale for breakfast, dinner and supper."

"Then the sooner we are out of this hellish place, the better," Tom said.

They followed the course of the river to Borough High Street. The main southern thoroughfare out of the City was filled with overflowing inns. Here Will and Church wore their swords prominently to deter the cutpurses who preyed on drunken travellers.

St Thomas Street was quieter. The printers, potters, glaziers, leather workers, brewers, sculptors and other craftsmen who had filled the streets around the hospital to avoid the restrictions of the City of London guilds had all shut up for the night.

Finally they arrived at London Bridge. Church was excited to see it before the massive alterations of the eighteenth century, with houses and shops built up cramped and towering on the span of the bridge. At any moment, the bulky structure looked as if it might crash into the slow, murky waters of the Thames beneath.

The drawbridge on the southern side had been partly raised when the gatehouse closed at nightfall. The sickening fruity smell of decomposition filled the air from the heads of two now-unrecognisable traitors spiked on the gateposts.

"Would it not have been wiser to come during the day when we could have walked onto the bridge with ease?" Tom said.

"As a hero of the realm, my face is well known in polite circles, and even amongst some of the uneducated mass," Will said. "It would not do for me to walk into the home of Dee's contact as bold as you please."

"How are you planning to get onto the bridge?" Church pulled his cloak tighter as the gusting icy wind brought a heavier fall of snow.

"A good spy knows the best work demands rigorous preparation." Will scanned the lit windows of the upper storeys overlooking the drawbridge and selected one. "Now keep watch. Make sure no idle eyes observe." As Church and Tom scanned the road running away from the bridge, Will gave a rapid three-note whistle blast. A moment later a rope weighted with lead flew from one of the windows and over the lip of the drawbridge to crash onto the road.

"Now," Will said, "we climb."

"I'm not climbing that!" Tom eyed the slick rope as it soared over the freezing waters.

"Then stay here, friend. Though it is said no man caught on this road after midnight lives to see the dawn."

Weighing his chances, Tom glanced back to the dark network of streets on the city's southern side. When he looked back towards the bridge, Will was already speedily climbing the rope into the gusting snow.

"Do you want to hang on to me?" Church asked.

"Don't be ridiculous! I am not some feeble woman."

Church found the climb hard going. His fingers were soon frozen numb, and intermittent gusts of wind blasted hard enough to threaten to rip him off. The grey waters churned around the bridge's pillars far below; he would not survive a fall into their icy depths. The physical exertions of his life over the past few months had hardened his muscles, but he was glad when he crawled through the tiny window and flopped onto dirty wooden boards. He quickly jumped to his feet to help Tom who followed a few moments later, his face rigid with fear. Church was proud of him, but knew Tom would be insulted if anything was said.

Will was waiting with another man who held a lamp aloft. The stranger had sensitive features and a wry turn to his mouth. His curly hair was cut in the current fashion and his beard and moustache were well trimmed and waxed. His clothes were also fashionable and expensive.

"Another spy?" Tom spat.

"An ally," Will replied obliquely. "Marlowe, meet Master Churchill and True Thomas, who hails from the brutish wilderness in the north."

Marlowe gave an ironic bow. "The pleasure is mine," he said.

Church realised who he was: Christopher Marlowe, the playwright, one year off writing *Doctor Faustus* and six years away from being stabbed to death during an argument in an inn. If Church recalled correctly, Marlowe couldn't have been in London long, having been recruited into the secret service by Sir Francis Walsingham while he was at Cambridge University.

"Enough talk," Tom snapped. "Let's to business."

"A man after my own heart," Marlowe said. "Our Lord awaits us."

Marlowe led the way down cramped, winding stairs and out onto the road leading across the bridge, where the snow lay thick and unspoiled. The houses and shops rose up high on either side, obscuring all views of the river. Marlowe took them to a nondescript door that lay between a butcher's and a milliner's.

"I shall wait here to ensure no one follows," Marlowe said. "Make haste, for I would not like to be found frozen cold come the morn."

"And then *Tamburlaine* would never be finished," Will joked with clear affection for the young man.

Inside, the furnishings were much more opulent than the exterior suggested. A small entrance hall opened onto a sitting room with expensive chairs and desks. Tapestries and paintings hung the walls and a fire roared in the grate.

A man of around thirty with an acne-scarred face warmed himself while sipping a glass of wine. He came over and clapped Will heartily on the shoulders.

"Robert," Will said. "It has been too long."

"It is good to see you, Will. I have spent far too long north of the border in the land of my grandfather."

"We have another of your family's countrymen here." Will introduced Tom and Church. "This is Sir Robert Balfour. We chased the Devil round the streets of Cambridge together."

"It is a mystery how we ever got an education." Balfour grew grave. "If Dee told you what lies in the catacombs, then these are dark times. That was a secret supposed to outlive us by many a generation."

"A device to communicate with angels," Will said.

Balfour snorted. "Dee and his angels. Gods, Will. Gods. There is more than one secret here, but all point to the true history that lies behind the one we know: of this country's secret communion with the Fair Folk over the years." He glanced at Church and Tom. "These can be trusted?"

"On my life, Robert."

"Then come. Let us venture into the bowels."

Lifting a lamp, Balfour took Church, Tom and Will into a panelled drawing room and then through a hidden door to a flight of stone steps that wound down into the dark. Church struggled to comprehend the exterior architecture as they descended, and it was only when the stone walls grew wet to the touch and drops of moisture began to fall with echoing splashes that he realised the steps must lead down into one of the pillars that supported the bridge, and then deeper still, beneath the river bed itself. Tom had clearly reached the same conclusion, for he was starting to grow uneasy.

"Will the stones hold?" he said. "The water drips through as if the first sign of a coming deluge."

"It sluices out into vast chambers below," Balfour said. "It has stood for three hundred and fifty years and will stand for hundreds more. In this construction, you will find the greatest secrets of the master masons, passed down from Solomon himself."

"Who built it?" Church was amazed by construction skill that would have stunned modern engineers.

"Robert's family can trace their line back to the Order of the Poor Knights of Christ and the Temple of Solomon," Will said, "and his kin have guarded their secrets with religious fervour since those days."

"On the thirteenth day of October, thirteen hundred and seven, that damnable Philippe of France set about the destruction of the Order," Balfour said. "Eighteen galleys left the Order's naval base at La Rochelle filled with Templar wealth and the accumulated mass of their wisdom, not just from the Holy Land but from across the known world. Of the two, this wisdom was the greater prize."

The stairwell opened out into a vaulted chamber with more rooms leading off through dark doorways on every wall. Water dripped from the low ceiling to puddle and run into drains set into the flagged floor.

"In this repository was placed one full quarter of the Templars' wisdom, including many of the magical artefacts they recovered from ancient sites across the lands," Balfour continued.

"And here we shall find the talisman that Dee has directed us to retrieve?" Will mused.

"A device to communicate with the gods and, for a short time, to bend them to your will." Balfour nodded gravely.

"Why has this not been gifted to the queen?" Will asked.

"Too dangerous an object to be allowed to fall into the hands of any particular political or religious sect," Tom noted.

"The Fey have had many dealings with our rulers across the long centuries," Balfour said. "'Tis written that kings and queens of Faerie have banqueted with our monarchs since the Flood. Indeed, one is said to be in our queen's court even now, kept in chambers far from prying eyes. 'Tis said she advised Sir Edmund Spenser before his trip to Munster. Some stood with

William of Normandy and turned the tide of battle. Others brought much amusement to Henry and his father before him. But the true dangers were revealed long ago when one of the gods went mad and had to be bound beneath Rosslyn Chapel not far from fair Edinburgh, where it is said his screams can be heard to this day. No man must have that power, nor no country, though they call me traitor."

"Yet you're letting us have it," Church noted.

"For a while only, and it must be returned. These are dark times, if the word I received from Dee is to be believed. Desperate times require desperate measures."

"Where does it lie?" Will peered into the gloom.

"There is a labyrinth. The Templars protected their treasures well. But stay left and you will find your way through to the repository. The artefact you require is a crystal skull. Legends say it was fashioned in the land of the gods themselves, and placed here as a lure for foolish mortals who chose to bring the powers to their home." They all fell silent for a moment until Balfour said, "Dee's coded letter spoke of a box? Some kind of doomsday weapon?"

"We have sent it north for safekeeping."

"To the safe house?"

"None would think to look for it there," Will said.

"Good," Balfour replied. "It would be dangerous to have the box and skull in close proximity."

A distant bell rang.

"What is that?" Tom asked.

"A warning." Balfour looked concerned. "An intruder in my home above."

"Marlowe waits without," Will said.

"Then I fear for good Kit's wellbeing. The alarm is in my inner sanctum. Go on ahead. I will return to deter any unwanted guests." Balfour left the lamp with them and slipped back into the stairwell.

Tom shivered. "This place makes my lungs ache. What loon would build rooms beneath a river?"

"No loon, but someone foolish as a snake." Will lifted the lamp and headed towards the first opening on the left.

The catacombs were as oppressive and confusing as they had feared. Every chamber was exactly like the last, with numerous doors leading off to other chambers, all alike. Church guessed the chambers formed some kind of extensive honeycomb structure where a man could wander for days or weeks without finding a way out. He marvelled again at the expertise required to construct such a maze in such an inhospitable place.

Water dripped everywhere they went, but in some places it streamed through the roof in a sheet, and at one point they had to wade knee-deep through a slow-moving current. Each new obstacle raised Tom's anxiety another notch, until Church could hear his wheezing breath above the drips and echoes.

But Balfour's guidance saw them through, and after a good half-hour they came to a large chamber bisected by rusty iron bars like a cell door. Beyond was a cornucopia of gold and precious jewels, chests, books, statues and other artefacts the purpose of which Church could not divine.

"Riches beyond measure," Will noted. "Why, I could buy my own country with these."

"Thinking of leaving the queen's service?" Church asked.

"We all have a calling, Master Churchill, and mine is to be a spy—the best in the world." Will gripped the rusted bars and peered with a faint yearning at what lay beyond. "I could no more give that up than you could turn your back on your obligation."

Church was sick of hearing of his obligations and responsibilities, but he said nothing.

"I have travelled far and wide," Will continued. "I have slit throats and duelled and poisoned. I have watched and listened and reported back. I have personally halted ten Catholic plots to take my mistress's life. The Catholics will never rest until England has returned to the call of Rome, and so I can never rest." His usual charismatic smile looked wan in the lamplight. "It is a hard life and a brutal one, and there are times when I would wish to give it up for a quiet life in the country, and a wife and a family. But this is the life we have, Master Churchill, and we do the best we can."

Church couldn't answer him.

"Will you get the damnable gates open so we can get out of here?" Tom snapped.

"Patience, True Thomas." Will moved the lamp along the railings until a shimmer of light revealed the crystal skull. "There. Now, where is the lock—and the key?" He looked around, but saw no sign.

"It would have helped if Balfour had told us how to get in there," Tom said with irritation.

"I think he hoped to follow us," Church said.

"And it troubles me that he is not here now." Will continued to search the length of the railings and the points where they disappeared into the stone walls. "If we try to tear them out—even if we could—we will have the roof down on us, and the river soon after."

"We can count on the Templars not to have made this easy," Church said.

"Their reputation speaks of tricks and traps," Will said. "Even if we find the key, we must beware."

"Enough talk!" Tom raged, his claustrophobia overwhelming him. "I cannot spend another moment in this place!"

He stormed to the shadows at the rear of the chamber where Church could hear him splashing back and forth through pools of water. After a moment he fell silent before calling out, "Here!"

Church and Will found him standing against the rear wall in one corner, pointing to the flags. Church looked at the floor and saw nothing at first, then finally made out a black square of water where one of the flags had been removed.

Tom held out a wringing wet sleeve. "It goes down an arm's length, then doglegs towards the railings."

"A tunnel to a lever, perhaps," Will mused.

"That's crazy. It's barely big enough to get my shoulder through," Church said. "It might just be a drain. You don't know how far the tunnel goes or if you could hold your breath for that long. You wouldn't even be able to turn around. You'd have to scramble backwards, underwater, in the dark."

Tom was ghost-white in the lamplight. He brought a trembling hand to his mouth.

"It is all we have," Will said. "We must try."

Church steeled himself. "I'll go." He began to unbuckle his sword belt.

Will caught his arm. "This is my place. My obligation. I'll do it now, before I have time to think again."

Will took a deep breath and then, before Church could protest, forced himself down through the hole.

11

Freezing water numbed Will's face and body in one shocking instant, and then he was engulfed in complete darkness. Using his hands for eyes, he felt for the dogleg Tom had described. It took an effort to twist his body around the sharp bend, and he knew then how difficult it would be to repeat the manoeuvre in reverse.

The tunnel was barely wide enough to contain his shoulders. His head bumped against the stone repeatedly and his elbows and knees dragged; only a hair's breadth separated him from becoming jammed in the restrictive space.

He could hold his breath for at least the count of ninety, the result of childhood days swimming in the sea off Kent. But if he continued to forty-five, would he not retreat at a much slower rate? What, then, should he set as his target, for his life depended on it? The first edge of panic increased its pressure on his mind.

Dragging himself forward, feeling ahead in the numb blackness, the water pressed as hard around him as an iron coffin. An ache began in his lungs. *Twenty-nine, thirty, thirty-one.* How much longer? He must have covered half the distance between the rear wall of the chamber and the treasure, locked under the stone on which they had walked. He dragged himself on. *Thirty-nine, forty, forty-one.* It was time to turn back or he would die there, horribly, fighting to hold on and hold on and hold on, until he could do so no longer, and then he would suck the icy water into his lungs, thrashing, unable to move backwards or forwards, wedged . . .

His fingers closed on a protrusion on the wall: a handle of some sort. Will grasped it and yanked down. At first it didn't move. He increased the pressure and it shifted slightly. Manoeuvring himself to gain leverage against the walls, he used both hands and all his strength.

The lever came down. Instantly, Will was driving himself backwards, the insane panic close to breaking through despite his best efforts. *Fifty-three, fifty-four, fifty-five.* He pulled himself along with the toes of his boots and his elbows, moving too slowly, barely moving at all.

His lungs were on fire, his throat as thin as a taper. Stars flashed across the dark inside his eyes. He was inching back. When he reached ninety he stopped counting.

His boot heels came up hard against something and at first he thought he'd gone insane, until he realised he had reached the upward shaft to the treasure chamber. But he had no more air left, and the urge to open his mouth and breathe in was almost overwhelming.

He tried to twist his legs around, could not. He forced himself, became jammed in the turn. He started to flail. He began to open his mouth to gasp.

Hands grabbed his ankles and yanked him upwards with such force that his flesh was torn against the stone. He smashed his head, blacked out momentarily, and then he was dragged out roughly onto the flags, where he sucked in burning air in huge mouthfuls. Finally, the darkness lifted from his eyes.

"Bloody hell. I thought you were done for," Church said.

It took another moment before Will could pull enough rational thoughts together to speak. "A little swim. 'Twas nothing." He steadied himself and forced a smile. "But I thank you for your aid, Master Churchill. You caught a fine fish today."

Will accepted Church's hand to help him to his feet, and he tried to contain the shivering that came as much from the shock as the cold. Yet as he glanced towards the treasure he saw the ordeal had been worthwhile. The gate was raised; the crystal skull beckoned.

12

The room in the farmhouse that doubled as the village tavern was small but warm. Lucia sat next to the fire, half-thinking of Church and Will, while watching her owl perched on the table. He had come when the Pendragon Spirit had first woken within her, and though she couldn't fathom the owl's depths, it had aided her on many occasions. Earlier she had dozed in front of the fire's warm glow and crackle and dreamed that the owl transformed into a man with eerie bird-like features who had watched over her when she slept. It was both comforting and disturbing.

Stretching, she went to the window, hoping Church and Will would join them soon. She missed male company, and the Mocker, who shared the adjoining room with Niamh, did not count. The panes were frosted, so she threw the windows open to take a restorative breath of the cold night air.

The fields all around glowed in the moonlight under a covering of heavy snow. Myddle was a small settlement deep in the Shropshire countryside where the inhabitants hacked out a harsh living in the common fields and hedged pastures. At its centre was the medieval Church of St Peter, and it had once boasted its own red sandstone castle. It had fallen into ruin during the 280 years since it had been built to protect the locals against the Welsh raiders who came down from the hills Lucia could see in the distance. Lucia understood why Will had dispatched them to the safe house there with the Anubis Box: the isolation of empty fields and woods was all-encompassing.

Just as Lucia prepared to return to the fire she saw movement. A figure trudged through the snow across the fields to the edge of Myddlewood. Lucia could tell from the upright posture and green cloak that it was Niamh.

Lucia's suspicion of the goddess had not diminished and so she grabbed her cloak and boots and set out in pursuit. The night was bitter and her breath clouded as she hurried past the church and along the winding lane out of the village. Niamh's tracks were clear in the deep snow, but the going was hard and Lucia stumbled several times.

As she closed on Myddlewood, she became aware of a faint golden light and the distant mutter of voices. Oddly, the temperature felt as though it was growing warmer and her breath no longer clouded.

There was a gathering at the point where the fields met the woods. Lucia kept low along the line of the hedge until she reached a place where she had a clear view. At first what lay before her faded in and out of her perception: a dream, a shifting shadow. Even when it fell into relief there was a magical aspect to it, as though it was not quite there, or on the edge of forming.

Niamh stood before a group of around thirty Tuatha Dé Danann. They were all tall, proud and beautiful, but behind them was a man with the head of an ass, another who resembled a giant toad, a woman with horns, another with scales. Tiny beings that could stand on the palm of her hand fluttered in and out of the stark branches like fireflies.

The leader of the group wore an Elizabethan doublet and hose in deepest purple, studded with tiny diamonds that shimmered as he moved. He wore a headdress fitted with ram's horns. Beside him was a woman as beautiful as she was otherworldly, with auburn hair and a dress of ultramarine.

"We welcome you to this last gathering of the Seelie Court here in the Fixed Lands, sister," the leader said in a voice like the wind in the trees.

Niamh bowed her head gracefully. "It is always an honour to attend to the king and queen of the Seelie Court."

"You are far from your own court, sister, in these wild lands." The queen regarded Niamh curiously. "Have you also developed a taste for the pleasures and enchantments of Fragile Creatures?"

Niamh chose her words carefully. "I am intrigued by their machinations."

"Ah," the queen replied. "That is always how it begins."

"Of all the twenty great courts, ours has the longest relationship with Fragile Creatures," the king said. "We observed them when they crawled, mud-stained and wild-eyed, from caves. We danced with them in the days of the tribes. We tricked and teased, loved and lost. There are many in our court for whom the Fixed Lands pluck a string that resonates deep in the heart." The king looked out wistfully across the snowbound fields. "We will miss these dreaming lands of wild emotion and tranquil thoughts."

"The Seelie Court's fondness for Fragile Creatures is well known in the Far Lands," Niamh said.

"And despised by some," the queen noted. "Misunderstood."

"Then why do you abandon these green glades?"

"The seasons are changing." The king held out one slender hand. Gold dust appeared to drift from his fingertips, and where it fell on the ground the snow retreated and the green vegetation of summer appeared. "An Age of Reason is approaching. There will be no place in the minds and hearts of Fragile Creatures for ones such as us."

"A sad time, then," Niamh said.

"Yes, there is sadness," the king replied, "but in the spirit of our court we will meet this parting with celebration and joy. This beauteous moonlit night is a time for music to enchant the heart, for dance and play and food and drink and perfume and wonders beyond imagination. No more words now, sister. Let us leave behind this land we love with a festival of pleasure."

At that moment, Lucia thought she could make out scores, if not hundreds, of the otherworldly beings stretching deep into the heart of Myddlewood, fading in and out of view as if they were falling somewhere between this world and the next.

The king held up his hand and when it fell, the air was suddenly filled with the most glorious and mesmerising music Lucia had ever heard. The members of the court began a dance that started slowly, but then grew faster and wilder as the music increased in intensity. Rich scents to excite the passions floated out from the now-summery branches, and magic held sway over all.

Lucia was caught up in the wonder of the vision, entranced by the music and the perfume, and it felt to her as if time had stopped, and there was only an everlasting now filled with astonishment and delight.

Engulfed by sensation, Lucia fell into a trance that would eventually become a deep, comforting sleep where the winter cold could not touch her. And so she was not aware of the five riders who came across the rolling countryside towards Myddle, scurrying black shapes moving across the pristine white.

Shivering after his immersion in the freezing waters, Will wrapped himself in the cloak he had abandoned and headed into the Templar treasure-store. Church watched him, marvelling at his bravery and hoping he could live up to his own obligations to the same degree.

Tom stared at the crystal skull. "I have heard tell of many of these artefacts in the Far Lands. They are said to scream at the touch and bring disaster."

"Then touch not." With a flourish, Will pulled a sheet of black velvet from the depths of his cloak. He plucked up the skull and wrapped it tightly.

As he did so, the rusty iron gate dropped down a foot from where it had been raised to the ceiling. They all started. "It must be on a timed release," Church said. "A drop every minute or so until it's back in place."

"Better we do not linger, then," Will said, "lest we become three more treasures to add to this fine hoard."

"You flatter yourself, Swyfte. More dull lead than shining gold." Don Alanzo stood at the entrance to the chamber with three other men more brutish than the refined Spanish aristocrat. Behind them, Church could just make out another figure waiting in the shadows. The sense of threat was almost supernaturally powerful.

Will's hand went to his sword, but before he could draw it the three thugs raised their crossbows. Will relaxed, but Church could see him searching for a solution to the predicament. "Where is Rab?" he said. "And Kit?"

"Poor guards for such a remarkable treasure." Don Alanzo could barely contain his smugness.

In his face Church saw something that triggered a revelation. "You let us retrieve the skull for you."

"We have been observing your little group since you first set foot on English soil. Our spies are everywhere." Don Alanzo nodded and his men marched forward. They clubbed Will and Church to the floor. Tom got down willingly. The men tied Will, Church and Tom's hands behind their backs and strapped them to a pillar as Don Alanzo retrieved the crystal skull from Will and slipped it into a leather pouch at his waist.

The iron gate dropped another foot. Don Alanzo stooped to walk under it, where he was met by the figure that had been waiting in the shadows. Church was shocked to see it was the silver-masked spider-thing that had controlled the Redcaps in Cornwall.

"Your master?" Will asked.

Don Alanzo swept an introductory arm towards the silent, black-robed thing. "Apologies for my lack of good manners. This is Salazar, a wise and powerful man who will ensure that the rule of Rome returns to this godless land."

"He's not human," Church said.

One of the thugs aimed a hefty kick at the back of Church's head. When his vision cleared, Don Alanzo and Salazar were already at the door. "And now," Don Alanzo said with a bow, "we only need to retake the Anubis Box and this business will have an end."

The gate dropped another foot; it was now only two feet above the ground.

As the Spaniards left, Church saw Salazar's blank silver mask turn directly towards him. In the movement, Church sensed a terrible note of finality.

Will strained at his bonds as the gate fell again. "Do not give up hope. This rope has been tied by a child."

Church's own bonds were too tight even to wriggle his hands.

"Hurry!" Tom snapped. "I do not wish to spend eternity with you two."

"I would prefer a beautiful woman," Will said. "Frankly, I would prefer a gap-toothed strumpet with the pox, but we are all beggars at the time of our passing."

He wrenched his hands free from the ropes just as the gate crashed to the flags with an echo like a tolling bell. Will jumped forward and futilely strained to lift it before turning back to Church and Tom.

"Balfour will be back to free us?" Tom said hopefully.

"Rab is likely dead. Don Alanzo will have sealed the hidden door. We must not look for help from outside, friends."

"What do you suggest, then?" Tom's voice broke with the strain. "The lever to open this gate is on the other side of the gate! There's nothing we can do!"

"Then 'tis a slow death from starvation," Will said blithely. He prowled the perimeter of the room looking for inspiration.

While Tom hugged his knees to contain his mounting panic, Church's attention was drawn to a stream of water pouring through the stone ceiling. It splashed on the flags and ran into a gutter where it flowed away.

"If we could prise out some of these stones we might be able to dig through the river bed," he said. "It can't be far above our heads."

"Are you mad?" Tom roared. "The waters would rush down upon us in an instant. Would you commit suicide by drowning?"

"To be honest, it's rapidly becoming an attractive prospect if it means I don't have to listen to you any more," Church snapped.

Will examined the point where the water rushed in. "I think you have hit on a good plan, Master Churchill."

"We hold our breath until the water has filled up this chamber, and then we should be able to swim up," Church said.

"'Twill be an icy dip, but our limbs should stay strong until we reach the bank," Will noted.

"You're both mad," Tom raged.

"He's right, you know," Will said.

"Yep."

"Still, desperate men lead desperate lives." Will searched in the depths of his cloak.

"I could attack you both. Beat your brains out with this . . . this . . ." Tom searched amongst the artefacts and randomly pulled one out. "This brass pig."

"We have swords," Church cautioned.

"Though, a brass pig . . ." Will mused. "As deaths go, the novelty would live on in history."

"If anyone ever found out," Church said.

"Ah!" Will plucked a small pouch from one of the many secret pockets in his cloak. "Save your sword, Master Churchill. I have an easier route to a watery grave."

"What's that?"

"Why, gunpowder!"

Church glanced at Tom who was as white as the wintry streets above, but he appeared to have resigned himself to whatever Church and Will had planned.

Will packed the gunpowder in the gap between the flags and pushed in a short fuse, also retrieved from the pouch.

"I wouldn't mind a cloak like that," Church said. "Something for every occasion."

"The first thing they teach you as a spy is always to be prepared," Will said. "Actually, the first thing they teach you is to beware a woman who opens her legs before her mouth."

He struck his flint and lit the fuse before diving behind the pile of treasures where Church and Tom were already sheltering. Church had the briefest moment to mourn the loss of Templar wisdom and artefacts and then the blast struck him blind, deaf and dumb.

It was followed by a torrent of water smashing into the pile of treasures.

Church, Tom and Will just made it over to the railings before the full force of the deluge knocked the wind from their lungs. The water was so cold Church wondered if they really did stand a chance before hypothermia set in.

Tom shivered uncontrollably as they climbed to the top of the gates. "You have killed me before my time! I should have known better than to entrust my life to two fools!" he shouted above the deafening torrent.

The sense of desperate claustrophobia and impending doom spiralled when the river extinguished the lamp and plunged them into darkness. Their bodies numb, they pressed their faces against the stones of the ceiling to fight for the last gasp of air. The water touched their lips, their noses, and then it was done. Church felt around for Tom and Will, then urged them both to move. They struck out for the gaping hole, feeling in the dark for its ragged edges.

And then Church was drawing himself up through rock and mud until he felt the river's current pulling at him. With frozen, tired limbs, he struck up and out towards what he hoped would be the bank.

Minutes later he dragged himself out onto the snow-covered mud flat. Will broke water seconds later, but after his ordeal in the lever tunnel he had no strength left. Church waded in and dragged him out.

"True Thomas," Will said through chattering teeth. "Where is he?"

Church scanned the slow-moving water, but could see no sign. Steeling himself, his limbs shaking uncontrollably, he dived back into the river.

It was impossible to see anything in the murky depths, so it was more by chance than design that he came across Tom's too-still floating body. Church grabbed him and struck back to the surface.

On the bank, Church gave Tom the kiss of life, pumping his lungs and massaging his heart but fearing the worst. After several moments Tom convulsed and vomited water.

"You realise," Will said, "that you will now have to endure a lifetime of grumbles and moans for what you have put him through."

On the brink of hypothermia, they made it to the road. Marlowe stood next to the rope overhanging the drawbridge, clutching a cloth to a gash on his head.

"I was afeared Don Alanzo had left you for dead," he said.

"He may still have lest you get us to a warm fire," Will said. "What news of Rab?"

"They took him," Marlowe said. "As I woke on the doorstep, I heard them in their passing. They know where the box is. They are on their way to Myddle."

14

Lucia woke at first light, swathed in a gradually fading warmth and hallu-cinogenic memories of startling potency that already felt like the remnants of a dream. The liminal zone between the snow-covered fields and the dark recesses of Myddlewood was deserted. Nor were there even footprints to sig-nify that anyone had been there apart from her and Niamh.

Trying to draw some understanding from half-remembered visions, Lucia followed her own tracks back to the village. Smoke from morning fires was already rising into the chill red sky, but behind the cries of the winter birds hunting for food there was another sound that she couldn't quite distinguish.

On the edge of the village, the doors of Tyler's farmhouse hung open despite the cold, and as she passed the parsonage heading towards Castle Farm House where her room was, she came across a small gathering of vil-lagers. They were animated and tempers were fraying. John Gossage was yelling at the parson, who was attempting to calm them down.

As she drew near, she saw a familiar figure hunched in the centre of the crowd. It was Jerzy, not wearing his mask. His white, grinning face was con-torted with fear as blows and kicks rained down on him.

"Leave him alone!" Lucia yelled.

As she ran forward to intervene, a hooded figure stepped out from under the eaves of Castle Farm House and pointed an accusing finger at her.

"Here she is—the witch!" he shouted. "She's come to call on the demon she's summoned up!"

The knot of villagers surged towards Lucia, men and women, young and old, and dragged her forward in a storm of scratching, pinching and biting. Stunned, Lucia was driven to her knees before the parson.

"A witch in our midst!" John Gossage raged. "She has brought the Devil to Myddle! You must act now, before it is too late for our souls!"

The parson nodded. "Take her to the churchyard. We must ask our Lord to deliver to us the truth. Bind her mouth to prevent her uttering spells."

"Leave her be! She has done nothing!" Jerzy shrieked, but it only inflamed the villagers more.

As Lucia was dragged towards the churchyard, her eyes locked on those of the hooded man who had branded her a witch. He smiled darkly.

"Better late than never," Veitch said.

15

The coach raced across the countryside, but however much the wheels bounced over the frozen, rutted lanes of middle England or threw Church, Will and Tom around the coach's interior, to Church it was still moving at a snail's pace.

To Will, used to a horse-based transport system, they were making rapid progress and he remained calm and in good spirits. But every time they stopped to feed and water the horses or to take detours to avoid bandits in the thick Midlands forests, or stopped at a roadside inn for an entire night, Church's anxiety increased. It wasn't just his concern for Lucia, Jerzy and Niamh, but his fear over what the Army of the Ten Billion Spiders planned to do with the Anubis Box and the crystal skull.

Myddle was far from the main coaching routes so they were forced to buy horses once they crossed the border into Shropshire. The lanes and tracks were thick with snow and the going was hard. They came upon the village in the late afternoon when the light was growing thin and the air becoming bitter.

Across the still fields where only the mournful sounds of birds rose up, they became aware of a commotion in the trees that clustered hard against the lane.

"What is that?" Tom strained to hear. "A hunt?"

Church heard the howls of dogs and the whoops of men. Vegetation crashed.

"It is too dark to see," Will said. "This is not the time of year to hunt with dogs."

Something broke out of the trees and lurched through the thick snow of the lane ahead. In the half-light, Church couldn't quite believe what he was seeing, but as the figure scrambled to get into the trees on the other side he accepted it was the Mocker.

Church urged his horse on. Jerzy shrieked and redoubled his efforts to get over a thick hedge. "Jerzy! It's me!" Church called.

The Mocker spun in a blind panic. "They come! They hunt!"

Church could hear the dogs drawing closer. The commotion in the undergrowth was loud enough to be made by ten men. Church reached down and lifted Jerzy to his saddle and then spurred his horse on, with Will and Tom riding close behind.

"You should have kept your mask on, you idiot!" Church called above the beat of the hoofs. But Jerzy only sobbed uncontrollably in response and Church felt guilty for his tone.

The Mocker had calmed a little by the time they reached the village. Church was hesitant about entering until Jerzy's face was covered but Will urged them on.

"The box?" he shouted to the Mocker as they rode. "Is it still here?"

"The riders have taken it. And my mistress!" Jerzy broke down in another bout of shrieks and sobs.

"We must find the direction they took and give pursuit," Will said. He grabbed Jerzy's shoulder to calm him and asked, "They have Lucia, too?"

The Mocker fell silent, and then pointed one trembling finger. In the yard before Castle Farm House, Lucia hung from a makeshift gibbet, as cold as the impending night. Her clothes had been partly torn to reveal white skin covered with the marks of torture. Her black hair hung across her face. The quiet of the yard was only broken by the creak of the rope as she swung in the breeze.

Church was frozen in his saddle, the horrific image seared on his mind. Will ran towards the body, slowing as he neared it. Lucia was dead, there was no doubt.

Will did not turn back to the others for a long moment, and when he did, his face looked like the winter fields. "There will be a reckoning," he said grimly. "Was this the work of Don Alanzo?"

The Mocker shook his head furiously and tears welled up in his eyes. "The people here found out she was a witch. They said she consorted with the Devil—" His voice caught in a juddering sob.

"She doesn't even believe in the Devil," Church exclaimed. "It's madness. This whole country is insane."

"The whole world, brother," Will said quietly. "Europe is gripped with a fear of witches and the priests fan the flames. I fear where it will end." The strain of the journey finally told on his face.

Jerzy said to Church, "A stranger drove them to this. A man who speaks like you . . . a tattooed man . . ."

Church bowed his head. He was overwhelmed by the sheer pointlessness of everything that he did. His fears crystallised into one clear certainty: things were only going to get worse.

16

They cut down Lucia's body in the bitter cold, beneath hard grey clouds that promised more snow. Church tried to keep in his head the image of Lucia sitting amongst the standing stones after they had left Rome, telling him not to mourn for her when she died. But faced with the harsh reality of her limp body and cold skin, and the unnecessary circumstances of her death, it was difficult not to turn towards dark thoughts.

Will remained cold-faced, all emotions locked tightly within. Church knew the spy had started to feel deeply for Lucia, and there was nothing Church could say to ease his pain. He couldn't even sustain anger for the ignorant villagers, manipulated into a brutal, false reading of their religion.

"We should bury her," Church said.

"The ground will be like iron," Will said. "Besides, these illiterate, superstitious peasants would never let her rest in peace if they knew the location of her grave."

"What, then? Cremation?"

They were interrupted by a woman's cry from a nearby house. Tom investigated, and after a moment beckoned Church to follow while Will stood guard over Lucia's body, though all the villagers had long since hidden themselves away.

The house smelled of woodsmoke and dried herbs. Tom led Church upstairs to a bedroom where a woman sobbed quietly. On the bed, her skin as white as the snow outside, was a girl of around seventeen. She was heavily pregnant and appeared to be sleeping though her breath was thready.

"She's dying," Tom whispered to Church. "She hasn't woken for days. She had a fever, then slipped into unconsciousness. The birth has started and the mother knows the baby will die, too." Tom indicated the woman in the corner who was trying to compose herself.

"What am I supposed to do about it?" Church said sharply, but his bitterness at Lucia's death drained away when he looked at the girl. Life was harsh, and in the absence of proper medical care, death remained close to every community. All the love and hope and dreams and art and music counted for nothing in the face of it. Where was the meaning in that, any rhyme or reason to Existence?

"My Alice suffers because we allowed the witch into our village. God is punishing us," the woman said.

"No," Church said. "That 'witch' was a woman like you, like your daughter, with the same feelings, the same thoughts. What kind of God would want to bring pain or death into her life?"

Tom caught Church's arm, but the woman was already crying. Church knew she needed some way to make sense of her impending loss; everyone did. It was so senseless.

As he watched over the pale girl, his thoughts flashed back to Carn Euny and the dawn celebration for Ailidh's stillborn child. Eighteen hundred years separated the two girls, yet their concerns were the same. Hope and sadness; humanity in essence.

Before Church could say something to ease the woman's grief, a powerful wind crashed against the tiny window and they all jumped. A snowstorm had come out of nowhere with an unnatural ferocity. Through the window, Myddle was gone. There was only a wall of white, as if the house was floating in a non-place. Flakes were already compacting to blanket the glass.

Church and Tom exchanged a brief look of unease before hurrying outside. So intense was the storm it was near-impossible to pick the right direction. Everywhere was white, and they were blinded by the snow driven into their faces by the bitter wind. For five minutes, they wandered around calling for Will, though they had left him only a stone's throw from the door.

And then the snowstorm abated as suddenly and mysteriously as it had begun. The wind dropped in the blink of an eye; the final flakes drifted to the ground.

A snow-covered mound lay where Will and Lucia's body had been. Church and Tom brushed the snow away and dragged Will to his feet. He was dazed, barely conscious, frozen to the bone and shivering. Lucia's body was nowhere to be seen.

"What happened to her, Will?" Church asked.

Will tried to reclaim his thoughts. "I saw . . . dark eyes . . ." was all he could manage.

Tom indicated a set of cloven hoofprints leading away from them.

"An animal?" Church said.

"That walks on two legs?"

Church and Tom helped Will back to the house to recover in front of the fire. Before they could talk further, the woman stumbled down the stairs, wailing hysterically. "My Alice! My Alice!" When they had finally calmed her, they learned that the pregnant girl had disappeared from her bed. The woman had looked to the window, and when she looked back the girl was gone.

"I'm going after Lucia and the girl," Church said as he pulled his cloak tightly around him.

"Is that wise?" Tom said. "The suddenness of the snowstorm, the hoofprints—it speaks to me of wild, dark magic."

"I can't abandon them, Tom."

The Rhymer nodded. "Then take care. I fear what awaits you."

The hoofprints led Church to the main street and then out of the village. Beyond the houses, they left the road and crossed the fields. Shivering, Church struggled through the thick snow until he came to Myddlewood, where Lucia had spent a night of wonder and mystery only hours earlier. The hoofprints continued straight into the heart of the wood.

Church hesitated on the boundary and stared into the desolate trees. Nothing moved. There was no breeze, no sound. He drew his sword and entered the dark world.

The strange, still atmosphere blanketed the edge of the wood, swollen with anticipation, like the moment before someone speaks. Church was ready for an attack from any direction, but he could not sense any impending threat.

As he progressed further into the wood, the claustrophobic atmosphere slowly dissipated, and with it went the snow as the temperature gradually increased. Eventually it felt like a balmy spring day. Snowdrops and then bluebells carpeted the floor of the wood, illuminated by shafts of sunlight, and birdsong filled the air. Words from an uplifting song sprang to mind: "The day is full of birds." Soon he stood amidst summer in the heart of winter.

Cautiously, he sheathed his sword. A rabbit hopped out from behind a tree and approached him without fear. It sniffed his boots and then looked up at him. He felt a frisson as he stared into its eyes: an unnerving intelligence lay there. As it lazily hopped away, the wood gradually came alive: a fox slipped amongst green ferns, mice and voles, more rabbits, birds landing so close it was as if he was not there. The same gleam of consciousness lay in all their eyes.

An abiding sense of peace came over Church, and then a sense of wonder that made him feel as if he was on the brink of something profound. The sound of a child's voice startled him and he broke into a run.

In a grotto formed by the gnarled roots of ancient trees and filled with woodland flowers sat Alice, now pink with life, her blonde hair gleaming. She was laughing in amazement, and her eyes sparkled when she saw Church.

"Look," she said with delight. "I have a baby now."

She pulled her newborn from the folds of her nightgown. It looked at Church with big, dark eyes, and in them Church saw everything for which he hoped, but had never dared believe possible.

Not enough time had passed for Alice to have delivered the child herself, and yet there it was, apparently healthy and filled with life. Alice too had recovered from her near-death state with unbelievable speed.

"Who delivered your baby, Alice?" Church said, as he moved towards the answer himself.

"Oh, 'twas wonderful. I remember it all," the girl said. "There was no pain, only a beautiful light and the scent of roses."

Church looked around the glade. The wildlife was everywhere, all looking towards him with the same fierce personality, one mind behind a hundred eyes. He could sense it, too, breathing with a deep peace in the trees, the ferns, the flowers, the rocks, the soil.

"It was a woman, a beautiful woman," Alice continued dreamily. "Long, dark hair that had stars sparkling in it, and dark eyes, and a smile that made me safe. I could feel her love. She delivered me from the dark and the cold and brought me to life."

The last vestiges of Church's sadness dissipated. Once again he was with Lucia, sitting amongst the stones on a balmy night, and this time her words did resonate with him. *Do not mourn for me, for I will travel into the heart of the mystery.*

Alice rocked her baby gently. "She was not alone. There was a man waiting for her amongst the trees . . . a handsome man. I think she loved him."

Church had no idea exactly what had taken place there, but he was certain of the result. In death, Lucia's adventure continued, and now her innate goodness permeated everything. She had moved on from the grief and the suffering and found her oasis of peace. He hoped Myddlewood would be a good home for her.

"Goodbye, Lucia," he said softly, and he felt as if he was answered, though it may have been just the breeze amongst the trees.

Church helped Alice to her feet, and then wrapped her and her baby in his cloak before picking them both up and carrying them. As they left the wood, Alice's face took on a strange cast. "There was something else . . . something I couldn't see . . . I remember . . . dark eyes, and laughter . . ."

Her words echoed what Will had said when Lucia's body had been stolen. There was a hidden hand at play here, and Church was unsure of what it might be, whether good or evil.

Back at the village, Alice's mother was hysterical with joy. The other villagers gathered round in amazement, proclaiming a miracle. Church considered telling them who had really delivered new life to their community, but knew they would not believe him. Even Will registered quiet disbelief when Church tried to explain what he had experienced in Myddlewood. The spy thought Church was merely trying to ease his grief, and thanked him for his kindness. In the end, Church accepted that only by being there and experiencing first hand could such a thing be believed; perhaps that was the heart of mystery.

"This is a hard world, filled with shadows," Will said grimly as they followed the trail north from the village.

"It's designed to make us think that," Church said, "but the light's there. You just have to look hard to find it."

They rode on through the cold without food or drink, but for a brief while Church felt that no misery could touch him again.

17

"We have to follow them," Church insisted over a much-needed meal of mutton and potatoes and ale in a vinegar-smelling inn overlooking the Liverpool docks. A ship had sailed for the New World not long before; the trail had gone cold.

"Of course, Master Churchill. I have a ship here, up my sleeve," Will replied tartly.

Church realised how ridiculous his statement must have sounded. The cost and logistical difficulties of chartering a ship at a time when war with Spain was threatened must have been the equivalent of trying to book passage on the Space Shuttle in modern times.

"All right," Church said, "but we can't just let it go. Whatever they're planning with the box and skull can't mean well for England."

"True," Will said. "And there is a matter of revenge, which I will not take lightly. I personally will ensure Don Alanzo and his men pay for what was done to Lucia." He punctuated the statement with a long draught of ale to mask the emotion that lay beneath the surface of his vow.

When Will went to relieve himself, Jerzy said quietly, "Do we have to pursue them? While Niamh is gone, we are free men. And if she does not survive we are free men for ever."

"That's right, think of yourself, you selfish creature," Tom snapped. "Never mind that whatever is in the box could mean that the Army of the Ten Billion Spiders will win this war."

"We do not know for certain that there will be a war!" the Mocker protested. "We do not know who they are or what they want!"

Church calmed him; curious eyes were already turning in their direction. "Tom's right. They're a threat to everything. That much is clear, even if we don't know the details. We have to find a way to get across the Atlantic."

18

Time passed excruciatingly slowly for Church. Winter had turned to spring by the time Will had negotiated passage for the two of them on a ship carrying more than 100 men, women and children to create a New England in the New World. Tom and Jerzy would have to remain behind in London.

Church could remember little of the voyage from his history books apart from a few sketchy facts: that the expedition had been arranged by Sir Walter Raleigh to capitalise on the riches of the land Elizabeth I had named Virginia after his scouts had brought back news of it three years earlier; and that Raleigh had originally intended for the colonists to settle on the shores of Chesapeake Bay, but that the ship's pilot had refused to take them any further than Roanoke Island on the coast of what was in modern times North Carolina.

The pain of Lucia's death grew less acute, but did not diminish for either Church or Will. Church often saw her in his dreams, when her face would line up with all the others who had died since he had set off on his long road home. In his darkest moments he wondered how many more would join them by the time his journey ended.

Will and Church kept themselves to themselves throughout the ten-week voyage. John White, the man who had been appointed governor of the new colony, knew from Raleigh of Will's status as a spy and gave them all the protection they needed.

The only person who paid any attention to Church was White's pregnant daughter Eleanor Dare, a thoughtful, sensitive woman who came to him one morning as he stood on deck looking out across the Atlantic.

"I have been watching you for a while, Master Churchill. You appear to be afflicted with a terrible sadness," she said with some concern.

"I'm worried about what lies ahead," he replied. "There are a lot of dangers in the New World."

"God will watch over us. But I fear it is more than that. It is an affair of the heart that troubles you." She smiled when she saw the shadow cross Church's face. "I knew it! You have left your love behind in England."

"Yes," Church replied truthfully. In England, 500 years in the future.

"And you fear you will never see her again?"

"There are a lot of obstacles, a great distance, many dangers between us."

"Master Churchill, you must not lose hope. Love overcomes all—that is the one, true rule of life and God." She unconsciously stroked the curve of her belly as she watched the swelling waves. "My child shall be the first to be born in the New World. She is a symbol of the hope I feel, that we all feel. We have faith in our future, Master Churchill, and you must, too. We will abide in this strange, new land, and grow, and thrive. And you will see your love again."

Eleanor caught sight of her stern-faced husband Annanias, and she hurried to meet him. Church wished he could feel the same bright hope that Eleanor had described. Instead, he was aware of a dark stain deep inside him that appeared to be growing by the day.

19

The ship anchored off Roanoke Island in July. It was a low, narrow island lying between the treacherous Outer Banks and the mainland, but it was green with oaks and marshland and teeming with wildlife. The colonists unloaded their supplies and set about repairing a fort that had been abandoned by Raleigh's men the previous year. Will and Church helped with the work for most of the day before scouring the island at twilight for any sign of Don Alanzo and the Army of the Ten Billion Spiders. They found nothing.

On 18 August, Eleanor Dare gave birth to a daughter she named Virginia after the land in which they had settled, and ten days later Simon Fernandes, the Portuguese pilot, departed for England. John White, who had grown anxious that the supplies they had brought were not enough, went with him to fetch more.

Despite the joy of the birth, the mood amongst some of the colonists had started to sour. Food was already running low, and cultivation of the surrounding area was not progressing as quickly as the colonists had hoped. They were also repeatedly being attacked by the Native American tribe that lived in the area, who had not forgotten the cruelty the English had meted out to them on their arrival in the New World.

And three nights after the ship had departed for England, the Army of the Ten Billion Spiders rose up.

It was twilight. Will and Church sat by the communal campfire watching the stars appear and the bats chasing the insects rising up from the marshland.

"Maybe Don Alanzo just stopped here, checking out the lie of the land," Church said. "He could be on his way back to Spain—"

"Don Alanzo is a man of purpose. If he were to charter a ship and sail across the ocean it would be for a great reason, not a mere dalliance," Will said. "The truth lies here somewhere. We have yet to find it."

A cry rang out from one of the huts near the stockade. Church and Will grabbed their swords and ran. Eleanor Dare was tearing at her hair on the front step of her hut, limned by the lamplight from within. The door hung askew in its frame. "He took my baby!" she cried.

Church pulled Eleanor to him to calm her. "Who took Virginia?"

She pointed towards the gate. "Tom Bowler. He took her out of the settlement." As Church turned to give pursuit, Eleanor caught his sleeve. "I fear the Devil has taken hold of him," she whispered, full of dread.

At the gate, Church and Will found the guard unconscious and the gate open. Will fetched a brand from the fire, but on his return Richard Cordell was already trying to force the gate shut. "You must wait till dawn," he said. "Go now and the savages will slit your throats in the dark."

"We can't wait," Church said. He drew Llyrwyn, and Cordell recoiled when he saw the blue glow dappling the blade.

"Sorcery," Cordell hissed.

Will threw him to one side and wrenched the gate open. Church followed him out into the night. Deep into the heart of the wilderness they ran, where the oak trees moved in the wind with threatening gestures. The paths through the thick vegetation were few and Will found regular footprints in the damp earth. Eventually they caught up with Tom Bowler, who was standing on the edge of a sticky expanse of marshland, looking around desperately. Virgina Dare was clutched to his chest, whimpering softly.

"Tom," Will called softly, "release the child. Her mother calls for her."

As Tom Bowler turned, Church saw in the flickering light of the brand what Eleanor Dare had meant: a black spider was embedded in the centre of his forehead. It appeared newly attached, for blood trickled down from the eight spiky legs. As the colonist's eyes fell on Church and Will, a clarity came to them. "I am afflicted with a madness," he stuttered. "What ails me?" He looked down at the baby as if seeing it for the first time. But when Church stepped in to take Virginia, the colonist clutched her even more tightly, his eyes crazed once more. "Stay back," he said. "With this gift I shall buy my future." He took a step backwards towards the sucking marshland.

Will held out an anxious hand. "Master Bowler! Your future lies this way."

Church's attention was drawn past the colonist to the expanse of marshland, the surface of which appeared to be moving in the light of the brand. At first Church thought it was marsh gas bubbling up from the depths, but it was too consistent and moving towards them in a direct manner.

Will caught sight of it, too, and then Tom Bowler whimpered and said, "They are coming again!"

Church seized the moment to grab Virginia. Off-balance, Bowler stumbled waist-deep into the marsh. He began to claw at his face and hair, howling like a madman.

"He has lost his mind," Will said. "Let us back to camp—"

He paused mid-sentence as the moving shadow crossing the surface of the marsh reached Bowler and they could both see clearly what was causing it. Spiders, some as small as the one attached to Bowler's head, others as large as dogs, were rising up from the depths and skimming across the surface of the marsh on scuttling legs. They surged towards Bowler, then over him, into his clothes, his hair, tumbling into his mouth, choking his screams with the multitude of their bodies.

As Church and Will spun around to race back to the fort, figures emerged from the trees to block their path. "Will Swyfte," Don Alanzo said with surprise and unconcealed glee. "Good sense, as always, escapes you. You have brought yourself to the end."

The spiders were all around now, a lake of wriggling black as far as the eye could see.

21

Church and Will were herded back into the fort, where the colonists had been rounded up by a small army of Spaniards. Eleanor Dare cried with joy when she saw Church carrying Virginia. Don Alanzo moved his men to one side to allow her to reclaim her child tearfully. Her brief words of thanks to Church were drowned out by the cries of the colonists as the multitude of spiders swarmed through the gates and over the stockade to seethe on every available surface. At Salazar's silent command, they came to rest.

"You have thrown in your lot with the Devil!" Will shouted furiously.

For a second his accusation appeared to strike a chord with Don Alanzo, but then the spider parasite on his neck reasserted its control and he smiled contemptuously. "You fear what you know is about to come to pass. England's days are numbered. Philip will triumph over the despised Elizabeth, who will finally be forced to explain to her Maker why she turned away from God's path. Even now our Armada prepares to sail—"

"Look around you, lumpkin!" Will shouted. "Since when did Spain ally itself with demons in the form of spiders?"

"There's no point, Will," Church said. "The spider controls his thoughts. I'm sure he thinks he's being perfectly rational in carrying out the king's business."

"If that is so, then why are we not all the mares of spiders?"

It was a question that had troubled Church since he realised Maxentius had fallen under the spiders' control in their bid to take Rome and prevent Constantine's succession to power.

The answer soon became apparent. One of the Spanish guards walked along the lines of colonists and selected a man who was on his knees, whining, and whom Church recalled had been one of the most prominent doomsayers about the declining supplies. The guards dragged him to the campfire and held him down. Salazar loomed over him and made a gesture in the air. Instantly one of the spiders scurried forward and climbed onto the man's cheek, where it raised one metallic-looking leg at a time and thrust them into the man's flesh. As the last leg went in, his screams subsided and he grew calm.

"Despair," Church said in a moment of clarity as all the evidence of his eyes over recent months fell into relief. "The spiders can only control people who've given in to despair."

"Then the nature of this war is clear, Master Churchill. It is not between Spain and England, but despair and hope."

"Spiders and snakes," Church whispered.

As the victim stood up quietly to join the Spanish soldiers, Don Alanzo said, "A short period of madness will afflict him intermittently, but then he will give in freely to our philosophy. Good shall win out in the end."

Will laughed hollowly.

Salazar communicated silently with Don Alanzo. "You are honoured indeed to be here, Will Swyfte," the Don said. "Tonight you will witness the very pillars of heaven shake. The angels are coming down to Earth."

A man walked out of the shadows at Don Alanzo's beckoning. It was Sir Robert Balfour, as refined and calm as the last time Church had seen him in the Templar store beneath his home.

"Rab? Have they hurt you?" Will questioned with concern, but Church could see Will already knew the truth.

"A change has to come, Will. Elizabeth must die. And she shall." Rab read the betrayal in Will's eyes. "My family is Catholic. We put our hope in Mary, but Elizabeth saw that threat off."

"The spiders have you."

"No spiders, Will. This comes from the heart."

"You're insane," Church said. "Two factions of Christianity fighting each other to the death while a greater enemy is destroying the human race. Can't you see how ridiculous that is?"

"Our roads are our own. We can walk no other." Rab motioned to the guards to bind Will and Church's hands. "I would not see you hurt, Will. I hold you dear, but I hold my religion dearer. Bind them tight. This is a wily one."

"Your betrayal came early, Rab—I see it now. You told Dee of the crystal skull because you had no idea how to retrieve it yourself."

"I knew you would find a way. You always were the clever one."

"And now you've given it to them." Will nodded towards Salazar and Don Alanzo who were marking out an area in the centre of the fort. "And they'll use it with the box."

"Politics and religion make strange bedfellows. But the end justifies the means."

"Why did you come here?" Church asked.

"This New World will teem with people one day. It will provide riches uncounted for whoever rules it. The Spanish will not see it fall into English hands."

"I don't care why you're here," Church said. "The spiders will wipe you out the minute you've served your purpose. Why are *they* here?"

Balfour looked uneasily at the mass of spiders sitting silently on every available surface apart from the small area at the centre of the fort. They moved as one, a single mind, a single beast breathing. "They serve our purpose," Balfour said, but everyone present knew the lie. He nodded to the guards to take Will and Church away.

They were dragged to one of the huts and thrown inside. When the guards had gone, Will said, "Do you know why the spiders are here?"

"Balfour was right. In the future, this will be a thriving, powerful nation. Whoever controls it controls the world."

"But only," Will said speculatively, "if they turn their backs on hope and give in to despair."

Church recalled the spiders rising up out of the marshland, and thought of them in the centuries to come, nestling down under the ground, rising up in ones or thousands to take control of those who would do their bidding; here in America, in Rome, perhaps London, Berlin, Tokyo, Beijing. Everywhere. The spiders were playing a long, long game. From this point forward they would be the nightmares of the human race, slipping out of the shadows to torment and direct, but never being seen in full light.

The door opened a crack and Eleanor Dare crept in, her face tear-stained and frightened. She crawled behind Church and began to saw at his bonds with a kitchen knife. "They have taken Richard Frasier and Judith Carter. They are taking all of them." Her voice was cracked and desperate. "Some walk of their own accord, putting their heads low for the spiders to climb on."

"Don't give in to it, Eleanor," Church urged.

"I shall not," she said defiantly. "I will survive for Virginia and for God. In life's long journey there are many threats. We do not bow down to them. We stand tall, we fight, we abide." She sawed through Church's bonds and he took the knife from her and moved on to Will. "I place my faith in you, Master Churchill, and you, Master Swyfte. Deliver us from this evil."

She slipped back outside as quickly and silently as she had entered. Will flexed his wrists to bring back the blood supply. "I am my own master, and I play by my own rules. I am not comfortable when faith is placed in my abilities."

"Neither am I, Will," Church said, "but it's too late now. They're trusting in us. Their lives are in our hands."

22

Church and Will retrieved their weapons from where the Spaniards had left them and found a good vantage point at the side of one of the huts. Salazar and Don Alanzo had finished marking out a large circle with torches burning at the four cardinal points. But it was what stood beside it that caught Church and Will's attention. It appeared to be a doorway rising up nine feet or more with a frame constructed of some substance that resembled meat— the same substance that had formed the enemy fortress in the Far Lands.

Looking at the abandoned clothes scattered nearby, Church wondered if it really was made from flesh. Within the frame the air shimmered, making it impossible to see through to the other side. Church sensed that passing through that doorway would take one much further than a mere step across the fort.

His fears were confirmed when Don Alanzo ordered his guards to make the colonists line up before the doorway. Some fell in easily, controlled by the spiders, but others had to be prodded sharply. Eleanor was near the rear of the line, holding Virginia.

"Where do you send them?" Balfour said uneasily.

"To a fortress in a land beyond the sunset." Don Alanzo's voice was strained. "They will not be alone."

Church understood: the spiders had been stealing people for centuries and taking them back to their fortress in the Far Lands where they would march alongside the Ninth Legion and all the others who had mysteriously disappeared. He saw Eleanor rocking her baby and forced himself not to consider what horrors waited on the other side of the door.

"Do you have a plan, Master Churchill?" Will hissed. "For I must confess I am bereft."

"There are two of us with swords and we're surrounded by a small army of Spanish soldiers and about a million supernatural creatures. Who needs a plan?"

Will laughed. "I will miss fighting at your side, Good Jack."

The first of the colonists were prodded through the doorway. It looked as though they passed through a gelatinous membrane—one moment of clinging, then gone.

Salazar was at work in the circle, drawing patterns in the air with one gloved hand. He had barely finished when there was a distant sound of rending, then another, drawing closer. To Church it sounded like a series of doors opening one after the other.

In the air over the circle the final doorway opened with a deafening crash and the smell of burned iron. An oblong of darkness obscured the night sky. Into it stepped a figure that made Church's blood run cold: Janus, the dual-faced god of doorways, radiating a primal dread that made men blanch and turn away.

"The preparations have been made?" The voice was like a funeral bell.

"Our power will rest in the dark beneath the earth until the season is right." The words came from Don Alanzo, but they were clipped and mechanical, and his eyes were glazed. Church had the impression Salazar was speaking through him. "Our power will rest beneath an island named Croatoan. And the word of power that will summon it is Croatoan."

"Then call them from their prison. Open the Anubis Box, and let the long-closed doors be thrown wide." Janus disappeared from view as a gust of icy wind blew through the camp.

Salazar took the crystal skull from its velvet wrapping and set it in the centre of the circle. Church and Will were transfixed as Salazar bent over it and made another strange gesture with his gloved hand. The skull began to glow with a faint purple light. A sound emanated from it, high-pitched and reedy, growing louder by the second until everyone present clutched at their eyes and ears. The crystal skull was screaming.

At Don Alanzo's summoning, two guards escorted a woman from one of the huts. Despite the hood placed over her head, Church could tell it was Niamh. She walked proud and erect; Church wondered what power Salazar had over her that she offered no resistance.

From the floating doorway, two golden-skinned angels emerged. One had the same refined, beautiful features as Niamh. Church guessed it was Lugh. At first the other's features swam, but when they settled Church could see he was slightly rougher in appearance, though still beautiful by human standards, his nose straight, his hair curly; he looked like a distant cousin of Niamh's branch of the family.

They dropped slowly down until they stood before Salazar and Don Alanzo. There was something in their sagging-shouldered, bowed-headed posture that suggested they had been broken by their experience. Church saw none of the arrogance he had witnessed in other Golden Ones.

Niamh tore off her hood. She looked frightened, and Church saw her mouth the words, "My brother . . ."

Salazar took the Anubis Box from a bag and held it before him. An unnatural silence fell across the camp; even the tramp of the colonists' boots as they walked through the doorway could not be heard.

"With this power, we bind you, known on this world by your worshippers as Apollo," Don Alanzo/Salazar said.

He held the box before the second god and raised the lid slightly. Black tendrils rose out like smoke, curling through the air until they suddenly lashed into Apollo's face. The tendrils spread out, driving his head back, forcing their way into his nose, his mouth, ears and eyes; and it seemed to Church that along those tendrils surged tiny creatures, pouring into the god's body.

Finally the tendrils retreated back into the box. They left Apollo's face with a malignant cast; the whites of his eyes were now black. Hesitantly, he opened his mouth and said, "We are one." It sounded to Church like a thousand voices speaking at once.

Church suddenly became aware he had been mesmerised by the strange ritual taking place. As he looked around, he saw everyone else had been affected the same way. He shook Will who said, dazed, "The box . . . it allows them to bend angels to their will."

Church launched himself forward. He was past the Spanish guards before they even saw him coming, drawing his sword as he leaped into the circle. With a powerful swing, he cleaved Salazar in half. There was a flash of blue molten sparks, and a terrible shrieking echoed through Church's head. Spiders of all sizes flew from Salazar's body and scurried into the vast mass of arachnids that covered the fort.

Church was too dazed to put up a defence as Don Alanzo drew his sword. Will threw himself in between them and engaged the Spanish aristocrat.

Niamh grabbed Church as he staggered and slowly came back to his senses. He looked around for the skull and the Anubis Box, but they were already disappearing beneath the sea of spiders.

"We must leave," she hissed. "There is no more that can be done here."

"They can't have the box . . ." His attention was drawn to the dwindling line of colonists and Eleanor and Virginia Dare near the back.

Before he could move to help her, he was grabbed and lifted into the air. Slowly he was turned to face Apollo; the sun god was now transformed into a malignant engine of destruction. Black spiders swirled around the edges of his eyes and crawled in the depths of his mouth. Church could feel a brutish power rolling off the god; it felt like the furious burning of a nuclear core. Church could feel it searing through his skin, driving into his centre, cooking him from within. He gripped the sword tightly, but couldn't lift it. Consciousness began to leak out of him.

Something wrenched him from Apollo's grasp and hurled him across the fort like a toy. He crashed to the ground near one of the huts. As he finally slipped into the deep black, he saw two things.

It was Lugh who had saved him, and now the god fought furiously with Apollo. Bolts of golden and black lightning lashed across the camp accompanied by peals of deafening thunder. At their core, Lugh and Apollo were two suns, their shapes indistinguishable in the burning incandescence of their fury.

The final thing Church saw was Eleanor Dare turn to look at him. Behind the sadness, her pale face still registered hope as she clutched her child tightly to her and stepped through the doorway into hell.

23

Church woke as dawn's first light fell across the camp. His head was nestled in Niamh's lap and he was looking up into her beautiful face. Her deep concern slowly transformed into relief by way of a growing smile.

"I feared you were dead," she said softly.

Church lifted himself onto his elbows to look around. The fort was deserted. There was no sign of the millions of spiders, nor of the transformed god who had almost burned Church's life from him. Church recalled that last lingering look from Eleanor Dare and felt a sharp stab of righteous anger.

"I'm going to get them back," he said defiantly. "Nothing's going to stand in my way, however long it takes. Eleanor, Virginia and all the other colonists are counting on me and I'm not going to let them down."

"Are you certain they still live?" Niamh asked hesitantly.

"The spiders took them alive for a reason. They need them that way. I'm betting they're being kept prisoner in the spiders' fortress in the Far Lands."

"Then you will never be able to reach them."

Logically, Church knew Niamh was right, but he refused to accept it. "Some day we'll be strong enough to attack that fortress and when we do I'm going to be right at the front, freeing Eleanor and Virgina and making whoever took them pay." He punched the ground in frustration. "If only I hadn't lost the skull and the box."

Niamh placed a cool hand on the back of his neck. "You saved my brother. You saved me."

Church nodded. "Maybe we'll call this one a draw."

"This is the start of a brutal war. I have seen that now. It will shake the foundations of the Fixed Lands and the Far Lands, and all lands beyond. This was but one battle. There will be many more."

Will emerged from one of the huts, munching with distaste on one of the hard biscuits the colonists had brought with them.

"Don Alanzo?" Church said.

"Escaped, and took Rab with him. We are too equally matched. I lost him in the blaze of . . ." He shook his head, unable to describe the details of the gods' battle. "My head is filled with wool and not a drop of wine has passed my lips." He took another bite. "We shall cross paths again. And next time the blades of Albion will triumph."

Will put on a brave face, but Church could see he had not forgotten Lucia. A moment passed between them, a bond, an unspoken agreement that neither of them would rest until justice had been done.

They walked out of the camp towards a large tree, where Will took out his knife and began to carve.

"What are you doing?" Church asked.

"Whatever dark power was here has returned to its lair to wait until its time comes round again. We must leave a reminder, and a warning, for those who come after."

When he had finished, the word "Croatoan" was carved into the bark.

"And now, Master Churchill, you will be wanting to return to that place where great heroes live, with your angel-love and her angel-brother." Church began to protest at Will's implications, but the spy silenced him. "I fear I may have a few months' wait until a ship comes this way, but there are fish in the sea and I will have time aplenty to lick my wounds and rest my bones."

"You're going to be okay?"

Will smiled. "I have my memories of the fair Lucia. They will keep me warm. And I like to think that what you told me in Myddle is correct: that she has found a better place, and, perhaps, that she watches over us still."

In the few short months they had been together, Church had developed a deep friendship with the spy. It gave him hope that Will would still be around holding the line against the Army of the Ten Billion Spiders on Earth once Church had departed.

Will looked out across the blue sea, the sun illuminating his face like a spotlight. "Shadows are approaching. This world changes faster by the moment, and the struggles that wait just beyond yon horizon shall be great. Yet I know this: in every man's heart there burns a light, a light that will guide us e'en in the darkest of the night."

CHAPTER SIX
THE FOOL'S JOURNEY

1

The Court of the Soaring Spirit was strangely changed. Though the dwellings, inns, stores and public buildings still pressed hard against each other in a bewildering jumble, there was something less oppressive about the place than the last time Church had walked its streets. More sunlight made its way past the overhanging eaves to illuminate the winding alleys and the people were brighter and friendlier.

But even the life and colour of the public square did little to raise his spirits. The Tuatha Dé Danann and the many strange races of the Far Lands loved their entertainment and nowhere was it more evident than in the Great Square. Across the cobbles and amongst the soaring fountains of water and fire, scores of different songs from a thousand different instruments fought to be heard. There were tumblers and jugglers, performers whose masks hid even greater grotesquery, beautiful olive-skinned dancers, actors and poets. In the centre, Church spied the eerie puppeteer from the Venice carnival with his stringless yet animated puppets. He was disturbed to see the puppeteer was now enacting Church and Will's confrontation with Don Alanzo in the Palazzo Ducale. The troublingly realistic Church puppet even turned and winked as the real Church passed.

"How can they enjoy themselves as if nothing has changed?" Church said. "There's a fortress being built on their border, an army amassing—an enemy that now has the power to summon and control them . . ."

Tom sucked on a briar pipe filled with a strange kind of tobacco he had found in one of the back-alley shops. "They are content in their mastery of all they see."

"By the time they get their rude awakening it may be too late."

"Who knows, perhaps the Lady Niamh will engender some change in their addled golden heads. You seem to have wrought a remarkable transformation in her."

"I've done nothing."

Tom let Church's response hang in the air for a moment. "Even now she is in deep discussion with her brother Lugh. He is a warrior and master of his own great court. Should Niamh persuade him of the seriousness of the growing threats, and should his own experiences carry weight, you may find yourself with allies."

"Can you see what the Enemy is planning?"

Tom shook his head.

"You saw the Anubis Box clearly enough."

"I thought I had explained to you that my ability is not as simple as looking out of a window," Tom said wearily. "I see images without context. Some make sense, some do not."

"Can you see where the Anubis Box and the crystal skull are now? We can't allow them to remain in the Enemy's hands."

"Of course not, but sadly you will have to use some of your own inspiration to find them," Tom snapped.

"We don't even know who we're supposed to be fighting. The Army of the Ten Billion Spiders? Janus? Who's the real enemy?"

"You'll find out soon enough." Tom puffed out a cloud of fragrant blue smoke.

"I'm sick of your riddles and word-games. You know more than you're saying. You're supposed to be True Thomas—why don't you tell me the truth?"

Tom laughed. "You know you're going to say nearly those very same words to me again?"

Church could barely contain his frustration while Tom inspected a stand selling hot cakes, pretending to be half-listening, but with a hint of concern that Church didn't see. "Just pull yourself together. You're whinging like a little girl," Tom muttered.

Before Church could continue the conversation, Evgen marched up with a cohort of Niamh's guards. "My mistress requests your presence in her quarters," he said.

Behind Church the puppetmaster waved his arm and the puppet Church fell to the ground.

2

Niamh sat on a balcony encircling the highest tower in her palace. She looked even more beautiful in the morning sun, her smile enigmatic and alluring. Lugh stood next to her, by comparison drawn and weary; the scars of his ordeal lay as heavily on his face as they did on his mind. Nearby the Mocker sang a lilting song softly to himself.

"Jack. Thank you for coming," Niamh said sweetly. "I would like to extend my thanks for the part you played in returning my brother to me."

Lugh bowed slightly; the move was awkward and clearly out of character. "I too would like to express my gratitude. I have never been close to Fragile Creatures, but my sister has recently spoken to me of the value of your kind, and in you her words are made flesh."

Church nodded. "You had a close call."

"We are already taking steps to ensure no other Golden One should fall under the spell of the Enemy in such a manner," Niamh said.

"But there are other gods beside the Golden Ones," Church pointed out. "That one at Roanoke Island was Apollo." He looked at Lugh. "Another sun god. I think they chose you two first to strike a blow against the light . . . against hope."

"We are aware of others like us, who reside close to the Far Lands, but we have never sought dealings with them," Lugh said.

"Because it would mean facing up to the reality of your 'unique' status. You're not so special, just another species vying for survival," Church said.

"The Golden Ones are singular in their blindness, like children who think themselves the centre of Existence," the Mocker said with a grin. Niamh glared at him. "You wished a jester to speak the truths that no one else would dare," he added.

"I think I have given you too much freedom," Niamh said.

"There is much to consider," Lugh interjected. "My capture was not meant to be. I saw ahead, as does your friend True Thomas, and nothing suggested the events of recent times. The Enemy is changing the course of things. What lies ahead is now fluid. We can no longer rely on the comfort of what could or should have happened."

"Can you rally your people to your side?" Church asked. "The Enemy must be confronted before they gain too much of an upper hand."

"We have already opened negotiations with the other great courts, but it will not be an easy task," Niamh said. "Some remain blind to the perils before us."

"As of now, my court and my sister's will stand with you and the Quincunx," Lugh said.

Though it was delivered in an understated way, Church sensed the importance of this statement for Lugh. Church thanked him graciously.

"One other thing," Niamh said with a note of sadness. "I promised I would free you from your obligation if you helped bring my brother back to me. I am true to my word. No more will you be at my behest."

Church's relief was tempered when he glanced at Jerzy squatting further along the balcony, humming to himself. The air of misery that always surrounded the Mocker was palpable.

"I have a request," he said. "Free Jerzy instead of me. He has a more pressing need. There are people here he may want to return to."

Niamh gave Church a puzzled but warm look and turned to the Mocker. "So be it. You have been a trustworthy if increasingly irritating servant under the guidance of Jack Churchill, Mocker. I hereby free you of your obligation."

Jerzy's eyes darted between Church and Niamh, at first unable to comprehend what he was hearing. The fixed grin lent a surreal aspect to the intensity of emotions playing out in his eyes.

"Good friend, is this true?" he asked with a quavering voice. "You would sacrifice your own wellbeing for me?"

"You deserve it, Jerzy. There'll be other chances for me."

Tears welled up in Jerzy's eyes, and for a moment Church thought the Mocker was going to be sick. Then he bounded past Church into the palace, a thin, desperate wailing trailing behind him.

3

Church searched their quarters, the music room and the extensive, steaming kitchens where Jerzy used to pass his time amongst the thronging cooks and their assistants. Afterwards, Church tried the Hunter's Moon inn and the maze of alleys that had become a regular hideaway for both of them. Jerzy was nowhere to be found.

As Church made his way back to the palace, Tom ran up. "You'd better come quickly," he said breathlessly. "The bloody idiot has finally lost what little sense he had."

At the palace, a crowd of bemused Tuatha Dé Danann stood in the central courtyard, looking up the vertiginous walls of the keep. Church could just make out Jerzy standing precariously on one of the gargoyles that vented water from the guttering.

Church sped up flights of stairs until he came to the window through which the Mocker had accessed the tiny ledge that led to the gargoyle. Church could see him balanced on its head, arms outstretched, eyes closed.

As Church threw one leg out of the window, Tom grabbed him. "What do you think you're doing?"

"I have to get him back in——"

"You're as much of a bloody idiot as he is." Tom averted his gaze from the dizzying drop.

"I thought it was enclosed spaces that scared you."

"Enclosed spaces . . . heights . . . anywhere there's the slightest chance I might lose my life ahead of schedule. You're telling me it doesn't bother you?"

Church glanced at the golden specks moving around the courtyard far below and felt sick. "I can't let him do anything stupid."

He climbed out. Instantly the wind threatened to drag him off the ledge, which was only as wide as his feet. He pressed his back against the stone and kept his eyes straight ahead. Each step was a battle. Vertigo made his perceptions shift so that he could easily have pitched forward, and he had to close his eyes continually to take a deep breath. Finally he was close enough to call.

"Jerzy, what are you doing?" He tried not to startle his friend, but Jerzy still wrong-footed himself in surprise. He went off the edge of the gargoyle and it was only his innate athleticism that allowed him to grab the carving with both arms and, feet kicking wildly, scramble back on top.

"Go back," he sobbed. "Go back."

"What's wrong?" The stone was hard against Church's back, the wind increasing.

"If you die here, I truly will be damned." Tears streamed down Jerzy's face.

"I'm not going back inside until you tell me what's wrong."

Jerzy took a juddering breath. "What is wrong is that I have betrayed the greatest man to walk any of the Lands . . . the best friend a fool like me could ever ask for."

"You haven't betrayed me."

"Oh, but I have, I have."

A sharp gust of wind dragged past Church and he clutched at the stone, his hands slick with sweat. "You'd better tell me quick, Jerzy, because I can't hold on much longer."

Jerzy stifled a sob. "It was I who took the lamp that contained your essence. I delivered it to the Court of the Final Word."

"Why?"

"I had no choice! They control me in a way that even the mistress cannot control me."

234

Church steeled himself to stop his head spinning. "If they control you, you had no choice. I can't blame you."

"You should, you should! I did it to buy my freedom!" He prepared to jump.

"Wait!"

Jerzy balanced precariously on his tiptoes.

"You're a friend, Jerzy, and I don't turn my back on my friends, whatever they've done. We'll sort it out."

Jerzy hesitated. "Friends, still? Even after my grand betrayal?"

"Friends, Jerzy."

Jerzy looked towards him, guilt conflicting with desperate hope. Tears streamed down his face.

Back inside the keep, Jerzy flung himself at Church, burying his face in Church's chest and sobbing uncontrollably. Church awkwardly gave him a brief but manly hug before prising him off.

Tom rolled his eyes and muttered, "For God's sake."

In the privacy of their quarters, with the doors securely locked, they huddled together as Jerzy retold how the Caraprix had been inserted into his head at the Court of the Final Word.

"And it drove you to take the lamp containing my Pendragon Spirit just after we left Rome," Church said.

"I was forced to deliver it to the old stones, where one of the Court of the Final Word crossed the barrier between worlds to collect it. You met me as I was returning from my terrible act." Jerzy unconsciously drove a knuckle into his mouth at the memory of what he had been compelled to do.

"Why did they want the lamp?" Church asked.

"The Pendragon Spirit is the very essence of Existence," Tom said. "For one who can divine its secrets, anything is possible."

"We have to get it back," Church said.

Tom and Jerzy recoiled as one. "No one ventures into the Court of the Final Word unbidden," Jerzy hissed.

"Those who enter never come out unchanged," Tom added. "Many do not come out at all."

"There has to be a way. The Pendragon Spirit is a part of me. I'm not whole without it."

"I know." Tom's gaze was unwavering.

"We can't leave the lamp in their hands. It might be the key to unlocking all sorts of doors."

"I know." Tom looked down at his boots.

"You're saying I'm on my own."

"You do not venture in there on a whim," Tom said. "Planning is essential. You must bide your time until a path presents itself."

"All right, we gather information. But we can't wait long."

Tom nodded. "I will begin discreet enquiries."

"The first thing we have to do is remove that thing from Jerzy's head," Church said. "But we have to be careful it doesn't get back to the Court of the Final Word."

"Who amongst the gods would be prepared to abort such a thing?" Jerzy asked.

"Somebody isolated," Church replied. "Someone who has more on their mind than idle talk. Get your things together, Jerzy. We have a long ride ahead of us."

4

The Court of Peaceful Days was as quiet and desolate as the last time Church had seen it, but it had undergone a subtle change. The gates were no longer barred and a carpet of colourful flowers spread out from the perimeter fence to the court's walls. Butterflies fluttered over them and honey bees buzzed back and forth in the stillness of the morning.

The door was opened by Rhiannon, also subtly changed. Her helmet and armour had been replaced by a plain dress, and her face had matured with a deep sadness with which she had finally come to terms.

She greeted Church and Jerzy formally before Church offered his condolences for the dreadful losses her court had suffered in the battle outside Eboracum.

"In war one must always accept defeat as a potential outcome," she said. "But for my people death was never a real consideration. Now everything has changed. The Far Lands are no longer comforting. They are new and strange and terrifying. The night is too dark and draws too close. I can no longer rest easily."

She motioned to Church to leave Llyrwyn inside the door. "Arms will no longer be carried in this court. It will no longer ring with the clash of martial anthems. No more shall thought be given to war without thought given to what comes after. This court now stands for healing, and quiet introspection, and study." She paused to stare at the sunbeams breaking through the glass roof of the atrium. "For what few of us remain."

In an empty dining room they ate fresh fruit while Church made his request for the removal of the Caraprix from Jerzy's head. Rhiannon asked no questions. She needed some time for preparation, and so Church asked for her leave to visit the Wish-Post. He hoped to see Ruth, but the first thing that came into view caused strange echoes in the depths of his missing memory.

5

The transport café was an oasis of light in the dark countryside. Large enough to dispense greasy fry-ups to 150 truckers at a time, its picture windows on three walls now splayed out rectangles of light across a largely deserted car park.

Shavi counted only three other diners, bleary-eyed and unshaven as they pored over outdated copies of the *Star*, one hand gripping a chipped mug of treacly tea. He was tired and his back ached from too long in the driver's seat of his van. For the last five days, he and the Bone Inspector had crisscrossed the Midlands, to the best of their ability attempting to follow the ley lines that radiated out from Avebury. They always spent the night at one of the nodes of the network of fiery power identified by the Bone Inspector—at Arbor Low stone circle in the Peaks of Derbyshire to the Rollrights and Belas Knap in the Cotswolds—knowing that whatever dissipated energy remained in the ground would at least make them invisible to the forces hunting them.

Whenever Shavi was tempted to make light of the cynicism that infected the Bone Inspector's rants about the powers secretly controlling the world, he only had to turn his mind to the numerous disturbing incidents that had dogged their path: the car with smoked windows that had attempted to run them off the road in a small village outside Oxford; the police road blocks that cropped up frequently, forcing detours; and the infestation of black spiders they had seen repeatedly along their route. Something terrible was out there, ready to attack if he ever let his concentration slip.

The Bone Inspector returned from the toilet, his lank hair now wet and slicked back after his cursory wash. Shavi had insisted it was a necessity after they had been refused entry to two cafés because of the Bone Inspector's heavy odour of sweat and loam from the nights they had spent beneath hedges or in ditches. He slipped into the booth and hunched over his mug of tea. Shavi was pleased to see that much of his stress-induced psychosis had faded; company in his misery had helped share the burden.

"We're in bloody trouble," the Bone Inspector muttered darkly.

"We do not know that."

"You want to stop with that optimism before I slap you. It's irritating."

"We can leave now—"

"No point. We'll never be there by dawn. If we hadn't run out of fuel this afternoon—"

"It could not be helped. You know we had to go fifty miles out of our way to avoid the roadblock."

The Bone Inspector slurped his tea noisily. One foot rattled in unconscious anxiety against the seat. "No point crying over it now. We'll just have to keep our eyes open." He glanced out of the window, but it was difficult to see much beyond the light shining through the café's windows.

"How long are we supposed to keep running like this?"

"Till you come up with a plan. I've spent months doing this—legging it at night from one old site to the next, burrowing under stones to get some shuteye during the day, bawling out curious tourists till they'd leave me alone. I can keep doing it, but it doesn't solve anything."

"How can I come up with a plan when I have no idea what is going on?"

"They've done their damnedest to run me to ground, but nothing like how they've gone after you. I never saw any men filled with spiders before now. They think you're important. So it's your bloody job. I'm just along for the ride."

Shavi had listened intently to the Bone Inspector's talk of the mythic Brothers and Sisters of Dragons during their long hours together in the van. The Bone Inspector professed never to have met any of the fabled heroes, asserting instead that it was information passed down through the Culture, the secret society of which he claimed to be the last living member. Shavi couldn't see himself as some legendary warrior, but there were elements of the story with which he felt a deep connection.

Headlight beams sprayed around the walls of the café as a car swung into the car park with a crunch of gravel. Shavi and the Bone Inspector watched intently.

"How are they going to come?" Shavi said. "Looking as normal as Rourke, so they can sneak up on us unawares? Or like the spiders, eating their way through everything?"

"It'll be whatever will do the job."

A man got out of the car and stumbled wearily towards the café door.

"Looks normal. But who can tell?" the Bone Inspector said.

"Do you think we are taking a gamble waiting here in plain sight?"

"What choice do we have? Would you rather face those things out there in the lanes and fields and woods where there's no light? And I'm betting they still don't want to draw too much attention to themselves or they wouldn't have gone to the bother of disguising those spiders as a man."

"I need to refresh myself," Shavi said. He'd walked a few paces before he added, "I cannot help but think I have met you before."

"You think if you'd met me before there'd be any doubt about it?" the Bone Inspector said. "Go on. *Refresh* yourself."

In the toilets, Shavi filled the sink with cold water and soaked his face. The jolt took the edge off his creeping weariness. He had decided that he liked the Bone Inspector, despite his curmudgeonly manner. There was something inherently decent about him, but he buried it as deep as the secrets of the stones that he protected.

As he stretched, cat-like, and performed a t'ai chi manoeuvre to centre himself, his attention was drawn to the graffiti on the wall next to the mirror. It read: *The Army of the Ten Billion Spiders wants you!*

There were other pieces of spider-related graffiti that had been scribbled out or hastily painted over, the ghost of their intent showing through the strokes. He felt a frisson. Was it a coincidence?

There was one other piece of graffiti that puzzled him: *The answer lies at Stonehenge: Heel Stone 45 pcs SW.* It was scrawled in every cubicle and on the back of the main door.

Intrigued, Shavi returned to the café to discuss the matter with the Bone Inspector, but found their table empty. Shavi scanned the room: nothing was out of the ordinary. The three other diners sat at their seats peacefully and the new arrival was carrying a mug of tea from the counter. He was a bohemian with a black greatcoat, long black hair and a pair of sunglasses despite the fact that he had driven through the night.

Shavi could only presume the Bone Inspector had gone to fetch something from the van. As he returned to his seat, the new arrival materialised at his side.

"May I join you?" His voice was wry and urbane. Before Shavi could respond, the stranger had sat down. He put six sugars into his tea and stirred noisily. "Nice night."

"It is," Shavi replied, "but I am just waiting for my friend. We must be on our way soon."

The man nodded and sipped his sickly-sweet brew. "Where is he, then?"

"He will be here soon."

"I've been on the road for hours and frankly I'm exhausted." The stranger stretched.

Shavi was distracted by a faint, rhythmic splashing. *A spilled mug of tea?*

"It's nice to find someone to talk to after so long behind the wheel with only the radio for company," the stranger continued.

Shavi smiled politely. "I am sorry. I am not very good company tonight."

The stranger laughed. "I suppose it's not really the hour for chitchat."

Shavi glanced out of the window. There was no sign of movement at the van, or anywhere around the car park that he could see.

Drip-drip-drip. The noise caught his attention again and this time he identified the source. A dark pool was slowly spreading over the recently mopped floor in one of the aisles. One of the diners sat over it, the entire sleeve of his jacket sodden. It was blood and Shavi could now see that the man was dead.

His heart thundering, Shavi quickly took in the rest of the café: the other two diners were also dead, propped up in the position they had been in when they were alive, or simply murdered so quickly with a flash of a knife across their throats that they had not had the chance even to register their own passing. On the floor, a hand was just visible reaching out from behind the counter.

"I'm sorry. We've not been properly introduced," the stranger said. Shavi thought he could see red coals glowing fiercely behind the sunglasses. "My name is the Libertarian."

"Why did you kill those men? They had nothing to do with this."

"I killed them because I could. To show you that in this world everything now falls before my will."

"Then you are the one behind everything that has happened."

The Libertarian laughed coldly. "I am the strong right arm. Nothing more."

"Then who——?"

"Don't waste your breath asking me." The Libertarian took another noisy sip of tea. "It's much bigger than your tiny little brain can deal with."

"Are you made of spiders, too?"

"I'm made of flesh and bone like you, only better."

Had the Libertarian already killed the Bone Inspector and was simply toying with him? "Why?"

"That's a good question. One of the big ones. Why are we here? Why does anything happen? Why do fools fall in love? Ah, I see. Why are we tormenting you? Why are we hunting you up hill and down dale? And why are we going to wipe you out of Existence as if you never were? Actually, we never intended to take this course. If you had kept on sleeping with your eyes open, and doing the silly, pointless things that mundane people do, like going to work for most of your waking hours, shifting things from here to there, picking up a few extra quid that might buy you a drink at the weekend or a shiny new piece of useless technology, and then repeating it over and over again until the day you died, none the wiser for having lived, then we could happily have left you well alone. But no, you chose to make trouble. You chose to give up your *job*. You fool. You chose to ask questions, and you chose to break the rules. Our rules. And make no mistake, we set the rules, all of them. And if we find a troublemaker, we take him or her out of the game. We don't allow anybody to ruin things for everyone else."

Shavi listened to the Libertarian's gently threatening mockery and realised that something unspoken lay behind it. "You are hunting me down because I am a threat to you."

The Libertarian's laugh was harsh but unconvincing.

"You let me 'sleep with my eyes open' because it was safer than taking the risk of trying to destroy me," Shavi continued. "For by doing so you might have brought about that very same awakening. And then . . . ?" Shavi let the words hang in the air, and in his mind. *And then what?*

"Let's get things straight." The Libertarian put another two spoons of sugar into the remnants of his tea. "There's as much point to you racing back and forth now as there was to your existence before. That Blue Fire you love so much? Gone. All those pretty little ley lines fizzing with energy, that hippie-shit network of love and power? Gone. All those Fabulous Beasts who are symbols of the power, who are the power, who feed on the power, or whatever . . ." He yawned theatrically. "All long gone. There's nothing here for you at all. You're an anomaly in a world that's moved on. Different things matter now. There are different rules. There's no point wishing, or praying, or carrying out little rituals and spells."

"What are you going to do?"

"My job." He smiled. "What anyone would do with an anomaly—take it out of the system and pretend it never existed."

"And then your world of work and money and power and consumption can carry on turning smoothly."

"Exactly." The Libertarian finished his tea. "All gone. Time to die."

The café was suddenly flooded with light. In the car park, one of the lorries had come to life with a loud growl. It began to move, slowly picking up speed, rushing directly towards where Shavi and the Libertarian were seated.

The Libertarian was rooted, uncomprehending. Shavi realised what was happening just in time to scramble over the back of the seat and throw himself down an aisle as the lorry ploughed straight into the side of the café. The deafening explosion of shattering glass and bursting brick brought the roof down around the point of impact.

Shavi crawled through clouds of dust and debris until he reached the door. In the car park, he saw the extent of his lucky escape. The lorry had rammed right across where he had been sitting. Flashing gold sparks of electricity arcing from torn cables lit up the night.

The Bone Inspector wriggled out of the lorry's side window and limped quickly towards Shavi, blood streaming from numerous cuts.

"I thought you could not drive." Shavi said.

"It's a bloody good job I paid attention to what you were doing all that time in the van."

"How did you get the keys—?"

"All right, all right, I picked up a few things in my long, miserable life," the Bone Inspector snapped. "Now stop your stupid talk. We need to get away from here before any more bastards turn up."

As they ran to the van, the Bone Inspector said, "I think we should head north. Maybe get over to Callanish, lie low for a while—"

"No," Shavi said firmly. "We are going to Stonehenge."

6

Church reeled as he withdrew from the images the Wish-Post had been imprinting on his mind. His shock at seeing the Libertarian was profound, but he was confused: had the Libertarian survived until the twenty-first century, or had he started his journey in modern times and moved into the past? With time and space and all of reality so fluid, it was difficult for him to get a handle on the truth.

One thing was apparent: the threat against the Brothers and Sisters of Dragons was as potent in the twenty-first century as in the earlier periods of human history Church had visited. The Army of the Ten Billion Spiders was already attempting to kill Shavi; how long before it turned its attention to Laura and Ruth?

What could he do? He needed to know more, and so he immersed himself in the Wish-Post again, desperately hoping it would lead him to Ruth.

Instead he found himself watching Laura in a park, transfixed by the flowers and the bushes. Church couldn't begin to understand what she was attempting to do, though she appeared to be alternating between talking to the plants and concentrating on them, growing more distressed by the moment.

Finally she stalked away in disgust, but behind her back Church saw a section of vegetation grow rapidly. It was clear to him that Laura had caused it in some way.

As she walked off, a figure separated from the nearby tree line and followed her. It was Rourke, the man who had been associating with Shavi, Laura and Ruth.

When Laura left the park, Church saw road signs identifying the area as Northampton. He began to devise a plan.

He made one more attempt to utilise the Wish-Post, and this time it did take him to Ruth. He was outside her flat, but as he attempted to use his ghost-like abilities to enter he became acutely aware of the same dark presence inside the wardrobe that he had experienced before, and it was aware of him.

Church felt a mounting sense of dread coming off whatever lay inside, and a sense that it would destroy him, Ruth and everything in an instant. However much he tried to force himself in, it pressed back harder, and eventually it drove him off.

He circled the premises, aware of it squatting inside, watching him with loathing. It would never let him across the threshold.

Fearful for Ruth's safety, he emerged from the reality of the Wish-Post in a cold sweat.

7

Church hurried back to find Jerzy and Rhiannon. During his two brief sessions at the Wish-Post, he felt he had come to understand the essential nature of his fellow Brothers and Sisters of Dragons, however deeply it had been buried so that the three of them could survive in the illusory situation in which they had been imprisoned. Shavi: calm, insightful, spiritual. Laura: prickly, iconoclastic, passionate. Ruth: empathic and introspective, someone who felt too much and was forced to pay the price for it.

They didn't recall their heritage as Brothers and Sisters of Dragons, and they didn't remember Church. Yet the truth was trying to break through. Church liked to think that the Pendragon Spirit was so strong that it couldn't be contained for long, but perhaps it was also that the bonds they had shared were so powerful that they resonated across time and even the Army of the Ten Billion Spiders could not break them.

How terribly must Veitch have suffered to turn his back on that bond? Something as terrible as being murdered by his closest friend over a woman they both loved?

With that disturbing thought pressing at his mind, Church found Rhiannon and Jerzy in a tranquil room subtly scented with rose petals. Jerzy lay on a thick blanket thrown over a table. He appeared to be either sedated or in a deep trance.

"Will you assist?" Rhiannon asked. Church nodded. "Then take his hand. The procedure is invasive and he shall need the support of a friend. The Caraprix will have nestled itself within his hopes and dreams. It will be difficult to remove."

She gently caressed the side of Jerzy's head. Gradually a soft white light like mist began to appear at the point where her fingers touched his temple. As the light increased, it was clear that Rhiannon's fingers were moving through flesh and bone and into the Mocker's head.

The atmosphere grew tense. Rhiannon probed for ten long minutes, and Church could see from her increasingly concerned expression that it was not going well.

Finally she withdrew. "I cannot help him," she said. "The Caraprix is resisting my call." She appeared deeply troubled by this discovery, as though something fundamental had been radically altered. "I fear only the one who placed it there may remove it without damaging this one's essence."

Afterwards, Jerzy took the result with equanimity. "My existence has been one of suffering," he said. "I have my life and my freedom, in so far as these things are possible. And I have a good friend, and that is more valuable than anything."

"We'll find a way to remove it, Jerzy," Church vowed, "even if it means we have to storm the gates of the Court of the Final Word to get it done."

Jerzy was both touched and disturbed by this. Yet as they left the Court of Peaceful Days another thought struck Church. He had dismissed the Caraprix as just another of the strange things that existed in the Far Lands, but perhaps the creatures were much more important than that.

He had been told that the more *fluid* things were, the closer they were to the heart of Existence, and the Caraprix appeared to be endlessly mutable. What, then, did that mean?

8

Niamh pored over her cards laid out on a small, exquisitely carved table, with only the light of the crackling fire for illumination. She was lost to whatever the cards were telling her and was startled by Church's approach.

"Did you see your love?" she asked.

He shook his head.

"I am sorry. It must be a great burden to yearn so deeply and yet not be able to touch or speak of what lies in the heart."

Church couldn't begin to express his fears for Ruth and so turned his attention to the cards. "What do you see?"

"The cards are confusing. They change constantly, as if what lies ahead and behind and all around is in a state of flux." Church could see the uncertainty scared her.

"I can't get my head around gods having gods."

She shrugged. "The rules of Existence are plain to see. Seasons turn in a continuous cycle. Existence stretches out for ever. There is no beginning and no end. That is the rule. And there is no smallest and no largest. No boundaries anywhere. As the Golden Ones are above Fragile Creatures, so there are others above us. There is always something higher."

A memory came to Church unbidden and he shivered: a face looming over him as he lay close to death en route to Boskawen-Un and his rendezvous with the Fabulous Beast. The thing saying to him, "Gods answer to gods answer to gods, and somehow the voice of Existence trickles through to men."

Church peered at the cards more closely. "Am I in there?"

Niamh pointed to the Fool. "The Fool is on a journey of enlightenment. When he reaches the end of his path he returns to the start again, for there is always something new to learn."

Church pulled up a chair and watched the logs crackle and spit. "Will Swyfte knew his position and what was expected of him, and he knew he had the abilities to deal with it. He didn't want to be a spy, I could tell, but he accepted his responsibilities whatever the cost to himself. I wish I had his confidence."

"Existence chose you for a reason, Jack Churchill."

Church looked up to see Niamh watching him tenderly. "I'm not going to be able to do this on my own."

"You have allies. My court stands with you."

In her face Church saw a whole host of emotions that had gone unrecognised for a long time. The realisation shocked him, but consideration of the implications was something for another time.

"I want your permission to travel to my own world," he said. "The fight back starts here, and I have a lot of things to put in place."

CHAPTER SEVEN
HELL IS A CITY

1

England, 1 May 1851

Beneath a dreaming night sky, the massive bluestones of Stonehenge stood sentinel on the windswept Downs, their setting barely altered since they had first been raised 4,000 years earlier. Church knew all that was about to change. In a few short decades they would be packaged and presented for the modern world, swarmed over by tourists, imprisoned by roads and traffic and watched over by new buildings that were temples of mundanity.

For now Church could enjoy the circle as it was originally intended, part of an ancient landscape of tranquillity where the only sound was the wind across the grass.

"Get a bloody move on. They're only stones." Tom had grown bad-tempered on the long walk from where the carriage had dropped them off.

"You know that's not true."

"Losing your lamp has addled you. Can you not feel it?" Tom rested one hand on the turf. "There's barely a flicker under here. The Blue Fire has gone to sleep. What did you expect? This is the Age of Reason. People these days haven't got any time for magic, if the journey here is anything to go by. They like big machines and stinking factories, and as much money as they can possibly make, and damn the consequences and the poorhouses."

"When I was looking into the Wish-Post, the Libertarian told Shavi that the earth energy was gone, and so were the Fabulous Beasts."

"Aye, well, maybe they are gone by then. Right now the energy's just dormant. It's linked to our unconscious. If we don't want it around it dies down. And this is the first time in human history when things we make are more important than things we feel."

Jerzy gambolled up like a monkey. Despite the failure to remove the Caraprix, his new-found freedom had left him changed: brighter, more optimistic, filled with passion and humour.

"Bloody hell!" Tom strode off, shouting, "Damnable ape! What I would give for some intelligent companionship."

Niamh followed Jerzy, her cape billowing behind her. "There is beauty in these Fixed Lands." She lifted her head to survey the sea of stars.

Jerzy did a little jig. "Methinks the beauty she has her eyes on is earth-bound."

Tom was sitting on a fallen megalith, smoking, when Church reached the circle.

"At least you're starting to use your God-given brains," the Rhymer said.

"You were the inspiration." Church searched for landmarks, then began to pace out the distance. "I needed to stop seeing time from my own narrow perspective. Start taking the long view." He weighed in his hands the stone he had brought from Niamh's court. "I need to send a message from now to then."

"You're starting to make as much sense as the monkey-boy," Tom observed.

Church reached the correct spot and then dug a hole with a silver trowel. He dropped the stone in it, replaced the soil and the turf and stamped it down.

When he looked up he was not where he had been standing and the shock of dislocation almost threw him off his feet. Stonehenge was nowhere to be seen, nor were Tom, Niamh or Jerzy. He was on the Downs some-where—he could tell from the rolling landscape. Struggling with his disori-entation, he walked a few paces, calling to the others.

"What, ho!"

Church jumped. Jerzy was standing a foot behind him, although he had not been there when Church had looked a moment before.

"Where did you come from?"

"Where did you come from?" Jerzy mimicked.

"This is no time for your jokes." Church looked around uneasily. "We need to find out where we are."

"We are here, and if we were over there we would be here, too."

Church ignored the Mocker's mischief. He was wondering whether this was the start of some attack by the Army of the Ten Billion Spiders, or if the Libertarian or Salazar or Veitch were going to descend on them.

"I must bid you farewell, to seek my fortune in London," Jerzy said.

"We're all going to London," Church replied, distracted. "You know that. I've got to start spreading the word."

"There is much mischief in these lands, and mischief is what I love the most. Things shall be turned on their head. What is down shall be up, and vice versa, and inside out. I go to serve at the foot of a master."

Church was puzzled by Jerzy's tone, and when he looked at him properly, he caught a strange cast to the Mocker's face. The unfamiliar expression may have been caused by a shadow passing across the moon, but for one fleeting moment it didn't look like Jerzy at all.

Church heard his name called, and when he looked up he saw he was back at the same spot where he had buried the stone. The others were walking across the grassland on the other side of the stones; and Jerzy was with them.

Church looked behind him, where Jerzy had been standing. He was alone. He shivered, not quite knowing why, and ran to the others. But when he rounded the circle he could only see Tom and Niamh.

"There you are," Tom snapped. "What are you doing, wandering off? I thought the spiders had got you."

"Where's Jerzy?" Church asked.

Tom and Niamh looked around, puzzled. "He was here only a moment ago," Niamh said.

Though they called his name for more than an hour, there was no sign of him. Church told the others what Jerzy had said about going to London, and they all agreed that they had little choice but to hope Jerzy would meet them there.

As their carriage pulled away from the moon-shadows sweeping over the Downs, Church felt that they had been at the centre of something very strange indeed.

2

The winding, pitch-black cesspit streets of the East End were almost lost beneath the ramshackle buildings that towered over them, seeping degradation and despair. Occasionally there were pools of light, the pubs where the locals attempted to make the best of their lot amidst the vinegary stink of sour beer and the thick smoke of cheap tobacco. But mostly there was darkness.

Veitch strode purposefully through the dire lanes. His sword was strapped to his back beneath his cloak. He could feel the blade calling out to the shadows, sense its subtle black energies permeating his own flesh and bone, hungrily seeking out his desire for vengeance, and his hatred and his bitterness.

He had grown up across the river in South London, an area of similar hardness and struggle. South Londoners and East Enders were rivals, but there was an affinity beneath the surface that forged an unspoken bond. They knew life wasn't easy, that it was about compromise, and attempting to mine whatever nuggets of happiness you could find in the thick seam of day-to-day hardship. That was life; no point moaning about it.

Though the East End had changed a great deal by his own time, thanks to German bombs and out-of-town developers, he could still find his way around. The old familiar markers were still there: Mile End and Whitechapel, Shoreditch and Ratcliff Highway. The names were comforting. They brought back memories of running with his brothers when he was in his teens, of hot nights and beer and girls, before his mother's death and his father's descent into booze, when their only option had become petty crime. That's when the shutters had started to come down.

"Mister, mister! A fuck for a farthing." The reedy voice floated out of a nearby alley. Veitch paused as a woman slowly emerged like a ghost from the shadows. She was hunched over, her hair wild, her arms like sticks. Veitch at first took her to be in her sixties, but only when she neared did he see she was a young girl of around thirteen. Her face and body bore the weight of life on the street; it didn't look as though she had many years ahead of her.

"What are you doing out here at this time of night, love?" Veitch already knew the answer.

"I'll suck for less. Or a quick handshake. Just a farthing, mister. You can put it anywhere."

Veitch went over and the girl's smile was filled with a pathetic gratitude. Behind the hardness of her face he saw something that spoke to him. "What's your name?"

"Annie, mister."

She looked as if she might faint, and when Veitch put an arm around her for support she felt like a bundle of sticks. "You shouldn't be out here, Annie. It's dangerous at this time of night."

Her look told him that the danger was ever-present. "I haven't earned enough for my lodgings yet, mister, and I don't want to spend another night under the arches in West Street." She looked hunted. "My friend was stabbed to death there the other night."

"Where's your mum and dad? You should be home with them."

"My mum died of the pox, not two years gone. I've never known my dad. Mum always said he was good for nothing, and spent her pennies on gin." She hacked a cough. "Will you come down the alley with me, mister?"

250

Veitch was horrified by her plain, workaday tone. He dug into his pocket and found the guinea that would have bought his own food and lodgings until the business was finished. He pressed it into her hand.

"You take this and get out of this shit-hole, all right? Get yourself some food. Get up West or . . . or . . . down to Bromley or somewhere. Get yourself a maid's job."

Even as the words left his lips he realised the hopelessness in them, but the girl didn't care. Gasping for breath and words that wouldn't come, she stared at the guinea on her palm as if it were a sign from God.

A shadow fell over them both. Veitch glanced around, saw nothing, then looked up as he caught a glimpse of movement dropping from on high. A figure landed before him. Veitch was not easily unsettled, but what he saw shocked him with its sheer strangeness. The figure was white and slippery, though he couldn't tell if it was clothes or skin for a black cloak billowed all around it. The hands were clawed where they clutched the material. As it raised its head, Veitch saw goat horns and blazing red eyes, a face that was part-human and part-bestial, but before he could fix on it, the thing opened its mouth to release a blaze of Blue Fire.

Grabbing Annie to protect her, Veitch threw them both backwards. Then the creature gave a remarkable bound and cleared a good twenty feet, where it turned and waited for Veitch to follow.

"God help us!" Annie shrieked. "It's Spring-heeled Jack!"

At her cry windows were flung open and men and women stumbled out of the rank tenements in various states of drunkenness.

"Oi, you bleeder!" one broken-nosed man yelled. "Be off wiv ya!" He ran for the creature, three other men quickly joining him. The thing waited until they were almost upon it before giving a massive leap that sent it sailing up to the rooftops, its cloak folding around it like bat-wings. It landed on the roof in a clattering of tiles, and turned to look back. Veitch thought he glimpsed a demonic grin and then it was away across the rooftops.

The broken-nosed man hurried up. "Are you all right, mate? Did he hurt ya?"

A prostitute in her forties came over wearing dirty white muslin and greasy blue silk. She reeked of cheap gin, and her face was seamed with smallpox scars and the scabs of some sexually transmitted disease.

"That was Spring-heeled Jack, that was. Lor', you were lucky," she slurred.

"What is it?" Veitch asked.

"The Devil hisself," the broken-nosed man said.

"He's been coming round these parts for thirteen year," the prostitute said. "Lost souls aplenty in the East End."

"Surely you've heard of 'im?" the broken-nosed man said. "Even the Lord Mayor of London talks about Spring-heeled Jack."

"He blinded poor Lucy Squires down in Limehouse with that fiery breath of his." The prostitute staggered around, talking to no one in particular. "Down in Green Dragon Alley. Only eighteen, she was, the little darlin'."

Veitch looked around for Annie, but she'd run off in the confusion. Irritated by the distraction, he pushed his way past the prostitute and marched into the maze of stinking alleys.

Ten minutes later he found his way to the courtyard. He could smell the horses and hear the rattle of their hooves and the hiss of their breath long before he saw them. In the shadows the Brothers and Sisters of Spiders stood like statues, dead eyes staring damnation.

Veitch kissed Etain on her dry, cold cheek. She turned the icy lamps of her eyes on him, and Tannis, Branwen and Owein followed suit immediately, like the gears of a machine turning.

"I'm glad you lot are here," Veitch said. "You need friends in a city like this. It's a sewer. All the poor left to fend for themselves in the shit, dying from diseases, killing each other slowly. And all the rich up West, sipping their claret and not giving a toss." He couldn't get the image of Annie out of his mind and he was surprised how much it troubled him.

"All right," he said. "No point moaning about shit you can't do anything about. I've found where the first one is. Let's get to business."

3

2,300 girders. 3,300 columns. 300,000 panes of glass. The Crystal Palace was a cathedral dedicated to Victorian ingenuity and excellence. It sprawled across the southern edge of Hyde Park for nineteen acres and soared up 108 feet to tower above the London skyline, encompassing several of the park's elm trees within its massive bulk.

Church stood in the shimmering celestial interior and marvelled; nothing that he'd read about the Great Exhibition had prepared him for the spectacle. A rich spectrum of hues burst from the displays on every side. In the centre a gigantic fountain rose up, illuminated by shafts of sunlight. To the north was a bank of forest trees and verdant tropical plants. Everywhere sculptures had been placed in the most harmonious settings, some of them colossal and of unrivalled beauty.

Niamh stood close, so entranced she appeared unaware her shoulder was brushing his. "Why, this is a thing of wonder. It would not look out of place in one of the great courts."

Tom snorted. "Open your eyes. It's a big shop to sell spoons to foreigners."

"You're just a cynic," Church said.

"And you are a small child, entranced by shiny things."

"Must you two bicker all the time?" Niamh sighed regally.

"I wish Jerzy could see this," Church said.

"Oh, will you stop worrying about the prancing buffoon." Tom sniffed. "If he's too empty-headed to accompany us on our jaunt, he deserves all he gets." He shuffled towards one of the halls displaying the wares of Persia, Greece, Egypt and Turkey. "Besides, the lad's only just gained his freedom. He should have some time to follow his own feet."

Church heard the half-buried note of sympathy, but Tom refused to meet his gaze.

"Where do we find this man with whom you wish to speak?" Niamh asked.

"He's here with the Archbishop of Canterbury on an official visit," Church said. "Queen Victoria opened this place with Prince Albert yesterday, and today all the other dignitaries get their chance at being big shots. So just look for a bunch of stuffed shirts pretending they're something important."

They moved through the crowded courts amongst the exhibits of arts and crafts from all parts of the globe until they came across a crowd of finely dressed men and women being led by a guide. The archbishop in his ceremonial robes was near the front with a small group of ecclesiastical advisors.

Church indicated a stern-faced man with a long, greying beard.

"How do you know he's one of your Watchmen? You don't keep that close an eye on them," Tom said.

"I visited a couple of days ago by our time, during the late seventeenth century in this timeline, when Sir Christopher Wren and Nicholas Hawksmoor were building a new series of churches to replace the ones lost in the Great Fire of London. I met with the Watchmen and we decided that there would always be a representative at Christchurch, Spitalfields, so I'd always have a contact."

"So you have got a brain in there. You manage to keep it well hidden."

Though Niamh wore the voluminous yet restrictive Victorian dress, her beauty and the faint glimmer of gold glowing through her make-up gave her an exotic appearance that drew many stares. Church watched the bearded clergyman's eyes fall on her, then move to Tom and Church. Realisation slowly dawned on his face, and he slipped away from the group.

"Is it true?" he said quietly to Church. "You are the one in the information passed down to me by my forebears? I have a drawing, a rough thing, but the likeness is uncanny."

"I'm Jack Churchill."

"Francis Cole. Sir, I must shake your hand." Cole pumped Church's hand furiously. "You have some new information for me? A mission, perhaps?"

Church handed him a crisp, white envelope. "In here are directions to a roadside café . . . a tea-room, if you like. It'll be meaningless to you, because it hasn't been built yet, but it will be. I want you to pass it down to your successors until the early years of the twenty-first century, when one of them must go to the café to write a message on the walls of the toilets."

"The lavatories?" Cole looked uncertain.

"A message to someone who will be born in around a hundred and thirty years' time."

Cole looked into Church's eyes, intellectual excitement growing on his face. "Remarkable! All they said about you is true. A message across the years, to times yet unwritten. Remarkable." As Cole slipped the envelope into his pocket, his face darkened. "I am afraid I have some distressing news, Mr Churchill. Before I set off this morning I heard word of a brutal murder in my parish. I have not yet had time to establish the truth of the matter, but I fear it is a gentleman who recently made my acquaintance—a bookkeeper by the name of Richard Tanner." He leaned in conspiratorially. "He announced himself as a Brother of Dragons, and had just made contact with two more of his group."

"Veitch," Church said.

"You're not thinking of confronting him, are you?" Tom interjected. "There's only one of you this time."

Church wavered. "I don't know."

"Veitch is playing the long game," Tom pressed. "You should, too."

"That's easily said. How do you walk away when you know something bad's happening that you might be able to influence?"

"Best stay away. You don't want to be forced into facing him before you're whole."

"If it is any help, there was another sighting of Spring-heeled Jack in the vicinity," Cole added. "If such a fearsome thing exists, it may well have been involved."

"Walk away, Jack," Tom insisted.

Church was torn, but before he could reach a decision he glimpsed a familiar figure through the crowd. It was fleeting, but Church was sure he had seen correctly. "Jerzy's here," he said.

4

Veitch leaned against the chimney stack, examining his silver hand. The view across the rooftops had been spectacular, to St Paul's and beyond, to the gleaming white manses of the West End. But now it was rapidly being obscured by the descending smog as thousands of fires pumped up greasy smoke from the cheap coal slack the poor shovelled into their grates.

Veitch clamped the mechanical fingers into a fist. "Not even a whole man any more."

He slipped his other arm around Etain, who was sitting next to him. "Who'd ever have thought a dirty little urchin from South London would end up here? When I was at school, the careers wanker told me I wouldn't amount to anything. Not smart enough to take my exams. I could train as a mechanic if I was lucky. No point having any *hopes*." He said the word bitterly. "Can you imagine telling a kid that? Basically saying, 'Sorry, mate, you life's over.' Wanker. All those nice middle-class kids, they have parents who tell them they can do anything. Then they're set up, no boundaries. They just head off and do the best they can."

He kicked a loose shingle, sending it slithering down the roof to pitch over the edge and shatter in the street far below.

"Then I started having all these dreams. Not the kind of dreams you might have. Like drug trips. Movies in my head. Every night. Drove me mad. Everyone thought I was bleedin' nuts." He unbuttoned his shirt to reveal the technicoloured tattoos dappling his torso. "Only way I could deal with them was to get them drawn up here. Turns out they weren't dreams. They were my . . ." He wrestled to find the right word. "Heritage. Who I was. Stuff that was going to happen." He traced his finger around the outline of a green dragon. "And then my life exploded from nothing into something. A Brother of Dragons. A Champion of Life." He laughed. "I hooked up with the others and we were going to change everything. Shavi, he was all right. Laura . . . bitch. And Ruth . . ." He fell silent. "Sorry, darlin', but she was something special. I loved her. I bloody loved her. And then that bastard Church came along and ruined it all. We were a team . . . they were the best friends I ever had. Or so I thought. I'd have done anything for them. We could have done anything. No boundaries. You get it? The sky was the bleedin' limit. All thrown away. Me, tossed back on the scrapheap. Left for dead. I *was* dead . . . until I got a second chance. This time I'm using it right. I'm not going to let anybody screw me over again."

He balanced on the pitch of the roof and stretched. The smog hung so densely all around that it felt as if night was coming in early.

"You going to help me, darlin'? I can't do this bit on my own." He held out his hand and Etain took it. Together they walked to the roof's edge, and then over, vertically down the face of the building. Veitch directed Etain to a window through which candlelight glimmered. Veitch leaned back and smashed the glass with his boot, at the same time drawing his sword. Black fire danced around the blade.

Inside, a young man and woman cowered in one corner. They held each other's hands, for strength; allies, not lovers. "Who are you?" the man said defiantly. He tried to push the woman behind him for safety.

"I'm your worst fucking nightmare, mate." Veitch lifted the sword and stepped towards them.

5

Church dashed through the halls of the Great Exhibition, pushing his way through the genteel crowds. He caught sight of what he thought was Jerzy in the Indian court and then again amongst the agricultural implements of the United States court. It was only ever a fleeting glimpse of white skin or a fixed grin, enough to identify the figure as the Mocker, yet rationally Church couldn't understand how it could be him: there were no shrieks, no swooning women or angry, shocked men.

Eventually his pursuit led him to the Russian court. There was no sign of Jerzy amidst the malachite doors, vases and ornaments, but as Church searched amongst the browsers he saw something else that put him on edge: a rapid movement, a blur of what looked like brown seal-skin and a sinuous, muscular shape that was definitely not human. It was something he had seen before, near Carn Euny and on the way out of Eboracum.

Before he could investigate further, a hand closed on his sleeve. He looked into the face of a woman of about twenty years old, with heavy Eastern European features, brown hair and dark, penetrating eyes.

"You are looking for your friend," she said in thickly accented English. "You will not find him here. He is with the Master now."

"I saw him."

"No, you did not."

Church searched for a sign that she was more than she appeared. "What do you know?"

"I know we all have masters who set us on a path to wisdom. My own Master is a Hindu man of imposing appearance who visited me many times when I was a child. I saw him this day and he directed me to you. Jack Churchill. The King Beyond the Water."

"And you are?"

"Helena Petrovna Blavatsky. I was born in the Ukraine, but I am now a child of the world."

"So why did this master send you to me?"

"Because you are at a fork in your life's path," said the woman who would help launch the Victorian era's occult revival with her Theosophical Society. "In the coming days, months, years, you can choose to go one way or another. I am to give you information to help you make your choice."

Helena led Church away from the crowds to a quiet area under one of the wrought-iron staircases that led to the upper level.

"The first thing you must understand is that the universe is built on a system of harmonious numbers," she said.

Five, Church thought.

"Numbers that have specific meaning, specific powers. The universe is an ordered system that contains chaos. Order implies intelligence. Who created it? That is the question. Two is a powerful number, for it lies at the heart of everything. Wherever you look, there is duality. Night and day. Good and evil. Zoroastrianism, which is the root of Gnosticism, believed the world was a battleground for two beings: Ahura Mazda, the god of light, and life, and goodness; and Ahriman, the god of darkness, corruption and death."

Her mention of Gnosticism triggered Church's memory of John Dee talking about the same subject in his university rooms in Krakow. Coincidence? Or more of the patterns Helena was talking about?

"You are meant to tell me about Gnosticism?" he asked.

"Gnosis means knowing through observation or experience."

Another connection: Church recalled what Hal, the spirit in the Blue

Fire, had said about not revealing what had happened because Church had to learn it for himself.

"By the time of Christ's birth, the fundamentals of Gnosticism were already ancient," she continued. "The roots stretch back at least six hundred years before that, when adepts used what many perceived to be 'magic.' You are aware of the Blue Fire?"

He nodded.

"Simon Magus, Valentinus, Marcion—all of them were attracted to Gnosticism. They understood the meanings of the serpent and the labyrinth. For centuries that knowledge disappeared from public view, but it was protected by the Knights Templar and the Cathars . . ."

Her words sparked so many links in his mind that it could not be random—this time with the treasure store under London Bridge that had held the crystal skull. Church felt the movement of great forces around him.

". . . who could only avoid persecution over the secrets of Existence by coding the information for others to decipher." She gave a teasing smile. "Did you know that the ancient Ophites sect worshipped the serpent as the source of forbidden knowledge? Did you know that the Peratae believed Jesus was the soul of the serpent? That the Naasseni worshipped the serpent? All Gnostics."

"You're playing with me now."

She took his hand. "I am simply showing you that there are layers upon layers. Strip away one to find the hidden knowledge beneath. The hidden structure that holds everything together. There are truths and untruths, and the mere act of searching for the mystery is in itself the uncovering of the mystery. In Eastern philosophies there is a technique known as raising kundalini. Kundalini means 'serpent fire.' This technique involves waking the dormant power of the sleeping serpent, the spiritual and psychic energy we all possess, and then raising the energy through the body to the head. Once it is in the head, anything is possible."

"All right . . . Gnosticism . . . serpents . . . secret connections. I hear what you're saying. I just don't see how it helps me right now. And, frankly, I'm not wholly sure I should trust you."

Church looked around the crowds. The glimpses of Jerzy had clearly been designed to lead him to this meeting with Helena Blavatsky, but who had arranged it? Would her information help him, or was there some malign intent behind her words? So many mysteries surrounded his life that he found it increasingly difficult to know who to trust and in which direction to go.

"The kundalini is symbolised by two entwined snakes, which is also the caduceus, the timeless symbol of healing. The truth is everywhere you look, Jack Churchill," she said, as if she could read his thoughts. "This may mean nothing to you now, but there may come a time in the labyrinth of your life when you will see this golden thread and follow its sinuous path to enlightenment."

The whole meeting with Blavatsky was starting to feel like a distraction from his original intention: to find Veitch and prevent him from killing any more Brothers and Sisters of Dragons.

"One more thing," she said, smiling. "Look to the Fool, for the Fool is the holder of wisdom. The Fool knows nothing. That is wisdom. Look to the Fool."

Blavatsky's cryptic comments were starting to irritate him. He was distracted by laughter echoing around the room; it sounded simultaneously very far away yet close at hand, and it had a quality that was not entirely human. When he looked back, Blavatsky was gone. Church searched for her, and when he returned to the point where she had stood he had a fleeting impression of a darkly mocking grin and searing inhuman eyes, fading like the Cheshire Cat.

Something brushed his temple and he fell into unconsciousness.

6

Veitch wiped the blood from his blade on the bedclothes. Etain stood nearby, staring out of the window into the smog-created gloom in a manner that Veitch pretended was yearning for the green, rolling landscape of her former life.

"Three down," he hummed. "Two to go. Wish I'd been keeping a running total. I stopped at a hundred and forty-five."

He sheathed the blade and turned back to the room. The man's head, which had been sitting in the centre of the room, was somehow back on his neck. The lips had been pulled into a mocking grin.

Veitch kept his hand on the sword. "Who did that?" he said incredulously to Etain. He'd only been wiping his blade for a second; no time at all for someone to steal in behind him and adjust the body. Then he noticed that the woman's head was missing.

Cursing, he rushed to the door. It was locked. He shattered it with his boot and stormed into a dark corridor that smelled of coal and damp and cabbage water. At the end, by the stairs, the woman's head hung by the hair like a Hallowe'en lantern, but he could not see who was holding it.

Veitch raced along the corridor. By the time he reached the end he could hear footsteps rapidly descending the stairs, and then the banging of the front door. Sprinting into the street, he coughed and choked in the smog, looking up and down. The head bobbed along, just disappearing in the haze.

Veitch hadn't got far when hands grabbed him roughly and hauled him into an alley. It was the Libertarian.

"What the hell are you doing?" Veitch raged. He threw himself back into the street, but he had lost sight of the head.

The Libertarian pulled him back. "What are *you* doing?" His red eyes blazed in the gloom. "You may well hold a position of some authority because of your peculiar abilities, though why you were given them remains beyond me. But you are still weak and pathetic, easily distracted and, I might add, none too bright. We cannot risk upsetting the delicate balance at this crucial stage." The Libertarian's sneer became a snarl.

Veitch threw him off and drew his sword. "Who cares what you think, you parasite?"

The Libertarian stared at the sword, then drew himself up and smiled menacingly.

Veitch was distracted by a shapeless mass in the alley, which he realised were two bodies, butchered so brutally they were almost unrecognisable. Scattered nearby were pieces of clothing—a shawl, worn but cared for lovingly, and a man's flat cap.

"What did you do that for?" Veitch said, disgusted. "They couldn't have hurt you."

"I did it because I could."

Veitch stared deeply into the Libertarian's eyes but couldn't fathom what he saw there. "You and me are going to have it out one day," he said.

"I relish the moment."

Sickened, Veitch sheathed his blade and ran back into the street. Candles and lamps were alight in the windows he passed. They revealed families, sometimes eight to a room, old men hunched over tiny fires, women old before their time, sobbing at a table or getting drunk on cheap spirits, children worn out from work, men in the act of robbery or violence. It was dark and it smelled sour.

Just when he was about to give up and return to Etain, the head dropped from above him and splattered at his feet before rolling into the gutter. On the edge of the roof, Spring-heeled Jack rocked on his haunches, his staring eyes seething. With a flourish, his cloak rose up around him and he was away across the rooftops once more.

"Right, you bastard," Veitch hissed. "I'm in a bad bleedin' mood and it's all coming down on your head."

Sometimes it was difficult to see the figure skittering across the rooftops, for the streets were narrow and the buildings high. But once they moved out of the East End it became easier. Past the Tower and St Paul's Veitch raced, determined Spring-heeled Jack would not outpace him. Finally, the West End rose up around him. There were carriages and people in fine clothes on their way to the theatre or stretching their legs after dinner. Veitch hitched a ride on the back of a carriage, keeping one eye on the roofs.

It was only when the buildings ran out that Spring-heeled Jack came down to ground level, and by then they were in Hyde Park. Ahead, the gleaming majesty of the Crystal Palace stood like a beacon in the night.

7

"Have you been drinking? Wake up!"

Church opened his eyes to find himself being roughly shaken by Tom. Tropical vegetation swayed all around him. He pulled himself to his feet and discovered that he was buried deep in the greenery near the trees inside the Crystal Palace. Niamh stood nearby looking as anxious as Tom. It was dark and the exhibition was deserted. Only a few lights burned at intermittent stages along the concourse and there was the eerie atmosphere found in all public places locked up for the night.

"We've been searching for you for hours," Tom said. "What do you think you're doing?"

Church could recall talking to Helena Blavatsky and then her disappearance, but nothing more. "Something made me black out."

"We had to hide in one of the exhibits when they started to lock up so we could carry on looking for you," Tom continued with exasperation. "What do you mean, something made you black out?"

Church pushed past Tom onto the echoing concourse. An even stranger atmosphere was apparent there, unsettled, like a room before an arrival. "Can you feel it?" he asked.

Niamh nodded slowly. She cocked her head, listening. "They come. The Seelie Court come."

Church wandered along the concourse, feeling the electricity in the air. Tom chased after him. "Let's leave. Now. We don't want anything to do with any more of *them*."

To Church, it appeared as though the glass and steel walls of the Palace were stretching out into Hyde Park so that the Exhibition encompassed the whole of the open space, then all of London, and finally it seemed there were no walls at all. Church could see the exhibits, the epitome of modern thought and industrialisation, and the statues, and then an impenetrable forest stretching as far as the eye could see underneath unrecognisable constellations in an alien sky.

"What's happening?" he asked. The atmosphere had taken on a dreamy, hallucinogenic quality.

Beside him, Niamh was smiling. "They could not stay away."

Figures were becoming visible amongst the trees, ghostly at first but gaining more substance as they approached.

"The Seelie Court is one of the twenty great courts, but they remain detached from my brothers and sisters. They prefer their own rules, their own culture, subtly different, unique, perhaps," Niamh explained. "They are wanderers across the lands, and have no palaces or castles, no walled enclaves. They have no banner and no name but the one the Fragile Creatures gave them. They have always had a great affinity with the Fixed Lands and with your people, but they believed this place was changing and that there was no longer a home for them here."

Some of the mysterious figures were clearly Tuatha Dé Danann, golden-skinned, ethereal and alluring. Some were grotesque, with strange faces that reminded Church of carvings on Gothic buildings. Others were simply monstrous, all scales and bat-wings, horns and tails and cloven hooves. The Golden Ones who were clearly the king and queen led the stately procession. They came to a halt in front of Church, Niamh and Tom.

"Sister, we see you again sooner than we expected," the king said.

Niamh gave a formal bow. "A pleasure, as always, my brother."

He turned to Church and surveyed him with a curious eye. "And you are the Brother of Dragons about whom we have heard so much?"

Mostly Church felt indifferent to the Tuatha Dé Danann and their interference in humanity, but he felt a strange connection with this group. He could tell from the way some of the more monstrous creatures shifted hungrily that they were dangerous, and at the least prone to mischief, but there was something almost paternal about the king. Church bowed. "I'm pleased to meet you. My name is Jack Churchill."

"Or Jack, Giantkiller," the queen said with a wry smile. "Tales are already being told of your exploits in the Far Lands. Of how you tricked the Master of Tongues to win the Cunning Key, and how you climbed the Malign Mount to free the daughters of the Lord Tempest from the Ice Dolls—"

"I'm sure they're exaggerated. You know how tales get."

"I do indeed, Brother of Dragons." The king gave an enigmatic smile. "We would introduce ourselves, but our names are legion amongst the Sons of Adam. We are the king and queen of the Seelie Court. Will that suffice?"

"It's good enough for me." Church noticed Tom had slipped several feet back and was skulking near the vegetation.

"You have returned, then, brother?" Niamh said.

"A brief visit, sister. It saddens us to see what is transpiring in the Fixed Lands. The rivers are filled with poisons. Smoke blackens the sky over foul factories. The cities sprawl across green fields. It is not surprising that the Blue Fire has fallen asleep in many parts of the land."

"But there are still places like this," the queen added, "where wonder is ignited in the Sons of Adam. We come to drink of their astonishment and delight. And we shall until Reason drives us away for ever."

The sound of smashing glass echoed from somewhere near at hand. Church turned to Niamh. "Police?" The Seelie Court did not look perturbed, although the king's face hardened as he scented the air.

His black coat swirling around him, Veitch strode out of the shadows to stand in the circle of light beneath one of the torches. "Well, what the bloody hell's all this, then?" he sneered.

Church grew cold, remembering Lucia and Etain, and all the others Veitch had murdered.

Veitch drew his sizzling black blade and pointed it towards the king. "Don't stick your nose in, all right? This is between me and him."

"I wouldn't get on their wrong side, Veitch," Church said.

"I'm not scared of them." Veitch held out his silver hand. "See this? A present from Dian Cecht and the Court of the Final Word. Only when you get presents from that lot they never turn out how you expect. They can't be trusted, any of them."

The Court of the Final Word: Jerzy, Tom and now Veitch. The connections were becoming clearer to Church.

He could see the cold hatred in Veitch's eyes, and the hot, barely constrained anger bubbling behind it. They were the eyes of a man on the edge. Church drew his sword. The blade sang and fizzed with Blue Fire, but it was much depleted from its original state and Church wasn't convinced it could stand up to the black fury of Veitch's sword.

Veitch saw it, too. "You're only half a man since Janus had his way with you. You're a joke now. You don't stand a chance."

"So what's the plan? Drag me off again so your vampire can suck out the rest of my spirit?"

Veitch's eyes narrowed. "Nah. This time I'm just going to kill you."

"Your bosses won't like that." Tom came forward defiantly. "You know they need the Pendragon Spirit. They're terrified of it—they must find a way to contain it. Only it can't be contained."

"Shut up!" Rage lit Veitch's face. "You always were a pain in the arse."

Church looked from Veitch to Tom. Veitch saw the betrayal in Church's expression and laughed. "I forgot—*you* forgot. In the future, you wankers. A hundred and fifty years from now. He was with the Five of us. And her." He nodded towards Niamh.

Veitch advanced a few steps. Church hefted his sword, but Veitch was lost to his bitterness. He jabbed his sword towards Tom and Niamh. "They both gave up their lives for the cause—that's how sick all this is. She loved you—" Niamh winced as if she had been slapped "—but you didn't care because all you wanted was Ruth. And that bastard thought you were some kind of hero. So you let them both walk away and die, and just carried on getting what you wanted. I wish you *could* remember so I could see your face. See if there's any guilt there. See if you care at all."

The rage finally broke though and Veitch rushed forward, swinging his sword. Church parried, and a massive explosion of energy lit up the whole Crystal Palace; black lightning flashed and Blue Fire erupted in wild bolts. Both men were thrown yards across the hard stone floor as though opposing polarities had been brought violently together.

Stunned, and with every bone ringing, Church staggered to his feet. Veitch had already recovered and was bearing down on him. Church avoided the arc of the black blade, but Veitch caught Church full in the face with his silver hand. The blow sent Church spinning across the floor once more until he crashed into the side of the fountain.

Through a haze of pain and blood, Church was aware of the Seelie Court watching silently; he felt like a gladiator fighting before the emperor as entertainment.

Veitch drove Church into the pool of the fountain. Water rained down in sheets all around, obscuring the rest of the exhibition. Their blades met again, and the cascading energy raged all around them, turning every droplet into a miniature sun.

Veitch forced Church back, pressing his face so close that Church could see the gleam of his snarling teeth. "See—you're too weak. I could gut you in a second."

Church was determined not to let everyone down. He drilled down into his depleted reserves and took the fight to Veitch, driving him back by rapidly changing between techniques he had learned in the Iron Age, Roman Britain and in Tudor times. It made up for the relentless savagery of Veitch's approach. He took his knocks, a cut here, a blow there, and came back just as hard. When he laid open Veitch's forearm, he felt a glimmer of satisfaction that he had paid Veitch back for the licks he had taken in Rome.

Amidst the explosions of light, they tumbled out of the fountain and battled their way up one of the winding wrought-iron staircases. On the balcony overlooking the concourse, Church realised how much he missed the Pendragon Spirit as his energy levels flagged while Veitch fought on as powerfully as he had begun.

It would have been easier to give up, or to run and hide, but Church wanted to find within himself the person that everyone else recognised, but he had never seen: the hero, the king. He fought back again just as hard, but now he was taking cuts all over his upper body and his blood was running freely.

Finally, he slipped on his own blood splattered on the floor and crashed back against the railing. Veitch moved in quickly, determined to drive Church over the top and onto the hard stone far below.

"Say goodbye," Veitch whispered.

But as he raised his blade for the final blow, a figure shot up behind Church. It landed on the railing and balanced perfectly. Blue Fire burst into Veitch's eyes, blinding him.

Veitch staggered backwards, clutching at his face, and Church prised himself away from the railing. Spring-heeled Jack's face was impassive. He balanced on the railing for one more second, and then he gave another enormous leap and was gone.

The intrusion was enough for Church to recover. He rebalanced himself and gripped his sword defensively as Veitch, cursing loudly, righted himself. But before he could attack once more, he cried out in pain. A small knife protruded from his back. Behind him, Tom quickly retreated, pale and frightened.

"You bastards!" Veitch raged, but the rest of his comments were drowned by the sound of breaking glass. Riding down the sheer face of the glass and steel wall were Etain, Tannis, Branwen and Owein. Church felt sick when he saw them, the feelings of what had been lost still as raw as when he had found their bodies in Carn Euny. Yet when he looked at their dead faces and saw their hate-filled eyes, he also felt scared, for he could see they were now capable of any atrocity.

The Brothers and Sisters of Spiders steered their demonic mounts onto the balcony and circled Veitch. Church backed away, knowing he did not have the strength to fight them.

They made no attempt to attack. Etain bent down to pull Veitch onto the back of her horse, where Church had once ridden not so long—or maybe an age—ago. Veitch's face was strained with pain, but he still had the strength to point one finger at Church. That simple gesture contained all his hatred and bitterness and a promise that revenge would be swift and terrible.

And then they were away, rising eerily up the wall to disappear through the hole in the roof.

Church sagged to his knees, what little energy he had dissipated by the shattering battle.

Niamh ran up and put an arm around his shoulders, while Tom helped him to his feet. "Thank you," Church said to Tom. The Rhymer nodded curtly. Yet they could barely look at each other after Veitch's statement that Niamh and Tom would give their own lives for Church's cause in the future. The revelation was both heart-warming and a terrible burden; none of their relationships would ever be the same.

8

While a handful of police officers investigated the disturbance at the main doors, the king and queen of the Seelie Court whisked Church, Niamh and Tom out of the Crystal Palace—one moment they were standing on the main concourse and the next they were on the edge of Hyde Park. Church sensed that what the Seelie Court had witnessed had changed them in some way, though he could not define how.

Everything Veitch had said haunted him, reopening old wounds and adding to his confusion about his purpose. Was he really as corrupted as Veitch made out, and if so, could he make amends?

There were other mysteries: what part was Spring-heeled Jack playing? What had happened to Jerzy? And what was the significance of Helena Blavatsky's cryptic words?

Church was so lost to his thoughts that he did not notice a carriage pass the edge of the park. In the back seat sat a thirteen-year-old girl called Annie, desperate and apprehensive at what the future might hold, but also hopeful. She had bought herself a fresh start in a new life with a guinea that had been delivered to her, one single moment of grace and charity that had changed her entire existence.

266

CHAPTER EIGHT
SATYR DAY AND SUN DAY

1

Church stood at the window and looked out over the Court of the Soaring Spirit. When he had first arrived it had been a grim, labyrinthine prison of the mind and soul. Now it was a source of transcendental magic with lanterns gleaming in every window and torches ablaze in the streets and public places. Music rang out from the inns and drifting fragrances were caught on the breeze. The Far Lands altered continually, like life, like emotions. You could never see the same view from a window twice.

He tried to recall Ruth—not her face, which was as clear as ever, but the subtleties that were the foundation of any relationship: the looks, the touches, the shared words, the fleeting moments in between the big occasions. They were all lost. Even his trips to the Wish-Post didn't help, for they only reminded him of the threat and what was missing, not the heart. He feared he was losing her.

He gently hummed "In the Wee Small Hours," taking refuge in the familiar: old songs, old friends, old times. The past had always offered him great comfort, but now he couldn't shake his troubled sense of foreboding. What had happened in London was so bizarre it betrayed any kind of understanding. The mysterious disappearance of Jerzy, the equally mysterious appearance of Helena Blavatsky telling him about Gnostic thought, the apparently coincidental arrival of the Seelie Court and the involvement of Spring-heeled Jack—Church was convinced they were linked in some way, but the connections eluded him. Patterns were forming all around him, then disappearing from view just as quickly. He felt as though he was being poked and prodded in a certain direction without any real understanding of why. The sensation was both creepy and infuriating.

At least his wounds had healed reasonably well. He was angry that he had not been able to prevent Veitch from escaping, but he had started to believe that nothing would be resolved until one of them was dead.

"They're ready." Tom leaned against the wall, casually rolling himself a smoke with some of the herbs he bought from one of the shadowy stores in the Gothic quarter.

Church reluctantly left the window and turned his mind to the struggle that lay ahead. As he passed Tom, he paused. "What Veitch said—"

"Forget it. He's a liar and a murderer. You don't want to start believing the words of scum like that."

In the moment of silence that passed between them, the lie in Tom's words was evident and he looked away, inhaling a deep draught of the aromatic smoke.

"All right," Church said. "I'm glad you were with me in the Crystal Palace and . . . I'm glad you're still around."

Tom nodded. "Don't let them push you about. You're the king, remember."

"I don't feel like it."

"Does any king?"

Church entered the vast Hall of Whispers, where every sound was magnified into a susurration of invisible beings, travelling back and forth until they slowly faded. In the centre was an ancient, huge oak table, and all around, some sitting, some standing, were representatives of Niamh and Lugh's courts. Church surveyed the faces, his perception swimming when his eyes fell on creatures he had never seen before until his disoriented mind settled on an image it found acceptable. Many were unfamiliar to him, but some echoed descriptions of gods from Celtic mythology. Math, the sorcerer with the four-faced mask, was there, as was Ceridwen, a nature goddess with flowing black hair and a sensitive face.

All eyes turned to him as he entered. Niamh rose from her chair at the head of the table and said, "The Brother of Dragons has arrived. Let the council begin."

"Do we recognise the authority of this Fragile Creature?" Math said gruffly from behind a bear mask.

Lugh stood and said, "I recognise his authority, as does my sister, and so our two courts shall also recognise him."

Math nodded but did not appear to concede the point. Church could see in some of the other faces the contempt in which Fragile Creatures were held; it would be a hard fight to overcome that prejudice.

"We are gathered here to discuss the information we have collected," Niamh announced, "and to discuss our response to the Army of the Ten Billion Spiders."

"Why should we respond? We are the Golden Ones," someone said.

"They mass on our borders," Lugh said. "Their fortress grows by the day and is now larger than any court. The army swells with stolen Fragile Creatures, and the lesser races who are easily controlled. They have Redcaps, Baobhan Sith, the Gehennis, and more."

Discussion about the relative powers of both sides ranged back and forth for a while, with the majority of the group unshaken in their belief in their innate superiority under any circumstances. Church grew angry with the arrogance and signalled to Niamh that he wished to speak.

Suspicious eyes fell on him as he stood. "You're seeing the Enemy in the wrong light," he began. "You consider them lesser because they're marshalling Fragile Creatures and Redcaps and all the others. But they're none of those things. They're not even spiders. Those things are just the surface, symbols representing what lies behind them. And what they will be, very shortly, is you."

Church looked around at the beautiful faces. "They have in their possession a magical artefact—a crystal skull. I don't know where it came from, but I do know what it is capable of: summoning you against your will. It's a lure for gods. That in itself is not enough. They have also obtained another weapon, the Anubis Box. With it they can corrupt any captured god and control them."

A ripple of angry voices ran round the room. Some called out for Church to be expelled.

"What the Brother of Dragons says is true," Lugh interrupted, "for I was almost corrupted by those very weapons. And I saw it take another."

"Who?" Math asked.

"A god from one of the other branches of your family that you pretend doesn't exist," Church said. "If you want to survive this, you need to change your thinking. You need to recognise that there were other races here in the Far Lands before you, who may well have been responsible for the creation of the crystal skull and other weapons like it. And you have to accept there are others like you who have been seen as gods across my world throughout our civilisation. And you and they could soon be working for the Army of the Ten Billion Spiders towards your own destruction."

Church was shouted down by angry gods, some of whom looked as if they were ready to kill him on the spot. Surprisingly it was Math who turned the tide of the debate, speaking through the boar's-head mask. "What the Brother of Dragons says is true." The crowd fell silent. "In my studies I have become aware of others like us, and some of you know in your hearts that we are not alone."

"If we, or others like us, fall to the Enemy, it will become a fight we cannot win," Lugh said.

"There is another matter," Niamh began hesitantly. She recounted how the Libertarian had killed her guards and how the Ninth Legion had "wiped from Existence" many of the Court of Peaceful Days. "We thought ourselves free of endings," she said, "but now we know that is not true. We are resilient. It takes much to eradicate us. But in the final reckoning we are no different from Fragile Creatures."

Her blasphemy stunned the room. Church had never seen so many rocked to the core of their being, but they could not deny the truths that had been delivered by the queen and king of the two courts. It would take them a long time to assimilate the information.

"Who are the Enemy? Truly?" one of the Tuatha Dé Danann asked, eager to change the line of conversation.

"We don't know," Church replied, "but they are extremely powerful, and they appear to be fanning out through history to achieve their ends."

"And what are those ends?"

"The Enemy thrives on despair," Church said. "I think they want to eradicate all hope. That's what they appear to be doing in their interference in the history of my kind."

A woman with long blonde hair and silver eyes stood up. Her voice had no trace of arrogance; it quavered. "Then what path should we take? To confront them could mean we will all be wiped from Existence." A tear sprang to her eye.

"I fear we have no choice," Lugh said.

"But we could be wiped from Existence," the woman repeated desperately.

"Their forces are already too strong for us to meet them head on," Niamh said. "Certainly not without the aid of the other courts."

"You will not convince the others," Math said adamantly through the mask of the fish, and Church could see that Niamh believed this to be true.

"The first thing we have to do is destroy the crystal skull or the Anubis Box, preferably both," Church said. "They may have the numbers, but those are their most potent weapons."

"We do not know how many have already fallen under their spell," Math said.

The silver-eyed woman clutched at her hair. "Madness! If we cannot confront the Enemy, how do we destroy these weapons?"

"I'm not going to pretend I know how these weapons work," Church said, "but it appears they have to be operated—if that's the right word—from my world, otherwise the Enemy would have summoned Lugh and Apollo to their fortress. They didn't. They did it in my world, and they chose their time very carefully. They didn't rush into it, so I'm betting they can't use the skull and the box at the drop of a hat."

"So the weapons must be found in the Fixed Lands," Math mused.

"And you can do that?" Ceridwen said to Church.

"There are people in my world who are my eyes and ears. They can look out for any activity, anything that might point me to the weapons."

"And you will fight for the Golden Ones?" the silver-eyed woman said in amazement.

Church considered this for a moment. "I will fight for Existence," he said.

2

Church and Tom rode to the top of the rise and looked down on the Court of the Final Word. It was like a Roman temple, majestic in gleaming white marble, with Doric columns supporting a portico that towered over a pair of brass doors that could have admitted ten men standing on each other's shoulders. The pure white light that reflected off the extensive complex spread for at least ten square miles across the floor of the sunlit valley. The court was so large that a river ran through the centre of it, and numerous smaller tributaries emerged from under the walls. At the point where the river flowed out of the court the waters ran red.

"One entrance, see." Tom indicated the brass doors.

Church could see the Rhymer was shaking. "Are you all right?"

"No," Tom snapped. "And if you ever get inside that place you'll see why." With trembling hands he rolled himself a smoke and dragged on it to calm himself. "I don't know if I can go any nearer. I don't know if I can carry on doing this at all. There's nothing written that says just because I can see what's coming, I should have to play some part in preventing it. I could walk away. I might just do that. Make the most of what little time I've got left."

"It's your choice, Tom. And nobody would think badly of you for doing that. But I'd miss your advice—"

Tom snorted.

"When you actually give me any. You're a cryptic, miserable bastard, but you're the only person I can rely on round here."

"By default, then," Tom said. "And isn't that a pathetic state of affairs. You're a poor excuse for a king, and I'm a pitiable example of a wise man. We both have a lot to learn and we need to find some fast ways of doing it."

Church looked back at the brooding presence of the Court of the Final Word. "There are too many priorities—get in there and retrieve my Pendragon Spirit, return to our world and destroy the skull and box, stop Veitch killing any more Brothers and Sisters of Dragons—"

"That's why there should be five of you. Can't do it on your own."

"So there's no other way in there?"

"One door. Like death, once you pass through it you're changed for ever."

Reluctantly, Church turned his horse around and headed back down the rise. Tom followed. "So how am I supposed to do this without Shavi and Laura?" he said. "And Ruth?"

3

Ruth lay on the sofa with her iPod on, eyes shut and drifting close to sleep. Aimee Mann was singing about someone looking like a perfect fit, for a girl in need of a tourniquet, and Ruth felt tears spring to her eyes without any understanding of why they were there.

Like Peter Pan, like Superman, someone would come to save her, the song said.

She wanted to make the most of the music because there was something wrong with her iPod. Her downloads kept disappearing into the ether every time she found a song that touched her heart. They were wiped from her PC, too, and CDs vanished, there on the table one minute, gone the next. She was increasingly convinced that her flimsy grip on sanity was fading by the day.

The flat smelled strange, too, as if something had crawled into her wardrobe and died. Ruth felt sick and sad, and couldn't shake the feeling that she too was dying, slowly but surely.

As she sank down into the music, dreams, half-memories and fractured images rose up to meet reality. There was Albert Bridge again, shrouded in mist. Why did it prey so heavily on her mind? There was fire, but not the kind of fire you see in autumn gardens. And somewhere she was calling, "I'll love you . . . always," and her sadness felt like a deep, dark pool.

And then, strangely, she dreamed she was lying on the sofa listening to her iPod, only there was someone in the room with her. At first she thought it was an owl flying here and there, but then she realised it was a man pacing the floor, except he had features like an owl. As he walked, his head swivelled unnaturally, his big, round eyes constantly surveying her. Ruth felt that he wasn't particularly pleasant, and probably extremely dangerous, but for now he had allied himself with her.

After a moment, he bent over her so that those eyes filled her entire vision. "You must wake from your slumber," he said in a harsh voice. "You are the most powerful."

"I can't wake," Ruth replied dreamily. "I'll never be able to find my CDs if I do that."

Ruth could smell his breath and that jarred her reverie. *Are there aromas in dreams?* she thought absently.

"Shake yourself," he pressed. "You must Craft a message, spell out your intent, unpick the fabric and weave new words of wonder. Fly again. Dream again. Tear out your heart and show it to another. Only a shared heart beats in time. Do it now, now, now. Two-day, for two is one, and one makes five. Do it now. Not on the Sun-Day or the Moon-Day, not on Woden's Day or Thor's Day or even Freya's Day. Do it today, the Satyr's Day."

"I can't." Ruth began to cry again.

"There are others who can help you. Your brother and sister. And more, four more. The Knight and his combat honey. The Broken Woman. The Warrior-Shaman with bloody clothes."

"I don't know what you mean!" Ruth called out.

The front door burst open with a tremendous crash. The owl-man retreated to the window as a dark shape that looked like a million tiny shapes joined together rushed towards him.

Ruth felt a huge weight on her chest preventing her from moving, but she was aware obliquely of a raging fight, flickering light and sucking shadows.

It ended suddenly and Ruth found herself being shaken gently awake. Rourke was sitting on the sofa next to her.

"You were having a bad dream," he said with a reassuring smile.

Ruth gently pushed him away. "I don't know . . . it was so strange."

He put his arm round her shoulders and leaned in to kiss her.

"Don't," she said.

Rourke pressed on. "I thought we might go to bed. You've been teasing me along for ages . . ."

Ruth's cheeks flushed. "I have not." She wriggled out of his grasp and stood up. "I'm sorry. I don't know how to say this, but . . . I don't really want a relationship right now. I thought I did, but I don't."

Rourke looked more surprised than hurt.

"I know I've not been fair to you," Ruth continued, "and I did agree to all those dates, but . . ." Her thoughts were moving too fast for words to express, faster than they had moved in a long time. "I'm just very sorry."

"I don't understand—"

"I don't either, really. I just know I've been acting like some sappy loser. For a long time. And I'm not like that. I don't *need* a boyfriend, but I thought I did, and you were around . . . I sound awful, don't I?"

"You're saying you don't want to see me any more?"

A slow sound echoed through the flat. Ruth was sure it was her wardrobe door opening just a little, perhaps stirred by a breeze. Suddenly she felt unaccountably frightened.

"Can't we just be friends?" Rourke was saying. "You know I love your company, Ruth."

"Okay," she replied hesitantly. "Sure. Why not?"

The feeling of dread subsided. Ruth went to the window and found herself looking into the night for a dream-owl. "What day is it Two-Day?" she asked dreamily.

"Today? Saturday."

"Satyr Day," she whispered. Mist was drifting along the dark street, reminding her of Albert Bridge, where she thought she had first met somebody special. And despite the dark, and despite the mist, it felt as if the sun was coming out.

4

Shavi inhaled deeply and tasted the night, the grass, the stones. A dangerous, uncertain future lay ahead, but he felt more at peace than he ever had.

"You're a bloody idiot." The Bone Inspector sat on one of the fallen menhirs, clutching his staff like a weapon. "Coming to Stonehenge on a fool's errand when we could be hiding out in Callanish. Do you want to get us both killed?"

"There is something here."

"Because some graffiti on a toilet wall says so? The wind must blow right through your head."

Shavi checked his position and began to pace out the distance.

"I tell you, Stonehenge's dead. As dead as Avebury. There's a thin bit of power in the ground, enough to keep us hidden, but that's it. And if you're looking for something buried, forget it. The bloody archaeologists have been all over the place with a fine-tooth comb."

"All of it?" Shavi found his spot and dropped to his knees to tear at the turf with his fingers. Eventually he found the stone Church had buried more than 150 years earlier.

On it was carefully painted the legend: "To Shavi. Laura DuSantiago, Sister of Dragons, is in a burger bar in Northampton. Ruth Gallagher, Sister of Dragons, is in an old people's home in South London. Church."

"Church," Shavi read out loud. It was a name, and it felt oddly familiar to his lips.

5

Laura stood at the window and looked at the sun baking the rooftops. The air was filled with the stink of cheap burgers on the griddle and a high-pitched whine as the electric carver cut slices off the puce, fat-seeping pillar of doner meat.

"Modern life is shit," she said. "It looks like shit. It sounds like shit. And it smells like shit."

"You're right at home, then, aren't you?" the burger bar owner said.

Laura served the three customers waiting without saying a word, and then turned to the two at the back. One was a rangy old man with a sour face and dirty clothes, but the other was a handsome Asian man with gleaming shoulder-length black hair and a pleasant, peaceful expression.

"Laura?" the Asian man said.

She studied his face for a moment and then said, "Yep. You just hit the jackpot."

6

"You trawled around every burger bar in Northampton looking for me?" Laura said incredulously as they sat at the back of the café in the main shopping area. "And you did it because a stone told you to. Okay. Sanity-challenged or drugs?"

The café was crowded and noisy, but it still felt like a refuge from the Sunday afternoon browsers in the street outside. Shavi smiled and Laura felt a brief tingle; he had sex appeal to spare beneath his aura of calmness.

"I cannot explain it," Shavi said, "but there are many mysterious things happening at the moment."

"Tell me about it." She tried not to think about the incident with the rapidly growing vegetation.

"Are you sure about her? She doesn't look like much to me." The Bone Inspector had barely taken his piercing eyes off Laura.

"You want to be careful you don't break a hip or something," she said.

He smiled darkly. "*You* want to be careful *I* don't break something."

Laura bristled. "What is it with you, you old fucker—"

Shavi interrupted. "We have travelled far to find you because we fear you may be in danger." Seeing he had Laura's interest, he continued, "I was pursued by a man by the name of Rourke, who was not all he appeared—"

"I know someone called Rourke." Laura watched as Shavi and the Bone Inspector shared an uneasy glance. "Creepy tosser," she continued. "Black hair . . ." She tried to describe Rourke but found she couldn't really put her finger on what he looked like. She settled for, "He's got one of those faces you always forget. Bland. Just merges into the background."

"That sounds like my Rourke," Shavi said.

"I don't get how he could be with you, because the wanker never seems to leave me alone."

"Because," Shavi said cautiously, "he is not human." He proceeded to tell Laura exactly what Rourke was, or as close as he could surmise. Laura watched his face carefully. He didn't appear to be lying, or a nut, but she'd heard numerous similar stories from those who couldn't tell their bad trips from reality.

"The Army of the Ten Billion Spiders," she said, recalling the graffiti she'd seen everywhere. "Of course. Close allies of the Thirteen Hundred Daddy Longlegs. Nice one. Well, some of us have a life to lead. You know, in this world."

As she stood up to go, the Bone Inspector grabbed her wrist. She fought to free herself, but his grip belied his appearance. Ignoring her vehement cursing, he pulled her slowly across the table to examine the tattoo he had spied on the back of her right hand.

He traced his finger around the circle of interlocking leaves. "You know what that is?"

"Yeah, it's a sign that any irritating old bastard gets a kick in the bollocks for touching it." She wrenched her hand free and rubbed the circulation back into her wrist.

"It's the Mark of Cernunnos. At least, that's one of his names. You might know him as the Green Man."

Laura tapped her head. "It's a tattoo."

The Bone Inspector smiled tightly. "He's marked you. Given you his patronage." He jerked his thumb at Shavi. "This one here's a seer . . . a shaman. You can tap into nature in all its power—"

Laura blanched.

"You know, don't you? You're trying to pretend you don't. Well, it doesn't wash. The two of you have got a job to do, or everything goes to hell in a handcart."

"It already has," Laura snapped.

"You know what? You're right."

His knowing smile was too much for Laura. She stormed out, knocking over a shopping bag that sent potatoes spilling across the café floor.

In the street she tried to laugh off the incident, but everything that had been said troubled her on some fundamental level. She weaved her way amongst the shoppers just in case the two of them followed her. She hadn't gone far when someone grabbed her arm. She threw it off, expecting to see the old guy. It was Rourke.

"Hello, darlin'," he said with a cheery grin. "Going somewhere in a hurry?"

Despite laughing off Shavi's story, Laura's blood ran cold. "You're like a limpet, you are." She made to go, but Rourke caught her arm again.

"You can't be allowed to communicate with them." His tone had become almost mechanical. "You might wake further. The risk is too great." Nobody was paying any attention to them and Laura was strangely sure Rourke had made it that way. "There is no longer any choice."

He clamped his hand over Laura's mouth. She fought him, but he was too strong. The moment he touched her, her lips sensed the flesh on his palm moving as though something was squirming just beneath the skin. Then whatever was in there broke through. Small, hard objects forced against her lips, her teeth, prising them apart.

She couldn't resist. As she opened her mouth, a mass of scurrying filled it to the brim, and Laura knew exactly what they were.

The scurrying continued down her throat and into her belly, hundreds of them, thousands. Although she wanted to vomit, she couldn't. Finally the terror and the sickening sensation were too much and she blacked out.

7

Shavi was about to catch up with Laura when he saw Rourke attack. At first he thought one of the many shoppers would rush to Laura's aid, but they all continued on their way, oblivious.

Rourke hauled the now-unconscious Laura down a side street. Shavi didn't know what had been done to her, but he could see her mouth bulging and that her stomach was bloated.

The Bone Inspector caught up with him. "Now what?" He watched as Laura was dragged away. "We can't attack him head on."

"And we cannot let Rourke take her away." Shavi slipped into the side street and kept close to the wall, but Rourke appeared to have no comprehension that he might be followed. Shavi weighed his options.

His thoughts were interrupted by a strange sight. Rourke had dumped Laura to the pavement and was carving a pattern in the air in the shape of a doorway. Chillingly, the view through the defined shape now looked oddly fake, like painted scenery in a theatre. Shavi could see a brick wall, and a flyer, now unnervingly two-dimensional. Rourke gripped the upper right-hand corner and peeled down. It looked as if he was removing a sheet of wallpaper. Behind it Shavi glimpsed something that his mind couldn't comprehend, and after a few seconds of queasy swimming it settled on the closest approximation it could present to him: a structure in darkness, like scaffolding, perhaps, or the workings of some vast machine. But what disturbed Shavi the most was a hint of movement: something lived there, behind the surface of reality.

Following that troubling revelation came another: that Rourke was going to drag Laura out of reality completely. What awaited her was too frightening to contemplate. Shavi acted on instinct.

While Rourke was occupied with creating his exit, Shavi ran forward. All he knew was that he couldn't abandon Laura, whatever the risk to himself. Rourke began to turn just as Shavi reached Laura. Shavi glimpsed Rourke's face becoming aware of his presence, and then starting to unfold to reveal the spiders beneath.

Shavi grabbed Laura's waist and there was a blue flash and a smell of burned iron. Whatever had happened, it had thrown Rourke several feet away, his face split wide open with long legs thrashing wildly out of it.

Laura had revived and, struggling to her knees, she retched violently. Her convulsions propelled spiders from her mouth, all of them dead. The flow appeared never-ending, but by the time Shavi had helped her to her feet she was only coughing up handfuls of the smaller ones.

Rourke was on his feet, his body breaking up into its component parts just as the other Rourke's had at Avebury. Laura clutched hold of Shavi, sick with terror born of incomprehension.

The sound of a protesting engine filled the street. Shavi's van appeared, being driven with insane disregard for its surroundings. It careered off three parked cars and mounted the kerb. Shavi had to thrust Laura out of the way at the last moment to save both of them from being killed.

The Bone Inspector threw open the passenger door. "If I'm going to keep doing this, you'd better give me some lessons."

Shavi pushed Laura in and jumped in after her. The Rourke-spiders were already swarming onto the nearside, and appeared to be eating at the very fabric of the vehicle.

The Bone Inspector had seen them, too. With deafening grinding and a fountain of sparks, he ran the van along the brick wall. With the spiders scraped off, he accelerated towards the end of the street, where Shavi took the wheel.

"Worst. Rescue. Ever." Laura's stomach was still churning from the thought of the spiders nestling inside her.

"You're alive, aren't you?" the Bone Inspector snapped.

"I was nearly mounted on the radiator grille!" Shavi thought she was going to cry, but then she put her head back and laughed silently. "Fucking head rush. Spiders, urrh!"

"Mad woman," the Bone Inspector mumbled.

Laura glanced at Shavi, her eyes bright. "I nearly died and I feel as if I'm flying. How fucked up is that?" She smiled to herself. "You can't go back to the day job once you've had spiders crawling around your gullet."

Shavi had been through exactly the same process of awakening: that the life they had been ushered into should be more terrifying and dangerous than anyone could bear, yet he felt more vibrant than he ever had in his safe, secure, mundane existence.

Laura turned on the radio and scanned across the stations until she found the Chemical Brothers singing "Hey Boy Hey Girl." She cranked it up to full volume.

"The blue spark that flashed between us," Shavi said. "I think it was important."

"You're right there. It means we're two of a kind, pretty boy." She put her feet on the dashboard and stretched like a cat. "All right. Now what?"

8

Wearily, Church tramped up the long, winding staircase to his chamber in the Court of the Soaring Spirit. His officer's uniform was filthy with the mud of Flanders, and he was sickened after seeing wave after wave of fresh, hopeful young men shot and gassed and blown to pieces over a few inches of soil. For the first time he could understand why the Seelie Court had turned its back on Earth.

Tom sat by the fire, smoking. "Anything?" he asked.

Church shook his head. "One of the Watchmen in Paris gave me a lead, but it didn't pan out. He said the Germans had the skull and box for some kind of ritual. I think it was just wishful thinking." Church flopped into a chair and tossed his gas mask to one side. "Tell you what, though—the spider-zombies are everywhere. All over Europe I came across people with spiders stuck in their neck, or arm, or whatever."

"The Enemy is exerting its influence. I imagine a war of that magnitude would spread despair like the plague."

Church could tell Tom had seen some of the horrors of the First World War with his premonitory powers. "That's it, I think. They're controlling people who can position themselves to generate despair. How do we fight something like that? It's like an infestation."

"You spread hope." Tom's eyes sparkled.

"I managed to save one of the Brothers of Dragons before Veitch got to him," Church said. "He's just a kid, but when you look in his eyes it's as if he's a hundred years old. The things he must have seen on the battlefield—"

"Death forges the Brothers and Sisters of Dragons," Tom said.

"Then he's going to be one of the strongest of all of us," Church replied bitterly. "I've left him with Decebalus and Aula. They're doing a good job with all the others I managed to bring back. Our recruits will be ready when we need them."

Niamh walked in clutching a letter. She looked troubled. "I found this on my bed," she said, puzzled. "I was in the other chamber. No one could have entered without my knowledge."

"Who's it from?" Church asked.

She handed it to him. The writing was copperplate and dignified. "Jerzy," she said. "He's inviting you to a show—and offers an answer to 'The Question of the Skull and the Box.'"

CHAPTER NINE
VAUDEVILLE

1

London, November 1940.

"Gor Bimey, you'll never see a night like it! Forget old Mr Hitler—he's a twerp! Goering's barmy, so's his army! Get inside for the time of your lovely lives!"

The man in the garish yellow and black pinstripe suit clapped his hands and threw his arms wide. Behind him the glittering lights of the Holborn Empire formed a golden halo that promised warmth and comfort amidst the thick, chilly fog and the bomb-blasted rubble-strewn street.

Church shivered even in the depths of his suit and thick woollen overcoat. From the shadows across the street he watched the couples in their Sunday best troop up arm in arm from all directions. Nothing appeared out of the ordinary, no gods, no spider-controlled politicians, no misshapen beasts or magical beings; just working-class people out for a night of beer, laughter and song to help them forget the day's labours and the rigours of war. Jerzy's message had specified the time and the place, and Church had no choice but to investigate.

The foyer was grand with a plush red and gold carpet, polished mahogany and chandeliers harking back to its music hall glory days in the Victorian era. Church eased his way through the chattering crowd and bought his ticket. The bar was packed to the brim with men swilling pints of bitter and women sipping on halves of mild beneath a fug of smoke. Raucous laughter and spontaneous song thundered around the walls.

"Wouldn't believe there's a war on, would you, mate?" a rat-faced man said as he pushed his way to the bar. "I wish they'd go back to the old days when they'd let you take your beer into the auditorium. Bloody Council."

Using the Far Lands glamour Niamh had provided him with for cash, Church couldn't resist indulging in a pint, the first he'd had for months, and then he made his way to the auditorium. Before the First World War it had been laid out with rows of tables where food and drink were served up all night long, but now it resembled any other theatre, with velvet-seated stalls, boxes and a balcony.

A man in a long fur coat was already on stage singing, "I'm 'Enery the Eighth I am, 'Enery the Eighth I am, I am," with lots of comic moves and face-pulling. In the stalls, where drunks were already heckling, there was a bear-pit atmosphere. "You're no Harry Champion!" Someone hurled what looked like a cauliflower at the singer. He ducked and then side-stepped two other pieces of produce with which the audience members had pre-armed themselves.

Church searched the darkened seats for any sign of Jerzy, but he was nowhere to be seen, not even in disguise. The unfortunate performer was driven off-stage prematurely and the compère came out to lead the audience in mass singing of "Roll Out the Barrel."

As the voices rose up to the rafters, Church noticed a subtle change come over the auditorium.

"It's not like this when Arthur Askey's on." A cockney man with slicked-back hair and an expensive-looking charcoal suit was now sitting in the next seat, though Church had not seen him arrive. The man put his feet over the seat in front. His shoes shone so brightly they reflected the man's radiant grin; there was something darkly mischievous about him that Church found familiar. "Still, there's a right load of riff-raff in tonight." He jerked a thumb over his shoulder.

Church looked back and saw the source of the shifting atmosphere. High up in the balcony, almost lost in the deep shadows, was the Seelie Court. Church could make out the shimmering golden skin of the king and queen in the front row, and the more monstrous members of the court loomed behind. Church guessed that no other audience member would see anything out of the ordinary, but when he turned to the fellow beside him to check, the seat was empty once more.

Church slipped out of his seat and made his way to the balcony. The audience was now singing "Knocked 'Em in the Old Kent Road." He was ushered forward by a being with bat-wings and a head like the Elephant Man. The king bowed his head slightly to one side and smiled faintly. "Greetings, Brother of Dragons. What is the nature of your business this even? More battles to fight and enemies to slay?"

"More women to romance?" the queen added with an enigmatic smile.

Church bowed. "I came by invitation, your majesty."

"As did we," the king said. "How curious. A mysterious assignation was promised, and a night of unparalleled entertainment. I must say the latter is certainly true. The Fragile Creatures have excelled themselves in this hall of wine and song." He tapped his foot in time to the robust singing of the audience.

"May I ask who invited you?" Church said.

"Another mystery." The queen stroked her chin thoughtfully. "The invitation was unsigned." She urged one of the Tuatha Dé Danann beside her to leave his seat. "Sit a while," she said to Church. "Fragile Creatures have always intrigued us, but the reputation achieved by the Brothers and Sisters of Dragons is most interesting. I had the pleasure of spending time with one of your kind who fought against the Northmen who invaded this island in their dragon ships. He had many great tales to tell of his adventures. And of you."

"Me?" Church took his seat. On stage, an escapologist was now being locked into his chains by a pretty assistant.

"Why, your exploits are quite legendary amongst your own kind. They speak of you and the Blue Fire in one breath, as one thing, interchangeable, immutable. The king who must be awakened from his deep sleep. The power in the land that will return in the darkest hour. As we know, there are two faces to everything."

Her beautiful features were inscrutable, but Church had the impression she was not simply speaking metaphorically. Was she alluding to Janus?

"I have heard tell in the same stories," she continued, "of a love that spans the vast sea of time, of two hearts torn asunder, striving to return to each other across the years, whatever suffering and hardship may be thrown in their path. Is this true? Can Fragile Creatures really feel so deeply, so strongly?"

"Yes, they can."

"Remarkable. This woman—she is special?"

"She is to me." Church watched the escapologist disappear into a sack that was tied at the neck. "I've lost a lot of my memories of us together, but I haven't forgotten a thing about the kind of person she is, and how much we mean to each other."

"It must be difficult to maintain those feelings without the structure of the memories to contain them."

Church didn't respond.

"Would you like one of those memories back?"

"You can do that?"

"One. For now. Too many would unbalance you." She smiled warmly at Church's hopeful expression. "Here."

She rested her cool fingers on Church's forehead and he felt a rush of colour and light that gradually coalesced into images. The early hours of the morning along the banks of the Thames in South London. Thick fog, shortly before dawn. A creeping feeling of despair over the death of his old girlfriend,

Marianne. A sound from beneath the shadows of Albert Bridge: a shape-shifting creature from the Far Lands. It was the incident that had propelled him into his new life as a Brother of Dragons. And Ruth was there, too. She'd arrived from another direction, drawn by the same sound.

But it was more than just a memory, for it explained everything about his love for Ruth. In the moment when their eyes locked for the first time, he saw a person filled with passion, someone with whom he had a deep, instant connection. She gave him hope, there and then, in one glance.

Church withdrew from the memory with a strong swell of emotion threatening to wash him away. "Thank you," he said. The queen nodded and smiled sweetly.

The escapologist slipped from the sack and his chains in a flash of light and a puff of smoke. He left the stage to thunderous applause.

With his new memory warming his heart and changing his perspective completely, Church felt he had much to consider and so made his excuses and left the Seelie Court.

By the time he was back in his seat, the compère had finished his patter and the next act was coming onstage to loud cheers—clearly a popular choice.

"And now Max Masque!" the compère announced. "The Dandy of the Dance, with a bag full of songs and smiles!"

A man in a lime-green suit shuffled on, did a pirouette followed by a back-flip. The audience cheered and clapped even louder.

"Now then, now then, stop yer trouble," he said. "A copper grabbed me on the Mile End Road, and I said, ''Ang on, mate. I'll tickle yer ribs for a guinea.' What did I say?"

He put one hand to his ear and the audience responded as one: "I'll tickle yer ribs for a guinea!"

The comedian wore a mask that was split down the middle: one side showed the face of tragedy, the other the face of comedy. It was Jerzy.

2

The Mocker soon had the audience reeling with laughter, with a constant stream of jokes that even had Church chuckling. Slapstick and satire, song and dance, his polished repertoire covered everything the crowd expected and more. Jerzy left the stage to tumultuous applause, with his catchphrase ringing to the roof.

Church made his way to the door at the side of the stage and bribed the attendant to let him in. A grizzled old stagehand was mopping the floor outside the dressing-room door.

"No point knocking, mate," he said. "Nobody sees Max Masque without his mask. It's his trademark."

"He'll see me," Church said. He ducked inside before the stagehand could stop him.

There was a shriek as the maskless Jerzy dived behind the changing screen. "Get out! Get out!"

"Jerzy, it's me. Church."

"I don't know you! Get out before I call the manager!"

"Jerzy—"

"I don't know anyone called Church!" Jerzy peered round the edge of the screen. Church caught a glimpse of the familiar parchment flesh. After a moment of thoughtful silence, he ventured, "Church—?" Gradually, he emerged from behind the screen, his frightened eyes making his frozen grin uncertain.

"What's going on?" Church asked.

"I . . . I do not know. I had forgotten about you for so long." He came over to scan Church's face before throwing his arms around Church. "I remember Stonehenge. And then I came here, to London. It seemed the most natural thing . . ." He shook his head, dazed. "What happened to me?"

"But you sent me an invitation. And you sent one to the Seelie Court. You said you had some information about the skull and the box."

Jerzy shook his head slowly. "I sent no invitations. I never gave my previous life a second thought." He plucked a silk dressing gown from a coat hanger and slipped it on before lighting himself a cigarette in a long holder. "Would you like a snout?" he asked.

Church had to smile at the comical image, but oddly Jerzy appeared more at home, and at ease, than he ever had before.

"Looks like you've been carving out quite the niche for yourself," Church said.

Jerzy's face lit up so it was almost unrecognisable. "Church, you would not believe the wonder that has entered my life. Blimey, it's a real thrill." His accent kept shifting between his natural Far Lands lilt and the cockney he had adopted for his act.

"How did you get into it?"

Jerzy thought for a moment, then shook his head. "All I remember is being an apprentice. Learning the ropes. Learning how to tell a gag. I have learned a lot of things." He grew pensive, and pointed to his mask. "I have learned that humour comes out of tragedy. That humour heals tragedy. I had everything good in my life stolen from me, the people I loved most of all. Every night the pain in my heart was so great I could not sleep. And then I found you, Church, and it eased a little, and then I found this." He wiped away a tear. "I feel at home with the show people. They accept my looks. They understand people may to all intents and purposes be different, yet at the same time be the same."

"I'm glad you're happy, Jerzy."

"I am. I truly am. We find humour in the darkest places, and humour is hope. Music is hope. Laughter and mischief are hope. And they come when you least expect it. They form the path to Existence, Church, out of darkness and into the light. And they give the lie to Mr Darwin's Theory of Evolution—yes, I have been reading! For it is possible to make the argument that we developed love to protect and develop the species, though I do not subscribe to that notion. But there is no argument for humour and song, except to uplift us spiritually. Blessed are the comic and the singer!" He raised his hands to the air like an evangelical.

"So you're not coming back to the Court of the Soaring Spirit?" Church said wryly.

Jerzy jumped to his feet and paced the room exuberantly. "The wonders that exist here and now! Every night the Germans drop their bombs. People die by the thousands. Homes are destroyed. There is not enough food to go around. Children are shipped away from their families. *But* . . . once a week everyone gathers around their radio to listen to Tommy Handley . . . *It's That Man Again*! If Mr Hitler chose to invade between eight-thirty and nine on a Thursday evening, he would have an easy job of it because *everyone* is tuned in to the show. You wouldn't believe it could be funny when Mrs Mopp the Cleaner says every week—every week!—'Can I do yer now, sir?' But it is! Or when Colonel Chinstrap laconically meets every remark with, 'I don't mind if I do.' We all laugh and it brings us together. In the music halls there's Flanagan and Allen singing 'Underneath the Arches' . . . and Gracie Fields, and George Formby, and Max Miller . . ."

His eyes took on a plangent cast. "No, Church, I am not going back. But if you ever need me, if there is anything I can ever do to help you in this great struggle that is unfolding, call me. I will come in an instant."

Church was touched. "You tell your jokes, Jerzy. The world needs more like you." In the moment's silence that followed their friendship grew stronger still.

"The questions remain, though," Church mused. "Who sent the invitation? Why did they want me here to see you, and what do they know about the skull and the box?"

"And," Jerzy added, "are they from the same one who spirited me away from you at Stonehenge?"

Before they could debate possible answers there was an outcry in the corridor. Jerzy grabbed his mask and ran out with Church to find an anxious man in a dinner jacket and bow tie, several stagehands and the escapologist's pretty assistant.

"Don't worry, Max. We're on top of it," the man in the dinner jacket said.

"No, you're bleedin' not!" the assistant shrieked. "He jumped right over the top of me!"

"Who?" Jerzy asked.

"Just some gadabout who fancies a life on the stage," the dinner-jacketed man said with theatrical reassurance.

"He was breathing blue fire!" The assistant looked as if she was about to swoon. "He was wearing a black cape and he had eyes like the devil! He was flying . . . flying—"

"Bouncing," one of the stagehands corrected.

"Leaping," the assistant said, "like he was a bleedin' India rubber man!"

With that, the assistant finally did swoon, and the man in the dinner jacket caught her flamboyantly. The grizzled stagehand with the mop pushed his way forward. "You know who that is? That's Spring-heeled Jack, that is. Hasn't been seen round these parts for thirty year or more."

Church pulled Jerzy to one side. "Things are starting to make a lot more sense," he said.

3

"My Old Man (Said Follow the Van)" was ringing around the auditorium as Church and Jerzy followed the trail of Spring-heeled Jack backstage. A man practising the trombone pointed them to the stage door, which hung open. Outside in the icy fog two women clutching each other in terror directed Church and Jerzy towards the East End.

They hadn't gone far when ear-piercing sirens rose up.

"It's another air raid," Jerzy said. "That's why there's a blackout—if the city is in darkness it is much more difficult for the bombers to find a target."

"I know what a blackout is, Jerzy."

"Ah. I forgot. This is all history to you."

"Come on, come on, lively up!" An ARP warden brought his bicycle to a wobbly halt. "You don't want to be out on the street with the Nazis dropping eggs on your bonces. Get down the Tube, pronto!"

Jerzy grabbed Church and started to haul him in the direction of the nearest Underground station. "He is right, Church. I have seen what it is like. The fires blaze like the furnaces of the Court of the Final Word. Even if you are nowhere near the bomb blast it can tear you limb from limb. I have seen arms and legs lying in the gutter . . . men, women and children. We can search later."

"It'll be too late then," Church said, but he knew Jerzy was right. They set off for the nearest Tube station, but after a few feet Church had a very strange feeling about the ARP Warden: something about him was familiar. He turned back, but the street was empty.

4

"You are a very strange creature, Ryan Veitch. I cannot quite fathom you." The Libertarian gnawed the last vestiges of his lamb dinner from a bone in the darkened second-floor room. Outside, the cry of, "Get that light out!" rose up at irregular intervals.

Wearing a too-sharp suit that made him resemble a local gangster, Veitch stood at the window looking out at the silhouette of the city skyscape. He lazily flipped a half-crown, a mannerism he'd picked up from a George Raft movie he'd seen at the Gaumont that afternoon. "What is there to understand?" he said without looking back.

"Hmm. Well, there is that. The point is, I feel you are completely lacking in self-awareness. Do you have any idea who you are?" He tossed the lamb bone into the corner of the room. "You collude with our forces to bring about our ends, yet at the same time you'll help some innocent or carry out some futile action to winnow the flame of hope. These two extremes are incompatible. Do you not comprehend that?"

"Don't know what you're talking about, mate."

The Libertarian sighed. "I really should know better." He stood up and stretched like a cat. "Are you coming to the ritual?"

"Nah. Seen one, seen 'em all." In the distance, searchlights swept the sky.

Veitch listened for the approaching drone as the Libertarian closed the door behind him. His footsteps disappeared down the creaking stairs.

Sometimes Veitch's thoughts felt like a black hole sucking him in, never to escape. He could understand the Libertarian's confusion, for nothing appeared to make sense, either outside in the world or within him. He was a good person aspiring to good things—it was the reason why Existence chose him to be one of that most select band, a Brother of Dragons—yet nevertheless, here he was, murdering, destroying, tipping the scales towards the darkness.

A column of flame rose up somewhere in the Kentish limits of the city. More indiscriminate deaths.

His own killings, however, were not indiscriminate. They were not innocents, but combatants in a war who knew, or would know, that they were legitimate targets. Veitch held on to that thought tightly, for to let it slip away would mean facing up to unpalatable truths.

He had been wronged, badly, and he should never forget that. Betrayed, when all he had offered was support for the cause, even at the risk of his own life. Treated badly by Ruth and Church, manipulating him even while they established their affair behind his back, secretly laughing at him. Ruth knew he loved her; Church knew he loved her. It didn't mean anything in the long run, and if love was meaningless, the whole premise on which his membership of the Brotherhood of Dragons was based was a pack of lies. He couldn't trust Existence at all; he could only trust himself, and what he wanted was revenge. That's what he learned when he was growing up: if somebody hits you, you hit back harder. He wouldn't be taken for a fool ever again.

The sky was filled with the thunder of war machines. The nagging thoughts that threatened to strip away the façade from his justifications slipped back and were lost in the noise. He turned from the window, secure in the knowledge that he was on the right path.

5

People were flooding into the Tube as quickly as they had entered the Holborn Empire, but the mood now was tense and fearful. The half-lit platform was packed. People made themselves as comfortable as they could. Men smoked in silence, or whispered to their wives and children. Young couples gripped each other's hands desperately, while the old folk huddled under blankets to keep warm. Babies woken from their cots were crying in unison, their voices merging into one constant wail.

And then the bombs began to fall. It was the pounding of a great machine whose job was to reduce the city to dust. *Thoom-thoom-thoom.* Dust fell from the ceiling. The babies cried more, and whimpering young children joined them.

Church looked around the faces and saw the dread grow stronger, reaching through the taut expressions and into their bones. He couldn't begin to guess how they coped with the horror night after night for months on end.

Suddenly a voice chimed up. "It's Max Masque. Oi, Max! Tickle me ribs for a guinea!"

"I'll tickle yer ribs for a guinea!" Jerzy responded. His eyes smiled at Church. "My public awaits."

"Go to it."

"How about a song?" Jerzy called. A cheer went up. In a clear, strong voice, Jerzy began, "You are my sunshine, my only sunshine . . ."

The whole platform joined in. "You make me happy when skies are grey . . ."

Jerzy moved through the crowd, his very presence transformative. Church leaned against the wall, feeling the vibrations of the distant rhythm section shaking the city, marvelling in turn at how Jerzy had been transformed by his experience. One simple choice had made him something better.

As he listened to the singing, Church noticed something flare briefly in the black mouth of the tunnel. It was bright blue, like the hissing flame of an acetylene torch. He could have dismissed it as men at work on the line, but it looked to him very much like the flaming breath of Spring-heeled Jack.

While the sheltering crowd was distracted by Jerzy, Church slipped off the platform and, keeping close to the wall, edged his way into the tunnel. Rats scurried away from him into the depths. When he reached the point where he'd seen the flare, there was no sign of any workmen, but there was movement further along the tunnel.

The emergency lights of the platform already looked distant. Church knew he would be crazy to venture any further into the tunnel, but another blue flare much further ahead drew him on.

For the next fifteen minutes he progressed slowly through a deep, uncomfortable darkness, punctuated only at irregular points by emergency lights. The sounds of movement and the occasional flare kept him moving, but he never appeared to draw any closer.

Then, on the edge of the illumination of one of the emergency lights, he came across a branching tunnel wide enough for two men to walk side by side. A security door hung open and inside chipped white tiles gleamed from a distant light. He could hear sounds coming from down the corridor.

Inside, it smelled of engine oil. The corridor led past empty storerooms, and then through a ragged hole where the tiles gave way to new wood. Church could hear voices ahead, like flies buzzing in the distance.

Eventually he came to a complex of rooms that he guessed were part of the civil defence system constructed in the early days of the war to house the government in case of devastating attack. They were newly built, the emergency lights still strung on temporary wires along the walls.

One door stood ajar, and it was from inside that the voices emanated. Peering through the crack, Church could see a group of men in dark suits. Some of the mutterings he heard were in German, others in English. Beyond stood Salazar, his silver mask glowing in the half-light, and next to him was the Libertarian. Between them, on a wooden table, were the crystal skull and the Anubis Box. Church thought of coincidence and the vagaries of fate, and decided none of it mattered. This was his chance.

The air was filled with a dark energy and heavy with anticipation. The gathered men were intense, as though they had been waiting for a long time. It felt as if something very bad indeed was going to happen. Another god was going to be summoned and corrupted. *Which one?* Church wondered. What new, dark powers would be lined up against him and his allies? He delved into his knowledge of mythology and then wished he hadn't, shivering briefly at some of the dreadful possibilities.

A man with a silver-grey moustache and florid jowls joined Salazar and the Libertarian and raised his hands to silence the congregation. "This time has been long coming," he said with the hint of a middle-European accent, "but here at this confluence of the old lines of power, we are in the right place. And after decades of waiting, events have conspired to make this the right time. The skull is now filled with power once again. We can begin the ritual. Are you ready?"

A murmur ran around the room. The Libertarian eyed the assembled group with unconcealed contempt.

Church wondered what the man meant by "the right place." Was it simply that the energies were right for the ritual, or was the god they wanted to call somehow tied to the place of the summoning?

"Tonight," the florid-jowled man continued in a tremulous voice, "we enter the halls of the Aesir. Tonight we dare to entice one of the great gods of our northern homeland—the trickster and shape-changer. Stand in awe—Loki comes."

Church felt another frisson. He didn't know enough about the Northern gods to anticipate the threat of a corrupted Loki, but the excitement evident in the crowd made him think it would be worse than he could imagine.

Salazar began his ritual before the crystal skull. Church threw off his overcoat and removed Llyrwyn from the harness on his back, but was still unsure how to proceed—there were too many people in the room to attempt to storm it. His window of opportunity was closing rapidly. If he didn't disrupt the ritual before the god arrived, he wouldn't stand a chance.

Light shimmered across the ceiling and walls from the now radiant skull. Shadows danced. The Libertarian and Salazar both moved back as the air began to peel open.

As Church searched for a line of attack, he heard a voice at his ear: "Over here." In the confusion of light and sound from the ritual, he presumed he had imagined it, but his attention was drawn to a store cupboard on one wall. It had been closed when he arrived, but now the doors hung open. Inside was a large box of the flares the workmen carried in case of emergencies while they were working on the rails.

As Church ignited one flare, he saw that Loki had emerged from the rift and Salazar was in the process of opening the Anubis Box. In the glare of the skull it was impossible to get a clear view of the god, but Church could still feel the power crackling off it.

Church thrust the lit flare into the full box, kicked open the door and hurled the makeshift bomb into the midst of the rapt crowd. He slammed the door briefly as the box ignited with a thunderous explosion.

When he darted inside there was horrific confusion. Men were on fire and screaming, and the air was filled with thick, foul-smelling smoke. Gripping his sword, Church drove through the stumbling bodies.

Salazar appeared out of the billowing clouds. As he had done once before, Church swung his sword and cleaved the thing from shoulder to hip. The blade met as little resistance as he expected. Spiders gushed across the floor.

And then Church was at the table where the crystal skull burned with an intense inner power. Beyond it, Church glimpsed feral eyes and a face marked with black runes carved into it by the Anubis Box. The god let out a bestial growl.

Church brought his blade down on the crystal skull and shattered it in an explosion of white light. Half-blinded even though he had shielded his eyes at the last, Church fumbled for the box. When his fingers closed on it, he ran to the wall, hoping to follow it around to the door while everyone else was disoriented by the smoke. Instead he came across another door. He wrenched it open and entered a shaft with a winding metal staircase.

When he was halfway up it, a chilling growl echoed from the darkness and the stairs vibrated from heavy footsteps in pursuit.

6

Church emerged from a manhole cover onto a hellish street. All around buildings blazed out of control. The heat seared his lungs and smoke choked his throat. Burned bodies, their identities, even their sex, unrecognisable, lay amidst piles of rubble. Searchlights washed back and forth across the night sky against the backdrop of the interminable drone of bomber engines.

Church futilely tried to get his bearings. A fire engine sped into the street, bell ringing. The fire team leaped out to perform their individual responsibilities with well-oiled efficiency.

One of the firefighters ran up to Church. "Oi, mate—you all right? You get caught in the blast?" Before Church could answer, the fireman's gaze fell on Llyrwyn. "Bloody hell. What you doing with that?"

Another bomb fell a couple of streets away, and they both ducked to avoid flying debris. When they rose, the fireman was looking past Church with mounting terror.

Loki was rising from the manhole further down the street. At first it was difficult to tell whether the god was closer to man or beast, for it moved slowly and menacingly on all fours, its grey hair streaming behind it. Its pupils were golden and filled with a wild frenzy, and its lips were pulled back in a snarl from pointed teeth.

"What the bleedin' hell is that?" the fireman said.

"Get out of here." Church thrust him away.

Loki broke into a lupine lope, accelerating with each step. When it leaped with a ferocious roar, Church threw himself to one side. The god continued to the fire engine and with one swipe of its talons tore the side of the vehicle wide open. The firemen who had been directing a gushing hose towards one of the burning buildings dropped it and dashed away. The hose snaked around and the full force of the water hit Loki in the chest. The god flipped over backwards and was driven against the burning house. The wall rocked and then came crashing on top of him.

Church had his chance to flee, but he was distracted by cries from one of the houses just being licked by the conflagration that was rapidly leaping from building to building. The firefighters were distracted trying to wrestle the thrashing hose under control.

Church dashed to the house and kicked open the front door. The interior was already thick with smoke and the heat was intense.

"Anyone there?" Church called. A weak, coughing voice answered from the kitchen. An elderly woman was sprawled on the floor next to the open trap door leading to the cellar that she had been using as an air-raid shelter. Church scooped her up in his arms and carried her out into the night. Two firemen took her from him and carried her away.

Church had lost his advantage. Loki rose up from the burning pile of rubble, showering bricks and mortar across the street. Flames licked all around the god, so that it resembled the Devil in some medieval painting.

Powerful muscles bunched in its legs as the creature propelled itself across the street towards Church. A chilling howl escaped its mouth as Loki transformed fully into an enormous grey wolf. The beast's slavering jaws just missed Church's neck. Church managed to swing his sword enough to clip the wolf's haunches. As it went down, he threw himself upon it.

But instead of grasping wolf fur, he found himself sprawling on a nest of writhing snakes. Their heads rose as one, snapping for his face. Church threw himself off them, venom sizzling on the back of his hand.

As he scrambled to his feet, he heard a voice calling, "Church! Over here! I can help!" Jerzy stood further down the street.

Church ran towards him as Loki began to reconfigure into another shape. "How?" Church gasped.

Jerzy smiled. "This is the punch line."

From high overhead came the whistling of a falling bomb. The firemen were already taking cover, but there was nowhere for Church to run. Behind him, Loki was loping in his direction.

Suddenly, the ground beneath his feet gave way and Church plummeted into the dark. The fall was only around ten feet and he landed hard with a splash. The stink told him he was in the effluent of one of the Victorian sewers, its integrity already damaged by the blasts.

The bomb hit a split second later. The explosion stunned him even in the depths of the sewer, but the fall had saved his life. Choking and spluttering, it took him a few moments to scramble out over the debris thrown into the hole.

A crater lay where Loki had been. Further along the street some unrecognisable shape was lowering itself into the manhole from which Church had exited the underground system; disappearing into the dark to lick its wounds, ready to return another day.

Jerzy was nowhere to be seen, but Church didn't think for a minute that he had died in the blast. Some other power was at play here. In his jacket pocket, Church felt the cold, malign presence of the Anubis Box. With the skull destroyed, it had been a victory. A great one.

One of the firemen rushed up, bleeding from a shrapnel cut on his forehead. The others were unharmed. If Loki hadn't driven them back, they would have died in the bomb-blast. A confluence of coincidences that were not coincidences.

"Blimey, mate, are you all right? Talk about luck!" the fireman said. He turned up his nose. "You really smell like shit, though."

7

Back at the Holborn Empire the atmosphere was as exuberant as ever. "The Windmill never closes, and neither shall we," the dinner-jacketed manager said with gusto, "Blitz or no Blitz. Alongside the rest of the British people, I offer a firm two fingers to Mr Hitler."

Backstage was chaotic, with garishly dressed comics mingling with tuxedoed song-and-dance men, jugglers, mimes, fire-eaters and a member of the orchestra taking a cigarette break. Church moved through the colour and activity with a calm and watchful eye, knowing that sooner or later an opportunity would be presented to him.

It came in one of the maze of corridors leading to the scenery store, where the smell of paint and turps was strong. Jerzy was leaning against a wall in his mask, humming thoughtfully to himself. This time Church took the opportunity to observe Jerzy's eyes, for that was the only way to divine the subtleties of emotion in a person whose face was frozen in an expression of horrific humour. They were not Jerzy's eyes. Through the slits, Church saw them dart with dark mischief.

Church sauntered up, then grabbed the impostor and thrust Llyrwyn to his throat. "Who are you?"

In the gleam of those eyes, Church saw the mysteries of the past unfold. They had watched him in Carn Euny and Eboracum. They had seen Lucia's body and watched over her transformation in Myddlewood. They had looked out of the face of Jerzy just before he had disappeared from Stonehenge, and from the frightening visage of Spring-heeled Jack; and there was the ARP Warden, and the music-hall lover who had pointed out the Seelie Court, and all the others who had pulled the strings that had danced Church around like a marionette. "Who are you?" Church asked again with menace.

The eyes never lost their mischievous sparkle. "I am trouble," he said in a voice that sounded like the wind across the wild countryside. Slowly, he moved his hand up to the mask. Church allowed him the unveiling.

As he whisked away the face trapped between tragedy and comedy, Church glimpsed many unnerving things, but what remained was a face as brown as oak-bark but with the soft texture of seal skin. He appeared at once human, animal and flora, yet none of them, and there was certainly something of the impish about him in the blaze of his eyes and the point of his ears, and the grinning row of needle-sharp teeth. Here was mischief, certainly, but also an uneasy darkness that could turn like a summer storm.

"Who are you?" Church asked a third time.

"I am that merry wanderer of the night." His smile brought a chill to Church's spine. "The one that frights the maidens of the village . . . and bootless makes the breathless housewife churn. I mislead night-wanderers, laughing at their harm."

The stranger chuckled and Church realised he was holding on to nothing but air. Several feet away, the stranger now crouched like a monkey ready to leap.

"I am that shrewd and knavish sprite called Robin Goodfellow," he continued, "called by some Hobgoblin, and Sweet Puck. Be kind to me and you shall have good luck."

Church watched the strange figure uneasily. The shape-shifting trickster lived on in the old stories. Kipling had called him "the oldest Old Thing in England," a figure more powerful than the gods and faeries of myth.

He smiled as if reading Church's thoughts. "In all cultures do I live. Call me *Pwca* amongst the Welsh, and *Puki* in Old Norse, *Pukis* in Lithuania."

And all agreed he could be as dangerous and malign a force as he was mischievous.

In the blink of an eye he was gone again. Church whirled to find the Puck a few feet behind his shoulder. "Call me faerie, goblin, devil or imp, but to lovers and fools I can be friend, for they are often one and the same."

"You led me to the skull and the box," Church said. "You're on our side."

"Robin has no side 'cept Robin's own. Sometimes our views collide, sometimes they stand poles apart. I seek out mischief and humour in the gloomiest vale, but in a world of darkness and despair, there are no laughs . . . no heart . . . no hale."

"I thank you for your help, whatever your reasons."

"Not all Robin's help has yet been reveal'd. There is yet more to see. A bond has been made with the Seelie Court. To the garden they will lead ye."

Church didn't understand what the imp was saying, nor did he know how much he could trust this Robin Goodfellow. There was an old Midlands term—"pouk-ledden"—used to describe how people were spun around, manipulated and misled by the sprite for mischief or spite.

"A merrier hour was never wasted here, but now the time has come to part our ways. Yet when you least expect it, there I'll be, more mischief done in future days. Anon. Robin is gone."

There was no flash or puff of smoke. The Puck was simply there one second, gone the next, and Church was left blinking at the space where he'd been.

Church was still contemplating the tricky creature's words and the victory that had been achieved that day when Jerzy walked up.

"Why do you look at me in such a strange manner?" he asked.

"I just wanted to check it was really you."

"You like your jokes, good friend. As if there could be two such as me!" Jerzy's eyes gleamed through the mask.

Church was warmed to see his friend so happily at peace, but he would miss him. "You're definitely staying?"

"This is my place now, bringing joy and laughter to people who really need me. This is home. But you know the words of the song on everyone's lips: 'We'll meet again. Don't know where, don't know when.'" He held out his arms and they hugged before Jerzy pulled back sharply. "Church—?"

"I know, I know!" Church snapped. "I'm going to get a bath!"

8

It was only when he was leaving the Holborn Empire into a night that smelled of smoke and dust that Church realised Robin Goodfellow had played one last trick. The pocket inside his jacket where he had stored his prize was empty. The Anubis Box was gone.

CHAPTER TEN
THE FINAL WORD

1

Niamh laid out the Tarot cards on the small table next to the roaring fire. Tom watched her intently. From the shadow that crossed her face, he knew the answer before he asked the question. "Still nothing?"

"There is a wall across what lies ahead. Beyond it exists only darkness." She turned over another card: the Nine of Ravens. "I try to summon the Messengers of Existence, but there are shadow-ripples flowing back from that wall, disrupting my pleas, perverting their answers. Changing everything."

"So the powers won't respond?"

"They do what they can, but even they are insignificant compared to what lies ahead."

Tom took out a brown leather pouch and began to roll himself a smoke. "And there's still no little ray of sunshine ahead for you and me?"

Niamh shook her head gravely. "Our time is nearly done. Soon we will make our choices to shuffle off the board."

Tom nodded as he crimped the paper and took out his flint. "That's what I see. That's what I've always seen. An ending, like a black cloud on the horizon. We go, but the world keeps turning."

Niamh turned another card: the Lovers. "It seems so futile, for even with our sacrifice the wall still stands," she said bitterly.

"No one knows how it all fits together," Tom said. "Existence is complex and we see only one dog-eared corner of the vast pattern. Through cause and effect, one simple action can change the world." He lit his roll-up and inhaled the blue smoke deeply.

"But it *can* change," she said hopefully. "Things can change. Nothing is fixed, anywhere. You know that. Existence is mutable. The structure can be altered by events . . . or will."

"And our friend lies at the heart of that."

Niamh moved her fingers over the cards. "It says here that if he chose me over the Sister of Dragons I would survive—"

"You are a god and he is a mortal." Tom fixed a searching eye on Niamh as she mulled over the cards. "One would think it would not be difficult to bring about that end."

She shook her head sadly. "His love would be meaningless if it were forced. I stand or fall by what lies in his heart."

"You love him very deeply."

"More than I can bring myself to believe. By doing nothing apart from being himself, he has altered my world completely. When I peer into my deepest thoughts I am not the same person I was before I met him. Far from it. He has awakened many great things in my heart, and though I have experienced wish-pain for the first time, I would not have it any other way." She smiled sadly. "I exist in hope that he will return my love."

Tom nodded, but could give her no reassurance. "And do you see his future in the cards? I fear greatly for what lies ahead for him. I see—"

He was interrupted by a knock at the door, and then Church entered. He was in unusually high spirits.

"Well, you have the smile of a winner," Tom noted.

"And with good reason. The crystal skull is destroyed. The Anubis Box has been taken. The Army of the Ten Billion Spiders can't entrap any more gods. I'd call that a result."

"Unless they have already trapped everyone they need," Tom pointed out.

Church plucked an apple from a fruit display and pulled up a chair. "You're a real glass-half-empty kind of person, aren't you?"

"I'd call it pragmatic."

"Okay, we don't know how many gods they've got on their side: Janus, Apollo and Loki for definite . . ." He shifted uneasily when he thought of Loki's ferocity. "All right, they're pretty terrifying and I wouldn't want to face one of them on my own again. But we've got twenty courts here to oppose them. That weights things in our favour, I think." He crunched on the apple. "Have you heard of Robin Goodfellow?"

"Stay away from the Puck," Niamh interjected. "He is dangerous."

"I don't know why he decided to focus on me, but he really messed things around. Changing his appearance, shepherding me this way and that—"

"The Puck has his own agenda," she warned.

"This time it coincided with ours. I would never have destroyed the crystal skull without his help. Okay, he absconded with the Anubis Box, but—"

"And you call that a success?" Tom said. "An artefact of such power in the hands of something so unpredictable?"

Church shrugged. "Whatever you say, I think things are turning in our favour."

Tom hesitated before saying, "I believe I have found a way into the Court of the Final Word."

"See? That's great," Church said. "So the next thing is to get the lamp and my Pendragon Spirit back." He didn't see Tom share a dark glance with Niamh. "I've put things in place to get Shavi, Laura and Ruth together in the future. Trust me. Everything is going to be fine."

2

"So, have we got to spend the rest of our days hanging out in churches? 'Cause, you know, it's not really me." Laura leaned against the wall of Waltham Abbey Church and watched the rising sun cast pointing shadows from the gravestones.

Shavi sat cross-legged on the grass. The atmosphere was still, perfect for meditation. "The power in the land was strong at all sites people considered sacred—not just churches, but stone circles, cairns, springs, hilltops, lakes. Perhaps people instinctively sensed its strength and worshipped there. Or perhaps the act of worshipping made the power stronger in some way. Who knows?"

"Sounds like a load of hippie crap to me." Laura sniffed. "So where's it gone now?"

"I do not know. But I believe locating the Blue Fire is important in freeing the world from the Army of the Ten Billion Spiders."

"You really believe all that bollocks the old git keeps spouting?"

"Behind his demeanour, the Bone Inspector is a wise man with a vast amount of knowledge that has been passed down to him across the generations—"

"So he says."

"I am inclined to believe him. Everything I have witnessed gels with his perception of the situation."

"So . . . dragons?" She rested her head on the stone wall, enjoying the sun warming her face.

"He says if we can find the Fabulous Beasts we can find the Blue Fire, for the two are inextricably linked. The latent Blue Fire in these places not only masks our presence from the Army, it appears to be anathema to them. You saw how Rourke was thrown when the spark flashed between us. It appears it can be used both to heal and to hurt."

"This Pendragon Spirit is the thing I don't get. The old git says we're supposed to have it because we're some kind of heroes. But, you know—and don't take this the wrong way—are we the best they can get? I wouldn't want to be protected by any army that has me in the front line. I'm a selfish, lying, cheating, promiscuous coward who will fuck anybody over if it will save her neck."

Shavi smiled. "I think you are being harsh on yourself. And I think you are presenting a certain face to the world to hide the truth. You fear people will think the worst of you so you try to show them that aspect to prevent your disappointment."

"You don't know anything, pretty boy. You think you do, but you really, really don't." She changed the subject with a dismissive gesture. "So there's supposed to be five of us, right? The magic number. Five Brothers and Sisters of Dragons. There's you and me—"

"Ruth Gallagher must be one, the other name on the stone."

"That's only three. Who's this 'Church' who left the stone for us? He must have been around a long time ago if the ground wasn't disturbed, as you said."

"I do not know. Now we must find Ruth."

"How? There must be about eight million old folks' homes in South London. You reckon we should knock on every door?"

"I have an idea I would like to try." Shavi's statement was simple, but it carried a weight of apprehension.

"Do you ever get the feeling that your life's not real?" Laura said thoughtfully.

The concept troubled Shavi to a degree that he couldn't understand, but he knew exactly what she meant. "I feel as if I am playing a part."

"That's it. It's as though it's all fake—memories and everything. I can remember my parents, but there's none of that real detail you should have. It's like I know they're my parents, but that's all. And they don't feel as if they really are. They're like actors playing a part." She paused, troubled. "How weird is that?"

The Bone Inspector came up so silently that Laura jumped. He held out his hands to show six eggs. "Breakfast," he said. "Then we get down to business."

3

Forty minutes later on the edge of the graveyard, Shavi sat alone, listening to the birdsong, the wind stirring the branches of the trees, trying to still his rapidly beating heart. Laura and the Bone Inspector had retreated, bickering, to the van to give him his meditative space.

He breathed in, breathed out, tried to attune himself to the rhythms of nature as he had done in his flat after his long, hard days at the office. He expected it to take a long time, if it happened at all, but within minutes he was surprised to find himself slipping into a trance state. The waking world receded and soon there was only the soft thrum of blood in his head. He concentrated on what he wanted to achieve.

Time appeared to hang. It could have been minutes or hours when a faint fizzing arose accompanied by the smell of burned iron. The air was bubbling and spitting like molten metal. Shavi forced himself to stay calm. A gap the size of a porthole opened up in the seething air, and then a hand snaked out, followed by another. The spirit-form hauled itself through until it hung out from the waist up. It was the same almost featureless thing that had manifested in his office.

It mewled in pain, then said, "You have called me from the Invisible World again, Brother of Dragons, forced me to endure the suffering of this world. Do you have a question for me this time, or do you merely wish to exhibit your cruelty?"

"I have three questions," Shavi said. The Bone Inspector had told Shavi that as a seer he should be able to communicate with the "Others," but Shavi hadn't understood the meaning of the statement until that moment.

"Then speak them, Dragon-Brother, but know this: there is a price to pay for the answers you seek."

"What price?"

"A small thing."

"You must tell me first."

"No, you must agree to the contract first. That is the way these things are done."

Shavi knew it was stupid to agree in advance, but he could see no other alternative; there was too much at stake. "A small thing?" he asked.

"A small thing."

"Then I agree."

The spirit-form made an unpleasant smacking noise and said, "Then ask, Brother of Dragons, and may the knowledge benefit you as much as you hope."

Shavi took a deep breath. Then: "Where, exactly, is Ruth Gallagher, Sister of Dragons?"

"Not a good question, Brother of Dragons. Ruth Gallagher is *exactly* in the Fixed Lands. She is *exactly* within a day's flight from this place. But with respect to you, I will offer the answer you require this time. Ruth Gallagher spends her days in labour next to the river, near a bridge."

Shavi decided the information was good enough for him to find her. For the second question, he strove to choose his words more cleverly. "I know there are supposed to be five Brothers and Sisters of Dragons. Ruth, Laura and myself make three. Who are the other two?"

"Jack Churchill, known as Church, and Ryan Veitch."

Shavi couldn't understand how Church could be one of their group and also have buried the stone all those years ago, but he couldn't risk asking. He had one more important thing to ask. "Where can I find the Fabulous Beasts?"

The spirit-form paused for so long that Shavi thought it was not going to answer. But finally it said, "There is only one Fabulous Beast left in this world. It remained behind in the hope that one day a voice would call out and waken it from its slumber."

It fell silent. Shavi waited.

"The Fabulous Beast sleeps beneath the Garden of Eden."

Shavi continued to wait, but it was clear the spirit-form was not going to volunteer any more information. "But that is meaningless . . . The Garden of Eden does not exist."

"I have answered your questions, Brother of Dragons, and now I demand my price."

"But—"

Shavi's protestations died in his throat. The spirit-form rushed from the hole in the air with outstretched grasping hands.

4

The howl of pain echoed across the Abbey grounds. Laura and the Bone Inspector rushed across the graveyard to find Shavi sprawled on the grass. Laura turned him over. His hands were clutched to his face and when Laura pulled them away she recoiled in horror. Shavi's left eye had been torn out leaving a blood-encrusted, gaping socket.

5

After detouring to a costume shop in East London, Shavi had a black leather eye patch covering the empty orbit. "Strangely, it no longer hurts," he said as he gingerly probed around his cheekbone.

"Good. So you're ready to answer some straight questions," Laura said sharply from the driver's seat. "You gave up your eye on purpose? Just to get a few answers?"

"I did not know that would be the price."

"Then you're more of an idiot than I thought," the Bone Inspector growled. "You think they're going to take something that's not important?"

Shavi was surprised by how hard Laura had taken his sacrifice. She had already gone through disbelief, tears and finally had arrived at a cold, hard anger that currently was directed at him.

"I think the eye patch from the costume shop is quite dashing," he said in an attempt to defuse the tension. It didn't work.

Laura pulled the van over with a screech of tyres. "Is this what it's going to be like, then? You give up an eye. I donate an ovary. You lose a leg. I hack off an arm. Is that it? Because if it is, I don't want it."

"The burger bar is better?"

"Yes, it is. Let somebody else do this stuff. We can go back to having fun."

"There is no one else."

"You two shut up." The Bone Inspector glared at them. "Here's how it is: you do this or the Army of the Ten Billion Spiders cuts you—and me—out of reality. Gone. Forgotten. Never existed." He turned to Shavi. "That's it, isn't it?"

Shavi nodded.

"Now find this Ruth Gallagher and maybe you'll make a bigger spark. And then you find the other two, and then maybe we'll discover what's happened to the world and what the Enemy wants."

They'd already tried a number of care homes near London's bridges after consulting the *Yellow Pages* and the *A-Z*. There was only one left.

"That's it," Laura said nodding to a large, old house. "I hope she's got more sense than you or we really are fucked in the head."

Ruth felt as if she was waking from a long, deep sleep. Her mind was sluggish, but she was sure clarity lay just on the other side of the fog. Her dream of the owl-man had set something in motion, but she was not yet sure what it was or how it would turn out. The first manifestation of her new state was that she had called in sick to work, and the elation she felt when she put down the phone made her think she should give up her job completely. If she couldn't afford the flat, she could always move out of the city.

Her phone rang. It was Rourke. "I just tried you at work—"

"I called in sick."

"Is that wise?"

Ruth bristled. She wondered why she had put up with Rourke's claustrophobic attentions for so long.

"I thought I might drop round to see you," he continued.

"No," she said firmly.

"We could go for lunch?"

"I've got things to do. I'll call you later." Ruth hung up quickly. She realised that in the past he'd always managed to talk her round when she tried to hold him at bay. Was she really that weak?

A noise in the bedroom. Ruth felt a familiar shiver, but this time she didn't shy away from it.

The bedroom was still. Her bedroom door was ajar. Before she could investigate further, she was drawn to the window by a magnetic sense that someone desperately needed to speak to her.

In the street outside stood the giant she'd encountered on the Underground. He was looking up at her window with an expression of abject concern. When he saw her, he motioned furiously for her to join him. Ruth was surprised to realise she felt no sense of threat. Away from the shadows of the Tube tunnel, the giant appeared benign. Every now and then he glanced from side to side. Ruth knew obliquely that he was watching for the spiders. At that moment, not really knowing why, she decided she would go to him.

The creak of the wardrobe door made her start. Ruth turned to see the door opening of its own accord.

Ruth was gripped by a terrible dread. As the eerie movement of the door halted, she looked inside the wardrobe and saw not her clothes, but a deep, sucking darkness. Within the folds of the impenetrable gloom, *something* lurked. Ruth felt the inescapable gravity of the presence, the weight of its malign intent. It hungered for her.

The darkness bulged from the doorway, gaining shape and form. Ruth just had time to turn back to the giant before whatever was behind caught hold of her. Fear came down like night. She gripped onto the curtains, but was dragged back inexorably. Her eyes locked onto the giant's, and she saw fear in them, too: for her.

The darkness pulled her back, and back, until she was sucked into the depths of the wardrobe. She felt the presence close behind her, its breath on the back of her neck.

Ruth had time for one final scream and then the wardrobe door slammed shut.

7

"She's not there. I've got an address for her flat." Laura marched down the path from the care home, Shavi and the Bone Inspector hurrying in her wake.

"They gave out her address?" Shavi said.

"Not exactly."

Laura paused as she neared the van. Someone leaned jauntily against it: long, dark hair, a grinning, charismatic face.

"Who the fuck are you?" Laura said.

"Ryan Veitch," he replied. "Ring any bells?"

"We were about to search for you," Shavi said.

"And I've been searching for you."

Veitch held out his hand. When Shavi took it he was surprised by the coldness of the grip.

"Yeah," Veitch said. "I'm not all there." He held up his silver claw.

Shavi felt he should be remembering something, but it failed to surface.

"See?" Laura said bitterly. "I told you—he's already lost a hand. Well, I'm too beautiful and sexy to give up any body parts."

"You're right there, darlin'." Veitch held his arms wide and Laura gave him a tentative hug.

"You don't get any more until you get me drunk. I'm not a cheap date."

"How'd you find us?" The Bone Inspector watched Veitch suspiciously.

Veitch tapped his nose. "It's a Brothers and Sisters of Dragons thing."

"We were looking for another of our group," Shavi said. "Ruth Gallagher?"

"I know exactly where she is," Veitch said. "Come on—I'll take you right to her."

8

"You don't really expect me to get in there?" Church stared with disgust into the ruby-red waters flowing out from under the Court of the Final Word.

"I think you're insane even to consider venturing inside. Given that, this is just a baby step." Tom smoked to make himself forget. He wouldn't look in the direction of the court, which lay further along the valley floor.

"It's disgusting. I think I just saw some clots." The river gurgled and spat.

The sky was also the colour of an opened artery. The bloated red sun sinking behind the distant mountains cast the featureless landscape in hellish tones.

"You've got time to turn back." Tom's voice cracked, and Church glimpsed tears in his eyes.

"You know I don't have a choice—"

"You always have a choice!"

"Tom, this needs to be done. I have to reclaim the lamp. I need the strength it will give me to deal with what lies ahead. And if the gods in there are as bad as you say, we can't leave the Pendragon Spirit in their hands."

Tom finished his smoke and stamped the butt underfoot. "Don't forget, the one you need to watch out for is Dian Cecht. It's his court."

"In the old stories he was the god of healing, right?"

Tom laughed bitterly.

"I thought he was in charge of some kind of spring that restored dying gods to life."

"A metaphor," Tom said. "But you'll find all that out when you're in there. Just watch your back. Never relax your guard, not even for a moment. The court is vast, but sparsely populated. With any luck you stand a . . . reasonable chance . . ." His voice faltered at the lie in his words. "Just take care."

Tom walked away before Church could respond. Church called goodbye, but Tom did not turn or even acknowledge Church's presence.

Church looked one last time at the gleaming white marble of the Court of the Final Word caught between the bloody landscape and the bloody sky and then he stepped into the red river.

It was warmer than he had anticipated and had the sickening consistency of oil. The butcher's shop smell made him gag. Keeping as close to the bank as he could, he waded towards the court.

It took him fifteen minutes to reach the complex. The river emerged from the dark mouth of a culvert under the external wall. Church mentally prepared himself for what lay ahead and then plunged into the shadows.

It was warmer still in the enclosed space. Through the walls Church could hear a deep throbbing that sounded like machinery. There were other noises, too—sharp staccato bursts and the crackle of energy discharges, along with others that Church didn't want to consider.

As he progressed slowly in the dark, trailing one hand along the sticky wall, he felt the movement of swimming creatures brush his legs and wondered what could survive in that foul stew.

When he thought his stomach could bear no more of the gruesome atmosphere, he saw a shaft of light ahead. Positioning himself beneath it, he looked up at a grille at the top of a short shaft in the roof—some kind of drain for sluicing down the detritus from the room above. An iron ladder ran down the wall of the drain, for cleaning, probably. Standing on his tiptoes, Church could just reach the lowest rung. He hauled himself up and began to climb until he heard muffled voices in the room above. He clung to the ladder and waited, glad to be out of the river.

After five minutes, footsteps approached the drain. Church held his breath and looked up at the grille. But instead of seeing the occupant he was suddenly deluged with hot, sticky liquid, rushing across his face and drenching what little of him remained dry after the journey along the river. It was only when the torrent stopped a minute later that Church realised it was blood.

Fighting the urge to be sick, he held on, dripping, eyes shut tight. No more sounds came from the room and he decided to continue. He pushed upwards against the grille and it raised easily.

The chamber was empty. It was about twenty-one feet square with walls, floor and ceiling of the whitest marble that gleamed unbearably brightly after the dark of the culvert. There were two vats in one corner that Church chose not to investigate, and nothing else apart from a channel in the floor down which the discarded blood had flowed.

Church pulled himself into the chamber and headed towards the doorway, leaving a telltale trail of sticky red footprints. He tried to wipe off as much residue as he could and hoped the remainder would dry quickly.

The doorway opened onto a long corridor with many other doors leading off it. Everywhere was brilliant white, distorting perspective. His heart beating uncomfortably fast, Church edged along the corridor. The constant machine thrum hung in the background, occasionally punctuated by a distant high-pitched whine like an electric saw.

Tom had suggested that the lamp with the Pendragon Spirit would be kept somewhere in the heart of the complex, where the Tuatha Dé Danann conducted their most important experiments into the nature of Existence.

He had no way to get his bearings, and so he had no choice but to explore randomly and hope he would find something that would lead him in the right direction.

After a while he came across the first signs of life. An archway provided a view across three adjoining chambers, and in the furthest one he saw six people wearing robes of the deepest scarlet. They wore matching masks and hats that reminded Church of surgeons. He guessed that was a good analogy, for they were gathered around a table involved in some kind of operation. Church could see no instruments in use, but something lay on the table twitching and jumping as they went about their business. He watched for a moment, but what little detail he could garner hinted at something that disturbed him immensely and he moved on.

As he stood at the junction of three corridors, he realised that the constant thrum was louder down one corridor and he selected that route. At one point he had to slip into a room to hide from a young male and female wearing white togas with gold braid at the edges and a gold brooch at the shoulder. They had the air of clerical assistants about them.

Beyond that was a door through which Church could hear a faint whimpering. It would have been wiser to ignore it, but some quality to the sound drew him inside. A central aisle stretched for as far as the eye could see. On either side were cells containing people sitting on marble benches. There were no bars, and any of them could have walked out at any time, but they had a beatific, slightly dazed appearance that suggested sedation. As far as Church could see, all of the inmates were humans and from their clothes appeared to have been brought from many different periods. Church saw a woad-painted Celt, a wild-bearded Viking, a monk in brown robes, a Victorian woman in an extravagant dress who looked as though she had been plucked straight from a ball. There were scabby-kneed guttersnipes and other children in smart school uniforms, and Church was disturbed to see a number of babies sleeping peacefully in cribs.

Church stopped at one cell in which a man in his twenties wearing the rough clothes of a Tudor peasant hummed gently to himself.

"Are you all right?" Church asked.

The man smiled and nodded.

"Who are you?"

"My name is Robert, the miller's son."

"How did you get here, Robert?"

"I fell asleep in the fields one night," he said dreamily, "and I awoke to the most beautiful music I had ever heard. The Fair Folk were dancing around their mound to a fiddle and pipe tune. I tried to hide, but they saw me. And the girls . . . the beautiful girls . . . asked me if I wanted to dance with them. How could I refuse? We whirled around and around beneath the light of the moon, and then afterwards they invited me back to partake of their . . . food and drink . . . beneath the hills . . ." His voice trailed away to be replaced by a satisfied smile. His out-of-focus eyes replayed the scene of wonder over and over in his mind.

Church asked several others, but the story was always some variation on the same theme: of people enticed from their homes and villages by the Fair Folk with promises of wonders beyond measure. And the babies? Undoubtedly stolen from their cribs, as the old stories always said, with a changeling or a corn dolly left in their place.

Church looked up and down the aisle. Hundreds of cells, perhaps thousands, lined up like the pens at an animal-research lab. Church vowed to himself that he would find some way to return to free them.

Filled with mounting dread, Church continued towards the thrumming sound, which grew louder by the minute. What he encountered next dwarfed all his feelings about the horrors of the court.

He passed through a door that was larger than all the rest, set in a wall at least nine feet thick. There was a sense that he had also passed into an area of greater importance. Though everywhere was still white, an oppressive gloom lay heavily on the rooms and corridors. The tiles were dirtier, the grouting thick with black grease. This was an area of industrial labour, not philosophic thought. The machine sounds were now loud and resonant, like enormous hearts beating just behind the walls. Church found himself holding his breath.

More of the Tuatha Dé Danann moved around this section, their scarlet robes like pools of blood in the gloom, their masks depersonalising them until they became machine-like sentries. Church slipped stealthily through doors and behind vats or cupboards, or strange, lathe-like machines of indiscernible purpose.

Eventually he came to rows of windows that looked onto a large area of interconnecting rooms. The first thing he noticed were the numerous drainage channels crisscrossing the floor, all of them running with blood. Here the machine-noises were so loud they almost drowned out all other sound, but gradually his ears became attuned to what lay beneath: screaming, hundreds of voices rising up, mingling, different pitches, different timbres, an orchestration of agony.

There was movement in each of the rooms. As his eyes grew accustomed to the subdued lighting he saw teams of red-garbed figures busy over tables on which lay humans. At least, Church presumed they were human, for they were all in various stages of dissection, and all of them were conscious. The surgeons did not use scalpels or saws. To Church, it appeared as though they passed their hands through flesh and bone, peeling open faces, delving into organs, investigating to the very atomic structure of their subjects. Here and there, where some procedure became particularly difficult, a Caraprix would be introduced to the operation, changing its shape as it delved deeper into the bodies.

On some tables the people were being put back together, but not always the way they had started out. Some lay shaking, on the surface quite normal, but Church had seen objects introduced into brains and hearts and lungs and eyes. Others woke to find themselves with scales or wings or fiery breath. Many died in the process and their bodies were quickly removed. Others suffered terribly. On one table a pile of component parts made a sickening mewling sound.

In that moment Church understood why Tom was the way he was, and what Jerzy had also suffered. And that vista over atrocity told Church what the gods thought of humans and why his role was so important: it was a battle for survival, species against species. But it also fanned into life the first black spark of despair, small but growing, for how could he or any other human combat a race that was capable of such things, that was not even the true Enemy but which simply considered humans so far beneath them that they were accorded the same degree of concern that an abattoir worker showed to the cattle trooping past his work-station?

Sickened and reeling, Church moved away from the windows, desperate to complete his task and escape. The further he moved into the heart of the complex, the stranger and more puzzling the experiments became. Here there were no operations on humans, for which he was thankful, but what he did see troubled him on a different level.

On a crystal as big as he was, every facet revealed a different view of reality—in his own world, in the Far Lands, and in other places he did not recognise. An orb contained within it a tiny boiling galaxy. A machine cut a door shape in the air, and then opened the door a minute fraction before it slammed shut. Then the process would begin all over again. There were arcs of coruscating energy, and shimmering beams of light, and whirring blades. A system of mirrors filled Church with a devastating dread when he glanced into it, but he blacked out before his mind would reveal what it had seen. When he came around, he moved quickly away, no longer sure whether he could complete his mission.

But then he came to a long corridor with windows on either side and the mood became profoundly different. The queasy sense of dread diminished and he felt oddly uplifted, almost heady. When he glanced out of the window, he realised why: it was like looking into starless space, with crackling bursts of Blue Fire illuminating holes darker than the surrounding space. And from these holes Fabulous Beasts appeared to be birthing. Their sinuous forms rolled and turned joyously as they soared on their leathery wings, their scales glimmering like miniature suns. At times they appeared to be made entirely of the blue energy.

Church watched them for a while, mesmerised. For those moments he felt an abiding peace that he had not experienced since childhood. It was with great reluctance that he continued to the door at the end of the corridor.

This new room was dark, and unlike the rest of the court had walls of studded iron. In the centre hovered a globe formed from interconnecting blue lines, which shifted every now and then so that the globe took on new dimensions and warped perspectives. After Church had studied it for a while, he decided it was a representation of how the Blue Fire ran through reality.

And there, on a platform scattered with instruments whose use Church couldn't divine, sat the lamp. Church felt an ache in his heart as it tugged him towards it.

"You may take it."

Church started at the voice. Behind him stood a red-robed figure with aristocratic features, a high forehead, piercing grey eyes and a Roman nose. His long, grey hair was tied in a ponytail. Church could sense his authority.

"You're Dian Cecht." Church cautiously lowered his hand to Llyrwyn, knowing that if he chose to fight he would not escape the court alive.

"That is the name by which I was known by the tribes of your people." He smiled warmly. It was difficult to reconcile his benign appearance with the horrors Church had witnessed.

"You can't be allowed to carry on with what you're doing here," Church said.

"And how far would your kind go if you were faced with the annihilation of your race?"

"Don't tell me this is all a response to the Army of the Ten Billion Spiders. You've been doing this for a long time."

"A race can die in many ways. By annihilation in one devastating attack or by the slow attrition of stagnation." He motioned to the lamp. "Your kind were chosen to be the receptacle of the Pendragon Spirit, not mine. We, who have always been at the heart of Existence, were not considered to be champions of Existence. At the moment you are Fragile Creatures, but soon you will supplant us. And what then for the Golden Ones?"

"So you're going to torture us? Try to stop us reaching our potential, is that it?"

"Here in the Court of the Final Word we try to understand what makes a Fragile Creature so valuable to Existence. What is Existence? And can we shape it to our will?"

"The simple fact of what you're doing here shows you will never understand."

Dian Cecht considered this for a moment as he searched Church's face. "There is a more pressing problem. The Enemy has changed everything that lies ahead—nothing now is fixed. Soon, very soon, your people will be enslaved, the rising and advancing of their spirit halted. And my own people will be eradicated. That cannot be allowed to happen."

"Then you have to find a way to work with us."

"Perhaps." Dian Cecht smiled. "Take the lamp. I had hoped to plumb the depths of the Pendragon Spirit, but its mysteries still elude me."

Keeping a wary eye on Dian Cecht, Church took the lamp. It felt warm and soothing to his touch.

"You still do not trust me. That is understandable." The god went over to a stone column that reminded Church of the Wish-Post in the Court of Peaceful Days, but this one glowed with capillaries of blue energy. "The Blue Fire lies behind everything we know . . . behind time and space, which are but the thin skin stretched across it," Dian Cecht continued. "By moving into the medium of the blue energy, it is possible to alter everything. To reconstruct reality from the smallest particle."

"Who could do that?"

"Why, someone in whom the Pendragon Spirit burns strongly. Fire and fire, one within, one without, one and the same. You *are* the Blue Fire. I believe that locked inside you is the very thing for which I have been searching, and which I have failed so completely to find."

Church felt uneasy at the way Dian Cecht was looking at him.

"You are the key. Once you discover how to turn the lock, anything is possible. You could save my people by altering what is to come." Dian Cecht shook his head, bemused. "The Golden Ones, in the hands of Fragile Creatures." The god turned to the stone column. "This Wish-Post is unusual. It is one of my small successes. It allows you to see what your heart desires across the spread of Existence. But for anyone whose will is strong enough it allows travel to that time and place."

More trickery, Church thought—Dian Cecht knew exactly what Church wanted and was tempting him. Yet he wanted it so badly, he couldn't hide it. He could join Ruth immediately. He could save her, help the others.

"Will you try?" Dian Cecht said.

Church stepped forward, knowing he could not pass up the opportunity, whatever his doubts.

"Be warned—when the opportunity arises you must step through the doorway swiftly, for it will not maintain its integrity long. Do not waste time on thought."

Church looked into the Wish-Post and felt it shift and look back. "Go on."

Blue energy burst briefly like a camera flash, and when his vision cleared he was looking at a reflection of himself in a blue mirror. The reflection faded to be replaced by Shavi, only now he wore an eye patch and his face was spattered with blood. He looked disoriented and anxious.

"Shavi?" Shavi looked startled. "I'm Jack Churchill . . . Church."

Shavi's eyes widened. "Church? You must come quickly. You are the only one who can help—"

"I'm coming." He prepared to walk into the blue rectangle.

"Laura is dead," Shavi continued. "Ruth, too. They are going to bring him back, Church. They are—"

"Ruth's dead?" The words hit Church like a hammer blow. Reeling, he staggered back. The blue light faded, the moment lost. "Ruth's dead?" he repeated. It felt as if everything inside him was crumbling to dust.

Dian Cecht stood impassively, his hands behind his back. "Love is the source of all hope," he said, "the absence of love the source of all despair."

9

Black thoughts filled Church's head as Dian Cecht led him into a gleaming atrium. In one corner, a man cowered.

"Tom?" Church said.

The Rhymer looked ten years older than the last time Church had seen him.

"We found True Thomas wandering beyond the walls," Dian Cecht said. "How could we not offer such an old friend our hospitality? True Thomas has revisited many acquaintances and many fondly recalled parts of the court."

Church helped Tom to his feet. The Rhymer was shaking. "Are you all right?" Church asked him, concerned, but Tom couldn't find a voice to answer. Dian Cecht showed them to the door.

"You are both friends of the Court of the Final Word and I hope you will feel free to return at any time." To Church, he said, "And you, Brother of Dragons, have seen and learned much this day. I hope it enriches your life and guides you on your future path."

Church and Tom left without a backward glance. The despair that had infected Church's heart so long ago spread quickly through his system. He thought of Eleanor Dare and her daughter, victims of an uncaring universe that heaped suffering on good people, and he considered how powerless he had been to prevent their fate. But more than anything he thought of what he had seen in the Court of the Final Word. Its horrors ate through his mind, beating down any hope he had for a better world. The sheer scale of the pain inflicted dwarfed any goodness that glimmered in humanity. Hope was an aberration. That sick cruelty was the true state of being.

By the time they had set off on horseback, the black despair had infected every part of him. "Everything I've done has been pointless," he said. "I might as well have died in Carn Euny."

Tom said nothing.

"We need to make a detour on the way back." Church urged his horse on into the night.

10

At the Court of Peaceful Days, Rhiannon welcomed Church and Tom warmly. "You come to look into the Wish-Post?" she said.

Church shook his head. "I want to return this." He held out Llyrwyn.

Puzzled, Rhiannon took the sword and weighed it in her hands. "Very well. I will keep it safe until it seeks out another owner." She looked at Church with concern. "You seem changed, Brother of Dragons. Is all well?"

"No," Church replied. "And it never will be again."

11

Days passed dismally in the Court of the Soaring Spirit. Church mourned, and wrestled desperately with his memory, but it would not give up its ghosts. In the end, he was left with a terrible heartache, but no remembrance of good times to light up his grief.

Then, one evening, Tom came to him with Niamh. "I've had enough of this," he said. "Without you, it's all a waste of time. I just want to make the most of what few days I've got left. I'm going home."

Church considered this, and said, "I'll come with you." He glanced at Niamh. "If you'll let me."

"Of course." A deep sadness shadowed her eyes. "I will come, too."

"But what about your responsibilities here in the court?" Church said.

Niamh bowed her head. "I have given up my throne. The first queen to turn her back on her court in the long history of the Golden Ones."

"Why?"

She smiled sadly. "Because it is the right thing to do."

"I was hoping for a bit of free time," Tom said sourly, "but it looks as if I'm going to be wiping your snotty noses for a while longer."

As he turned away, the others didn't see his smile.

CHAPTER ELEVEN
FEEL LIKE I'M FIXIN' TO DIE

1

Neshoba County, Mississippi, December 1963

The radio played bluegrass while men in short sleeves with fists like ham-hocks and bellies like barrels drank from the bottle and played cards for nickels. Church, Tom and Niamh huddled around a table in one corner, their clothes sweaty and the dust of the road coating their boots.

Niamh looked transcendentally beautiful in a floaty cotton dress. Tom had decided to grow a beard and had adopted a down-at-heel beatnik chic. Church barely noticed any of the changes that had come over his travelling companions, or any of the towns they had passed through during the last week. Ruth's death haunted him day and night, and he was starting to feel as if he would never get over the empty-headed, hollow-hearted feeling.

"Those men keep staring at me," Niamh said, puzzled. "Are my clothes not correct for this time and place?"

"They're perfect," Tom said. "You'd better start getting used to it."

"Church?" When he didn't respond, her hand sought out his and gave it a warm squeeze.

"Sorry. I was miles away."

"Where do you want to go next?"

"Does it matter?"

Tom pulled a collection of flyers from his haversack. "I like the look of this San Francisco." He studied the information, as he had done many times over the past week.

"One place is as good as the next," Church said.

The door swung open and an intense young man of around eighteen stepped in hesitantly. He had a sensitive face emphasised by large brown eyes that took in detail quickly.

The barman bristled. "I told you—"

"I'm just looking for someone," the teenager interjected.

"I know who you're looking for, and you won't find her in here. Or any of her kind."

The teen opened his mouth to protest, then resigned himself to an exasperated silence.

One of the men chuckled as he checked his cards. "You had J. Edgar Hoover round yet about those Little Green Men?"

The teenager's cheeks flushed. "It wasn't Little Green Men."

"Aliens killed Kennedy!" Another of the card-players brayed with laughter.

The teenager stalked over to their table. "You can laugh all you want. There was a conspiracy."

The men continued to mock loudly. Niamh leaned into Church and whispered, "Who is Kennedy?"

"Used to be the president. Assassinated last month in Dallas. A lot of people who didn't have a voice loved him. A lot of people with conservative views hated him."

"It was the same in the Court of Alexander of Scotland," Tom said. "Politics and conspiracy go hand in hand."

"They arrested one man for killing Kennedy," Church explained. "Lee Harvey Oswald. But lots of other people thought Oswald was set up, that other people had a hand in the murder."

"Who?" Niamh struggled to grasp what Church was saying.

"Criminals like the Mafia. The government's own agencies. Political protestors. Businessmen. Renegade politicians and military types. In my time, it's become a kind of . . . myth." Church shrugged.

"Why would anyone want to kill their king? Unless it was for sacrificial purposes—"

The teenager was growing more passionate. "There is evidence! My dad worked at the Kodak labs when they brought in the Zapruder film of the assassination. It definitely showed a guy with a spider on the back of his neck making a signal . . ." The table fell silent. The teen looked from face to face until the card-players all burst out laughing as one.

"How come LBJ hasn't got the exterminators in?" one of the men said through tears of laughter.

"Because there's been a cover-up." The teen was red-faced with anger. "When *Life* magazine borrowed the film to copy it they said they damaged it. Six frames were cut out and it was spliced back together. They were the frames with the spider-guy in them."

As the jeering rose up again, the teen turned on his heel and marched out. Church followed a moment later.

The teen was sitting in an old pick-up on the dirt road. The Beatles were on the radio singing "I Want to Hold Your Hand" and the youth was beating the rhythm on the steering wheel.

Church leaned into the passenger window. "I heard what you were saying in the bar."

"Hey, you're English. Like these guys."

"My name's Jack Churchill. Church to my friends."

"Gabriel Adams. Gabe. So what—you come to laugh at me, too?"

"I've seen them."

Gabe's eyes grew wide. He snatched a cardboard box from under his seat. Inside were newspaper clippings, sketches, maps and pages of detailed notes. "JFK couldn't have been shot by a lone gunman. It's impossible. And I can prove it."

Church stopped him getting out the sheaf of papers. "I just wanted to say stay away from the spider-people. They're dangerous. Don't waste your life chasing this kind of stuff. Enjoy yourself."

Gabe looked hurt. "You don't want to hear my theory?"

Church's attention was caught by a blaze rising up away through the trees. Gabe blanched when he saw it.

"What is it?" Church asked.

"I don't know . . . I think . . . Marcy?" Gabe turned the ignition.

Church hesitated, then got in. "Trouble?"

Gabe's pale face revealed the answer as he gunned the pick-up in the direction of the fire.

2

Church could smell the thick, tarry smoke long before Gabe crashed the truck through vegetation into a field next to the woods. A twelve-foot-high cross blazed brightly against the night sky.

Eight men stood around in white robes and hoods. At the feet of the Ku Klux Klansmen sprawled a woman of Gabe's age, a noose tied around her neck. One of the men held the other end like a dog leash. She was mixed race with long hair tied up in bunches. Her eyes were wide with terror.

Gabe brought the pick-up to a juddering halt. "That's Marcy," he said. He was shaking.

One of the Klansmen raised a shotgun and called out, "You want to back off, boys. This ain't for you."

Gabe had frozen. Church released the handbrake and jammed his foot on top of Gabe's on the accelerator. Dirt sprayed in a fountain behind them as the pick-up lurched forward. Church dragged Gabe down as the shotgun blast frosted the window.

"They're going to kill us," Gabe said, but he kept the pick-up racing towards the Klansmen.

The Klansmen scattered as the pick-up rammed the base of the burning cross. It crashed down on the man with the shotgun, the impact killing him before his robes ignited.

Church jumped out to retrieve the shotgun. One barrel was still loaded. He brandished it at the remaining Klansmen while Gabe raced out to pull the noose from Marcy's neck. Crying and coughing, she rubbed at the sore flesh as Gabe helped her into the pick-up, with Church close behind.

One of the Klansmen threw himself onto the side of the vehicle to try to wrestle the shotgun from Church. As he forced his upper body through the passenger window, the gun discharged, killing the Klansman instantly. He slumped limply halfway through the window just as Gabe prepared to reverse the truck away at speed.

"I know you, Gabriel Adams," one of the Klansmen yelled in a thick Southern accent. "You want to get out of town before sun-up, or we're gonna pay your momma a visit."

"Your kind don't belong here," another yelled. "Consorting with niggers. Knew you were no good the minute you and your momma set foot here."

As they sped away, Gabe yelled, "Dump that damn body!"

"I need to check something," Church replied. "Just keep driving for now."

Church told Gabe to pull the truck over when they were a couple of miles away. Marcy had already recovered from her ordeal, and her fear had given way to a cold anger. Church pushed the dead Klansman back through the window onto the side of the road and jumped out. He stripped off the Klansman's robes and searched his body for any sign of a spider. There was none, which Church found even more disturbing. He returned to the pick-up where Gabe was hugging Marcy tightly.

"Are you all right?" he said. "If we hadn't seen the fire—"

"They dragged me out of the house, Gabe. They beat my momma with sticks but they came for me."

"I know the Klan lynched a lot of men, but girls . . . ?" Church said.

"They did it 'cause I'm dating a white boy," Marcy said bitterly.

"But look at you, Marcy," Gabe said. "You're nearly white yourself—"

Marcy glared at him. "What are you saying? I'm black—black in their eyes, black in mine. Having some white mixed in there doesn't mean they'll suddenly leave me alone 'cause I'm *normal*."

Gabe flushed. "That's not what I meant—"

"I'm sorry." Marcy hugged Gabe, and then Church. "And thanks for risking your neck, whoever you are. You saved my life."

Church was touched by her response. He had acted on instinct, and now the adrenalin rush had gone he was surprised by how quickly and decisively he had responded when he saw the gun.

"We can't stay here after this," Gabe said bitterly. "They'll come after my mom, and yours."

"I don't want to run away from them. They'll think they've won," she said.

"We can't fight them," Gabe said.

"It's none of my business," Church interjected, "but maybe you could hit the road just for a while, until it's calmed down here."

Gabe took Marcy's hand. "It's for the best. For our moms."

"You can come with my friends and me if you want," Church said. "We don't know where we're going or what we're doing. But on the plus side, we've got some cash to see us through for a while."

"We could go to Dallas," Gabe said thoughtfully. "I need to see for myself where the president died." He glanced at Church and added, "I want to prove that spider-guy is real."

Church felt sorry for the teenager. The road Gabe was about to walk wouldn't end happily.

3

Dallas, 1964

Dallas was like a bad hangover, even weeks after the assassination. In shops and bars and in the streets, people felt guilty, as if they had been personally responsible for the president's death.

Gabe got nowhere with his investigation, as Church had expected and secretly hoped, but it was clear Gabe wasn't going to give up easily. Church saw something of himself in the teenager's innocence and unfocused desire for justice, but they were echoes from long ago, before things had started to go so badly wrong.

On February 9, they stood outside a TV store in downtown Dallas watching the Beatles on the Ed Sullivan Show on the sets piled high in the window display.

"I wish I could hear them," Gabe said. "I reckon they're really going to shake things up."

"You could be right." Church smiled wryly to himself.

"I can't believe they let them on Ed Sullivan."

"You, me and seventy-four million others." Church watched Gabe's face light up with a simple joy and felt like an elder brother. "So why the obsession with JFK?"

Gabe fell silent for a moment. "My dad died a couple of days after he worked on the film of the assassination. Hit and run. They never caught the driver."

"I'm sorry."

"I remember how excited he was when he told me what he'd seen. And how angry when those frames got cut out. It was a big deal to him." He shrugged. "I'm just trying to make sense of stuff. These days nothing makes sense at all."

4

In April, Marcy persuaded Gabe that he wouldn't find anything else in Dallas and if he still wanted to dig for information, they should head east, to New York first, and then to Washington if he could find anything concrete to pursue.

Church was surprised by Tom's developing affinity for American culture and the music of the times. In the damp-ridden apartment they found for themselves in Queens, he installed a record player on which he would listen to Paul Revere and the Raiders and the Beau Brummels at full volume until the neighbours banged on the walls. He went to clubs on his own, and developed a wide network of eccentric friends. Church began to understand that for Tom, the ultimate outsider cut off from his own time and race by what had been done to him at the Court of the Final Word, this was finally somewhere he could feel at home. In the end they were all trying to forget the past and lose themselves in the present.

As the days grew longer and the leaves started to appear on the trees in the park, Tom returned one afternoon and told Church there was someone he needed to meet.

"A psychologist," Tom said, "by the name of Timothy Leary. He evangelises about a drug called LSD. He believes it can unlock areas of consciousness, and set off a big evolutionary leap for mankind."

"I've heard of him," Church said. "Nixon called him 'the most dangerous man in America.'"

Tom snorted. "He has a research centre in a mansion. Good work is being done."

"What have you been doing with him?" Church asked.

"None of your business." Tom pulled out a screwed-up magazine article. "This is what he said about his first drug trip: 'I could look back and see my body on the bed. I relived my life, and re-experienced many events I had forgotten . . . The discovery that the human brain possesses an infinity of potentialities and can operate at unexpected space-time dimensions left me feeling exhilarated, awed, and quite convinced that I had awakened from a long ontological sleep. A profound transcendent experience should leave in its wake a changed man and a changed life.'"

Church realised what Tom was proposing. "You want me to drop acid with Timothy Leary? To get my memory back?"

"Yes."

"No."

"Hear me out—not just for that," Tom said. "Leary's research has given him some perception of the structure of reality—"

"It's over, Tom—you've got to understand that. I'm not fighting this war any more. Every time I get involved people close to me die. Next time it could be you, or Niamh . . . Somebody else can do the heavy lifting now."

Tom folded the article carefully and returned it to his pocket. "He's seen the spiders," he said quietly.

"And don't go dragging Gabe into all that. He deserves some kind of life before it all goes pear-shaped. If he ignores the Army of the Ten Billion Spiders, they'll ignore him—"

"You think that's how it works?" Tom said sharply. "And what kind of philosophy are you promoting there? Look after yourself and everyone else be damned?"

"Why not? I haven't done any good. What's the point in carrying on, tell me that?"

Niamh and Marcy walked in laughing, but their high spirits ebbed away when they felt the tense atmosphere.

"Then I'll just take Gabe," Tom said slyly.

Church glared at him. "I'll come. Just to make sure you don't screw up someone else's life."

5

"LSD will, in the very near future, liberate minds and create a free society." The Most Dangerous Man in America had the look of a genial college professor as he sat cross-legged on a cushion in his airy study in the sprawling Millbrook Mansion. His greying hair was swept back from a tanned face and he was dressed all in white with an Indian motif embroidered in red around the collar.

"You're convinced of that?" Church asked.

"A sceptic." Leary smiled without offence. "It will, unless the Establishment prevents it."

Tom eyed Church suspiciously. "Let's not get into an argument," he cautioned. Beside him, Gabe listened intently.

"There is no inherent danger in hallucinogens if they are treated with a sacred and respectful attitude," Leary said. "That is, they should not be used for hedonistic purposes. Let us not forget that psychedelics have been utilised for sacred purposes in all major religions throughout history, including early Christian rites."

Gabe looked shocked.

"The drug is only a tool to contact the Godhead," Leary continued. "A catalyst. It has no inherent value beyond its ability to trigger that part of the brain, which we all have, that is responsible for spiritual experience. From that perspective, one's view, intention, attitude, personality and mood are just as important in achieving the right state."

"So in the wrong hands psychedelics can be dangerous," Church translated.

"The same as anything. But for someone who wishes to transform spiritually, hallucinogens *can* be a catalyst. They *can* lead to an understanding of your own destiny, and insight into the basic spiritual realities. This is what the ancient Greeks called gnosis—"

Church had a flash of a deeper connection stretching across the centuries, of the Universe itself giving him information to shape his path. "That's the same thing John Dee was talking about," Church said to Tom.

"John Dee?" Leary interjected. "You mentioning his name is a very weird coincidence."

"Yeah, there seem to be a lot of those going around," Church said.

"I was on a trip to North Africa with my wife Rosemary, and a friend, Brian Barritt," Leary said. "We took acid in the desert at Bou Saada, and Brian had a vision of a cowled man in a cloud of dust—a dust devil. He heard the name 'Doctor John Dee,' and an image of a giant scroll took over his mind, followed by visions of golden vessels with the faces of Egyptian gods. Weird, but true."

"What's Gnosticism got to do with it?"

"Everything. My life, and my understanding of everything I see around me, changed just over three years ago when I first took psilocybin mushrooms in Cuernavaca in Mexico." Leary closed his eyes and let his head drop backwards. "You understand the mystery religions of ancient cultures? Every one had outer mysteries, which consisted of myths that were common knowledge —the stories of the gods and the like—and rituals that were open to everyone. And then there were the inner mysteries, which consisted of a sacred secret known only to those who had undergone a powerful rite of initiation. During *my* initiation I learned what that secret was, the one all ancient seers understood fully. The secret that is at the core of Gnosticism."

Church could see why Leary annoyed as many people as he inspired. He had a taste for showmanship that often meant his message was lost.

"So what's the big secret?" Church prompted.

"That we're all living in hell." Tom's voice rang with echoes of the Court of the Final Word.

"At the heart of it is the nature of evil," Leary said. "If you believe there is a creator-god, why did he introduce evil into the world? The orthodox Christians found the answer. They put the blame for evil on mankind, particularly Eve, who allowed evil into the world when she accepted knowledge in the form of the apple from the snake in the Garden of Eden. The Gnostics took a different approach. They are, essentially, dualists: two sides, two faces, two worlds, two great opposing powers."

Church began to see more connections in the recent events that had shaped him and brought him to this point. He had a strange impression that Leary, and the study, and Millbrook Mansion, were an illusion and that in fact Existence was speaking directly to him.

"Do you ever wonder why children are murdered or suffer in poverty? Why diseases devastate our bodies? Why wars destroy generations? Why there is such an overwhelming drive to make money even if it brings about more human suffering? That we all know these things are wrong and that it is in our power to put them right, yet we do nothing about it?" Leary pressed his palms together as if he were praying. "Because this creation is a defective work. The material world is a trap for man and always has been, in the control of a force that we characterise as 'Evil,' but which is simply the opposite of what life should be. Dark to Light. Anti-Life to Life."

"Despair to hope," Church said.

"The Gnostic Secret says there is a solution," Leary continued. "The sacred secret that has been taught for thousands of years is this: that at the point when Light and Dark split into two, sparks of the divine light became embedded in what would be humanity, like slivers of glass from a broken mirror. The aim of all Gnostic teaching is to awaken those who contain the divine spark so they can find a way back to the Light, or Life."

Tom leaned forward eagerly. "You understand what he's saying? You know who these people are with the 'divine spark'? You thought you were fighting to save this world from the Army of the Ten Billion Spiders. The truth is, they're trying to stop you from leading a revolution that will overthrow their master, who created this world and who has let it tick over in his absence."

"And now he's back to take control of his creation?" The concept was so huge Church found it difficult to comprehend. "You're saying the Army of the Ten Billion Spiders are the foot soldiers of this . . . this power . . . this force for Anti-Life?"

"It has many names," Tom replied. "The Void. The Demiurge. The Tuatha Dé Danann know it as the Devourer of All Things."

"You suddenly know a lot of things you've never seen fit to mention before," Church said sharply.

"Life itself is an initiation, Church." In Tom's words, Church heard echoes of what he had been told so many centuries ago by the spirit in the Blue Fire. "Once you pass the test, you gain the knowledge."

Gabe turned to Leary. "Tom said you'd seen the spiders."

"In some trips, one in particular." Leary shifted uncomfortably. "They were moving behind the scenes of reality, keeping things the way they should be in the Void's world."

"But now they're in this world because you're here," Tom said to Church.

"Because now Existence has champions, and it's finally a threat to the rule of the Void. Because humanity is now rising and advancing, and there's a chance that everything could change. Everything."

"What's this got to do with the president's assassination?" Gabe interjected with frustration.

"Everything is connected," Tom said.

Leary nodded. "When you're up hard against the pattern, you can't see the pattern at all. What I'm going to tell you now you have to keep secret for your own safety."

More showmanship, Church thought.

"A couple of years ago I was contacted by a woman named Mary Pinchot Meyer at my office at Harvard University. She'd been following my experiments with LSD very closely. Mary is an artist in Washington, and she wanted to organise an LSD session for some friends." He paused for dramatic effect. "Mary was JFK's principal lover. Forget Marilyn—Mary was always the one."

Gabe was aghast. "You're saying the president took drugs in the White House?"

Leary smiled at the teen's naivety. "JFK smoked pot and took cocaine, which was his favourite. But the important point here is that he turned on to acid. Mary arranged several trips for him. He was expanding his consciousness . . . starting to see the way the world really works."

Gabe looked as if he might be sick. "My dad . . . I mean JFK . . . He really did this? I'm sorry. I'm starting to get confused."

"The day after JFK was assassinated, Mary called me up." All traces of showmanship had been replaced by a deep unease. "These were her exact words: 'They couldn't control him any more. He was changing too fast. He was learning too much . . . They'll cover everything up. I gotta come see you. I'm scared. I'm afraid.' They've left Mary alone so far, but she's still living in fear."

"You're saying JFK was assassinated because he dropped acid?" Church couldn't hide the note of incredulity in his voice.

"Not because he dropped acid—because he began to understand some universal truths. I'm saying he was a charismatic, influential and powerful person who, although flawed, was starting to open his eyes. It doesn't matter whether we're talking metaphorically or not—'spider-people' is a good way of describing those who buy into the whole Anti-Life agenda—kind of like the pod people in that Body Snatchers movie. The spider-people are everywhere, and every year that passes they control more and more of the world. But they have to carry out their business from the shadows, because otherwise they'd ruin the illusion of what they're trying to create."

"How do you recognise them?" Gabe said anxiously.

Leary thought about that for a moment, and then said simply, "You don't."

6

"I know what you're doing, Tom," Church said when they were back at the apartment. "You've learned a lot of manipulation skills out there in the Far Lands. But if you think you can get me back wasting my life in a fight I can't win, you'd better think again."

Tom shrugged and acted as if Church was speaking nonsense.

"Especially now you've told me I'm supposed to be fighting some kind of universal god of darkness. It's just insane."

With infuriating aloofness, Tom ignored Church completely, dropped an LP onto the record player and turned the volume up full.

7

In July, author Ken Kesey took his first Magic Bus Trip to New York on an LSD-fuelled quest to discover America, at the same time as President Lyndon Johnson was signing the Civil Rights Act.

On the night of 19 July, Niamh dragged Marcy into the apartment. Blood streamed from a gash on Marcy's head and Niamh had a stunned expression that Church had never seen before.

Gabe ran to help. "Who did this?"

"The police," Niamh said. "They came at us as if we were vermin being driven from a sewer."

Marcy sat in a chair in the kitchen, clutching a towel to her wound. "It was a Congress of Racial Equality protest in Harlem," she said. "The cops went crazy. Shot one guy dead, hundreds more injured. There was blood all over the sidewalk." She stared into the middle distance with an expression of mounting horror. "We only wanted a voice, just black people saying who we were." She smiled weakly at Niamh. "Sorry for dragging you into it, darlin'."

"Do not apologise. I need to see these things." She rested a hand on Marcy's shoulder. Church could see that a bond had grown between them similar to the one between Gabe and himself.

"We need to get out of this city," Gabe said, demoralised.

"No," Marcy replied defiantly. "We need to fight."

They buried their differences for the rest of the summer and into the autumn. But then in October, as the cold winds blew harder, Tom came across a small article in the newspaper. Timothy Leary's presidential contact, Mary Pinchot Meyer, had been murdered as she walked along the Chesapeake and Ohio towpath in Georgetown. It looked to have been the work of a professional hit man. The first bullet was fired into the back of her head, and when she did not die immediately, a second shot was loosed into her heart. The evidence showed that in both cases the gun was almost touching Meyer's body when it was fired.

Immediately afterwards, Church, Niamh, Tom, Gabe and Marcy left town and headed west.

8

While President Johnson was outlining his Great Society, they were holed up in a leaky warehouse in St Louis. By the time the US had started bombing North Vietnam in earnest on 8 February 1965, they had moved to slightly better surroundings in an old meat-packing plant in Chicago.

There was no sign of the Army of the Ten Billion Spiders anywhere near their lives. Church couldn't make the guilt go away entirely; he knew they were being left alone because he had chosen to walk away from the battlefield. With the lamp containing his stolen Pendragon Spirit still safe in his bag, he could claim to be little more than an average person, trudging through life below the radar of the forces that controlled everything.

On 21 February, black revolutionary leader Malcolm X was shot and killed. Marcy cried all night and there was nothing Gabe could do to drag her out of her growing despair at the worsening political situation.

All around them the misery continued to mount. On 6 March the first American soldier officially set foot on Vietnam's battlefields, and two days later 3,500 marines landed to protect Da Nang airbase. In between, Alabama state troopers attacked 500 civil rights workers preparing to march, and by the end of the month the Ku Klux Klan had murdered another civil rights worker in the same state. At home and abroad, the spider-people—in metaphor and reality—continued to take control, spreading despair, crushing hope.

"Existence needs its king to lead its troops," Tom said to Church as he browsed a day-old paper one morning. Church gave his standard response: it was somebody else's job now.

Over the months, to Tom's annoyance, Niamh had sided with Church. She pointed out that people were fighting back of their own accord. Martin Luther King Jr. and 25,000 supporters took the fight for civil rights back to Alabama. A further 25,000 marched on Washington in April to protest against the spiralling Vietnam War.

"Music is the voice of hope," she pointed out to Tom as he listened to his growing record collection, and he had to agree: Phil Ochs, Joan Baez and Judy Collins joined the anti-war marches, and the Rolling Stones and Bob Dylan spread the message of discontent.

On 5 September, writer Michael Fallon applied the term "hippie" to the San Francisco counterculture in an article about the Blue Unicorn Coffeehouse where campaigners for sexual freedom and the legalisation of marijuana met.

And on Christmas Day 1965, the Libertarian came to town.

9

"You don't get it, Gabe. Standing up and fighting for what you believe in is the only way. Malcolm was right. If you turn the other cheek they'll just keep slapping it." Marcy had changed more than all of them in the months they had been together. She'd developed a flintiness as a defence against the attacks that were coming from all quarters.

She trudged through the snow towards the convenience store in her boots and ragged jeans, a thrift-store coat pulled tight for warmth, annoyed at the childish frivolity of Church and Gabe who had stopped for a snowball fight.

"If you get involved in violence and confrontation you're just as bad as the people you're opposing," Gabe protested. "There's always a peaceful route. JFK could have bombed the Communists like all the hawks in the White House wanted, but he talked his way out of it and saved the world in the process."

When she was trying to keep her anger inside, Marcy always held her head in a way that made her appear haughty. "This is a war, and you're on one side or the other. There's no room for sitting on the fence. If you're not with us, you're against us. If you're not part of the solution, you're part of the problem. Sooner or later you've got to choose, Gabe."

"You know I'm with you." Gabe turned to Church. "What do you think?"

Marcy snorted. "There's no point asking him. He's already dropped out."

Her comments were delivered off the cuff, but they stung Church. The hardest part was that he couldn't argue with her because she was right.

While Gabe and Marcy went into the store to pick up supplies, Church watched the children playing in the park across the street and the gulls swooping across the Windy City's skyline. It was a grey and white world of dirty snow and industrial smoke, the kids' anoraks the only colour.

Every day his thoughts turned back to that day in Leary's study and the revelation of why the world was the way it was. He hoped that soon it would fade and he could drift into a soporific acceptance. Marlowe must have known the truth all those years ago when he briefly broke off from his spy games to write *Doctor Faustus*: *Why this is hell, nor am I out of it.*

After ten minutes the cold began to get to him, and Gabe and Marcy were still not at the checkout. He ventured into the store, but they were nowhere to be found.

When he came back out into the cold, puzzled, he was met by a boy with red cheeks and a nose caked with dry snot. "Mister, your friends have gone over there." He pointed to a derelict tenement further down the street. The windows were broken and the walls were scarred with graffiti. Scrawled in big white letters were the words "Watch out for the Army of the Ten Billion Spiders." The message was everywhere these days and it gave Church a kind of black satisfaction to know that he had set it in motion. When he turned back to ask for more information, the boy had already skipped away to rejoin his friends in the park.

The building smelled of damp and turps and long-dead fires. Church couldn't understand how Gabe and Marcy had slipped past him even though his back had been turned, nor why they had come to such a desolate place. He called their names, but only echoes replied. He started to wonder if the boy had been playing a trick on him.

But on the top floor he came to a large space where all the walls had been knocked out, and there he saw two people sitting on chairs in the middle of the floor, their backs to him. It was Gabe and Marcy. Their heads rested against each other and they were unmoving. A pool of blood grew beneath them.

Church backed against the damp plaster, torn between the recognition of what was clearly a trap and the devastating shock of grief for his friends.

"Is it really so bad? I'd have thought you'd have been used to it by now." The fruity voice rolled out from behind a pillar of bare brick and yellowing wallpaper. The Libertarian stepped out, dressed all in black, coat swirling around him like some silent-movie villain. A crescent of blood darkened the fabric covering his chest. He removed his sunglasses to wipe stray droplets off the lenses and fixed his lidless, red gaze on Church. "Surprised to see me again? I suppose you thought you could just slip back into the woodwork with all the other vermin."

Church wished he had Llyrwyn and imagined himself hacking the Libertarian's head from his body. He glanced at the dripping corpses of his friends, tongue-tied, trying to comprehend how things could slip away so quickly after months of inactivity.

"Why did you kill them? There was no need." He hated himself for the pathetic tone he heard in his words.

"There's always a need for death. It reminds us why we're alive." The Libertarian circled the bodies slowly.

Church followed, wanting yet not wanting to see Gabe and Marcy's faces one last time. As they came into view, he was surprised and relieved to see that the two bodies were not his friends after all, but had been carefully selected to resemble them from the rear.

The Libertarian smiled as he watched realisation dawn on Church's face. "It's important to make an impact to drive a message home."

"You killed two people randomly to send me a message?"

"You've been very good recently. No dashing around waving a sword trying to upset the apple cart. That's very satisfying. And it's how things should continue."

"I've walked away. There was no need for this."

"But you're a contrary sort. I wouldn't want you having second thoughts. See this as a subliminal affirmation. Picture the image you saw the moment you walked through that door. This *will* happen to your friends, wherever they are, if you start getting ideas above your station."

"You come anywhere near them or me again, and I'll kill you."

"Wooh!" The Libertarian flexed a mock-defiant fist.

Church backed towards the door.

"You should be careful," the Libertarian continued. "We're getting very close to the Source now. We're getting stronger. Soon you can shine your little blue light all you want and it won't do any good. You'll be just like them." He nodded towards the two bodies.

Church marched out of the tenement and back to the apartment, where Gabe and Marcy were putting away the groceries. Church took Gabe to one side. "We need to split up. For a while."

"I thought you liked us travelling with you."

"I do."

"We're like family, man."

"That's why I'm doing this. There's danger. I want you away from me until I'm sure it's safe."

"We could go to San Francisco." Marcy was leaning in the doorway thoughtfully. "There's a lot of energy out there, a lot of kids moving down . . . organising."

"All right," Gabe said. "But you'll join us, right? Every month we'll put a small ad in the local paper, telling you where we are." He masked his sense of abandonment and went to pack his bag.

Tom was smoking in his room while Niamh lounged nearby, listening to music. Church told them about the Libertarian. "We need to hit the road, keep on the move."

"He'll find you wherever you are," Tom said dismissively. "This is his world."

It was Niamh who raised the most pertinent question. "If he could have found you at any time, why did he feel the need to come to you now, in this place?"

Church considered this and realised Niamh was right. The Libertarian would not have seen the need to send a message unless he perceived a threat. But what was it?

10

After Gabe and Marcy left, the atmosphere in the apartment was tense. Tom had very little patience with Church and showed it at every opportunity. Church wanted to head to New Orleans. Tom flatly refused to set foot in the south while civil rights were being resisted. Tom wanted to go to Mexico to check out the sacred mushrooms that Leary had investigated. Church wasn't interested.

Finally Tom stormed out and disappeared for two days. When he returned he had an armful of cheaply produced magazines, all of them garishly illustrated. He tossed them at Church.

"See what's happening? Existence is organising. People are hearing the call, rising up. But if they're going to make a difference they need a king to lead them."

Church flicked through the magazines: articles on ley lines and Earth power, calls to arms against the Vietnam War, for civil rights, against the force for repression that was manifesting across the world, academic discussions of the occult, Wicca, Sufism, all sorts of Eastern spirituality.

"Freedom equals Life. Love equals Life," Tom said. "Control equals Anti-Life. This is war. And you're needed."

"You sound like one of those hippies out on the West Coast."

"When you want to destroy something you give it a name so you can mock it. Even the *filids* of the Celts knew that. But maybe these hippies are right."

Church lay back on the cushion and closed his eyes. "I don't want to argue, Tom," he said wearily.

"Well, I do. You sank into depression after your woman died, and I can understand that—I've fought against it ever since I walked out of the Court of the Final Word. A broken heart's a terrible thing, but you can't stay sinking down in the black waters for ever—"

"It's not just Ruth. What I saw in the Court of the Final Word showed me that the human race is nothing—"

"That's what they want you to think."

"The Demiurge, the Void, whatever you want to call it—it rules this world already and pretty soon it's going to control the Far Lands, too. It's beyond powerful, Tom. Surely you can see that. I'm one man. I can't make a difference."

"One man or woman can change everything."

"More stupid hippie talk."

Tom studied Church for a moment and then began to collect his magazines.

"What are you doing?" Church asked.

"What you should be doing. I've been living in fear ever since I was dragged out of my life and into this whole miserable business. But I don't have the luxury of being scared any more."

"You're very clever, Tom, but you're not going to make me feel guilty."

"The Blue Fire and everything it represents has been sleeping for a long,

long time, since the Age of Reason came in at least. But now it's being woken again. By ordinary people, Church—normal, everyday people filled with hope, who need help. Somewhere out there are new Brothers and Sisters of Dragons, who may well be the most powerful in generations. They need someone to shape them, before Veitch gets to them, or the Libertarian, or Salazar."

"How are you going to find them?"

"That's my problem now."

Church listened to Tom in his room packing his haversack, and soon after the front door slammed. He'd left all his records for Niamh with a warm, affectionate note, but for Church there was only a silence that spoke volumes.

11

1966 was a year of running away. Church and Niamh travelled to New Orleans and then to Boston, and finally to Maine, as far away as possible from the conflict that was beginning to grip the rest of the nation.

In San Francisco the Grateful Dead staged the first light show in front of 10,000 people, and Jefferson Airplane and Big Brother and the Holding Company performed at the Fillmore with Janis Joplin. Anti-Vietnam War protests brought tens of thousands onto the streets of New York City in March, and two months later another 10,000 marched on Washington DC.

At the same time the FBI was working hard to ensure that LSD had a bad press, and the Bureau launched a raid on Timothy Leary's Millbrook Mansion, arresting him for possession of marijuana. Leary, in true showmanship style, refused to take it lying down. In September he held a press conference announcing the formation of a psychedelic religion, the League for Spiritual Discovery, where he called on the world to "Turn on, tune in, drop out."

Church found himself growing closer to Niamh by dint of shared time and experience; they were rarely apart. At first she was difficult to comprehend. Over meals she would tell him sad stories of the Golden Ones unable to find their way back to their mythic homeland where they would finally feel complete. She wove tales of adventure, magic and mystery that reached back long before humanity ascended. The gods in those stories were alien and unknowable, but gradually he came to understand Niamh as a woman who was a product of her culture, struggling to come to terms with her own mortality and emotions that had been repressed by her upbringing.

And as she listened intently to his own account of his childhood, and the dreams he had nurtured in his formative years, he accepted that she had fallen in love with him. The moment when he finally recognised her feelings for him was ironically banal, as she sat next to a beaten-up mono record player, listening to *Songs for Swingin' Lovers* over and over again as she struggled and failed to comprehend his love for the music of Frank Sinatra. She felt more at home with the bands Tom had championed, the groundbreaking guitar music of the Yardbirds, the Beatles and the rest, and she was unaccountably happy when Church would sit and listen to them with her.

It was in the late autumn that everything changed. The trees were a mass of red and gold and the leaves rushed back and forth along the empty sidewalks of the small town in which they had rented a white clapperboard house. As they walked, deep in conversation, through the late-afternoon woodsmoke and wind hinting of coming snow, Church became aware of a man waiting under an oak tree ahead. His hair was fashionably long and he wore frayed denim and a battered military surplus jacket. It was only as they neared that Church realised it was Lugh, his golden skin resembling a honeyed Californian tan.

Niamh was understandably happy to see him, yet underneath it Church sensed a deep unease. Lugh hugged Niamh and then greeted Church with surprising warmth, but his smile faded quickly.

"Sister, dark days are drawing in across the Far Lands. The Enemy is growing in power, and their forces are making incursions into our territory. I fear war is imminent."

"I am sorry to hear that, brother, but it is not unexpected."

"Some of our people who have an affinity with the Fragile Creatures have fled here to the Fixed Lands. Those who remain refuse to acknowledge the threat."

"They still can't see it?" Church said. "They'll be indulging themselves while their courts burn around them."

"As you are aware, Brother of Dragons, my people are slow to recognise the nature of reality beyond their own fields." He turned to Niamh. "My sister, I ask you to return to the Far Lands to attend to the needs of your court. Defences must be established. The ruling council you left in place has neither the wisdom nor the popular support to do what is necessary."

Niamh turned to watch the leaves falling from the tree to hide her conflicting emotions, though Church could see the sadness in her body language. "This is a beautiful place, brother, and there is an abiding peace, too, if one looks carefully. I understand my responsibilities to my court, but here—"

"I understand, sister," Lugh interjected without judgment. "I wish you well and hope to see you again in more glorious times." He made to go, but then turned to Church. "Take care of my sister, Brother of Dragons. There is fragility even in the hearts of the Golden Ones." And with that he walked away until he was lost in a flurry of golden leaves, and when they had passed, he was lost to the Earth itself.

"Why didn't you go with him?" Church asked.

Niamh's eyes brimmed with tears. He had never seen her cry before. "You know why."

"Don't do it for me, Niamh."

"That is what Fragile Creatures do, is it not? They make sacrifices for love."

"I—"

Niamh pressed a finger to his lips to silence him. "I know you do not love me. That is not the point. Love is not an arrangement that demands reciprocation. I know my heart, and I must be true to it, whatever the outcome."

He stood beneath the tree amidst the falling leaves and watched her walk away, a small figure, lonely and sad, not a god at all.

12

Later he found her in her room, listening to the Beach Boys. "Pack your bag," he said. "We're moving on."

"I thought you were happy here."

"This last year with you, just travelling and thinking, it's been as close to idyllic as I've ever experienced in my life. But it's time to get back to work."

"Where are we going?"

"Put some flowers in your hair. We're heading west."

13

San Francisco, October 1966

San Francisco was a city on the brink. A diaspora had swarmed across America to the city by the Bay, building their capital in just six blocks centred on Haight Street and Ashbury Street. In 1965, 15,000 people lived there. Within two years it had exploded to 100,000, with more arriving every day off the buses from the sticks, in their Swinging London miniskirts or Beatles haircuts, their denim and tie-die, and Victorian and Edwardian fashions raided from thrift stores. The freaks and the hippies had their own stores, their own newspapers, their own medical centres and legal advice, their own bands and their own currency, usually LSD and marijuana, but sometimes sex and food.

It was a place that hung between worlds. To the east was the poor, black Fillmore neighbourhood and to the west the wealthy Pacific Heights. To the north was the Panhandle, an idyllic green retreat that led to Golden Gate Park, and beyond that was the political activism of the University of San Francisco.

The minute Church stepped off the bus into the swarming crowd, most of them barely old enough to be out of high school, he could feel the influence of the Blue Fire. This wasn't like Krakow when they had visited John Dee. There the atmosphere had been pure, invigorating and electric. Here it was conflicted, ebbing and flowing, and at times there was almost a sourness in the air that was suffocating the energy.

"Can you feel it?" he said to Niamh. "This place is gearing up to be a battlefield."

"It is . . . exciting." Niamh looked around at the strange faces and extravagant costumes with a faint sense of wonder. "It reminds me of the Far Lands."

San Francisco was filled with big, old Victorian houses where rooms could be cheaply rented. They found a place on Page, just up the street from a condemned mansion where Big Brother and the Holding Company and some of the other San Franciscan bands hung out. As Church stashed his clothes, he realised this was a lull before the ground started shifting under his feet. Big things were coming, events that had been 2,300 years in the making. He hoped he was up to it.

Police were everywhere, watching the colourfully dressed men and women with contempt and barely repressed aggression. As he moved through the streets, Church realised he was being watched, too. One cop followed him for half a block before making a phone call.

As they made their way to the newspaper offices to check the small ads, they came across a disturbance. A freckle-faced woman in a gold-starred headband was raving about *monsters* that had killed her boyfriend in Golden Gate Park. Church wondered if she was having a bad trip, but she didn't have the telltale disoriented look about her.

"It's started," Church said.

In the park, a group called the Diggers were handing out free food to the hungry kids, and leaflets urging the local businesses to distribute their profits to the community. One of them directed Church to a thick copse where a huddle of people had gathered.

The victim was young, probably still shy of his eighteenth birthday. His face was covered with weeping sores that looked like the latter stages of some plague. Fearful of infections, Church pulled Niamh away, but not before he had noticed something else: where the skin was peeling it looked as if there were scales just beneath the surface, and on his forehead two protrusions had broken through like horns.

Church caught one of the Diggers, a pale-faced man in a leather hat named Jerry. "I don't know what's going on around here any more, man," he said, concerned. He doled out a bowl of rice to a painfully thin girl. "People seeing far-out things—"

"What kind of things?"

He shifted uncomfortably. "Monsters, they say." He shrugged. "It's just crazy talk, but . . . It's not just one or two. Not the real freaks. A lot of regular guys. That chick said she saw something weird kill off her boyfriend. It's like the *Outer Limits*, you know?" He returned to the food, but Church could see he wasn't alone in his uneasiness. The sour mood was visible in the faces of many who passed, jumping from one to another like a plague as the strange stories were passed on.

14

After two days of exchanging notes, Church and Niamh finally met up with Gabe and Marcy in the I-Thou Coffee Shop, a hippie hang-out filled with beatnik poets, polemicists, writers, musicians and other movers and shakers of the local scene. They were not alone. Tom was there, surly-eyed and suspicious, with a young woman with long, black hair and hypnotic grey eyes.

The first thing that struck Church was how much they had changed. Marcy's delicate features only emphasised the hardness of her new militancy, with her Malcolm and Martin T-shirt, tight denims and biker boots. Gabe had grown his hair long and wore a Day-Glo "Never Trust a Prankster" T-shirt. A camera hung around his neck. Tom, too, had embraced the hippie aesthetics. His prematurely greying hair was tied in a ponytail and he wore glasses with one red lens and one blue.

"Better late than never," he muttered.

Gabe hugged Church warmly and Marcy kissed him on the cheek before fetching coffees. Tom introduced the other woman as Grace. He fixed Church with a stare: "A Sister of Dragons."

Grace opened her eyes wide. "This is the one? The first?"

Church felt uncomfortable with Grace's uncontained awe, but Tom said pointedly, "She recognises the important role you are supposed to be playing in events."

"I'm here now," Church snapped guiltily.

"If it's not too late. Things are already in motion." Tom contained himself and changed the subject. "Grace is a member of a coven up on Divisadero. Two weeks ago her use of the Craft started achieving astonishing results."

Grace looked scared. "I had to leave the coven. I mean, there are more witches in San Francisco than musicians, but suddenly everyone started getting spooked out by me."

"She's the first," Tom said. "We'll find the others soon. This is the time, this is the place."

In the performance area at the side of the floor, a poet was chanting, "The doors of perception are opening," over and over again.

"But first," Tom said, "we have to make you whole."

15

In the twilight, the mist rolled up the streets from the bay. For once the Haight was unnaturally still. Inside, the atmosphere was tense. The ambience had been designed for introspection with candles, incense and soft, ethnic music in the background. Gabe and Marcy had agreed to retreat to Niamh's room; they appeared to have been arguing. Grace had pushed the furniture back in the lounge so she could mark out in salt her sacred space. Tom, Niamh and Church sat at three of the cardinal points and in the centre of the circle was the lamp.

"So, like, do we get a genie if we rub it?" Grace said.

"Something like that." Church had yearned for the missing Pendragon Spirit to be a part of him for so long, but now it was about to happen he was apprehensive. Once he was whole again he would be out of excuses. "You know that once it's inside me again I'll light up like a flare in the Enemy's perception."

"You can still turn away from this," Niamh said.

Tom had been watching Church all afternoon as if he expected that very thing. "Sooner or later you're going to have to take a stand. Might as well be sooner."

"That's easy for you to say."

Grace completed her ablutions and began the ritual. For ten minutes she chanted and whispered, and just when Church thought nothing was going to happen, the atmosphere in the room altered perceptibly: the shadows lengthened and the temperature dropped several degrees. Their breath clouded as webs of frost formed on the inside of the window.

Grace sat silently for a moment, and then blue sparks began to crackle around the lamp, building in intensity. They became tiny jagged lines of lightning until suddenly a column of Blue Fire roared up from the lamp's spout. In the flames, Church saw a familiar face.

"You made it, Church," Hal said. "I could have told you everything you needed to know to get to this place, but you did it yourself. And on the way you learned a lot about who you are that will help you in the trials ahead."

"Haven't you been bored sleeping in that lamp all this time?"

The flames shimmered as Hal laughed silently. "You're still seeing things from your perspective. To me, all time is happening at the same moment, remember? While I'm talking to you now, I'm also talking to you in Rome and in the space you entered through the circle at Boskawen-Un."

"That must be confusing."

"To a human. I'm not one of those any more, which is kind of a relief."

"If all times are happening now from your perspective, you know exactly what's going to happen to us in the future. So what's the point?"

"It's not like that. Reality isn't fixed. It's just a house that's been built for us to live in. Knock out a few walls here and there and the whole configuration changes, past, present and future. Don't go thinking of it as cause and effect—that's all pre-quantum stuff."

Church looked around the circle. Tom, Niamh and Grace were entranced by the column of fire, their expressions beatific.

"The Army of the Ten Billion Spiders have already changed what *did* happen considerably," Hal continued. "You can change it, too. People who will die in the current version of events don't have to. In the time when I made my sacrifice, nearly all the Tuatha Dé Danann had been eradicated. That doesn't have to happen. Remember, people who sacrifice themselves don't have to die." The comment was pointed, though Church didn't know at whom it was aimed. "The thing is, Church, it's all down to you. If you don't stumble, if you stay true to yourself, you have the power to change everything. And I mean *everything*."

"No pressure, then." Church steeled himself and asked the question he had dreaded voicing: "You're telling me I can save Ruth?"

"Ruth's not dead, but she's in a very bad place."

"I saw—"

"You can never be certain about what you see. Everything depends on perspective, and whatever information you have to hand. In the moment that you're talking about she's alive, Church, but she's hanging by a thread."

The euphoria that rushed through Church was so powerful he almost bounded from the circle and shouted aloud.

"Keep it together, Church. This is a crucial time. The closer you get to home the more powerful the Enemy becomes. They still recognise you and what you represent as a threat to them, but they won't take the path of least resistance any more. See you, Church—in time."

The Blue Fire lashed across the room at Church. There was no heat, just an overwhelming feeling of wellbeing. When the rush had passed and the flames disappeared beneath his skin, Church felt stronger and more focused than he had done in a long time.

"Wow." Grace sprawled on her back, beaming. "That was a trip."

16

14 January 1967 was a turning point for the counterculture. The Human Be-In attracted 30,000 people to the polo field in Golden Gate Park to hear the Grateful Dead, Jefferson Airplane and other bands on the brink of breaking through to the big time. Timothy Leary was in the audience along with the poet Allen Ginsberg and the Berkeley revolutionary Jerry Rubin. The Diggers handed out turkey sandwiches with LSD in the bread mix.

It was an unqualified success with waves of positivity rippling out across the country and the world. Church and the others experienced many strange things around the event, and soon after it was clear that something else had changed.

More people were found dead in the Haight with the same weeping sores and partial transformation that Church had witnessed on the youth in Golden Gate Park. The authorities refused to take any action despite mounting claims that there was some sort of plague loose in the quarter. Rumours began that it was sexually transmitted or in the batches of LSD and marijuana that flooded the streets. Some people turned to amphetamines and heroin, and violence, rape and overdoses increased accordingly. The Haight was awash with sightings of "monsters." More rumours spread through the enclosed community; no one could separate fact from fiction.

Yet of the spider-people there was no sign. They had slipped into the background, subtly manipulating from positions of power. But when the Haight was flooded with heroin the day after all the soft-drug dealers were arrested, or when the police brutally beat up people for jaywalking, Church knew who was behind it somewhere up the chain of power.

Gabe's new job as a freelance photographer for the local counterculture news-paper, the *San Francisco Oracle*, took him to the centre of what was happening in Haight-Ashbury. But Church found it also raised his own profile. Thanks to Gabe, people all over the quarter knew who Church was, and that he was doing "good works," though the nature of those works was always left vague.

And then, as he got used once again to the full force of the Pendragon Spirit flooding his system, he realised he was aware of nodes in the city where the earth energy was particularly strong: in the Panhandle, and on the uni-versity campus. And then he became aware of the energy in Grace. If he allowed his consciousness to settle into a peaceful state, he could almost pic-ture where she was in the city. Subtle connections began to come to light, and that was when he realised he could use the Spirit to his advantage.

17

The Whiskey-a-Go-Go was a smart, compact club on Sacramento Street, the mirror image of its more famous Los Angelino sister. On Valentine's Day the Doors were performing to push their debut album. The crowds were heavy and curious about the mounting reputation of the band.

"Their singer is a very interesting fellow," Tom mused as he surveyed the poster outside the venue.

"We're not here to see the band." Church watched the people streaming in; nothing had alerted him yet. "I want you to stay out here with Niamh to keep an eye on Gabe and Marcy. Any sign of trouble, get in the rental and drive away as fast as you can."

"You don't have to baby-sit us," Marcy said with irritation.

"Yes, we do." Church nodded to Grace. "Just keep your eyes open."

"What am I looking for?"

"You'll know it when you see it. We're like magnets. The Pendragon Spirit brings us together. He or she is inside."

"You're sure?" Grace said, still uncertain.

Church closed his eyes: he could feel the presence like a torch in the dark. He nodded.

Inside the club, they separated. People were several deep at the bar, but when the band came on ten minutes later there was a crush towards the stage. Soon after, Jim Morrison was singing "Break On Through."

As the night wore on, Church started to doubt. There were too many people, too much distracting light and sound. But as the band began to play the eerie opening chords of "The End," Church saw all the evidence he needed. On the other side of the club, his back to the stage searching the crowd, was Veitch. His hair was longer and wild, and his hard face had the first shaggy signs of a beard. He wore a denim jacket, and as he turned, examining every face, Church saw a peace sign emblazoned on the back.

Morrison was singing about a danger on the edge of town. Church saw Grace heading towards Veitch. He hadn't seen her yet, but she was hypnotised by the band and Church couldn't catch her eye.

"Hey, man—do I know you?" It was a Hell's Angel, a good six feet six inches tall. He towered over Church, in a cut-off denim jacket covered in badges, and a black T-shirt with the devil's face in red. His wild hair and beard made him look like a mountain man.

Church was about to wave him off when he felt a crackle of energy. The Hell's Angel was the one.

"Yeah, I think so," Church said. "I need your help. There's a girl over there in trouble—long black hair, see her?"

"The witchy chick?"

"That's the one. There's someone here who wants to hurt her. Can you get her outside to our friends? I'll cause a diversion."

The Hell's Angel grinned. "*A diversion*," he repeated in a mocking English accent. "Sure thing." He clapped Church on the back and ploughed through the crowd with no resistance.

Veitch was still searching faces, and close to fixing on Grace. As Morrison threw himself around the stage in an orgiastic daze, Church clambered onto the edge of the speaker stack where Veitch couldn't fail to see him.

The expression that came over Veitch's face as his eyes locked with Church's was utterly chilling. So great was his hatred he forgot everything else, as Church had anticipated. Without breaking his stare, Veitch pushed through the crowd, relentless but controlled. Behind him the Hell's Angel caught up with Grace.

Church jumped from the speakers before the bouncers caught him and headed to the side of the room, hoping to get back to the exit, but Veitch was already bearing down on him. Veitch broke into a run and they both crashed through the doors into the toilets. Even as they hit the floor, Veitch was raining vicious blows. Church blocked them as best he could and threw Veitch off. He knew he lacked Veitch's brutal instinct and street thuggery; a straight fight would be too one-sided.

"You're one of us," Church said, trying to blunt Veitch's attack. "Existence must have seen some good in you to make you a Brother of Dragons."

"You're talking to me as if I'm the bad guy." Veitch's furious attack split Church's lip and bloodied his nose. "I'm the one who was betrayed by his mates." He grabbed Church and smashed his head against the urinal. Church kicked out, ramming his boot into Veitch's gut and propelling him into a cubicle, winded. Church threw himself after Veitch, punching rapidly. This time it was Veitch's blood that splashed across the graffitied wall.

"This is about more than you and me," Church said.

"You're right there. Once we find what we're looking for here, it's game over for you, and all that bollocks you stand for."

Veitch thrust them both out of the cubicle and as Church fell, Veitch planted a boot in Church's face. Church saw stars, but just as Veitch was about to stamp on his face, he rolled out of the way and brought his head and shoulders up into Veitch's groin.

"You're a dirty fucking bastard," Veitch said, staggering backwards. "I like that. Shows I'm right. No pedestal for you, Jack fucking Churchill."

Before Veitch could attack again, the door swung open and the Hell's Angel stepped in. He took less than a second to size up the situation before hammering a rabbit punch into the base of Veitch's skull.

The Angel hauled Church out and dragged him through the crowd. "The name's Ice Cream Al," he said with a maniacal laugh. "Or just Ice."

One thing was on Church's mind: what was Veitch searching for in San Francisco, and could it really be as powerful as he had implied?

18

Back in their rooms, Niamh mopped the blood from Church's face and tended to his wounds. "We won this one," Church said. "Unequivocally."

Tom sat next to the record player listening to Bob Dylan. "What could be here in San Francisco that's of such importance to the Enemy?"

"A weapon. Can't be anything else," Ice said. He sat with Grace, struggling to come to terms with everything she had told him.

"This is the epicentre of the resurgence of the power opposed to the Void," Tom said. "They must be worried about that, especially the way it's spreading across the world. It undermines everything they've put in place."

"Then what they are searching for must be designed to stop that," Niamh said.

Marcy paced the room with irritation. "You've gotta stop sittin' around. We've gotta take action. Get out there."

They all knew she was right.

19

To find out everything that was happening across the city, Gabe drew on the resources at the *Oracle* and his friendship with the reporter Jack Stimson. The mysterious deaths and terrifying sightings that were destabilising the community continued apace. Fear was rising amidst all the hopeful protest.

Church, Grace and Ice located another Brother of Dragons, straight off the bus from Ohio. He called himself Doctor Jay, a tall, thin twenty year old with a green crushed velvet suit, a hat, cane and never-removed sunglasses.

It was another victory, and as spring moved into summer it felt as if the Void and the Army of the Ten Billion Spiders were losing ground. In New York, 10,000 attended the Human Be-In. In April, 400,000 marched from Central Park to the UN to protest against the growing horrors of the war in Vietnam. And in June the Beatles sang "All You Need Is Love" on TV.

Shortly after the broadcast, Stimson arrived at the apartment in a state of excitement. He was a flamboyant character who matched a double-breasted suit with intensely colourful flowered shirts, and always smoked using a long cigarette holder.

He gave his familiar welcome—"Greetings, Chicks and Chicklets"—before urging Gabe to run for his camera. "This is a once-in-a-lifetime scoop, ladies and gents. We all know the greedheads and the suits are trying to shut down the positive energy we're brewing up here, but now we've got proof. Crazy, crazy proof."

"What's up?" Church asked.

"Got a tip-off from my man with the fuzz. They're on their way to a pad on Waller. There's something inside that could blow open the whole conspiracy." He paused. "Sorry. The mescaline's kicking in." He shook his head, slapped his cheek and continued, "The cops have to get it out before your intrepid reporter brings the news to the people." He smiled enigmatically. "Here's the rub, brothers and sisters. They say what's in that pad is an alien— a sick and dying alien." He saw Marcy's disbelieving expression and held out his hands. "Hey, I'm just telling you what my contact said, and they've been wrong before. The truth must wait until your reporter blows away the cobwebs. But there's a story there, brothers and sisters. A big, big story."

Despite Stimson's protestations, everyone piled into his car and they were at the house on Waller in no time. A skeletal youth haunted the brightly lit hallway. "Don't go in there, man. It's the plague."

Stimson pushed by him and led the way up the stairs. On the third floor an apartment door hung open. Stimson paused when he saw what lay within, but Church and Niamh slipped by.

Sprawled on the floor was one of the Tuatha Dé Danann dressed in local clothes. He was dying, his face covered with weeping sores, his body partly transformed into something reptilian. As Niamh knelt beside him, his eyes flicked towards her.

"My queen. Help me," he said weakly.

Niamh took his hand. "What has happened to you?"

"When you abandoned our court, like many I came to the Fixed Lands, and to this place." His eyelids fluttered as he fought to hold on. "There are wonders in this world . . . many wonders . . ." he said deliriously. "The Enemy has bound a god. She spreads plague before her. Until now they have not harmed any Golden Ones, but they grow more desperate . . . They demanded information from me. I escaped, but not before I was infected by her touch."

Sirens sounded in the distance, rapidly drawing closer. Niamh squeezed the god's hand to force him to stay awake. "What do they seek?"

"They are searching . . . for the Extinction Shears."

Niamh's breath caught in her throat.

"They wish to sever the ties that bind the Blue Fire to Existence. They wish to slay all the Fabulous Beasts."

His hand slipped limply from hers as he expired and his body began to break apart. Beams of golden light shone from within, and gradually his corporeal form transformed to golden moths that swirled upwards, and through the ceiling. Soon there was no sign he had ever been.

Niamh bowed her head in grief at her fellow's death, but there was no time for mourning. They fled into the night just as the police pulled up and raced into the building.

"That was an alien?" Stimson said in confusion.

"A god. The gods walk amongst us. Aren't we lucky?" Doctor Jay said wryly.

Stimson gazed at his notebook blankly. "This is beyond crazy. Who's going to believe that?" He stalked off to his car.

"What are the Extinction Shears?" Church asked.

"A legacy," Niamh replied. "They existed long before my people came to the Far Lands. Some say they were created by the gods above the gods themselves. They have the power to cut through the very fabric of Existence."

"If they're so powerful, what are they doing here?"

"They went missing long ago. None know where they are." She clutched at Church's hand. "If the Enemy uses them to cut through the Blue Fire, it will sever us all from Existence. Everything will be under the control of the Void for all time."

20

Haight-Ashbury was like a medieval street fair. People swarmed across the streets in outrageously colourful clothes, with jugglers, mimes and musicians moving amongst them. Many were on some drug or other, acting strangely and disconnected from the behaviour of straight society. It was hardly surprising that Church had not been aware of the people from the Far Lands who had made their home there. In the Haight, their strangeness was the norm. Church once again encountered the eerie puppeteer whose marionettes moved without strings, but when Church approached him he quickly packed up his stall and disappeared into the crowds.

Church and Niamh questioned as many as they could about the whereabouts of the Extinction Shears, without any luck. Their investigation had to be conducted surreptitiously, for the spider-people and their agents were everywhere—brutal police officers, men in dark suits who could have been FBI or government agents, violent criminals who raped and robbed and beat up all who got in their way.

By October, the freewheeling mood in the Haight had changed irrevocably. Ice caught up with Church as he questioned one of the Tuatha Dé Danann near the entrance to Buena Vista Park. "Man, you don't want to go back there. There's some kind of mass protest. Everyone's been pissed since the drugs bust on the Dead house. It's going to get ugly."

"All right. I'm done here. We're getting nowhere."

"One other thing." Ice held up a jewel that sang a strange, lilting song whenever he pressed it.

Church recognised its otherworldly nature. "Where'd you get that?"

"Took it off a kid a couple of blocks back. Told me he lifted it from some stall in Hippie Hill. The Market of Wishful Spirit, he called it."

Church recalled the bizarre travelling market he had seen in the Court of the Soaring Spirit. "What are they doing here?"

"The kids said the market comes and goes, like magic. I thought he was tripping."

They bypassed the disturbance at the Haight-Ashbury intersection to get to Hippie Hill, the lower part of Golden Gate Park that swarmed with beggars and the homeless.

As they passed through the crowds, the quality of the light changed. Mist drifted in and suddenly the air was filled with the aromas of perfumes and spices. They broke through the mist to find a great many stalls populated by people who were unmistakably not of this world. Their odd and grotesque appearances were often masked by wide-brimmed hats and cloaks, medieval gowns or Elizabethan doublets. To a person, their faces had a waxy sheen that made them look like masks over their real faces.

A few hippies passed amongst the stalls in a trance, beckoned here and there by the owners, and offered delights or nightmares disguised as such.

Church moved through the stalls, asking one purveyor after another about the Extinction Shears. Finally he came to a skeletal man in a black robe made of tatters who rubbed his hands together obsequiously when Church questioned him.

"Ah, so sorry. Just sold," he said. "But I can offer you even greater wonders . . ." From the mass of items on his stall, he plucked a glass globe that appeared to have a world at its centre.

"Who bought the Shears?" Church snapped.

"A Fragile Creature."

"We'll never find him," Ice said.

"Perhaps you can." The trader's eyes glittered. He picked up a small hand mirror; in its centre, a faint light shimmered like a torch on the horizon. "Follow the light and it will lead you to your heart's desire. Yours for just a small price . . . a very small price."

Church glanced at Ice. The Hell's Angel snatched the mirror and they ran from the market as fast as they could, the cries of the trader rising up behind them.

21

"We've got to get to the poor bastard before the Enemy finds him. Or before he tries to use this bargain he's picked up and accidentally ends all Existence," Church said as they exited the park. "You get the others and meet me back at the house."

Ice headed towards the centre of the Haight while Church held the mirror before him. The light was no longer visible in the glass, but as he turned the mirror it slipped back into view. He moved towards it.

22

Night was falling as Ice reached the chaos that had erupted at the intersection of Haight and Ashbury. A cacophony of screams and shouts thundered in the air as the heaving crowd surged in panic. Police were all around and tear gas drifted on the breeze.

Grace and Doctor Jay came running up with a young man with short hair, horn-rimmed glasses and a University of Berkeley T-shirt, and a woman with long auburn hair and an abundance of beads and bangles.

"They're killing us out there," Grace said breathlessly.

"They're making their move tonight. They're going to catch us all in one go," Doctor Jay added.

Ice nodded to the new arrivals. "These the last two?"

"James and Deanna." Grace looked over her shoulder at the seething crowd.

Ice could already feel his affinity for the two. In their faces he saw confidence and hardly any fear despite their situation. "Okay, that's a full packet. Where are the others?"

"Gabe's taking photos. Marcy's lost it. She's on the front line, stoning the cops. Tom and Niamh are trying to drag her away," Grace said.

"Let's help them. We have to return to the house."

They pushed their way back into the crowd as a wave of movement and screams came from their right. Ice stood his ground as a terrified mob washed around him. Behind them staggered five men and women clutching their faces where weeping sores were rapidly blooming.

And behind them, floating two feet above the sidewalk, was a voluptuous woman, nearly naked apart from a few wisps of gossamer veil. Her black hair flowed out all around a terrible face with wide, staring eyes and enormous fangs that looked sharp enough to tear off a man's arm. Her fingers and toes ended in jagged claws.

A young woman ran by, so busy looking over her shoulder at the police that she didn't see what she was passing. With rattlesnake speed, the floating thing lashed out and caught the woman across the side of the face with her claws. Instantly, the woman faltered. Her shock turned to discomfort and then agony as the sores began to appear.

"What the hell is that?" Ice said.

"Rangda." Doctor Jay's sunglasses made him impassive. "The demon-queen of Bali. Spreads plague. Leads an army of evil witches."

"You read too many books," Ice growled. He herded them back into the crowd as Rangda darted forward.

"The police aren't going to let us out of here," Grace squealed. "That thing's going to pick us off one by one."

"We'll get out," Ice said. "Church is counting on us. We don't let him down, you hear?"

The crowd swallowed them up and the screams grew louder.

23

The light in the mirror blazed so brightly that Church could barely look into it. He was outside one of the Victorian mansions near the Grateful Dead's house that had been raided only four nights earlier. He could already tell something was wrong. The front door hung on twisted hinges and the hall light blazed out into the night.

He entered cautiously. A man lay dead on the stairs, his throat torn out. On the first-floor landing, a woman hung over the banister, both eyes missing. His heart pounding, Church followed the trail of blood to a door on the second floor. It swung open at Church's fingertips.

The first thing he saw was writing on the walls in blood: *Helter Skelter. Death to Pigs.*

The Libertarian was admiring his handiwork. He turned to Church blithely. "Just getting in a little practice for nineteen sixty-nine. Or repeating what I will do then, depending on your point of view. Charlie's spelling is atrocious."

A ponytailed man with sunglasses sat on the sofa as if watching TV, a hole punched through his chest to where his heart had once been. The missing organ sat on a side table next to a lava lamp.

"You've got the Shears," Church said flatly.

"There was never any doubt. We've been searching for them for a long, long time, Mr Churchill." He dipped into the inside pocket of his long, black coat and pulled out what at first looked like a blinding white light. As Church forced himself to peer into it, he saw something that resembled a giant crystal snowflake, and then a series of circling orbs, and finally a pair of gold shears with ornate handles.

The Libertarian smiled at Church's unease. "Oh, don't worry, I have no intention of using them now. One wrong snip and the whole thing could start to unravel. We will take our time, ensure everything is just right, safe for us, not so for you, and then . . ." He made a snipping motion with two fingers of his free hand. "Things fall apart. The centre cannot hold."

Knowing he had no choice, Church advanced. The Libertarian smiled mockingly just as Church saw movement in the corner of his eye. Hands like dry wood clutched at his wrist before an arm moved across his throat. In the mirror opposite he could see Etain's dead eyes staring back at him. The loamy smell of her filled his nostrils.

"Despite what you might think, we really do know what we are doing." The Libertarian strode to the door and paused. "Oh—remember when we met not so very long ago in that cold city? I told you then what would happen if you ever chose to re-enter the game."

"Don't hurt Gabe and Marcy." Church strained in Etain's grip. "They've got nothing to do with this."

"I can't go back on my word," the Libertarian said indignantly. "Well, perhaps just one of them. I shall attend to that piece of business before I take a very long flight to the East. Have to see how our boys are getting on scaring up a few Fabulous Beasts with their napalm."

Church could hear him humming merrily as he walked down the stairs. Etain closed the crook of her elbow tighter around Church's throat. In the mirror, her unblinking stare never left his face.

"Etain, I'm really sorry about what happened to you," Church said hoarsely. "I don't know if you can hear me, but I wanted to say that. There hasn't been a day gone by when I haven't regretted what Veitch did to you, or felt guilty for getting you into it."

Etain didn't register a flicker of emotion.

"But I can't go on beating myself up over that. There's too much at stake now and too many people relying on me. I hope wherever you are you understand that."

While he was talking, Church had been shifting his position. He drove backwards with all his weight and smashed Etain into the wall, then pulled forward and did it again. While she was off-balance, Church jackknifed at the waist. Etain flew over his shoulder and crashed into the TV set. Amidst the flash and the sparks there was the smell of burning dead flesh.

Church didn't wait to see the results. He was soon racing into the night to save his friends.

24

The panic at the intersection had subsided when the police allowed some of the crowd to flow up Ashbury. Unmarked vans were already being loaded with body bags containing the plague victims. The demon-queen was gone.

Church found Ice and Grace helping some of the people who had been hurt in the crush.

"Bummer of a way to end the Summer of Love," Grace said.

Gabe came up, dismayed. "The fascist pigs took my camera," he said.

"Where's Marcy?" Church looked around, then pushed his way through the crowd in time to see Marcy being dragged into the back of a black car with smoked windows. The Libertarian saw Church, nodded and climbed in after her before the car sped swiftly away.

25

Back at the apartment, Gabe was beyond consoling. Church left him to Niamh's ministrations while he consulted with Tom.

"You did your best," Tom said.

"It's not over," Church responded defiantly.

"If they have the Extinction Shears, it really is. Existence will be remade in the image of the Void for all time. No ebb and flow of hope against despair, no Blue Fire to hold back the dark. We will live in the best of all possible worlds, and the best of all worlds will be the worst imaginable." Tom sat on the edge of the bed, staring into the middle distance.

"The Libertarian wasn't planning to use them straight away. Now that the Enemy has them, they can take their time. And if the Shears are as powerful as everybody says, they can't afford to rush into using them blindly."

"So what are you saying—that you're going to parachute into Vietnam?"

"If I have to."

"I can help." Gabe was at the door, his cheeks flushed.

"I know how you must be feeling," Church began, "but the likelihood is that Marcy isn't alive."

"You don't know that. You never turned away when the odds were against you. You're not doing it now. You've taught me a lesson there—blame yourself. I'm not going to give up on Marcy until I know for sure she's dead."

"All right. What do you suggest?"

"I got an offer from *Life* magazine to do some work for them. They need photographers in the war zone. Tim Page, Errol Flynn's son, a few others— they're doing good work, but there aren't enough of them. Nobody wants to risk their neck."

"You can get accreditation for me?" Church said.

"As a writer, maybe. If you're ready to take the risk."

"Ten thousand Americans have already died there this year," Church said. "The chances of getting out alive aren't good."

Tom nodded. "Then it's a suicide mission. Can I have your Frank Sinatra records?"

26

Vietnam, 31 January 1968

A heat haze hung so heavily over the thick jungle vegetation that Vietnam appeared to be boiling in the afternoon sun. In the sweaty, oppressive atmosphere clothes became sodden in minutes and Church's brain thudded inside his skull with every beat of his heart.

As he looked out across the treetops from the open door of the chopper, Church accepted that while he thought he had come to understand despair on the long, weary road from the Iron Age, he hadn't really come close. Below him, soldiers were being slaughtered, blown apart, tortured, burned alive, turned into quadriplegics. Civilians were being murdered, their livelihoods destroyed. Troops turned against their own leaders. Countrymen killed each other by the thousand. And as the sickening death toll mounted day by day, and the waves of escalating violence washed out across the region, across the world, it was clear there was no point to it at all. Vietnam was a machine fuelled by human suffering and it would go on for ever if they let it.

Church knew from the hindsight of history that it wouldn't. Instead, the Enemy would get smart and simply shift the conflict to new venues around the globe, from Africa to the Middle East, a perpetual world tour of misery.

"Are you ready for this?" Gabe was checking his camera equipment in the next seat.

"As much as I'll ever be."

They'd only been in Vietnam a few weeks, but already Church could see the horrors they'd witnessed etched into Gabe's once-innocent face. His fears for Marcy had turned him into a different person. No longer the laid-back hippie with the JFK fixation, he made contacts, wheeling and dealing and bribing military men jaded by the rigours of war, doing anything he could to find leads to the Libertarian's whereabouts.

The intelligence had been sketchy, but there had been a few references to spiders in Vietcong transmissions coming out of what had been known as the Iron Triangle, a highly dangerous area of forty square miles bordered by the Saigon River to the west and the Thi Tinh River to the east.

And so Gabe had spent several hundred dollars buying them places on a small incursion into the heart of the area: just twenty-seven soldiers and a handful of men from the 1st Engineer Battalion to investigate some of the 1,000 miles of Vietcong tunnels that crisscrossed the area.

"The mirror's still working?" Gabe asked quietly.

Out of sight of the soldiers in the helicopter, Church showed Gabe the artefact he had retrieved from the Market of Wishful Spirit. A bright light glowed in the centre.

The choppers came down one by one in a clearing in a dense part of the jungle that had not been razed to the ground during Operation Cedar Falls the previous year. The troops piled out, keeping their heads low beneath the whirling blades. Church and Gabe were amongst the last on the ground.

"Dust-off in six hours!" the captain yelled before the helicopters took off into the haze.

The captain was college-educated and had a decent nature, but couldn't mask his belief that he was out of his depth. Like many officers, he hadn't had the chance to build up any experience before being thrown into the thick of combat. "Stay close. Don't wander off the track," he said to Church and Gabe. "This area is rife with booby traps. We're supposed to have cleared out the VC, but nobody believes that. There'll probably be snipers." He eyed his men, the majority of whom were not yet out of their teens and as green as he was. "We've been tasked to head south. There's been some kind of vague intel that Hanoi's planning an offensive. That's all crap. It's Tet. There's a ceasefire every year so the Vietnamese can observe their holiday."

Church kept a poker face: he couldn't reveal that the Tet Offensive in 1968 would be the turning point in the war. The all-out military assault by the North Vietnamese Communists finally showed the American public they weren't winning the war and brought despair to the US homeland.

"If they've been told to head south, we need to go north," Church said to Gabe.

"You think the Enemy knows we're here?"

"I don't think the Army of the Ten Billion Spiders cares where we are any more, but their surrogates in the military and the CIA aren't going to let anybody get too close to their operation."

The point man led the way into the bush and the rest of the troops fanned out behind, rifles at the ready.

"If I get out of this alive with Marcy I'm going to ask her to marry me," Gabe said.

Church looked away so Gabe wouldn't see his belief that it was a futile hope.

"Will you be the best man?" Gabe asked.

"Sure." So his answer didn't sound too flat, he added, "I'd be honoured."

It was hard going through the thick undergrowth. The heat was merciless and the tension from constantly searching the shadowy vegetation for enemy soldiers was intense.

After a long period of silent contemplation, Gabe said, "I still don't get why we're here."

"Tom has a theory. The earth energy has nodes where it's stronger— Avebury and Stonehenge in England, Krakow in Poland. The Fabulous Beasts are drawn to these sites."

"Why? Because they feed on the energy?"

"They feed on it . . . they are it, to a degree. It's difficult to explain. There's a powerful tradition of dragons in the Far East, linked to the lines of force that run through the Earth. Tom thinks there might be some kind of source here—a place where the Blue Fire is created, or comes into our world, or something."

"So it would be more powerful, or pure, and it would attract more of those things?"

Church shrugged. "It's a theory."

After a few miles they broke for a rest. The soldiers sat around smoking and talking. Church and Gabe passed the time with the captain and a couple of engineers, the so-called "Tunnel Rats." They had the worst job in Vietnam, making safe the booby-trapped, vermin-infested tunnel system of the Vietcong.

One minute the jungle was filled with only the sound of insects and birds, the next it was torn apart by machine-gun fire and explosives. Panic hit instantly. The soldiers were up and firing randomly into the trees while their friends were cut down around them. The captain yelled for order, but there was too much gunfire for him to be heard.

In the nozzle bursts amongst the trees, Church could see the Vietcong, like ghosts. They were everywhere. The captain saw them too and gave the order to retreat. Some heard, some didn't. In the disarray that followed, a grenade blast tore apart three men.

And then everyone was running, Church and Gabe amongst them, heads down, pounding wildly into the thick bush. Sizzling lead streamed all around. Men fell, though it was impossible to tell if the shots came from friend or foe.

Finally they reached a place where the gunfire sounded like distant rain. Gabe was there, the captain, an engineer and two soldiers. The captain was shaking. "We have to regroup," he said uncertainly.

Church checked the mirror. The light in it was blinding.

"Over here." One of the remaining soldiers, a grizzled veteran of twenty-two, was indicating something hidden in the undergrowth. Church pulled aside the fronds to reveal ancient stonework covered with weather-worn carvings. Half-buried at the foot was an image of a snake eating its own tail.

"Some kind of ruins." The captain pointed out other stonework scattered amongst the underbrush.

They found large pieces of rubble that appeared to be the remains of a complex of buildings: an arch, a column carved with ferocious faces with snakes for hair and the stumps of walls now overgrown with creepers.

"This place is spooky," said the veteran who had found the site.

Amongst the ruins, no birds sang and no insects buzzed. The air was flat and sound deadened. It wasn't an unpleasant atmosphere, but it was eerie enough to put everyone even more on edge.

"Got a tunnel," the engineer called from the skeletal remains of a large room. He pointed out a cover made of interwoven branches and creepers.

"Okay," the captain said, distracted. "Do it."

The engineer checked around the trap door for booby traps and then threw it open. A short drop of around four feet opened into a tunnel running east-west. The Tunnel Rat dropped in, flopped to his belly and wriggled along one of the branches, which was barely a foot and a half high.

They waited around the entrance as the shadows grew longer. In the silent atmosphere, time stretched interminably. After an hour and a half, the captain said, "He's not coming back."

The words hung heavy in the air until the veteran soldier said, "Captain, maybe we should head towards the dust-off point? Any other survivors might already be there."

The captain nodded wearily; in the growing twilight he looked twenty years older.

It was Gabe who first heard the movement in the undergrowth. He tugged on Church's arm. "There's someone out there."

The captain and the two soldiers had their rifles at the ready. "Don't shoot until you get identification. Might be our guys," the captain said.

Church peered into the gloom and saw what appeared to be a long shadow lengthening towards them.

"What the hell is that?" the captain said in a dead voice.

The shadow rolled over bushes, around trees, submerging the stones of the ruins. Church realised what it was before it washed over the lip of the wall closest to them and was already pushing Gabe towards the tunnel entrance.

"Spiders?" the captain said.

They came in their thousands from every part of the jungle, a wave of scurrying blackness that hit the captain with the force of a breaker. Church hung onto the lip of the hole for a split second, watching in horror as the spiders reduced the captain to nothing. Wherever their tiny, ripping mandibles touched, strips of blackness appeared across his body; looking into them was like staring into the depths of space. And then, in a whisper, he was gone.

The other two soldiers were firing and screaming. Church thrust Gabe into the hole and piled in on top of him, and then they were scrabbling for their lives along the suffocating tunnel. Soil rained down on Church as he dragged himself forward, filling his mouth and eyes. The roughly dug tunnel was close to collapse. It was like crawling through a sauna, and the claustrophobia pressed down hard.

Gabe was whimpering. "Are they coming? How close? How close?"

Church tried to reassure him, but it was pointless. They both knew that if the spiders were flooding into the hole behind them, they would not be able to crawl fast enough to escape.

They rolled into a small room shored up with planks. A table and radio equipment sat to one side and two further tunnels led off from it. In a desperate panic, Gabe threw himself into one randomly. Church followed, aware they were now in danger of getting lost in the extensive tunnel network.

They crawled for five more minutes, and then Gabe suddenly cried out insistently, his voice quickly growing muffled. Before Church could ask what was wrong, he was assailed by a wave of undulating, greasy fur. Rats by the score forced their way past him, sharp claws tearing the flesh of his hands, tails lashing his face as they wriggled into any space to get past him, pressing tight against his head and face, forcing their way through the small gap between his back and the tunnel roof.

When they had finally passed and his queasy, primal fear had subsided, Church wondered what had driven the rats away.

Another room lay just ahead, with several others leading off it. Gabe was shaking and Church put an arm around his shoulders to comfort him.

"Are they gone?" Gabe brushed imaginary spiders from his arms.

"The fact they're here shows we're exactly where we should be," Church said. "You sure you're up to going on? It could get worse."

"Worse?" Gabe laughed hollowly. "Yes. 'Course." The thought of Marcy drove Gabe on. Church wondered sadly how Gabe would cope when he discovered the inevitable.

In the next room they discovered the engineer's body. The random brutality of the slaughter suggested the trademark of the Libertarian. In the room beyond, there were more signs of the ruins that lay a few feet above their heads. Someone had been excavating. Intricately carved columns had been uncovered, twisted faces and curling snakes hinting at ancient belief systems. Between the columns was a flat stone wall.

"Now what?" Gabe said.

Church stared at the blank wall. Amidst all the detailed carvings, it appeared out of place. As his adrenalin buzz subsided, he became aware of another sensation, out of place in the dank, oppressive tunnels: the electricity that was an unmistakable sign of the Blue Fire. He narrowed his eyes and focused intently. Gradually thin tracings of blue fell into relief on the floor and walls that reminded him of the first time he recalled seeing the effect at Boskawen-Un. The lines of power became stronger, converging on the blank wall at a point in the centre where they formed a continually revolving circle. Church pressed his hand into the centre of the circle. He felt the fire crackle around his fingers, almost a greeting. Instantly there was a shaking in the earth and more streams of soil fell from the ceiling. With a judder the wall pulled itself apart to reveal another tunnel behind, big enough to walk along upright. Gabe gave Church an uncertain look and then they both entered. The wall closed behind them with a worrying note of finality.

27

The air smelled of burned iron, but it had the invigorating quality of the seaside or a mountaintop. The tunnel sloped gently downwards. Instead of the absolute dark Church and Gabe had anticipated, they were surprised to discover a soft blue radiance leaking up from somewhere ahead.

After a while they could hear echoing voices. The light grew brighter, then brighter still until the tunnel opened onto a vista that took their breath away.

A cavern large enough to contain St Paul's Cathedral stretched ahead of them, and through it ran a river of Blue Fire as wide as the Amazon. The flames rose and splashed and undulated like a liquid, the light so bright after the darkness it made their eyes burn. They felt like children on Christmas morning.

Within the depths of the blazing river, a dark shape moved. It broke the surface showering droplets of fire, its head soaring up twenty feet or more. The Fabulous Beast was majestic, its scales shimmering in the firelight, its wings folded across its serpentine back. Church and Gabe were overcome by wonder.

This wasn't the same Fabulous Beast that had communicated with Church beneath Boskawen-Un. It was more distant and alien, yet just as affecting.

"Look." Gabe pointed into the river around the Fabulous Beast. Smaller shapes swam, and as they sinuously rose and fell, Church could see they were tiny Fabulous Beasts, still only partly formed. He considered the abundance of young and said in hushed tones, "This must be the source. This is where they're birthed into our world."

The mesmerising awe gave way to a harder reality when Church became aware of voices echoing up to the rocky roof of the cavern. Leading away from the tunnel down which they had walked, a thin path ran along the edge of the Blue Fire. They crept along it until they came to a smaller adjoining cavern containing more of the mysterious ruins, though these buildings were much more complete. Church recognised hints of Mayan and Incan architecture in a stepped pyramid and long arcades, but there were also echoes of the jungle temple complex of Angkor Wat, and ancient Egyptian styling coupled with the megalithic culture of Western Europe.

The ruins swarmed with spiders, some tiny, some as big as horses. Gabe chewed the back of his hand until blood rose up.

Around the nearest building stood a small group of people. The Libertarian was in the middle of what appeared to be an argument with Veitch. A metal chest lay between his feet. Etain stood nearby, half her face burned black from where Church had thrown her into the TV set in the Haight. Tannis, Owein and Branwen waited by her like statues. Salazar stood further back, the spiders running all over him and through him, making it difficult to separate one from the other.

"The whole sick crew in one place," Church whispered.

"Where's Marcy?" Gabe said.

Church shook his head. There was no easy answer to that question.

"I can't decide whether I question your loyalty, your sanity or your intelligence," the Libertarian was saying superciliously to Veitch.

Veitch levelled a murderous stare at him. "Without me—us—you can't do anything with the Brothers and Sisters of Dragons. You're like some bloke who can't get it up after a night on the beer."

"I wouldn't presume to understand your analogy. Suffice it to say you have done a remarkable job eliminating many of the novices, including those who don't even yet know they serve Existence. Yet you have had no success whatsoever with the most immediate threat." The Libertarian opened the chest and took out the Extinction Shears. They appeared to radiate no light, yet a white glow mysteriously washed over those present. "You are, of course, aware that your usefulness is coming to an end? Your unique relationship with the Brothers and Sisters of Dragons has allowed you to strike at them, but as we move closer to the Source and the strength of Anti-Life increases, that sport will be open to us all. And what then for you? Perhaps I could use a valet?"

"Yeah, maybe I should just gut you and be done with it." Veitch drew his sword. The black fire crackled in stark contrast to the white glow emanating from the Extinction Shears. An unsettled expression flickered across the Libertarian's face.

"Brawling is so vulgar," the Libertarian said. "Can we get down to the matter at hand?"

Veitch looked at the Shears. "You're sure you know what you're doing with those?"

"Salazar has made all the calculations. We are nearly ready. A small demonstration will give us the final information we need."

Church quickly weighed his options, and while Gabe's attention was fixed desperately on the Libertarian and Salazar, he edged back along the path until he reached the riverside near the Fabulous Beast. "I need help," he hissed, hoping that it was possible to communicate with the creature while fearing he could end up flash-fried or eaten alive.

There was no response so he called again. As he leaned forward, his hand slipped into the river of fire. He felt a surge of energy, and then a disturbing dislocation. It was as if he was actually in the Blue Fire while simultaneously still able to feel his body crouching by the river. His perception moved through the river like a fish swimming, and he realised obliquely that he was guiding it by thought. It reached the Fabulous Beast, and then, with a shiver, passed inside.

Church's shock was muted by the sudden rush of sensation; he could feel the Beast's great power, the energy flowing around it and through it; and he could see a blue world through its eyes, with lines of azure fire running through the rock, through his own body on the bank, through Gabe, all joined. The Fabulous Beast's mind lay alongside his own, unknowable yet completely accommodating his own desires. With surprising ease, Church turned the Fabulous Beast around and directed it towards the Libertarian.

28

Gabe glanced back. Seeing Church with one hand in the Blue Fire, he returned his attention to the congregation that had moved from the adjoining cavern to the shore of the blue lake. Lying on his belly, he wriggled as close as he could without being seen.

The Libertarian held the Extinction Shears gingerly. A figure emerged from the ruins behind him, and Gabe's heart leaped when he saw it was Marcy, though her movements were leaden and unnatural. A creeping horror paralysed him when he realised that a black spider was embedded in her left cheek.

"Why are you putting her through this?" Veitch said.

"Perhaps you would like to volunteer." The Libertarian cast a supercilious glance at Veitch. "It will be interesting to see what happens to her once the lines that tie her to Existence have been severed."

The Libertarian opened the Shears and a sound like a tolling bell rang across the cavern. Gabe felt a blast of Arctic wind. Shaking, he climbed to his feet. "Don't hurt her." He felt ashamed at how weak his voice sounded.

The Libertarian registered a moment of shock, then began to search the cavern for any sign of Church.

Gabe blinked away his tears. "Her name's Marcy. She's always tried to help people—"

"You're talking to me as if I really care about your species," the Libertarian said.

"Please," Gabe said. "I love her, and . . . and . . . she doesn't deserve this."

With a shrug, the Libertarian beckoned for Marcy to stand beside him.

The Fabulous Beast rose out of the Blue Fire with a beat of its mighty wings. Its shadow fell across the Libertarian, Veitch and the others, and the Beast opened its mouth. Fire surged out, exploding in liquid fury on the ruins and engulfing many of the spiders. Gabe thought he could hear a high-pitched screaming, like wind through winter trees. The Fabulous Beast soared into the heights of the cavern and then swooped down sinuously, releasing another blast of fire. Gabe couldn't believe that both attacks had almost magically left Marcy uninjured.

The Libertarian turned from Marcy and angled the Shears towards the Blue Fire. Gabe had the strange impression that instead of shears he was seeing an enormous crystalline weapon. The Libertarian snipped the blades together and the tolling bell sound rolled out again.

One of the young Fabulous Beasts leaped out of the river in convulsions. Lines of blue force lashed around it, unravelling. The Beast opened its mouth to emit an unnervingly human cry of suffering until the final line had unwound and it was gone.

Overhead, the larger Beast twisted and turned with a roar of despair. By the riverside, Church convulsed, looked around in a daze and then ran for Gabe.

"Delicious," the Libertarian said.

"You don't know what you're doing," Veitch yelled at him. "You were only prepared to deal with the girl. You're going to do us all in."

The Libertarian pulled Marcy to him and shouted to Church, who had appeared beside Gabe. "You have control over your forces, Mr Churchill, but

I have the Extinction Shears. So here is an interesting dilemma for you—the snake or the girl?" He opened the blades and held them high. "One is released without harm, the other loses its puppet strings." He smiled at the devastating dilemma.

Gabe silently pleaded with Church, but he already saw the decision had been made. "No," he said hoarsely. "You have to help us."

"You won't understand this now, Gabe," Church said gently, "but we're insignificant. This is about something greater than us." Gabe could see the heartbreak in Church's eyes, but knew that it wasn't enough to stop Church from doing what he had to do.

"Ah, fuck it." Veitch's voice floated up to them as he darted forward and wrenched Marcy from the Libertarian's grasp. Etain and Tannis moved to block the Libertarian's lunge as Veitch dragged Marcy towards another tunnel.

The Libertarian realised immediately that the balance of power had changed and brought the Shears together with a sound that made Gabe's ears ring. In the blink of an eye, the river of Blue Fire was severed. At the source it appeared to stop at an invisible barrier, and what remained in the cavern rose up in a funnel of flames and entered the Fabulous Beast, which thrashed wildly. Gaping wounds scythed across its scales.

One final blast of purging flame washed through the cavern, taking with it all hint of darkness.

29

Church and Gabe scrambled along the tunnels as fast as they could, unsure whether Marcy or the others had been destroyed in the inferno. But as they clambered out of the hole that gave access to the tunnel network, they found Marcy staggering around amongst the trees, a ragged scar marking her cheek where the spider had been. Gabe lurched towards her across the rolling ground.

"He took it out," she said, dazed. "I don't know how, but he did."

The sound of shelling and gunfire surrounded them. Plumes of smoke rose up through the vegetation and jets blazed across the sky. The Tet Offensive was in full swing.

Church stopped uncertainly a few feet from Gabe and Marcy.

"You were going to do what you had to," Gabe said. "I don't hold it against you."

They were all thrown off their feet as trees, vegetation, soil and rock erupted upwards in a deafening explosion. Rising up through the rubble came the Fabulous Beast with slow, heavy beats of its wings. Two Phantom jets roared by to attack the Vietcong positions and had to take evasive action to avoid the creature. As the Beast flew towards the west, Church's ears rang with a long, low, plaintive cry that broke his heart.

"Is this a win?" Gabe said.

Church shook his head. "The source of the Blue Fire has been blocked. We're cut off from it, and whatever energy is left here is going to dwindle. No more Fabulous Beasts will be born into this world."

Church was devastated by the thought of what had been lost. Magic was gone. The lifeblood of the world had been stanched. The Fabulous Beasts that brought such majesty and wonder to Existence were now threatened with extinction. He fought back the wave of despair that rose up in him, determined never to give in to it again. Church, Gabe and Marcy watched the Beast until it disappeared.

There was a disturbance in the trees. Church expected to see Veitch, but instead it was the trader in the tattered black robe from the Market of Wishful Spirit. He held the Extinction Shears, somehow recovered from the conflagration in the cavern. One pale hand was extended towards Church, a simple gesture that was somehow innately threatening. Church handed him the mirror.

He bowed obsequiously. "There are always many wonders at the Market of Wishful Spirit. These items may not be available for a while, but buyers will find something for their heart's desire. Drop by, drop by." He edged backwards into the trees and was soon lost to the shadows.

30

The flickering black and white image showed heaps of bodies in a Vietnamese village piled high like firewood. A US soldier was about to shoot a two year old desperately pulling herself out of the mound.

"March sixteen. My Lai. That's Lieutenant William L. Calley Junior with the rifle. He led First Platoon. Somewhere between two hundred and five hundred villagers massacred. We're not sure of the exact figures. Scores of women and children gang-raped by US forces." The low, drawling voice was impassive.

The room was dark and filled with tobacco smoke. Men in dark suits or military uniform sat or stood, watching the images of atrocities projected onto the screen.

"In his report, Calley said the Vietcong had captured one of his men shortly before," another voice said. "Calley and his men could hear the guy screaming all night, from seven clicks away. Calley thought the VC had amplified the screams. They hadn't. They'd skinned the guy, apart from his face, soaked him in salt water, torn his penis off."

"Yes, atrocities on both sides," the first voice agreed. "A moral vacuum."

The image changed to a smart-suited black man lying dying, a bloodstain spreading across his shirt. Several other black men in suits surrounded him, their faces torn by grief and shock.

"April 4. Martin Luther King Junior shot and killed in Memphis. The nominal assassin is James Earl Ray. With Malcolm X also dead, both voices of the black civil rights movement have been silenced." The narrator coughed, then took another drag on his cigarette. "The following week there were black uprisings in a hundred and twenty-five cities across the nation."

Another image. Robert F. Kennedy, brother of the assassinated US president, lying in a hotel kitchen, more blood spreading across a shirt, more expressions of grief and shock.

"June 5. Bobby Kennedy shot moments after winning the California primary. His presidential run was ended almost before it began. The nominal assassin was Sirhan Sirhan."

"Another lone assassin," someone else mused. "JFK. Malcolm X. Martin Luther King. Bobby Kennedy. That joke's wearing a bit thin."

The projector moved to a picture of a chaotic crowd scene showing police and demonstrators clashing brutally.

"August twenty-five to twenty-nine. The Democratic Convention in Chicago. Ten thousand anti-war demonstrators fight running battles with eleven thousand Chicago police, six thousand National Guard, seven thousand five hundred army troops and one thousand agents of the FBI, CIA and other services. Public support for the war plummets, as does trust in those opposing the war and those prosecuting the war. The hippies are demoralised. The legalize-marijuana campaign and the pro-LSD supporters are broken. There's been a seismic shift amongst the youth from soft drugs to heroin and amphetamines."

"And that brings us to the election tomorrow. When Nixon and Agnew win, will we see any changes?"

"In tone. There'll be a move away from the political arena for a while. The music industry looks vulnerable. Rock stars and the like, opinion formers. John Lennon has been trying to invigorate the marijuana campaign. Morrison is always trouble. The Rolling Stones. That black guitarist."

"And don't forget we're going to have Charlie out in the desert with his Family." The lights came on and the Libertarian strode past the man who had been giving the commentary. "He really does have a remarkable capacity for brutality, yet so charismatic! You have to admire him."

He marched around the room, looking like a rock star in his black coat and sunglasses. "Things did not go as planned during our excursion in Vietnam, that's true, but in retrospect I think we can mark it up in the victory column. The forces of Existence have been turned back on every front. There will be no global insurrection. Our influence moves across the world, quite rapidly in some quarters. There is still a minor problem in the United Kingdom—some of the nodes of Existence's network are still quite potent, but it's only a matter of time."

"Good one. Nice and confident." Veitch put his feet on the mahogany table. "'Course you've still got Jack Churchill and his people out there, and while Stonehenge and Avebury and all the other places are still pumping out the Blue Fire, he's a threat. Or did you forget that bit?"

A flicker of annoyance crossed the Libertarian's face, but he hid it behind a contemptuous smile. "It's very brave of you to bring up your singular failure to contain the threat of the Brothers and Sisters of Dragons, Mr Veitch. After all, that is your sole purpose in life. There are some who might say it was rather foolish to allow you to maintain any position of responsibility after your unfortunate display in Vietnam."

Veitch knew the Libertarian would never be able to act against him because Veitch answered to a higher power that the Libertarian would never risk offending.

"However, I don't quite see it that way," the Libertarian continued. "Frankly, where else could you go? You've systematically been burning bridges your whole, sad life. I think it may be a symptom of a self-destructive nature, sadly. The result is that you cut rather a pathetic figure. Friendless, without any direction or purpose apart from the one we give you, unfortunately not particularly blessed in the intelligence department . . . I really do pity you." He turned to the assembly. "I consider Mr Veitch our mascot. Where would we be without him?"

The men laughed.

Veitch's cheeks reddened. He wished he was with Etain, lying next to her, stroking her hair. He wished the Libertarian wasn't right.

31

Woodstock Music and Art Fair, Bethel, New York, August 1969

Church made his way past the naked men and women dancing in the August sunshine and scanned the half-million-strong crowd. He didn't really need to see the familiar faces—he could feel their pull in his head, just as Robin Goodfellow had told him.

On stage Country Joe was performing his "Fixin' to Die Rag," and the Woodstock Aquarian Music and Art Fair eased its way slowly into history as the last gasp of the Love Generation.

Church found the Seelie Court high up on the slope of the natural amphitheatre, watching the proceedings on what was, at the time, the largest performing stage in the world. Men and women in various stages of blissed-out euphoria wandered around the fringes of the court, oblivious to the collection of odd figures.

"Brother of Dragons." The queen greeted Church with a warm smile.

Church gave a bow. "Your majesty. It's good to see you again."

"And you. I feel your presence in my head. This is an unusual development."

"Something Robin Goodfellow arranged from the time we met at the music hall."

"Ah, the Puck. He is a merry fellow. But you would do well not to keep him at your back, Brother of Dragons."

The king finished watching Country Joe's set and turned his attention to Church. "The Fragile Creatures have excelled themselves this time. This is a spectacle beyond all others."

Church had to agree. The performers included some of the most celebrated bands of all time—The Who, The Grateful Dead, Jimi Hendrix, Crosby, Stills & Nash and Sly and the Family Stone. The organisers had only expected 50,000 people a day. Ten times that number had blocked all roads leading to the isolated farm where the festival was being held, a population equivalent to the third biggest city in the state.

"Would you like to spend some time with the Seelie Court?" the queen asked.

"Thank you—that'd be great. And I would like to ask for your help in a very important matter."

"A boon?"

"You have always been friends of my people. The years to come are going to be very hard for them. They're going to need all the help they can get, as will I."

The queen patted the grass beside her. "Sit, then, Brother of Dragons, and tell us your heart's desire."

32

On the stage, Santana were playing, their samba rhythms a jaunty contrast to the lowering clouds. It was the following day, and Church was apprehensive despite a good night's sleep. It felt as if they were on the brink of a disaster. In the Far Lands, the courts of the Tuatha Dé Danann were refusing to unite despite the fact that the forces of the Army of the Ten Billion Spiders were increasing by the day. And here in what he still humorously called the "real world," the Enemy appeared to have reshaped much of the globe into the Void's image of Anti-Life, where power and money and war and brutality ruled, and there was no room for hope, love or wonder. He saw only one opportunity to turn back the tide and that depended upon the vagaries of the Seelie Court.

Gabe came up to him as he watched the band. "You ready?"

"Are you?"

He grinned. "Never been surer. Marcy and me, we're poles apart in the way we see the world, but without her I haven't got a point." Gabe glanced up the slope to where the preparations were being made for the wedding.

"You're never going to forget the bands you had for the reception," Church said.

"It just felt right. The vibe here . . . it's what we believe in. Things are falling apart all over, but we'll remember this day, and what it meant, and if things do get dark we'll have something to keep us going."

Church considered this for a moment. "I'm worried about you, Gabe. You're starting to talk some sense."

"Blame Marcy for that." He laughed quietly. "Thanks for being best man."

"It was me or Tom, and frankly if he's the best you can do, there's not much hope."

"Wavy Gravy and the Hog Farm are doing the food. I'd better check everything's on schedule."

He headed off just as Niamh wound her way through the crowds. She looked perfectly at home, barefoot in a hippie dress, her ethereal beauty drawing stares from everyone she passed. She pulled his arm through hers.

"Tom's helping some kids who took some bad acid," she said.

"He still doesn't want to go back to your court?"

"He says his heart is here in the Fixed Lands at this time. He says he will do what he can here to mount a resistance to the Enemy's plans."

"That sounds as if he's admitting defeat."

"No. He says he has faith in you."

"Good old Tom. Never one to pile on the pressure." Church felt sad that they would be parting ways. For all his curmudgeonly ways, Tom had been a good friend.

Niamh looked towards the stage and her grip on him grew tighter. "It will not be long now before you are reunited with your love."

"Just over thirty-five years here. A blink of the eye in the Far Lands." Church noticed the subtle cast of Niamh's face and silently cursed himself for his insensitivity. "I'm sorry," he added.

"Why?"

"Because I can't return what you feel for me."

"If anyone is to blame it is me. You have no choice. I choose to love you regardless." She forced a smile. "Besides, it will all be meaningless in a short while."

"What do you mean by that?"

Gabe was hailing him from further up the slope. The wedding was about to begin. Niamh urged Church gently towards the ceremony, and soon he forgot he had even asked the question.

33

It was Sunday evening and hundreds of campfires blazed across the festival site. For a moment, Church thought he was back in the Iron Age at some vast gathering of the tribes. There was the same feeling of hope in the air, that no matter how dark the night, a new dawn was never far away.

The wedding had gone well and Gabe and Marcy had taken their tent to another part of the site for some honeymoon privacy. Tom and Niamh had gone off, deep in conversation. Their mood was restrained, but they refused to tell Church what was on their minds. More secrets; he was sick of it all, the undercurrents and the manipulations. He longed for simpler times, for some fabled golden age when there was no responsibility.

Someone announced over the speaker that it was midnight and Blood, Sweat and Tears were about to come on stage.

"How very fitting."

Church looked around to see the Libertarian sitting next to him. He held out a paper bag. "Would you like some brown acid? I've been giving it away in the crowd."

Church tried to jump to his feet, but he was thrust roughly back to the ground. It was Veitch. Etain, Tannis, Owein and Branwen stood nearby.

"No need for any anxiety. Chill out. That's what they say here, isn't it?" The campfires were reflected in the Libertarian's sunglasses so that it looked as if his eyes were burning. "I just want to talk. No fighting. No blood, sweat or tears. Just a quiet chat in the hope that we can reach a mutual agreement."

Church bristled. "You think we're going to find some common ground?"

"I do. Really, it's the only sensible course. We both have needs . . . obligations . . . If we can both achieve our ends without any further death, surely that is the way forward?"

"Why the change of tune? Afraid you're going to lose?"

"Oh, no. There's no chance of that at all, now. Which is why the time is right to discuss futility and wasted effort, and hope and despair."

Church eyed Veitch's cold, hateful stare and Etain's dead eyes. He couldn't fight, he couldn't run. "Go on."

The Libertarian stretched out on the grass and put his hands behind his head, watching the spray of stars. "A few short decades away from here we have the love of your life. She hovers on the brink of death. One tiny push will send her over the brink into oblivion. We have your two close friends, as well. It is the time of the Source and our powers are at their height. There is no protection for Brothers and Sisters of Dragons. You're all rabbits waiting for the gun."

"Is that supposed to be a threat? It could easily be a lie."

"It could be, but it is not. I think you already know I'm speaking the truth."

Church recalled what Hal had told him when he reclaimed the Pendragon Spirit from the lamp: *Ruth is in a bad place.* "What are you saying?"

"I'm offering you a simple trade. A pact." He glanced around at the crowds and smiled. "A *Pax Americana*, if you will."

"Go on."

"You surrender yourself to us and we promise not to kill your love or the other two. We won't free her from where she's being held, but she won't die."

Church glanced at Veitch; his face gave nothing away. "So I get executed, and Ruth, Shavi and Laura live."

"Nothing so vulgar. There is no need for execution if we can simply remove the king from the board."

"What, then?"

"A sleep that will be like death. I knew you would not willingly give yourself up to die, knowing how strongly you hold your obligations to Existence. I fear you would even sacrifice your love for that. The big picture, and all. But a sleep like death? That would allow you a glimmer of hope that you might return to the field, and I know how much you value that slippery little fantasy. 'While there's life there's hope,' and other fairy tales."

"You think I'm going to trust you? That's the fairy tale."

"It has nothing to do with trust. With you locked away, the world will carry on the way it's meant to be. We would have no need to kill Ruth—or you, for that matter. The same ends are achieved, and it saves us wasting unnecessary effort."

"If you agree to this, you have my word Ruth won't be hurt," Veitch said.

"I trust you even less than him," Church replied.

"Just to sweeten the pill a little more," the Libertarian continued, "I also guarantee that your friends Gabe and Marcy will live. I watched the wedding. Touching."

Church glared at him.

"What? You thought the vow I made to you in Chicago was forgotten just because you staged some dramatic rescue? Their lives will always be hanging by a thread until I decide to cut it."

Church thought of Gabe and Marcy dancing together at the ceremony, how happy they were, how hopeful.

"One long rest for you. Five lives saved. That seems a very straightforward equation."

"I don't have a choice, do I?" Church said.

"Of course you do. What are five more deaths on top of the hundreds you've already got on your conscience? You must be inured to it by now."

The music rolled out across the dark field. Everywhere people were holding hands, making love, dancing. "All right," Church said. He turned to Veitch. "You're the scum here, but I reckon you must have some values buried somewhere in that dead heart of yours. I'm counting on you to see this is done fairly."

Veitch said nothing.

"Oh, good." The Libertarian jumped to his feet. "An epic sacrifice in the great tradition. It almost brings a tear to the eye."

"I want to say goodbye to my friends."

"No goodbyes. You come with us now."

Church took one last, deep breath of the smoky, dreamy air. Overhead, a cloud was blotting out the stars.

34

The sun was coming up in the Far Lands, the sky a glorious pink and fiery red. But in the Forest of the Night, beneath the thick canopy of leaves it was still and dark and cool.

Far from the path that wound through the forest was a casket of gold and ivory with a heavy lid of frosted glass. On the side was the legend: *Here lies Jack Churchill, Brother of Dragons—his final battle fought.*

"A nice touch, do you not agree?" the Libertarian said.

Church examined what was supposed to be his final resting place. He struggled to swallow a rising feeling of dread.

Veitch watched from the nearby trees with his dead brothers and sisters.

"You finally get your revenge," Church said to him.

"It's not enough."

Church climbed into the casket, desperately focusing on the tiny flame of hope that still flickered in his heart. He was doing this for Ruth, Shavi and Laura. If they were alive, there was a chance they could find a way to oppose the Enemy's plans. His sacrifice would be worth it.

The Libertarian took out a small green bottle and a goblet. "Apologies," he said. "It hasn't been marked with the skull and crossbones in the traditional style." He poured the fizzing liquid into the goblet and offered it to Church.

It smelled of sour fruit. Church held it for a moment, still gripped with uncertainty. Finally, he swilled it down in one go. The liquid burned like acid, but then left a freezing cold as it passed.

The Libertarian nodded appreciatively. "Enjoy your long, untroubled sleep. If it's any consolation, your name and reputation will undoubtedly live on in mythology. There's little we can do about that, sadly."

Church lay down in the casket. His limbs were already growing leaden, his heart beating slower. Yet his thoughts remained active, and he could see, hear and feel everything. He wondered if he would eventually go insane as the days turned into months and years, with him conscious but unable to move a muscle.

The Libertarian loomed into his field of vision. He removed his sunglasses so those hellish eyes would be the last thing of the world Church would see.

"I imagine the most devastating part of this will be the unending loneliness," the Libertarian said. "I am not without compassion, so I have arranged for you to have company."

From the forest floor, Church could hear rustling. It rose up the foot of the casket. It felt like pebbles were being dropped on to his legs, rustling rapidly up to his chest. And then the spiders crossed his face and his eyes and he realised what the Libertarian intended.

The spiders flooded into the casket until it was brimming, every piece of his body alive with the movement of tiny legs and writhing bodies apart from one small circle of his face.

The Libertarian leaned in again, smiled and nodded farewell and then closed the casket lid.

CHAPTER TWELVE
TEN BILLION SPIDERS IN EDEN

1

Suffocating darkness enveloped Ruth. Something pressed against her then moved away, a rustling up her spine, a sour, cold breath against her neck. Filled with such a deep dread she could barely think straight, she had forgotten her flat, the giant who beckoned outside. She had forgotten being pulled into her wardrobe.

All she knew was the malign presence biding its time only a whisper away.

2

The procession moved through the Forest of the Night at dawn. As the birdsong began, and the butterflies fluttered amongst the trees, the king and queen led the Seelie Court at a measured pace. There were scores of them, stumbling and shambling, slithering and flying, but the mood was sombre and respectful. None spoke. Heads were bowed. It was the first time the Seelie Court had ever come together to share their grief and respect for a Fragile Creature.

With them were Niamh and Tom, still adrift, uncomprehending of what had come to pass. The procession stopped at the casket of gold and ivory, and the court formed a circle amongst the trees.

Niamh could contain her grief no longer. She began to cry silently.

"Do not hide your tears, sister, for this Brother of Dragons is worthy of the sorrow of all creatures under Existence, though he did not recognise that himself," the queen said gently.

"I do not understand how this could be," Niamh said. "If the Enemy attacked at the festival we would have known."

"He went willingly, as a sacrifice to save the lives of others." Tom spoke with the authority of someone who had glimpsed the truth.

"Know this, sister," the king said. "The Brother of Dragons is not dead.

Nor is he alive. He hovers on the brink between the dark and the light until a way is found to break the Enemy's spell."

Niamh smiled sadly. "Then there is hope. But it is not something I will see. Or True Thomas."

"Sister?" the king asked, puzzled.

"We have both seen the patterns that lie ahead. Our own lives will be sacrificed in the coming conflict. I had dared to believe that path might change, but now I see it cannot. I am resigned to my fate, as is True Thomas."

A murmur of appreciation ran through the assembly.

"The Seelie Court recognises your great sacrifice, sister, and yours, True Thomas. You will never be forgotten in the stories of the Golden Ones. May we all learn from them." The king offered Niamh a candle that burned with a blue flame. "This light shall never go out as long as the Brother of Dragons lives. Take it, sister, and keep it by you in remembrance for whatever time remains you."

As Niamh accepted the candle, Tom was deep in thought. "I wish to leave a gift in the casket," he said.

"As do I," Niamh added.

"Then do it," the king said. "The spiders will not attack unless you attempt to move them or the Brother of Dragons."

One of the attendants opened the frosted glass lid. Niamh recoiled from the seething mass of spiders, but steeled herself to lean in. Church's face remained uncovered and he looked as though he were sleeping.

Into the casket she slipped the pack of Tarot cards. "Take these with my love," she said softly. "If the gods would contact you, or you the gods, the ravens shall fly swiftly." She kissed him on his cold lips before turning away in grief.

Tom stepped up and pressed something between Church's lips that the others couldn't see. "A present from Doctor Leary," he whispered. "Use the sacrament wisely."

The attendant closed the lid, and then they stood in silence, listening to the birds and the breeze rustling through the trees, thinking of times past and yet to come.

3

"You shouldn't have tried to run, you idiot. I didn't mean to hurt you." Veitch thrust Shavi roughly onto the sofa in Ruth's flat. Blood splashed from the wound on Shavi's head, ran down his face and puddled in his good eye. Veitch tossed him a towel to stanch the wound.

"How can you say that? You killed Laura."

"She was always a bitch. She deserved it." Veitch laughed quietly to himself.

Shavi was disoriented. After Veitch had met them outside the care home, he had led them to Ruth's flat. It had felt as if they had turned a corner: three of the Brothers and Sisters of Dragons together, with a fourth, Ruth, soon to join them. The mysterious Church was the only one still missing.

But the moment they had stepped through Ruth's door, Veitch had turned on them with breathtaking brutality, clubbing the Bone Inspector unconscious and plunging a knife into Laura's chest when she had gone to the old man's aid. Veitch had dumped her in the bath and filled it with water. Stunned, Shavi had tried to get out to raise the alarm, and in the struggle that followed had received the gash to his head for his troubles.

"You're wasting your time here," Veitch said. "There's nothing you can do. We're bringing him back."

"Who are you bringing back?" Shavi said.

Veitch laughed, shook his head. "You always were a smart bastard, Shavi. And you were a good friend. You were." Veitch grew disturbed. He stalked across the room and kicked over the coffee table. "The five of us fought hard, and we won, in a way. We thought we were lining up against some big old devil, the enemy of those golden-skinned bastards—which we were. But it turned out he was just one aspect of something bigger . . . something immense."

"You are raving, Veitch. I do not understand you."

"You will, matey. You will. That bigger thing . . . well, that's here now. All around you. In every bit of this world. It rules it. But at the moment it's like . . ." he struggled for words ". . . the mist. We're going to give it a shape. We're going to bring the King of all the World back for some fun and games."

"Does it have a name?"

"Call him the Void, or Anti-Life. The golden-skins call him the Devourer of All Things."

"That does not sound good, Veitch."

Veitch laughed bitterly. "Tell you what, mate, the world he's built is a damn sight better than the one that was on the cards before. The one where I got fucked over by my friend, and then murdered for my troubles."

"What about Ruth? Have you killed her, too?"

There was a long pause before Veitch answered. "She's gone." He locked the front door and pocketed the key before going to the bathroom.

Shavi ran to the window, but it was locked and he couldn't see where Ruth kept the key. As he turned back to the room he noticed an overpowering odour, like burned iron. The air pressure dropped a degree, and then a doorway of shimmering Blue Fire appeared.

At first it was like a blue mirror reflecting his own blood-spattered features, but then it shifted and became a window on another place. In it, Shavi saw a man with a troubled but strong face; he too was stained with blood. Behind him was another man dressed in red robes.

"Shavi?" the bloodstained man said. "I'm Jack Churchill . . . Church."

Shavi glanced past the doorway. Veitch had still not emerged from the bathroom. "Church?" he said quietly. "You must come quickly. You are the only one who can help—"

"I'm coming." Church took a step forward.

"Laura is dead," Shavi continued. "Ruth, too. They are going to bring him back, Church. They are—"

"Ruth's dead?" The shadow of devastation crossed Church's face, and a second later the burning doorway winked out.

Before Shavi could consider what he had seen, the bathroom door crashed open. "Oi. Come here," Veitch called.

Shavi found Laura submerged in the bath, the knife still embedded in her chest. Grief and horror twisted in his heart to see her that way.

"Watch this," Veitch said. "Beats any party trick you've got."

After a moment, Laura's eyes flickered open. She looked at Veitch and Shavi through the water, and then became aware of her situation. She jack-knifed upwards, gasping for air, before coming to a sudden halt when she saw the knife protruding from her chest. "Shit—"

Veitch yanked out the knife.

Laura recoiled and crashed back against the taps. "Oww!"

"So you can still feel something," Veitch said. He grabbed her shirt and dragged her out of the bath and into the lounge where he flung her on the sofa.

"Please, don't hurt her," Shavi pleaded.

Laura jumped to her feet, eyes blazing. "Yes, you cunt. Come near me and I'll tear your bollocks off." Her gaze was drawn back to her chest. She searched the wound for the blood that had not materialised.

"You can't hurt a bleedin' plant," Veitch said.

"What do you mean?" Shavi was as stunned as Laura by her survival.

Veitch grabbed Laura's hand and pointed to the tattoo of interlocking leaves. "See this?"

"The mark of the god Cernunnos," Shavi said.

"No one told you the price she had to pay to get it?" Veitch laughed. "You're not human any more, love. To get all those weird nature powers you had to cross over—from animal to vegetable." He laughed again. "Or something like that. Lop off an arm, you grow another. Stabbing, drowning—no good. Weedkiller . . . not so sure." He laughed at his joke until tears came.

Laura slumped onto the sofa in shock. "I think I remember . . . something—"

"You did not have to reveal the information so cruelly," Shavi said. "You could simply have told us."

Veitch wiped his eyes. "Yeah, well, me and her didn't really get on."

"I wonder why," Laura said sourly.

"She was always having a go, always making me feel like I was nothin' . . ." Veitch shrugged. "Thought I'd get it out of my system here and now."

Veitch was clearly unbalanced, but Shavi couldn't tell whether Veitch planned to kill them both or if he had something else in mind. He decided the best course of action was to keep Veitch calm. "There is a great deal I do not understand," Shavi said. "Why have our memories been altered, but yours have not? If we were once friends, why do this?"

Veitch wandered to the window and looked out across the city, his mood suddenly pensive. "All right. The first thing you've got to get your head around is that nothing out there is what it appears. The world we grew up with is just a cover for what's going on behind the scenes. Which is basically a big bleedin' street fight with knives and bottles and chains and no rules. Humans, we think we're top of the pile here, but out there in the real place, no chance. We're scrapping with every other species just to stay in the game. The Brothers and Sisters of Dragons were designed to give us a chance. Five people, better together than they were on their own. And on our own we really were a bunch of losers." He turned back to Shavi and Laura and smiled sadly. "As you probably remember."

"Speak for yourself," Laura snapped, but it was clear she accepted the truth.

"So the five of us were brought together when everything went pear-shaped," Veitch continued. "Technology started failing. Weird supernatural stuff was breaking out all over the place. The golden-skinned bastards decided they were going to set up camp here. And to top if off, their old ene-mies the Nightwalkers invaded."

Laura glanced at Shavi, wondering how much of Veitch's commentary they could believe.

"In the old myths, they were called the Fomorii. Shape-shifting fuckers. The Tuatha Dé Danann defeated them thousands of years ago, thought they'd driven them off for good. But they came back with their leader, Balor. The God of Death."

"And this Balor is part of the bigger thing . . . the Void?" Shavi said.

"Look, a lot of this stuff goes right over my head. The way I see it, there's an ongoing battle between two sides—Life and Anti-Life, light and dark, whatever. It shifts back and forth all the time, but Anti-Life has the upper hand because it decided the way the world should be, and what all the rules were, right back at the start. But then we came along . . . us . . ." Veitch said, bemused, ". . . and we started to tip the balance the other way. We defeated the Fomorii, we destroyed Balor—it could have been a new Golden Age—"

"So what happened?" Laura said.

"Human nature." Veitch toyed with the knife he had pulled out of Laura. "Church and me were both in love with Ruth. She couldn't decide between the two of us. So right at the point when we'd won, Church thought he'd get rid of the competition. He killed me and Balor at the same time. Everything got fucked up by Balor's death . . . time and space and all that shit . . . and Church ended up getting thrown back in time two thousand years or so."

"You're not looking too bad for a dead man," Laura sneered.

"I got better."

"That was handy."

He looked from Laura to Shavi. "You'd be surprised how often it hap-pens. I was given a second chance—"

"By the Void," Shavi said.

"What the five of us did shook things up. It got us noticed, and not in a good way. The Void couldn't have us turning the world over to Life so it came back—or part of it did—and it made sure that the world stayed the way it was supposed to be. There was another group of Brothers and Sisters of Dragons after us, and the Void put paid to them."

"And it wiped our memories so we would not fight back," Shavi said.

"It didn't just make you forget—it changed everything. It can do that. Like I said, all the stuff outside the window is just scenery. And the Void moved it all around—"

"To create the illusion," Shavi finished. "No one is aware of the possibilities any more. There is no hope. No wonder. This is simply the way things are meant to be, so we have to make the best of it. And the Blue Fire drains away because the people who kept it alive do not believe in anything any longer. A dead world—"

"And you helped this happen?" Laura said in disbelief.

"Blame Church. He made sure I couldn't stay on the other side." Veitch wouldn't meet their eyes. He gripped the knife tightly.

"So now you're getting your revenge. Feel good?" Laura's eyes blazed.

"Yeah, it does." Veitch stared back unflinchingly.

"What about us?" Shavi said in an attempt to calm the rising tension. "You said we used to be friends. Are you going to kill us, too?"

Veitch gnawed on a knuckle. "Ruth and Church are out of the picture. The Brothers and Sisters of Dragons who came after you can't remember a thing about who they are. But you know how things can be changed, so you're a threat. I know what you're like . . . the two of you could still screw everything up. That's not going to be allowed." He weighed the knife in the palm of his hand. "I'm sorry, mate, I really am, but I haven't got a choice."

4

The constant churning of the spiders all around him was becoming a distant memory. Church was falling backwards down a long, dark tunnel, occasionally punctuated by starbursts of Blue Fire. It was a place of refuge, and he knew the deeper he could go the more he could escape the thinking and the feeling and the guilt and the sorrow.

Falling, falling, and then standing. He'd done it, broken the shackles, got away scot-free, and wherever his mind was telling him he was, it was better than where he had been before.

Everywhere was dark. He wandered around for an age, listening to distant voices come and go, louder and softer, like the sound of the blood in his head. He became aware of rock underfoot, a cavern of some kind. And then, across the dark, he glimpsed himself, although this was a younger Church, clean-shaven, shorter hair, face so surprisingly innocent and free of worry that he could barely remember being that way.

He convinced himself that he'd made his way to his own past, and he was taken by the urge to warn himself away from all the terrible things that lay ahead, that at the very least he could make sure he could take the one step that would change his current predicament.

His past self was staring at him, confused.

"Is this it? Is this the right time?" the modern Church said to his past-self. "You have to listen to me. This is a warning." He looked around, confused himself. "*Is* this the right place? Am I too late?"

"Tell me what you have to say," his past-self said.

"When you're in Otherworld and they call, heed it right away. They're going to bring him back. They're—"

"Calm down. You're babbling," his past-self yelled. "*Who* is going to bring *who* back?"

Church had the unnerving sensation of a presence behind him. An irrational fear gripped him. In panic, he yelled, "Too late!"

And then he was running from himself and into the dark.

5

Church didn't know how long it took for the blind panic to fade, but eventually he realised he could see a faint blue light ahead. He continued to run towards it until he saw it was a lantern with a blue flame flickering inside.

"The Wayfinder guides your path as ever, Brother of Dragons." The lantern was being held aloft by a giant at least eight feet tall, with a thick beard and glowering eyes beneath overhanging brows. He wore a shift made of sackcloth fastened with a leather belt.

"Who are you?" Church asked.

"I am the Caretaker. I keep a light burning in the darkest night. I serve all who come to me, whether their hearts are filled with hope or tainted by despair."

"Do you know me?"

"We all know you, Brother of Dragons." The Caretaker stepped to one side and motioned for Church to pass by. Beyond was an entrance to a cave.

Inside a cauldron bubbled over a small fire. Two figures stood around it. One was a man in old, tattered clothes, one hand clutching a long staff that had been subtly worked into a particular shape. His grey hair formed a wild halo around his head. Beside him was a woman who could have been his sister. She was painfully thin and wore a long black dress stained with tree-bark green and white dust. Her skin was almost grey and barely hung on her bones. Her hair was also grey and wild. But her face was smeared black with dirt or grease so that her grey eyes stared out of it with terrifying intensity.

Church realised he had seen her before, when he lay close to death on the journey to Boskawen-Un. She had come to him in what he had thought was a dream or hallucination, while Etain and the others talked nearby.

While the Caretaker felt benign, these two unsettled him. He felt they would turn on him at any moment if he said the wrong thing.

"Draw closer." The woman beckoned, cackling.

"Who are you?" Church asked. "Gods, like the Tuatha Dé Danann?"

"We are intermediaries," the Caretaker said. "A conduit to higher powers."

"What higher powers?" Church asked.

The wild-haired man looked as if he was about to fly into a rage, and Church fell silent.

"Look into the cauldron," the woman said.

Church peered into the bubbling, greasy liquid and saw an image of himself as a child asleep in bed. Niamh watched over him, fading as the young Church woke.

Church understood. While he had been sleeping in the casket of spiders, time in the real world had marched on into the seventies and he had been born. His head spun trying to encompass the possibility that he could exist in two different places at the same time: as a grown man in the casket in the Far Lands, and as a young boy growing up in the seventies on Earth.

The image changed as he watched. There was Tom, growing older as he wandered America, revelling in the hippie subculture in which he had felt so at home.

Another change: Church again, growing older. He met and fell in love with a woman, Marianne, who was killed, and he was overcome with a crippling grief. It only began to clear when he met Ruth on that misty early morning near Albert Bridge, when the great adventure began.

In a Britain isolated by the Blue Fire, Church saw Tom, and Niamh, and Lugh, and many other Tuatha Dé Danann. He saw Laura and Shavi and Veitch join them, and how they became the kind of friends that everyone dreamed of having, the kind you would trust with your life and your dreams.

He saw a dark power pressing in on life, the Fomorii, the monstrous race-enemy of the Tuatha Dé Dannan, and within it were echoes of the Army of the Ten Billion Spiders. He saw battles and setbacks, victories and heartbreak. He saw himself once more wielding the sword Caledfwlch, which he had been carrying when he walked out of the mists and into the Iron Age.

But what followed was dark and mournful, and revealed to him the true depth of the scars he carried on his conscience. He watched as Tom sacrificed his own life to save Church from a brutal attack by the Enemy. He saw Niamh sacrifice herself for him, turning into a glorious cloud of golden moths as she disabled a weapon that could have destroyed all five of them. The grief he felt was compounded by the knowledge that they loved him and trusted him more than he did himself, and he had never really seen that.

And he saw that they had both known for a long time that events would culminate in their deaths, yet they had continued regardless. They were the true heroes, going to their fate with a resolute silence.

The image shifted again to an apocalyptic final battle: Church, Shavi, Ruth, Laura and Veitch against the embodiment of that dark power, a thing that Church could now see was but a minor aspect of the Void. In a black tower, they came together. The Enemy was defeated, but as it passed it tore open the fabric of Existence behind which the spiders swarmed.

And then Church saw what he had dreaded seeing for so long: the moment when he plunged a sword through Veitch, just before he was sucked into a rift and hurled back through time. He was as evil as Veitch had said. No hero at all. He bowed his head, unable to watch any more.

The Caretaker rested a hand on Church's shoulder. "Things are not always as they appear."

Filled with guilt and self-loathing, Church ignored him. The Caretaker gently urged Church to look back into the cauldron. "Ryan Veitch was in the grip of other powers. Both the Tuatha Dé Dannan and the agents of the Devourer of All Things manipulated him. The Caraprix in his head attempted to steer him towards disaster."

"I knew?"

"You knew. You had no choice but to kill him."

"Then Veitch is a victim, too."

"You may say that. He does not see it so. Others might not see it so, either."

Church looked back into the cauldron. The days moved on after he had fallen back in time. He saw Ruth mourning him, thinking he was dead. He saw the Blue Fire becoming stronger due to the events Church and the others had set in motion when they defeated the Fomorii.

But in their victory were the seeds of the crisis to come, for they had awoken a power that slept beyond the edge of the universe, and then the Void came to put the world back the way it had been. The Tuatha Dé Danann were destroyed. The next five Brothers and Sisters of Dragons were stifled—only

Hal escaped into the medium of the Blue Fire where he would attempt to bring Church back into the fray. And then the world was remade. Magic, hope and wonder were swept aside. Money and power and violence and despair became the common currency, all the things that the Army of the Ten Billion Spiders had spent the last 2,000 years putting into place.

In America, the word of power "Croatoan" echoed across the landscape and the spiders rose up from their hiding place to spread across the world, corrupting and controlling.

"And that was when the Army of the Ten Billion Spiders began to move back through time, attempting to eradicate anything that might bring hope or change things in the modern time," Church said.

"They sowed the seeds of despair wherever they went, but the power of Existence is everywhere—in a song, in laughter, in a dream, in the caress of lovers. It cannot be destroyed, only contained."

"But it's so bleak," Church said. "Why does it have to be this way?"

"It does not." The woman cackled as she gave the cauldron a stir.

"Nothing is fixed in the Fixed Lands." The Caretaker smiled.

"You're saying things can be changed, even though they've happened?"

"What is *happened*?" The woman cackled again.

Church's mind experienced a sudden, radical shift and he was briefly back in Timothy Leary's study talking about the structure of reality, and the spiders moving behind the scenes to keep the world a certain way.

And then he was in the Court of the Final World with the strange globe of interconnecting blue lines in Dian Cecht's inner sanctum, watching as one slight movement changed the position of all the other intersections without altering the globe's integrity. And Dian Cecht was telling him that Church *was* the Blue Fire, one and the same: *You are the key. Once you discover how to turn the lock, anything is possible. You could save my people by altering what is to come.*

Church was back in the cave. "I could still change things?"

"He does not yet have the ability to alter much," the wild-haired man shouted.

"A tug here. A push there. Little changes make big changes." The woman laughed hysterically.

There was a nightmarish quality to the moment that made Church queasy. The Caretaker caught his arm to steady him. "What would you change?"

"I'd save Ruth and Tom and Niamh . . . and . . . and the Tuatha Dé Danann," Church said without a second thought. "I'd change it all."

"Is that a small thing?" The woman pondered. "I think it is!"

"Come, then," the Caretaker said. "Let us see the strength of your will."

As he led Church out of the cave, the wild-haired man ranted, "Changes ring changes ring changes. Who knows where this will turn? Bad or good! Good or bad!"

Dreamily detached, Church followed the Caretaker and his lantern. He passed another cave inside which stood three hooded women, their faces lost in shadow. He had an overwhelming feeling that if he did see their faces he would die.

"Beware the Daughters of the Night." The Caretaker urged Church onwards.

Church glanced into the cave one final time and saw that one of the women was unravelling a spindle, another measured out the thread, while the third brandished a pair of shears that reminded him oddly of the Extinction Shears.

A chill ran through him, but then the women fell from view and the Caretaker brought him to a third cave. When Church stared into its depths, his consciousness failed to grasp what he saw. His perception slid greasily across a slowly revolving crystal, then a series of flashing lights, a mandala, a Mandelbrot set. Finally it settled on a portion of some enormous machine filled with cogs and gears. The Caretaker held up his light so Church could see a lever nearby.

"That's all it takes?" Church said.

"It is more than most could manage. To push the lever is like pulling a sword from a stone." The Caretaker smiled.

Hesitantly, Church took the lever in his hands; it didn't feel how it looked. He put his shoulder to it and pushed. Nothing happened.

"I can't," he said.

"Do you always give up so easily? It takes much to turn the axis of Existence."

Church tried again, and again, gritting his teeth and straining. Eventually the lever shifted a fraction, and then a fraction more, and then it was moving easily. He had a sudden sense of everything shifting around him, as if he were in a theatre with a revolving stage and the scenery turning around him. The feeling was shockingly powerful, and for the briefest moment it felt as if he had been cut adrift from the universe and was spinning off into a dark chasm. He was floating, floating, and everything he saw was fake, a construct to keep him calm so he would not go insane.

The cogs and gears turned and shifted, and Church was back in the cavern, shaking with a terrible fear that he had done something that should never have been allowed. *All an illusion*, he told himself, knowing it wasn't. Exhausted, he staggered back. "Did that do it?"

"Soon we will know."

Church felt himself flagging. "This is all a dream, isn't it?"

"Yes, it is a dream."

Church rubbed his hands wearily over his eyes. "And soon I'll be back in the casket. With the spiders."

"Yes."

"Take me to Ruth," Church said. "One more time. Before all this fades."

The Caretaker nodded, and this time his smile was more enigmatic. He held the lantern aloft and led the way.

Church didn't know how he got out of the cavern, but soon they were walking along an odd corridor-like structure that was like scaffolding on one side and a wall of frosted glass on the other. After a while, the frost disappeared and Church was looking out on London. It was like being behind a two-way mirror that reached to the sky. On the other side, people shopped and chatted, cars drove by, planes flew overhead.

The Caretaker led the way through a door, up some stairs and into a flat. On the other side of the glass, Shavi sat next to Laura, staunching a wound on his head, and Veitch toyed with a knife. He looked menacing.

"What's going on?" Church asked, concerned.

"You cannot influence this," the Caretaker said. Reluctantly, Church moved on.

They went into the bedroom and came to a wardrobe, and then passed through the doors and into darkness.

"I can't see," Church said. "Raise your lantern."

The Caretaker's enigmatic smile grew wider.

6

Ruth held her breath and thought that she might die. In the dark the presence hovered behind her, all around her. Any second it would attack, she knew, and then it would tear her soul apart.

She bit her lip and tasted blood, forcing herself to hold on. And then she glimpsed a firefly moving far away. After the intensity of the gloom, she thought it might be a hallucination. But it stayed, and drew closer, and she realised it wasn't a firefly but a distant light. Hope flared in her heart.

Tentatively, she began to move towards it. She felt the malignant presence surrounding her fill with rage, rise up ready to strike, but she kept moving, focusing on the light ahead and not what lay at her back.

Her pace increased. She could scarcely believe it after so long amongst the horror and the dread; it felt as if she'd been there for a thousand years.

As she neared, she could see it was the light from a lantern, but it was blue. The malevolent presence made one final, futile effort to drag her back, but Ruth was moving too quickly now. All she could see was the light.

Briefly, she passed another presence, but this one filled her with the sense that everything would be all right. And then, without reaching the lantern, she was stumbling out of the wardrobe and into the light of her bedroom, blinking.

It took a moment to ground herself, but the dark presence in the wardrobe was already receding so fast she could barely recall it. There were voices coming from her lounge.

She peeked through the gap in the door and saw the back of a man with a knife who was clearly holding prisoner the two others who were there. A third, an elderly man, lay unconscious on the floor. Disoriented, she leaned against the wall, one hand over her face. What was going on?

The man with the knife was saying, "Don't worry about Jack Churchill. He's a prisoner in a gold and ivory casket in the middle of a forest way out there in Fairyland. You'll never see him again."

Ruth opened the bedroom door a little more. Shavi and Laura noticed the movement, and Ruth motioned to them not to draw attention to her.

Veitch agonised over what he had to do. Finally he jumped to his feet, holding the knife tightly. "I've got to do it, I've got to do it," he said to himself. He advanced on Shavi. The look in his eyes left no doubt that he was going to kill them.

Ruth crept into the room, unsure of what she could do. She was still dazed, but her heart was thundering fit to burst. Veitch drew back the knife. Shavi closed his eyes.

Ruth snatched up a metal box in which she kept her keys and phone. She stepped quickly forward and smashed it into the base of Veitch's skull. He crumpled instantly.

"You are Ruth!" Shavi jumped to his feet. "He implied you were dead."

"Somebody needs to tell me what's going on." Ruth was distracted by a flapping at the window. An owl was now sitting on the ledge, staring at her with its eerie eyes. Strangely, she felt comforted. "Why was that man trying to kill you? And what are you doing in my flat?"

"Better sit down," Laura said. "It's a trip and a half."

7

Twilight was drawing in as they stood on the edge of Stonehenge. The English Heritage workers had long since gone home and they could proceed without fear of interruption. Ruth was still reeling from all she had been told, but somehow her life made a lot more sense than it had done previously. For the first time in a long while she felt positive, and excited, whatever dangers lay ahead.

Laura surveyed the megaliths rising up against the darkening sky. "So we dance like pixies and a magic doorway appears," she said sarcastically.

"On the other hand I could just crack you on the head with my staff," the Bone Inspector said. "Now get a move on. Soon Veitch or one of those spider-people will be here and I don't intend being around when they arrive."

"You are not coming with us?" Shavi said.

"My place is here, not over there. I've got a job to do."

Shavi turned to Ruth. "Are you up to this?"

She glanced up at the owl flying overhead, and grinned. "Oh, yes."

8

The journey across the Far Lands took longer than they anticipated, but as they passed through its mysteries and wonders it began to feel as though they were awakening from a long, dreamless sleep. Earth and its grey streets were a distant shadow. The Land of Always Summer was more real, and life there was lived fully.

They encountered many strange beings, were guided with a paternal curiosity by some of the Tuatha Dé Danann, overcame untold dangers and magics and eventually arrived at the dark heart of the Forest of the Night.

The casket stood lonely and unmourned, gleaming in a solitary shaft of sunlight that broke through the dense canopy.

"Veitch said Church is being held prisoner in that," Laura said in hushed tones. "I hope they've been feeding him."

"I think he meant Church was being held magically," Shavi said.

"How are we supposed to break the spell, then?" Laura asked.

"I think that's down to me." Ruth gathered herself as her owl settled in the branches of a tree.

"Why you?" Laura eyed Ruth suspiciously.

"I don't know . . . instinct. I think we all have particular roles to play—"

"Archetypal roles," Shavi interjected. "Seer, warrior, king . . ." He looked to Ruth. "Are you ready?"

She flung open the casket lid. The spiders roiled in the depths.

Laura screwed up her face. "That is disgusting."

Ruth was oblivious to the spiders. All she could see was Church's face; it pulled her in and refused to let her go, speaking to some deeply buried part of her. It was distressing, for on the surface she did not know the man at all, yet in the well of her unconscious he was all she knew. The bonds that had been forged were unbreakable, tying them together for all time, however many miles or years lay between them. Now she knew why her recent life had been swathed in sorrow, why she felt as if she had been frozen in a living death, like Church.

Her heart swelled until it felt as if it was pressing against the prison of her skin. The sadness and the loneliness were part of the past. Now she could return to life.

Without thinking, she leaned in and kissed Church on the lips. There was a discharge of blue light and the spiders rushed from the casket. She heard their torrent hit the ground and the loud rustling as they fled into the undergrowth.

And still she kissed. His lips were cold at first, but gradually warmth came back to them, and they moved in union with hers. She broke away as his eyes flickered open.

He sat up and looked around. "How long have I been asleep?"

"A while, but you're awake now," she said softly.

"I had the strangest dreams."

His eyes locked on hers, and gradually realisation dawned in them. His smile was like the sun coming up. They embraced again, passionately this time, and for that moment no darkness could touch them.

9

It was the strangest reunion Church had every experienced. Though it felt as if they barely knew each other, a deeper part of them recognised the coming together of best friends, with bonds forged over time that were now unbreakable.

Shavi hugged Church warmly. "I do not understand it, but you feel like my brother."

"I am," Church replied. "We're Brothers of Dragons. Apart, we're just who we are. Together we're something better. Or so I'm led to believe."

Shavi nodded, smiling. "That sounds right."

Laura threw herself at Church, embracing him with a tangle of arms and legs. She kissed him passionately on the lips. "I don't feel as if you're my brother," she said with a wink.

And then his eyes fell on Ruth, who was standing away from the group in the shade of an elm tree. She was studying Church fiercely, uncertain emotions playing across her face.

"Give us a moment," Church said quietly to Shavi and Laura. He took Ruth's hand and led her away into the trees. She went compliantly, but he could feel her desperately trying to make sense of what she was feeling.

"You don't know me," Church began.

"No. But I also feel as if I know you better than anyone else in my life. I feel—" She caught herself.

"That's good. Because I was afraid when it got to this moment, I'd be just another stranger." He could feel her curious eyes on him. "You won't believe how long I've been thinking about this meeting," he said.

"Was it worth the wait?"

"Yes. It was worth everything I've been through to get here. And more." He was shocked to realise how true that statement was. The weight of his feelings as he stood there, trapped in her gravity, crushed all the terrible things he had experienced on the long road from the Iron Age. "Do you want to know," he began, barely daring to hope, "about you and me, about what we've shared, and what we lost . . . ?" He wanted to add, *And what we've found again*, but it was still too soon to presume.

"I do. More than anything."

The hairs on his neck stood erect. And so he began, with his clearest, earliest memory—of their meeting at Albert Bridge one misty morning, and how their eyes met, propelling them into a shared journey of adventure and fear, struggle and victory. As the memories surfaced of what he had witnessed in the depths of the cauldron, he spoke clearly and profoundly of his feelings, of how they had matured and deepened and transformed him from base metal into gold. He told her of the ache in his heart that felt like bereavement as he stood on the slopes above Carn Euny, and of his times before the Wish-Post, of Rome and Krakow and Roanoke and London, when the gulf of years separated them while in his heart and his head she was as close as this, close enough to touch.

When he had finished he waited for her response, but there was only silence. Dreading what he might see, he turned to her only to find tears in her eyes.

She grasped his hand so tightly it was as if she would never let it go. "I knew it all. In my heart, I knew. That feeling like someone I loved had died, only not knowing who, not being able to mourn. Feeling that my life was winding down to nothing."

As he looked into her eyes, he saw the despair that had consumed her for so long shrivel to nothing, and behind it rose a bright consuming light. In her smile there was everything he had ever wanted.

Church took her in his arms and she came to him easily. The weakness they had both felt fell away and a new strength was forged.

"There was a song I kept playing, one they tried to take away from me," she whispered in his ear, "and I wondered why it meant so much to me. It was called 'Save Me,' and that's what you've done. You've brought me back from the land of the dead."

They kissed, not like strangers, and suddenly everything became possible.

10

Once they were beyond the brooding confines of the Forest of the Night, they made camp amongst the ivy-covered ruins of a crumbling watchtower. Church was still shaky and finding it difficult to differentiate between the reality of his experiences in the casket and the wider reality he was now in. From what the others had told him, he had clearly observed the scene in Ruth's flat, but how much of the rest could he count on? His description of the Caretaker gelled with what Ruth told him of her own experiences, but if he had shifted the Axis of Existence, what effect would it have? Had he achieved what he had hoped?

Despite his disorientation, he could barely believe he was back. Jubilation came slowly, in small increments that left him smiling for no reason that the others could tell. It had been a long journey from the Iron Age back to his own time, and it had changed him in ways he was still trying to comprehend. He had looked into the darkest part of himself and still found a light that would lead him on. He had found deep, innate reserves that existed beyond the Pendragon Spirit, and now he felt able to cope with what lay ahead. Hal had been right. The journey itself had been all the training he needed.

But it had not just been about what was inside him. He had received an education on humanity, that throughout history people were essentially the same, struggling against hardship, finding depths that helped them transcend their origins. Good people were everywhere, doing the best they could—Will Swyfte, Gabe and Marcy, in Carn Euny, Eboracum and London. Against the constantly clustering darkness of the universe, he found that fact eminently reassuring.

As the day drew on, they talked through everything they had faced and saw how their differing perspectives came together to create a fuller picture of events. Their conversations were tentative at first, but gradually they got to know each other, and Church felt they had begun to tap into the real depth of their friendship that had been denied them by the Void.

"So let me get this straight," Laura said as she threw wood onto the campfire Shavi had built when twilight started to draw on. "It's the four of us against God. Or the god that created our world, at least."

"That's about the size of it," Church said.

"And it controls an army of ten billion supernatural spiders."

"Unless the number is meant metaphorically. Could be more," Church said.

"And this god controls an unspecified number of lesser gods, any one of which could probably bring the world to its knees."

"Yep."

"I think you're going to need a bigger sword."

"It sounds like a suicide mission to me," Ruth noted.

"Ah, don't let that get in the way of your thinking," Laura said. "Life's a suicide mission. It's not a case of if, it's when."

They all thought about this and then laughed. Though he wouldn't have said it to their faces, Church was proud of them; everything he had heard suggested they would be fine additions to the long heritage of the Brothers and Sisters of Dragons. Ruth was right—it was a suicide mission. Yet that didn't bother them in the way it would have troubled other people, a fact that was both absurd and uplifting.

"So how do we conduct a fight like that?" Shavi mused thoughtfully.

"I've been thinking about that. Laura was right in a way—we do need a bigger weapon," Church said.

"If you only knew how many times in my life I've had to say that," Laura said.

"What kind of weapon?" Ruth edged closer to him.

"The Extinction Shears," he said. "I saw what they could do. I think if we had them we could inflict some serious damage on the Void. Maybe even destroy it for good."

"You want to kill god," Laura said. "Nobody's going to accuse you of aiming low."

"Then we need to find that market you mentioned—" Shavi began.

"The Market of Wishful Spirit," Church said. "It travels around, from place to place. You never know where it's going to be until you stumble across it. The trader implied that the Shears were going to be off the market for a while, but we're not going to let a little thing like that stop us, are we?"

"Any idea where to start looking?" Ruth said.

"Not yet. But there's something else we need to do first. Tomorrow."

"I don't know about you," Laura said, "but I need to get some shut-eye. Finding out you're a plant is pretty exhausting." She made light of her comment, but Church could see in her eyes how much it troubled her.

The others fell asleep quickly, but Church stayed awake for almost an hour, watching Ruth, and feeling an abiding peace. Finally, after so many years and so much struggle, they were together.

11

The moon was full and milky in a star-spangled sky as they left the comfort of Stonehenge and made their way to Shavi's van. Church took the wheel, enjoying the prospect of driving much more than he would ever have anticipated before he turned up in the Iron Age.

"So where are we going?" Laura asked as she climbed into the back with Shavi.

"I don't know yet."

"Doesn't exactly fill me with confidence."

Church tapped his head. "It's all up here. I'm going with instinct."

Laura rested her head in Shavi's lap. "I'll say, ditto."

"I have to say, in my experience of the last few days, we cannot afford to stay in one place too long," Shavi said.

"Yeah, everywhere is enemy territory," Laura said. "How fucked up is that?"

"I don't see how we're going to be able to do anything positive," Ruth said.

"The enemy will have us on the run continually." She searched the shadowy hedgerows and the lonely Downs as Church pulled onto the main road. She half-expected Rourke to be waiting there, ready to throw himself at the van.

"That's the first thing we're going to tackle," Church said. "Some of this land has to be our land."

"Sounds like the man has a plan," Ruth said.

Shavi stretched out. "It is Veitch I feel sorry for. He was one of us, and though I cannot remember it, we must have been good friends. He has been a victim in these events."

"He was a victim, but he's also slaughtered hundreds of Brothers and Sisters of Dragons over the years," Church replied. "He chose to cross a line a long time ago." Of all their enemies, Church was convinced Veitch was the most dangerous. He would never stop, never walk away, until he felt he had got his revenge, even if rivers of blood were spilled and the land looked like a charnel house.

"Sounds like you've got a downer on the Veitch-dude," Laura said lazily.

Church glanced in the mirror and thought he saw a faint movement on the skyline. It was impossible to discern the cause, but it troubled him immensely.

12

They headed west through the ancient heart of England, over rolling downs and past silent golden cornfields, through market towns still dreaming of the Tudors and woods where the oaks were twisted with age, and onwards to the M5 motorway. They followed it south to Exeter, and then west through Devon and into Cornwall, stopping only briefly to refuel. Every time they slowed at junctions, Laura, Shavi and Ruth turned to the windows, searching for anything that might hint of an impending attack. But there were only lorry drivers heading through the night from the port at Bristol, or tourists trying to beat the daytime jams.

"I don't get it," Laura said. "They wouldn't give us a free run. Maybe they don't know where we are."

"They know," Church said.

"They are biding their time." Shavi leaned on the back of Church's seat, searching the road ahead. "After our escape they are not taking any chances. They want to get us into a position from which there is no escape."

"Because they're scared of us," Ruth said.

"They're scared of what we represent," Church corrected. "They're scared of the Pendragon Spirit."

They followed the granite spine of Cornwall towards the land where Church had begun his journey 2,300 years earlier. Before they reached Carn Euny, Church took them south, past patchwork fields and stone walls and trees bent double by Atlantic storms. In the distance the lights of St Austell rose up, with the beach and sea just beyond.

"Nearly there now," Church said. "I can feel it." The light in his head was brighter; he could almost hear the Seelie Court singing.

The roads beyond St Austell were poorly lit and the dark appeared to be closing in on every side. In the shadows they thought they glimpsed faces and movement, but they sped by too fast to be sure.

The road continued up a steep incline; at the top Church slowed and peered over the steering wheel. "I think I know where we are."

Ruth looked out into the night. "Don't stop here," she said uneasily.

From there it was downhill all the way. They left the main road and passed through some gates onto a private road. Ahead a soft golden glow rose up from somewhere below their line of sight.

And there Church did bring the van to a halt. While the engine idled, he looked at the faint glow. "This is either a coincidence or the weirdest synchronicity," he said. "This particular part of my journey is ending where my journey as a Brother of Dragons began this second time round. Metaphorically speaking."

"It is the ouroboros," Shavi said, "the serpent eating its own tail. A full circle. Every ending is a new beginning, and so the cycle continues."

"I have absolutely no idea what you're talking about," Laura said, "and to be honest, no interest. But you've clearly done a lot of drugs in the past."

Ruth had been staring out of the side window, not at the glow, but at the vast sea of darkness that surrounded it. "Something's not right," she said.

"What do you mean?" Church asked.

"The shadows are moving. See? All over." She indicated a wide arc.

Ruth was right: the darkness looked like a black sheet with something squirming underneath.

They were all mesmerised by it until Church realised what they were seeing. "Spiders."

They covered every inch of the fields and hillsides surrounding them, billions of them drawing in on the golden light ahead.

Laura pointed through the windscreen. In the cone of illumination from the headlights, the spiders streamed towards them.

"We'll never get past them," she said.

"If we don't get down there to the light, it's all over," Church said. "We've got nowhere else to go."

He revved the engine and popped the clutch. The van jumped forward with a squeal of tyres and Laura and Shavi were thrown across the back seat. Laura let out a stream of foul-mouthed abuse. Ruth gripped the dashboard until her knuckles turned white.

The van ploughed into the wave of spiders at speed. Some of them burst like overripe fruit, others crunched like gravel. It was difficult for the tyres to gain traction on the pulped remains, and the van skewed before going into a slide. Church wrestled with the wheel and kept the vehicle moving forward.

As the tyres spun wildly, Church realised it was already too late. The spiders were sweeping onto the vehicle from every direction.

"Keep away from the sides," Church yelled over the racing engine. "They're going to be coming through any second." Ahead, the sea of spiders appeared to stretch for ever.

Holes began to appear in the metal walls of the van. It wasn't as if the spiders had eaten through, but rather that they had cut through the fundamental force that tethered the molecules together in this reality. Laura positioned herself on the floor of the van and kicked out at any emerging spiders. They flew off into the slipstream before they could get a grip on her boots. Shavi snatched up a wheel brace and did the same.

Church kept the pedal to the floor. The road led downhill at a slight incline and the van skated from side to side. As they glimpsed a large, empty car park, a metallic scraping rose up.

"They've stripped away the tyres," Church said.

"Are we going to make it?" Ruth tried to hide the concern in her voice. Church didn't answer.

The sides of the van were suddenly ragged. Too many holes were forming for Laura and Shavi to stop the flow.

"They'll be in any second," Laura shouted. "How much further?"

"Not far," Church lied.

The spiders had gained purchase on the front of the van and were spreading across the windscreen. Church used the wipers to little effect.

"You're the one who works the Craft, aren't you?" Church said to Ruth. "Can't you do something?"

"I don't know how . . . I . . . I can't remember—"

"This junkheap is falling apart," Laura yelled. "I'm going to be sliding on my arse in a second."

Ruth bowed her head and closed her eyes. During the journey back through the Far Lands, Church had told her how one in every Five always had mastery of the Craft. It explained the owl, her familiar, but she had no idea how to access the abilities she must have developed in her past life. She concentrated intently.

The rear doors fell off with a clatter. Streams of golden sparks trailed behind them from the wheel rims. The windscreen was now fully covered by the wriggling black bodies. Soon the glass would disappear and hundreds of the writhing creatures would surge in.

There was a white flash, like a lightning bolt, and the entire windscreen flew out with the spiders still clinging to it. Ruth convulsed and spat a mouthful of bile to the floor.

"You did it," Church said.

Ruth smiled weakly before slumping back into the seat. Even that little effort had drained her completely.

The road noise grew drastically louder and Church saw there were no longer any spiders ahead.

"They are leaving," Shavi exclaimed. He watched the creatures fly off the van and return to the mass that waited along a clear line a few yards behind them.

"I don't get it," Laura said. "They had us. Why are they holding back now?"

Church stopped the van and jumped out, and saw that she was right. The spiders had halted in a wide arc as if held back by an invisible fence. "It doesn't matter," he said. "We're through."

The others clambered out. Laura jumped onto Shavi's back, laughing, and playfully bit his neck. He gave her a piggy-back to where Church was supporting Ruth, who was slowly recovering.

Church nodded to a winding path that led towards the light. "Let's go."

"I'm not looking forward to getting out of here later," Laura said, eyeing the darkness where the spiders waited.

They followed the path around to a large visitors' centre. Beyond it was a landscape that looked as if it had been plucked from a 1950s science fiction movie. In a 108-foot-deep former china clay pit stood two enormous geodesic domes surrounded by a massive, lush garden filled with plants from India to Russia. Shavi, Laura and Church recognised the place immediately.

"What are those domes?" Ruth said. The view was so impressive it made them all stop and stare.

"Greenhouses," Laura said. "They're called biomes." Everyone looked at her, puzzled. "I happen to like the environment," she said tartly. "Inside one of those domes are trees and plants from the rainforests and tropical islands. The other one has stuff from the Med, California and South Africa. They're temperature-controlled to match the local climates. You can't really tell from here, but there are full-grown trees in there. They've been calling this place the Eighth Wonder of the World." She gave a hard smile. "An environmentally friendly paradise."

Shavi read the sign by the entrance. "The Eden Project. Dedicated to the environment—" Shavi recalled the words of the spirit-form just before it took his eye: *The Fabulous Beast sleeps beneath the Garden of Eden.*

"Nature. That makes sense," Church mused.

"You're still not filling me with confidence that you know what you're doing," Laura said.

"Ten minutes ago, I didn't. Now . . . maybe."

The visitors' centre was lit up brightly, but eerily still. Church led the way inside.

"Look at this." Behind a desk, Ruth pointed out two security guards, both of them in a deep slumber, faint smiles playing on their lips.

They passed a deserted cafeteria and empty ticket desks. It felt as though all the occupants had suddenly vanished. Doors led outside to a viewing platform on the lip of the crater. Beneath them, a path wound around the side of the pit through the thick vegetation to the floor far below where the biomes and other buildings were located.

"Do you feel it?" Church said as they looked out over the evocative combination of ancient nature and futuristic design. The atmosphere was electric with the same vibrancy Church had felt at Boskawen-Un and Krakow.

"I do not understand," Shavi said, intrigued. "I thought the provenance of this power was the ancient sites."

"So did I," Church replied. "But it's here."

"Get a grip. We're not alone." Laura leaned over the rail of the viewing platform and pointed towards movement on the floor of the crater. Torches bobbed amongst the shadows near a large covered stage. Not far away, in a puddle of electric light, Church could see the tail of a procession of strange beings.

"The Seelie Court," he said.

"The travelling court of the Tuatha Dé Danann?" Ruth said. "What are they doing here?"

"When I was in London during the Second World War I developed a bond with them," Church answered. "I can feel them in my head, wherever they are, and they can sense me. When I was in America in sixty-nine I asked them for a favour."

"Drugs or sex?" Laura said.

"A search, for the one thing that could help us."

They jogged down the winding path towards the court. As the route opened onto the floor of the pit, they finally comprehended the huge scale of the biomes gleaming in the lights. For Ruth, Shavi and Laura it was the first time they had experienced the otherworldliness of the Seelie Court, and for a moment they could only stand and gape.

The king and queen approached Church with their attendants.

"Brother of Dragons," the king said. "So good to see you recovered from your previous predicament. Of course, we knew it was only a matter of time."

"Your legend grows by the day," the queen said lightly.

"And these are your fellow Brothers and Sisters of Dragons?" The king surveyed the others. Laura was fixated on a man with a hawk's beak and the legs of a goat, while a woman with silver eyes and grey skin was examining Ruth's long hair, much to Ruth's discomfort. Church introduced the three of them.

"You're here at my request?" Church asked the king.

"This is where our quest led us, Brother of Dragons. The task you set us was not easy, for the prize did not want to be found. We had to listen quietly to the whisperings of Existence, follow the scents on the wind—"

"Thank you. I'm in your debt. Where—?"

The queen brought a hand to her temple. Her brow furrowed. "Beware. The hunters have come."

On the lip of the crater high above, five riders were silhouetted against the lights of the visitors' centre. The spiders couldn't enter the peculiar magical atmosphere of the site, but Veitch and his four followers had no problem; they had all been touched by the Pendragon Spirit and the Blue Fire held no fear for them.

Veitch fell into relief as he urged his horse down the winding path. The others followed.

Church turned to Ruth, Shavi and Laura. "We have to find some way to hold them off until I can do what I need to do."

"Go," Shavi said. "We will do what we can."

The king pointed towards the tropical biome. Church ran for the entrance with the sound of the approaching horses in his ears.

13

Sparks flew from the iron-shod hoofs of the horses as they thundered from the path towards the biomes. Ruth was drawn to Veitch, whose dark eyes never left her face. Something crackled between them, but what it was she did not know; he scared her and intrigued her in equal measure.

She braced herself for a confrontation, but he continued past her, never breaking his stare, which, like her feelings, had a strange duality: accusing and yearning.

She heard two words as he passed: no quarter.

It was the second rider who almost brought her down, a once-beautiful woman, her face now half-scarred by burns; Church's description hadn't captured the true horror of Etain's dead, menacing stare. Ruth threw herself out of the way at the last moment.

Not far away, Tannis, Owein and Branwen focused their attention on Shavi and Laura. The monstrous horses attacked with a terrifying ferocity. Laura threw herself into the dense vegetation with Shavi close behind. The riders moved along the network of paths to head them off.

Etain tried three more times to run Ruth down, but Ruth felt infused with energy and desperate to make up for all the time she had spent sleeping through her life. Etain remained cold and aloof, as efficient in her attack as a machine, but Ruth sensed some well-hidden part of her that was not that way.

As they continued their cat-and-mouse game, Etain successfully backed Ruth into a corner. As Etain rode her down, Ruth's owl swooped from the sky and raked a chunk of dead flesh from the charred side of Etain's face. Once Ruth had escaped, the owl retreated before Etain could strike.

Deciding on a change of tactics, Etain leaped from her mount and drew a rusty, bloodstained sword. As she advanced, Ruth realised what was hidden behind those dead eyes: jealousy.

14

The heat hit Church like a wall the moment he stepped through the door. In an instant he went from the cool of an English summer evening to the oppressive cauldron of a humid tropical night. High overhead the hexagons and pentagons of the biome roof were just visible through the thick canopy of lofty, flourishing trees. The sound of rushing water thundered all around from artificial waterfalls and streams pouring into languid green pools. Standpipes sprayed a mist of water at regular intervals to maintain the humidity.

His heart pounding, Church hurried along the twisting path amongst the dense tropical vegetation. He had no idea where he was going—the path branched, leading down to dead ends or rising high up along a rock wall. His clothes were already drenched with sweat.

He forced himself to calm down. Closing his eyes and letting his breathing become deep and regular, he allowed himself to feel. The Blue Fire called to him. He only had to let himself be drawn into its embrace.

When he opened his eyes, his perception had changed, yet though he searched along the path there were no blue lines of force. If there was no Blue Fire to guide him, how could he do what had to be done?

As he turned slowly, ducking down to examine the surface of the path, he caught a glimmer of blue deep in the undergrowth. Peering in, he saw a barely visible sapphire filigree, secret, only for those who really wanted to find it. His prize had been as well hidden as the king had said. Scuttling on his hands and knees, he followed the thin blue line into the vegetation.

He only heard the padding footsteps at the last moment before the full weight of a body slam sent him sprawling across the path. Veitch loomed over him, the black fire of his sword casting swirling shadows. Church rolled out of the way as the blade came down. He was half-up when Veitch caught him in the face with a boot and he toppled over a railing and into the warm waters of a pool. Taking a breath, he swam beneath the surface.

Veitch dived in, raising torrents as he chopped wildly into the water with the sword. He finally caught Church beneath a deafening waterfall where the cascade eliminated the outside world, and the two of them were enclosed in a private prison of sound and fury. Church dodged another thrust, but instead of retreating he darted forward and smashed a fist into Veitch's face. His knuckles rang with pain, but Veitch pitched backwards into the churning water, spraying blood behind him.

Church leaped out through the waterfall and scrambled up a steep bank, using thick vines and overhanging branches for purchase. He eventually hauled himself over a railing and back onto the path. In the pool, there was no sign of Veitch.

He wrenched free a piece of railing; a poor weapon, but it would have to do. Quickly, he ducked down and searched until he found the near-invisible line of force. Keeping low, he followed it as fast as he could until he came to a hut on stilts, constructed to show how people lived in the tropics. The line continued underneath it.

A supplicant serpent, Church wriggled on his belly until he came to a spot in the most inaccessible area where a barely visible circle of Blue Fire formed in the soil. He slammed his palm down into the centre of it. The Pendragon Spirit within him spoke to the Blue Fire hiding in the earth. The ground rumbled and a small hole opened up. Church threw himself in.

15

Laura scrambled through dense bushes that tore at her skin, but however much she tried to hide, the riders somehow knew exactly where she was. Tannis drove his mount into the vegetation, hoofs smashing inches from her head with the force of a steam hammer.

She pressed further into the thicket, only to realise the sounds of Tannis's pursuit had changed. Looking back, she saw the bushes moving with a life of their own, growing and changing as they wrapped around the horse's legs.

Laura knew she had caused it, but had no idea how. As Tannis drew his sword and prepared to pursue her on foot, a branch shot out like a spear and burst through his chest. It pinned him like a butterfly in a collector's case, and though she knew he was already dead, Laura was still sickened by the way he tried to tear himself free.

She escaped from the undergrowth onto the path. Across the base of the crater, she could see Branwen and Owein trying to trap Shavi in a pincer movement. Further down near the biome, the Seelie Court had given Ruth cover so she could escape Etain's attack. Ruth was slipping quietly along a raised walkway and into the biome. Yet it looked to Laura as though Etain knew exactly where Ruth was going; indeed, that Etain had herded her that way on purpose.

16

After falling down the hole, Church found himself in a tunnel that sloped steeply downwards. The heat was as heavy as in the biome and added to the claustrophobic atmosphere. He skidded over damp rock gleaming in the half-light and came to a cavern that was barely the size of half a football pitch with a ceiling only the height of three men. A small pool of Blue Fire crackled in the centre, and in it slept the Fabulous Beast that had fled Vietnam, coiled tightly in the sustaining energy, its wounds still visible on its scales.

Church approached cautiously. The heavy-lidded eyes were closed and its breathing sounded like the rumbling of a traction engine.

When he had asked the Seelie Court to search for the Beast's hiding place, he knew it was the key to his ability to fight back, but he wasn't sure if even the Tuatha Dé Danann would be able to locate it.

As Church considered how to wake the Beast from its long, recuperative slumber, he heard movement behind him. Veitch stood in the entrance to the tunnel, his blade fizzing and spitting as if in opposition to the Blue Fire.

"Stay away, Veitch," Church said. "It's too late now. Once I wake this thing you'll be toast."

"You always used to call me Ryan." His face gave nothing away.

"You've wasted your time trying to get revenge. I didn't kill you over Ruth. I did it because I had no choice. You were being manipulated by the gods and you were going to wreck everything."

"We're all puppets in one way or another." He pointed the sword towards the rocks and the black flames snapped angrily. "When we met, you treated me like an equal. We set out on that road and there was a lot of death and a lot of pain, but for the first time I felt as if I wasn't on my own. I had friends like I'd never had before, who listened to me and trusted me." He looked away and Church was surprised to see tears in his eyes.

"We can—"

"No, we can't!" he raged. "You don't get it, do you? Things always work out for you. Born to be the king. The worst thing is to start out with misery, get shown a bit of hope and then have it taken away. If you lived in misery all your life you wouldn't know any difference. Having that bit of hope makes all the bad stuff a hundred times worse. A thousand. I wish I'd never known you. I wish I'd never been a Brother of Dragons, just so I wouldn't have to keep thinking how things might have been."

He gripped his sword with two hands and raised it. In the glare from the black flames, his face took on a monstrous cast.

"That's why I'm going to kill you, and then I'm going to kill that." He jabbed the sword towards the Fabulous Beast. "And then I'm going to make sure there's no more Blue Fire, and no more hope, so nobody has to go through what I've been through."

Church backed up until he was ankle-deep in the Blue Fire, and felt it call out to his own Pendragon Spirit. He held up the piece of broken railing and thought how pathetic it looked.

As Veitch brought his sword closer to the pool of earth energy, it began to emit a sound like static that set Church's teeth on edge. The unrestrained hatred in Veitch's face was almost too much for Church to bear.

Behind him, the Fabulous Beast still slept. Church prepared to fight, knowing his likely options were die now or die later.

He turned and placed his hands on the Fabulous Beast. Its scales were hard and cool like gems beneath his fingers. His consciousness flowed through him and into the Beast as it had done in Vietnam, and once again he had the bizarre sensation of being in two places at once: in his own body and in the creature's head.

The Fabulous Beast opened its eyes, and he had the even more disorienting sensation of watching himself. Veitch was behind him, sword raised to deliver the killing blow.

The creature reared up to the roof of the cavern in one fluid motion. Its uncoiling form propelled Church backwards and knocked Veitch off-balance. It released a burst of liquid fire along the roof of the cavern that illuminated another tunnel at the far end. The furnace heat of it seared Church's lungs and almost drove him unconscious.

For one instant, he looked into its glittering eye and saw the untamed power there. After a long recuperation from its agony in Vietnam, it was now ready to return. With serpentine grace, it glided across the pool of Blue Fire and disappeared into the tunnel at speed.

Church staggered to his feet, still reeling from the fiery blast. Veitch was already up, silent and intense.

"You can kill me now," Church said, "but now the Beast is out our side will have a chance."

"Aren't you the big hero winning the day," Veitch sneered.

He stepped forward. Church ducked the first blow, using the piece of railing to deflect the sword, but being careful to ensure it didn't take the full force that would shear through it in an instant. They performed a vicious ballet across the pool of Blue Fire. Veitch grew more furious with each passing second, forgetting his expertise, hacking and slashing almost randomly. Church was filled with grace and power. He could almost anticipate Veitch's attacks, slipping away at the last second. He wielded the railing like a sword, ripping open Veitch's cheek, tearing open his shirt, raising blood in a hundred places. Veitch's eyes blazed; Church was convinced his opponent's rage eliminated any pain.

As Veitch increased the ferocity of his attacks, Church grew calmer; he felt at peace in the centre of a storm. He sidestepped a vicious thrust, and then rammed the railing between Veitch's calves, using his weight to pitch Veitch to the ground. As Veitch sprawled in the Blue Fire, Church brought one jagged end of the railing to Veitch's throat.

"It's over," Church said.

"You know it's not," Veitch said. "It's not over till one of us is dead. You know that."

"It doesn't have to be that way."

"Yes, it does."

Their gazes locked. In Veitch's eyes, Church saw a deep sadness hiding behind the anger. For a moment, everything hung. All Church had to do was put his weight on the railing and Veitch would be gone.

As he continued to search Veitch's face, he caught a flicker: slyness. Veitch's eyes glanced to one side. Church followed his gaze; only the tunnel entrance lay that way.

With a rapid movement, Veitch knocked the railing out of Church's hand and jumped to his feet. His sword came up. Church had no defence.

At the last, Veitch hesitated. A dark smile crept across his face.

"What are you doing, Veitch?"

"Nearly time now," he whispered.

Confused, Church followed Veitch's gaze towards the tunnel leading to the biome. Ruth had just emerged in the entrance

Before Church could divine what Veitch was planning, Veitch flipped his sword fluidly. Church caught it instinctively just as Veitch threw himself forward. The blade burst through his chest and out of his back. Stifling his agony, Veitch turned himself on the weapon. A gout of blood burst from his mouth and splashed down his chin.

"Like I said," he croaked, "you're fucking scum." His smile became cruel, then victorious.

Veitch slumped down, sliding off the blade as his life flickered out. In that instant a bolt of black lightning crackled from the sword. It leaped into Veitch, then Church and finally into Ruth, uniting the three of them in a blaze of darkness. Church's mind blacked out for a moment, and when his thoughts returned, Veitch lay dead at his feet.

Ruth staggered over. "What just happened?"

"I don't know." Although his teeth were ringing and his stomach turned queasily, it appeared that the black fire had had no lasting effect.

Ruth knelt beside Veitch, examining his face, still bearing the cast of the pain he had suffered in his final moment. "Why did he do that?"

"Probably realised he couldn't win." Church knew he was wrong, but there was no way to guess what had gone through Veitch's mind at the end. Veitch's motivations had always been complex and unpredictable; a man who was prepared to remove all hope from the world while simultaneously risking himself to save innocents. Who knew what really drove him?

"At least he's gone," Ruth said, but her tone was flat, and Church felt the same way. It was difficult for him to accept, but despite all the death Veitch had wrought over the centuries, Church still felt as though he had lost a brother.

"Come on," Church said. "We're done here."

17

Church carried Veitch's body out of the biome and laid it on the ground under the stars. He backed away as Etain and Tannis came forward, their staring eyes accusing. They reclaimed the body and laid it with surprising gentleness over the saddle of his horse. Without a backward glance, the four Brothers and Sisters of Spiders led their friend and leader on a final ride up the winding path and away into the night.

The king and queen came over. The rest of the Seelie Court were in an unprecedented state of excitement, their strange cries and jubilant calls ringing off the walls of the pit like the sounds of a jungle at sunset.

The queen pointed towards the sky where the Fabulous Beast rolled and turned, its fiery breath mirroring the lights of the Eden Project far below it.

"This day you have struck a great blow for Existence, Brother of Dragons," the king said. "Magic has returned to the land. Wonder and mystery live here once more, and darkness cannot stand in the face of the light it brings."

"We have something for you, Brother of Dragons, to celebrate this new age." The queen was smiling strangely.

Behind her, the ranks of the Seelie Court parted to admit two attendants bearing items lost behind a blinding white light. The glow faded as the queen took the first and handed it to Church. "Do you recognise this?"

"The sword Caledfwlch." Blue flames danced along the blade and Church felt them calling to him. He took the sword in his hand and felt its power surge through him as exuberantly as it had done the last time he had held it, more than 2,000 years ago.

"Dark times lie ahead." The queen had grown sombre and Church felt an ominous but indefinable weight behind her words. "This is a weapon of the gods, and too great for most Fragile Creatures, but you will need it for what is to come."

"Thank you. I aim to repay your trust in me."

Church thought he noticed a hint of sadness flicker across the queen's face, but she quickly turned to take the second item. Now the glow had gone, Church could see it was a spear, the wood carved with mysterious runes.

"To the tribes this was known as the Spear of Lugh," the queen said. "Another weapon of power." She held it out.

It took a second before Ruth realised the queen was offering the spear to her. "I don't deserve this," she stuttered. "I wouldn't know how to use it."

"Nevertheless, Sister of Dragons, it is yours. Your awakening has already begun. Great things lie ahead for you."

Ruth took the spear hesitantly. Church could see from her face that she was experiencing the same sensation that had coursed through him when he took the sword.

"Can you feel it?" the king said suddenly. "Can you feel it?"

From nowhere, a bitter wind rushed over them, as cold as if it had blown from the Arctic. When it had passed, the king and queen both appeared grave.

"Across this land, the Army of the Ten Billion Spiders is gathering its strength," the king continued. "It fears you, but it will not rest until you are destroyed. Wherever you go you will be hunted. Your safe havens will be few and far between."

"We know what we're up against," Church said. "We're not going to turn away."

The king nodded. "I knew that would be your response, Brother of Dragons."

As the Seelie Court moved off towards the biomes, Church saw lights appear amongst the trees like fireflies wherever they passed. Soon the whole of the Eden Project was alive with flickering blue will-o'-the-wisps. Ruth, Shavi and Laura were transfixed by the spectacle, but Church had seen it before, long, long ago and far away in the megalithic complex on the road out of Rome.

"The spirits of the dead," he said softly.

The atmosphere was exhilarating and filled with the promise that everything would be all right. Emotions rushed through him, but the strongest was hope, and when he looked around he could see that the others were feeling the same. He slipped his arms around Ruth's shoulders and she fell in close to him. He revelled in the scent of her hair and her skin and the warmth of her next to him.

"It's going to be all right, isn't it?" she said.

"It's all right now. We'll deal with the future when it comes."

Nearby, one of the wisps took on more substance until it became a figure of burning blue flame. Church recognised the smiling features.

"Hal," he said. "My own little genie."

"The god in the machine," Hal replied, the flames sizzling with each word. "You've done well, Church, all of you have. But it's only what I expected."

"I'm guessing you're not about to give us time off for good behaviour."

"What, when you've just emerged from your chrysalis? You're ready now for the big struggle that lies ahead."

"It doesn't feel like it." Church felt uncomfortable giving voice to the doubts that he had long buried. "How are we supposed to stand up to the Void? Four miserable little humans against . . . what? A god? The ultimate force in this universe?"

"Do you really think Existence would have brought you to this point if there wasn't a hope? In you, in everyone, there is a little sliver of that original force for good that existed at the beginning of time. Most people don't get to find it, or put it to some use. But you and your little group have done that. If you could see what I see, Church . . . You, the four of you, you're burning like stars. You can all tap into the power that opposes the Void, you just haven't yet learned exactly how much you can do."

Church took a deep breath and felt the peace of the night fill his lungs. Hal's words had steadied him. "All right," he said, "we carry on. But what do we do next?"

"You take the battle to the Void. You're knights of light, dispelling the darkness. The Void isn't omnipotent, Church. Duality, remember? It's all there in Janus—two faces, equal. Sometimes one looks, then the other. You have to turn away the face of the Void and by doing so usher in a new golden age. Drive back the Kingdom of the Spider, and raise the standard of the Serpent."

"Okay," Laura said, "I'll ignore the fact that I'm talking to a pillar of fire and ask—are you going to give us any specific help, or just talk in wanky generalisations?"

"He can't tell us anything," Church said, "because knowledge is only power if you earn it."

Laura snorted derisively. "What a waste of space."

"I may not be able to tell you anything much, but I can point you in the right direction," Hal said. "Your battle can be helped by two young men. One is imbued with a force for destruction, the other with a force for life. Existence has hidden them from the Void. You have to find them, bring them back into contention."

"Anything else to go on?" Church said ironically.

"The force for life goes by the name of Jez Miller. He has the power to heal. The other one is another Jack—yes, just like you, Church. I wonder what that means."

"Surname?"

"He didn't have chance to find out before the Court of the Final Word snatched him from his cradle and implanted a Wish-Hex inside him, and that is a very powerful force indeed. With those two, and the Extinction Shears, anything is possible."

"That's not enough to go on," Ruth protested. "We wouldn't know where to begin."

"The last generation of Brothers and Sisters of Dragons who came after you—of which I was one—will be able to help you. Seek them out."

"You've got a lot of faith in us," Church said. "I hope we can live up to it."

Hal didn't reply.

"I'm just sorry so many Brothers and Sisters of Dragons had to die to get us to this point," Church continued.

The blazing figure smiled as it raised one hand to indicate the will-o'-the-wisps flickering all around. "Death is not an ending, Church. Your fallen comrades are here in the vast blue eternity, supporting you in your struggle. Lucia was right when she told you not to mourn. Take strength from their sacrifice. I'm going now, Church. Good luck to all of you, and remember, we're here. We're always here."

Hal flickered and then slowly faded away, but he left behind an atmosphere so strong and uplifting that Church could almost touch it. Everyone remained silent for a moment as they weighed what they had heard, and as Church looked around at their bright, open faces he knew that whatever lay ahead, he would be proud to stand beside them.

"I suppose this means you want to be the leader," Laura said. "You're such a show-off."

"Do you really think we have a chance?" Ruth asked.

"We've earned ourselves a breathing space today," Church said. "I can't guess how this is going to turn out, but we've been given a huge responsibility and we can't turn away from it, whatever lies ahead."

"I thought you were going to say that," Laura said sourly. "So it's us against the whole world. Seriously, who would bet against us?"

18

In London, a light rain fell. Tom hurried from doorway to doorway beneath the colourful wash of Soho's lights. Every moment filled him with astonishment. The doom that had dogged him for most of his life had dissipated and in its place he was filled with a remarkable optimism that almost moved him to tears, so unfamiliar was it. A deeply buried part of him half-thought that he should be dead, but he had no idea why he should feel that way. Instead, he sensed that he was about to embark on a new adventure.

Somewhere there were Brothers and Sisters of Dragons preparing for a struggle against odds that they could never overcome. But he had a plan that could help them, and perhaps, once he was at their side, they could challenge fate itself.

19

In the Far Lands, a hooded figure hurried through the driving rain towards the Court of the Soaring Spirit. The guard threw open the gates to reveal the oppressive jumble of buildings and the heavy gloom that clung to every street.

"Who goes?" the guard challenged.

The figure threw back its hood to reveal beautiful golden features.

"My queen." The guard bowed deeply and stepped aside so Niamh could enter her court.

She hurried past without speaking and headed towards her palace, ready for the struggle that lay ahead. And none who saw her knew of the spider that now nestled deep inside her head.

20

Church, Ruth, Shavi and Laura climbed wearily up the winding path to the rim of the crater to look out over the rolling Cornish countryside. The full moon cast its milky light across the fields, and the stars glittered in a universe that was vast and unknowable and unpredictable.

The Fabulous Beast had disappeared from view, but in the distance bursts of red and gold lit up the clouds.

"Look at that," Church said in awe.

The Blue Fire that the Fabulous Beast had taken into itself in Vietnam now ran in lines across the landscape, crisscrossing, interconnecting, and here and there shooting up in a column of power towards the heavens. It was releasing the remaining energy back into the earth, bringing the land alive, driving the spiders and the darkness they represented back to where they had originated.

"That's amazing," Ruth said quietly. "Beautiful." All four of them were mesmerised.

"It's still weak," Church said, "and it won't get stronger until we reconnect it with the source. But for now it's alive. The king was right. Magic has returned."

In their hearts, the Pendragon Spirit burned brightly and not even the clustering darkness could dim its light.

21

As they moved away from the Eden Project towards the lights of St Austell, a figure separated from the shadows and bounded onto the roof of the visitors' centre. In its mischievous eyes was the wildness of nature. In its enigmatic smile were mystery and a hint of secrets untold. Sly and dangerous, Robin Goodfellow gave a mocking bow.

"And so this tale must end,
With questions to be posed.
No rest yet for our players,
Though these pages soon will close.
New adventures lie ahead,
Love, lust, death and betrayal.
A world in shadow, a threat so great
As to make you quake and quail.
Yet life is but a game,
Mere sport before you die.
Where the rules are never told,
And the stakes are always high.
Sleep well now, Fragile Creatures,
But consider as you doze:
Your strings may be invisible,
Though like puppets you repose.
The puppetmaster makes you dance,
But keep your eyes tight shut.
For when you least expect it.
Snip, snip!

. . . the strings are cut . . ."

ABOUT THE AUTHOR

A two-time winner of the British Fantasy Award, Mark Chadbourn was raised in the United Kingdom's East Midlands and studied Economic History at Leeds University before becoming a jouranlist. Now a screenwriter for BBC Television Drama, he has also run an independent record company, managed rock bands, and worked on production lines. He is the author of the celebrated The Age of Misrule, The Dark Age, and Swords of Albion sequences. He now lives in a forest in a two-hundred-year-old house filled with books.